# TONI MOUNT

# THE COLOUR OF LIES

# The Colour of Lies

## A Sebastian Foxley Medieval Mystery
### Book 7

# M
MadeGlobal Publishing

For more information on
MadeGlobal Publishing, visit
our website
www.madeglobal.com

# Dedication

For my Gravesend History Class; they have been with me for many years and their love for history continues to inspire me to further study

Why not visit
Sebastian Foxley's web page
to discover more about his
life and times?
**www.SebastianFoxley.com**

# Prologue

H E HAD waited a long time for this moment – nigh two years of wandering, homeless and friendless, sneered at for a stranger and suspected as a foreigner. Somehow, he had survived such miserable journeyings. He had hated the German Lands, loathed France and everything about its people but, most especially, he despised the Low Countries, if for no other reason than that was where he had been abandoned, discarded as of no account. 'Revenge is a dish best served cold,' so they said and, in this case, there was not a vestige of warmth remaining.

There had never been a plan but always an intention. And now he had both a means of avenging the waste of years and making money out of it. God knows, he needed money; sick and tired of being a pauper.

The theft had been as straightforward as any impulsive action could be: a sharp blow from behind to the unguarded head of the unwary watchman, and the prising open of the locks – at least he had thought to bring an implement for that. And once the door had yielded to his efforts, the wondrous items had been his for the taking. The deed was done, and the matter should have ended there. But now this! Too many accursed foreigners had made his life a torment. All across the northern lands of Europe, merchants, lords and blackguards had vexed him, swindled him, plagued him. And now one more fool – from the Low Countries, as was almost to be expected – would deny him his desire. It could not be. He would not allow it.

The largest of his ill-gotten prizes was as fine a weapon as nature could devise. He raised it high, holding it in both hands

1

like a mace and brought the blunt end crashing down upon the fellow's head. It made a most satisfying sound in the half-light: the crunch of bone and the liquid slap of a brain destroyed. The wretch fell upon his back, bleeding on the withered clumps of grass in the darkness, but it was not enough to appease the sudden flare of anger that overwhelmed him. He reversed the exquisite weapon and plunged the spear-like point into the victim's chest.

It was done. Breathless and weary of a sudden, he withdrew it and wiped its beauty clean of blood. Nothing should mar such a fine and valuable thing. It was worth a king's ransom. Now it was his and, after years of desperation, revenge tasted sweet indeed.

# Chapter 1

## Tuesday, the eighteenth day of August in the year of Our Lord 1478 London

The city greeted us upon this summer day, sweltering in the heat and enfolding us in its same old stink made worse by our months of absence. I could see poor Adam – a newcomer to the stench of London – nigh gagging upon the unwholesome airs. No doubt but the unaccustomed sultry weather made it more intense. I could not think it healthful for our newborn son either, yet he alone made no complaint of it, sleeping soundly in my wife Emily's arms. Our walk from Norfolk had taken more than six weeks, what with a fortnight passed in Huntingdon after Emily became unwell. I dare say that was my fault, having forced her to travel so soon after birthing our son. It could not be helped, however, since my nemesis, Anthony Woodville, the queen's brother no less, had been about to visit Foxley village, of all places, where I had sought refuge with relatives. Then, during our journey, there were days spent in washing and drying linen for the babe, resting blistered feet and – in my case – a hip joint that caused me to limp by the end of a long day's trudging. The thought that our travels were at an end at last put a smile upon my face and I could forgive the city its shortcomings, knowing we were home.

There were five of us, including my dog, Gawain. Myself, Sebastian Foxley, reverting now to the surname I was known by in London. My goodwife with our tiny son, Dickon who was nigh unto two months in age. And Adam Armitage, my nephew by a much older brother I only discovered but lately during our sojourn in Norfolk. Adam was of an age with me and had become more like unto a brother. I was wary of how these two new members of our family would be received, particularly by my true brother, Jude.

To Adam, it was all utterly new. He gaped at the market crowds, the towering buildings, the bustling streets. I wondered what he would have thought of the city's Midsummer Watch – a festival we had missed, unfortunately – and St Bartholomew's Fayre still to come in a week's time, when the crowds would be greater by tenfold. As we entered the city by Bishopsgate, I was able to show him Crosby Place, the mansion that was lately the Duke of Gloucester's London home, and Adam's eyes grew wide as cartwheels as he stared at its grand portal, its pinnacled gables and numerous chimneys. Yet the buildings wore a coat of dust that muted its colours, the result of a few weeks without rain, as well as the lack of activity within its walls since Lord Richard had departed for the North Country. All London wore a similar pale shroud in the shimmering haze.

Despite the heat, life went on as usual. The noise of the city was deafening after the quietude of the countryside, and as we pushed through the afternoon crowd in Cornhill, I saw Adam pull his cap down to cover his unaccustomed ears. Apprentices cried their masters' wares, each trying to out-shout his neighbours. Cattle bellowed in the Stocks Market, a gaggle of geese squawked their raucous shrieks of feathered alarm and a laden donkey brayed in protest at the birds swirling about his hooves. Costermongers yelled, iron-rimmed cartwheels clattered over cobbles, and goodwives argued for a bargain. These were the sounds of an ordinary day in London, as Adam would discover. Emily saw a group of her friends gathered by the conduit in Cheapside and, of course, they wanted to see the babe and hear all her news, but she waved them away, promising with a weary smile to tell them everything on the morrow.

Thus, we reached our home by St Paul's – its towering spire another reason for Adam to crane his neck and gasp – but if I believed in returning home to London we could resume our life as it was before, how wrong was I? The house and workshop were still standing in Paternoster Row, having neither burned down nor collapsed in disrepair during our enforced absence and I expected some things to have changed since March last. For one, my brother Jude should have wed sweet Rose. But so much was not as I thought it would be.

Our little party arrived hot, tired and travel-stained, entering the familiar yard through the side gate as we always did and making for the kitchen. We were greeted in the kitchen by a squeal of delight from our gap-toothed serving wench, Nessie, who flung herself at me with such enthusiasm that I staggered under her weight which was more considerable than I remembered.

'Master Seb! You're back!' she cried, breathing onions in my face. 'I knew you'd come soon. I told everyone you would. Mistress Em, is that the babe? Let me see.'

'Nessie, I pray you, let us draw breath,' I said.

Emily sat down with a sigh of relief upon a bench by the board and eased the babe into her lap, flexing her arm now released from its burden.

Adam gazed around in wonder at the kitchen which was of a size with the entire cottage we had dwelt in back in Foxley village.

'This place is a palace, Seb,' he said. 'What must you have thought of the dog kennels we call home?'

'I thought they were wholesome and full of kindly welcome. What more did we need? We were content, Adam. Now, Nessie, pour us all some ale, if you will? And water for Gawain. Where be your manners? This is Adam Armitage. He will be biding with us. Come now! I know he be fine and handsome, but cease gawping at him and fetch us drink.'

Adam laughed, seeing her staring and fluttering her eyelashes. He would learn soon enough that Nessie fell in love – aye, and out again – with every pair of breeches that crossed the threshold, be they butchers' apprentices or noble knights. She had been smitten by both in the past.

I kicked off my dusty boots, flexing cramped toes, and bade Adam do likewise. After a sip of ale, I knelt and unfastened Emily's shoes for her as she began unwinding the babe's swaddling bands to change his wet tailclout. I passed her the bundle of linen we had brought with us from Norfolk, though there was little left that remained clean, but that could be put to rights now.

'Where are the others?' I asked Nessie as I put a ladleful of cool water in a bowl for the dog. He lapped it up gratefully.

She shrugged.

'Out.'

'What? All of them? Who be attending to customers in the shop? What of our work?'

She shrugged again.

'Can I hold the babe?' she asked Emily, holding out her arms. This was Nessie's way of avoiding making answer.

I sat on a stool, thankful at last to ease my hip. Warm weather aided it considerably, but we had walked so many miles these last weeks, rest was welcome.

'You may hold him after you answer Master Seb's question,' Emily said, sounding stern as she re-pinned the swaddling bands in place around the babe. Fortunately for us all, he was proving a placid little soul, our Dickon.

'Well, I don't know, do I? Nobody tells me what they're doing; just "do this, Nessie; do that, Nessie; fetch water, sweep the floors, chop the onions, wash the pots". Master Jude goes out first thing, Tom and Jack disappear to the Lord knows where, and me and Mistress Rose do all the work. That's all I know. It'll be better now you're back. Is that great hound really Gawain? Ain't he growed so.'

Feeling disquieted by Nessie's words – though how true they might prove was not to be relied upon – I went along the passage to the workshop. Mayhap, I should have been pleased to see it was neat and spotless, not a sheet of paper nor a quill pen nor a pot of ink out of place. However, it did not please me in the least for it was clear that not a stroke of work had been done there all day, perhaps all week. In the shop, the counter board was not lowered, opening on to the street, that prospective customers might see our books and pamphlets for sale. In fact, the door was firmly closed, inviting no one in to browse or buy. The shelves were well stocked and dusted, but I swear the items for sale were the same ones as had sat there back in March when we had left London. Had Jude even opened the shop during our time away? I began to have my doubts.

Back in the kitchen, Emily was already inspecting the larder for stuff that might go in the pot for supper. The bacon, onions and peas that had been intended to feed five mouths would now have to stretch to three more, and I was hungry indeed. No doubt, Emily and Adam were also. My wife was grumbling about the lack of provisions.

'There's naught worth having on these shelves but a morsel of cheese and wilting herbs,' she complained.

''Tis otherwise in the shop,' I said. 'The shelves be as full as when we left and with the very same items still for sale. Nessie, has Master Jude sold anything of late?'

'Can't can he? Shop's shut, master.' Nessie blew her nose upon her apron and turned her back to me.

'I can see that, but why?'

'Not allowed,' she muttered.

'What is it that be not allowed? Tell me.'

'Shop's shut 'cos the guild says so. That's all I know.'

'The guild says so? Why would they? This makes no sense to me.'

7

'With that wretched brother of yours, naught ever makes sense,' Emily said with a heartfelt sigh. 'This is his fault, of course.'

'Now, Em, you must not apportion blame afore we know the facts of the matter. This may have naught to do with Jude.'

'You never should have trusted him to run the business, Seb. It was doomed to go awry.'

'What else was I to do when we had to leave in such haste?' I turned my hands, palms upward: empty.

'I cannot say, but I know who will have to sort out the mess – you! Now you must excuse me. I have a babe to feed.' With that, Emily swept out and retired to the parlour. Like Nessie, she would turn her back on the problem. I wished I could too.

'Not the welcome you would have hoped for, eh, Seb?' Adam said, reaching out to touch my arm in a gesture of reassurance.

'No. Nor the best way for you to come join us. I apologise for the lack of comfort and warmth of greeting for you. This is not how it should be. Nessie, more ale for Adam, if you please?' I watched her refill his cup, spilling droplets on the board, careless as ever, but what was the point in reprimanding her? She would never change. 'When Jude gets home, I be sure he will explain everything. 'Tis all a misunderstanding, no doubt, about the shop.'

'Aye, no doubt,' Adam said, sounding unconvinced, pulling at his close-shorn beard as he often did when thinking. We heard sounds in the yard: a woman's light step and Rose came in, laden with a basket of vegetables.

'God give you good day, Rose,' I said, feeling my heart skip with the same pleasure I had every time I saw her, the greater for months of parting.

'Seb! My dearest, dearest friend.' She set her basket upon the floor to embrace me.

I kissed her soft cheek, fragrant and cool as flower petals, and returned her joyous smile.

'How do you fare, lass? You be well?'

'In good health, aye. And you? Where is Emily?'

'Nursing our babe in the parlour: a boy-child. We named him Richard. But I must introduce you both. Adam, this is Rose, my brother's wife. Rose, this is Adam Armitage, my near relation and, by happenstance, a fine scrivener. He will be staying with us and working here until he be settled.' I saw Adam's eyes brighten and his lips part as he took her hand. She affected most men thus.

'I-I must correct the, er, introduction, I fear,' Rose stammered, shaking her head. 'I am wife to no man.' Her voice roughened with unshed tears.

'How so, Rose? What of the wedding? It was all arranged.'

'There was no wedding. Oh, Seb, Seb. It was the worst day of my life.'

How blind and foolish had I been not to notice that she failed to conceal her hair as a goodwife must, nor was there a ring upon her finger.

'Never turned up, did he, that Master Jude,' Nessie said, unasked, as she took parsnips and coleworts from the basket and flung them in a bowl of cold water.

'Oh, I be that sorry, Rose. He seemed so set upon it. Oh, sweet lass, I apologise for his lack of thought. If I may make amends in any way?' I held her close, feeling her tears soaking through my clothes.

'Well, I've never met him,' Adam said, 'But if he turned from taking you to wife, then he must be the greatest fool on God's earth.'

I set a stool for Rose and gave her my ale to drink, that she might be restored somewhat.

'Can you speak of it, lass?' I asked. 'If it doesn't distress you beyond bearing to tell of it?'

She sipped the cup and dried her eyes.

''Tis such a tale of woe as you never heard, Seb. All was ready upon Easter Sunday: the food for the marriage breakfast, my new gown, everyone invited... I was so happy at the thought that next day Jude and I would be man and wife. Then he went to the Panyer Inn with his fellows, as they insisted, to celebrate his last few hours of freedom from the yoke of wedlock. He didn't return. The following morn, we all assembled in the porch at St Paul's: the priest, the guests, everybody. But not Jude. He never came. Eventually, one of his so-called friends arrived, still stinking of drink and piss, his nose bloodied, to tell us Jude was in Ludgate lock-up. There had been a brawl in the tavern and Jude was the cause...' Rose took a shuddering breath.

'My poor lass,' I said, stroking her hair in an act of consolation.

'But that is only half the story and not the worst of it,' she went on. 'You see, the fellow with whom Jude picked the quarrel ended with a broken arm and half-blinded in his eye. Being a scrivener like Jude, such injuries made it impossible for him to work for many weeks and even now he can't see properly, though his arm is mending.'

'Who is he that suffered so?'

'That is the sorriest part of it: 'tis Ralph Clifford, may God aid us.'

'Sweet heaven. Jude could hardly have done more harm if he had betrayed the king himself.'

'Why is that?' Adam asked. 'Who is this Ralph Clifford?'

'The son of John Clifford, the Warden Master of the Stationers' Guild.'

'Oh. That's bad indeed.'

'Now Jude is in the good graces of no man,' Rose said. 'Warden Clifford has had him fined and banned from trading for bringing the guild into disrepute; the Dean of St Paul's has fined him for failing to turn up for our wedding, and even the innkeeper at the Panyer has forbidden him to drink there again, since the place was wrecked during the fight. Oh, Seb, you have returned to find us in such straits as I would not wish upon my vilest enemy and never upon my dearest friend. We have all betrayed your trust so dreadfully.'

'No, Rose. Not you. Never say that. This be Jude's doing and no other's. Where is he? Do you know?'

'At his new favoured tavern, I suppose, drowning his sorrows, as usual, having naught else to do these days. He'll be at the Hart's Horn in Giltspur Street, if you know it?'

'Aye, I know it. 'Tis run by a respectable woman, Mistress Fletcher. He'd better behave himself in her tavern for she won't allow any troublemaking under her roof.'

'We see little of him, in truth,' Rose said. 'I think he is too ashamed.'

'Does he sleep here or lodge yet at Dame Ellen's place as before?'

'Dame Ellen has turned him from her door. As I said: he is in no one's favour now. His bed in his old room here sometimes looks to have been slept in but often not. He rarely eats with us, preferring the food at the Hart's Horn, I believe. Every now and then I find a heap of his soiled linen in his room and clean shirts disappear from the clothes press, but that seems to be his sole reason for coming home. When he is here, he barely speaks to any of us, spending his time in the parlour, shunning our company to sit alone, brooding and scowling. If I ask how he fares or if he has need of anything, he ignores me. He has never once mentioned the wedding...' Rose drew a long, quivering breath to steady herself. 'I know not where I stand concerning this last, Seb, whether we will ever be wed or no. It seems unlikely.'

I wondered at her words; that she should even want to marry my brother after what had come to pass. She must have read the query in my eyes.

'Aye, I know 'tis utter madness, but I am fond of him still, Seb. He has suffered such misfortune of late, but it was just one moment of foolishness that caused it all. If only it hadn't been Ralph Clifford that he struck.'

'But it was, and now we all suffer the consequences. First thing upon the morrow, I shall go to the guild and see what may be done to restore our business and our reputation, though the damage to both sounds serious indeed. At least I have not offended the guild insofar as I know. Mayhap, I will be permitted to reopen the shop and commence trading once more, even though Jude be forbidden. I pray it may be so. But what of Tom and Jack? What have they been about all this while?'

'Little to the good, I fear, and naught to improve our standing. They take no heed of a word I say. Gossip has it that Jack has been seen crossing to Bankside too many times of late. I know not where Tom goes. Perhaps they go together.'

'Bankside be a den of brothels, gambling houses and unlicensed taverns on the far side of London Bridge. Such shady dealings go on there as you would hardly believe,' I explained to Adam who pulled a face but said naught. What was there to say? Matters went from bad to worse. A master was responsible for the good behaviour of his apprentices, and it seemed mine were running wild.

Almost as if the speaking of their names had conjured them from the air – it being nigh suppertime by now – the unruly pair entered the kitchen with a racket that sounded more like a riotous mob than two youngsters. They stopped short at the sight of me. They were unkempt and smelled of strong ale and more unwholesome things also.

'M-master Seb. It's you, ain't it?' Jack said, being the first to recover. I noted the faint bloom of manly fluff upon his chin, and I swear he had grown another hand's span since Lent.

'Aye. 'Tis me, Jack, in the very flesh.' I drew myself up as tall as I might: we were much of a height now, but he hung his head and slouched over to a stool. Tom would not meet my eye either. Both lads knew they were disgraced without my speaking of it.

Supper was served, somewhat tardily. We sat at the board as of old, but with Adam taking Jude's place. I introduced him to the lads, and he spoke briefly of his home in Foxley and why he had come with us to London. Otherwise, little was said at all, and I could not say what we ate. The lads were silent as grave markers. Emily and Rose spoke in whispers to each other, mostly about the babe, with Nessie adding her occasional heedless pennyworth.

For myself, I was, of a sudden, so beset by problems, I felt overwhelmed and unable to voice my tumultuous thoughts coherently. My mind was in such turmoil as to what should be done to begin to mend matters. I ought to speak with Jude afore I did anything but, in truth, I hardly dare contemplate what I should say to him that would be other than a torrent of curses. Mayhap, it was for the best if we did not meet afore I had calmed myself and done what I might to order my thoughts, aye, and my tongue. But, as with all events this day, the avoidance of just such a meeting proved impossible, for my brother came home as we finished our supper.

Although by no means incapable, he was plainly the worse for drink, belligerent and maudlin by turns.

'What the bloody hell are you doing here?' That was his greeting to me.

''Tis good to see you, Jude,' I said, despite his words. I went to embrace him, but he stepped aside to avoid my gesture of brotherly affection. 'Oh, well, mayhap I should introduce you to our close relation from Foxley village, Ad...'

'Why are you here, Seb? What have you come for? Go back to bloody Norfolk, can't you? I don't need you here.'

'It seems to me that you do need me, Jude,' I contradicted him. 'What in heaven's name have you done to our business, you witless idiot?'

'Sod the business. Is that all you care about? Bloody guild ruined it, not me.'

'But our good name and reputation: what of those?'

'Get off me!' Jude snatched his arm away, and I realised I had been grasping his wrist. He turned on me, teeth bared in a snarl, his fist raised to strike me full in the face. But the blow never landed. Adam was there, twisting Jude's elbow so much that he cried out that it was breaking. Adam released him but shoved him back onto a bench and Emily clouted him with her favoured weapon: the broom. For good measure, Gawain seized his boot betwixt his teeth.

'Who the hell are you, you damned bastard? Wrenching my bloody arm like that,' Jude demanded of Adam once things quieted. He was rubbing his arm and wincing. 'And get that bloody mutt out of here.' His booted foot lashed out, but Gawain was sufficiently nimble to avoid it.

'I'm your nephew and all legitimate, upon my honour,' Adam said, grinning and holding out his hand in greeting, though Jude ignored it. 'So pleased to make your acquaintance, dearest uncle!' He burst out laughing. 'You should see your face: a smacked arse never looked so shocked.'

It took the lads a moment or two to understand Adam's words, what with his broad Norfolk way of speaking, but then they were chortling with merriment, and I was hard put not to join them. Jude's scowl was more fearsome than a basilisk's.

'Don't you dare bloody mock me, else I'll knock you into the midst of next month, you miserable dog turd.'

'Miserable? Indeed not, Uncle. Dog turds are a nuisance, 'tis true, but the dog always feels better for having made them, and they are greatly appreciated by the tanners' craft. Now, shall we not shake hands and be friends, as well as relatives?' Adam offered his hand a second time.

'Relatives be damned. You can all go to hell!' With which parting shot, my brother stormed out, slamming the door as hard as he could. He was still cursing us from the yard. We heard him even through the thickness of oak, and all of us sighed with relief, though I was saddened that our reunion had gone so badly. I was none the wiser as to our difficulties with the guild either, but no doubt I should learn the worst of it in the morning.

We retired early: Rose to her lonely bed in the little room she used to share with Kate, my talented young apprentice whom I hoped might return to us soon. Tom and Jack went to their attic and Adam had our old bedchamber at the back of the house – that which should have been Rose's bridal bed with Jude. Emily and I were to occupy the refurbished large chamber above the parlour where the glazed window – aye, there were eight glass panes in it – looked out across Paternoster Row to St Paul's. Rose had made a splendid job of cleaning out the mice and spiders that had inhabited the room for so long, making new hangings for the bed and a woven rush mat for the floor. Pride of place though went to the rocking cradle, intricately designed and wonderfully made by Stephen Appleyard, Emily's father, for his first grandchild. It even had a hinged canopy that folded back, so there was no danger of catching the infant's fragile head as he was lifted in and out of the bed. Little Dickon would sleep in princely comfort there.

In truth, I did not expect to sleep at all that night, not only because my mind was a-swirl with the troubles of the day, but because of the noise of the city even after dark, what with the ringing of church bells, the shouts of the Watch and the constant barking of dogs: sounds I had forgotten in the quiet of Foxley village. Yet my exhaustion was such that I slept deeply. Even the midnight wails of the babe failed to disturb my slumbers.

# Chapter 2

## Wednesday, the nineteenth day of August
## The Stationers' Hall in Ave Maria Lane

THE STATIONERS' HALL was not so grand as those belonging to the Goldsmiths' or Mercers' Guilds, but it was, nonetheless, an imposing building, backing on to the Bishop's Palace and facing the ageing but overly ornamented facade of Pembroke Inn across the way. The hall's pale stonework had shed much of its customary lichen cloak, the dry heat of recent weeks having scorched it away. A gull, up from the river, perched on a cornice, fixing me with its evil yellow eye. I made the sign of the cross to bless myself. I needed no additional superstitious fears to weigh upon me; I had burden sufficient as it was. I always admired the gargoyles; one, in particular, reminded me in a kindly way of my old master, Richard Collop, and of habit, I usually smiled up at the carving. But not today.

Despite the blazing sunshine, the hour was yet early, and Stationers' Hall was still in shadow. Above the grand entrance, the vivid paintwork of the guild's coat-of-arms – my own handiwork of a twelvemonth since – was dulled to sombre shades. I suppose it suited my downcast humour that it should look so colourless. The great studded doors might have been Hell's portal, and I dreaded what might await me on the other side.

One half of the door stood open, and I went in, wondering how my fellow stationers would receive me. The perfumes of parchment, paper and hot humanity eddied in the gloom. A knot of men stood just within, all of them known to me.

'I greet you well, good masters,' I said, touching my cap. 'May God grant you blessings this day.' The group parted to make way for me, like the sea before Moses, gowns rustling softly as wind in the trees. 'Good day, Master Benedict,' I said to one. 'How do you fare? I trust your wife and children be well? And Master Jameson, is your mother improved in health since last we met?'

Both men regarded me as if I carried some vile contagion.

'Master Foxley,' Benedict acknowledged brusquely and then turned his back. Jameson ignored me, saying naught, but returning to his conversation with the others. I did not speak to the rest for they all moved away, shunning me. I went further into the hall, seeing Warden Clifford standing by the dais, talking with Richard Collop, who had previously held the same office. Since I had worked hard as Master Collop's apprentice not so long since, surely, he at least would still prove a friend. As I approached, Warden Clifford saw me. His brow drew down, and his face darkened as an approaching storm.

'So you've returned,' he growled. 'I am surprised that you dare show yourself here.'

'Good day, Warden Clifford; Master Collop. I greet you well. God's blessings be upon you both.'

'We have no business dealings with you Foxleys. You're no longer welcome in this company. Be off with you!' Clifford's anger was blatant as he shook his fist, but Master Collop smiled at me.

'Now, now, John,' he said, laying a hand upon the warden's shoulder. 'The trouble was not of young Sebastian's making. Don't blame him for the hurt done to your son.'

'I pray that Ralph is mending, sir,' I said to the warden.

'Aye, no doubt you do, but we're still suing that wastrel brother of yours for compensation through the Lord Mayor's Court for the grievous harm he did. We are determined upon it.'

'Oh? I know naught of that, Master Clifford. In truth, I have exchanged so few words with Jude since my return yesterday; I be here to discover what came to pass precisely and to enquire as to when I may reopen my shop.'

'Never, if I have anything to do with it. You Foxleys are a disgrace to the guild.'

'That's not fair, John,' Master Collop said. 'Sebastian is a highly respected and industrious member of our fellowship.'

'They're folios cut from the same inferior parchment: each as bad as the other.'

''Twas not Sebastian who brought the stationers into disrepute. And remember,' Master Collop added in a whisper which perhaps I was not meant to hear, 'The Duke of Gloucester is his patron. We wouldn't want to offend the king's beloved brother, would we?' He winked at me, and I smiled in return. Richard Collop was indeed still my friend, God be thanked.

About one hour later, I returned home with a more spritely step and a somewhat lighter heart. With ill-grace and grudgingly, Warden Clifford had permitted me to open the shop and trade once again, though it would require the approval of a full meeting of the guild to reinstate the name 'Foxley' in the memoranda rolls from which it had been struck out – a revelation which had shocked me indeed. At length, he had heeded the wise counsel of Master Collop, however reluctantly, admitting I was not at fault in the matter. Thus, I had good tidings to impart – with one unfortunate proviso for the resumption of business: Jude was not to be a part of it. This distressed me, but mayhap it would not bother my brother so much?

I entered through the front door, rather than by means of the side gate, calling out:

'Tom! Jack! Come. Let down the shutter-board straightway. We be open for trade, directly. Hasten, everyone. 'Tis business as usual.'

At least Rose answered me, hurrying into the shop.

'You mended matters with the guild, then? I knew they would listen to you, Seb,' she said as we lowered the shutter onto its trestles to form the shop counter. She began arranging a few of the best books upon it, hoping to entice customers, polishing the covers with her apron so they appeared bright as possible.

'Aye, after a fashion, at least.'

'Is there still a difficulty then?'

'Our name is not yet reinstated. That will take a while, I fear. A-and... well, Jude is forbidden to be my partner. How long he may be barred from the trade, I know not, but there it stands. That be the situation for now.'

Rose nodded but said naught. I suppose, like me, she wondered if Jude would care.

Adam appeared in the doorway.

'So it's back to work, after all, Seb?' he said with a grin. 'You'd best show me what's to be done then, if I'm to earn my bed and board.'

'I shall be delighted to do so, shortly, but where are those two scallywags? I told them to await my return, did I not?' I strode along the passage to the kitchen. Emily was suckling the babe at her breast. Nessie was scrubbing the board clean. But of Tom and Jack, there was no sign.

'You had success with the guild, I hear?' Emily said, lifting little Dickon onto her shoulder and patting his back to wind him. 'That's a relief. Our funds from Lord Richard are all but spent. We need money, husband, and swiftly.'

'I be aware of that, Em, but a master also needs his apprentices. Where are they?'

'After breaking their fast – which you have yet to do – they went out to the yard. Tom said he would see Gawain did his business out there and Jack claimed his boots needed cleaning. I should have been suspicious of Jack cleaning anything, but I had Dickon to see to. Neither of them has come back since. They must have gone slinking off like a pair of miscreants as soon as your back was turned. They need a good thrashing with my broom, and they'll get it when next I see them, the idle young scoundrels.'

Emily was right: I had not had breakfast, so I helped myself to ale.

'Is there bread and cheese, Nessie?' I asked.

She shoved a platter at me, all ungraciously.

'And don't go dropping crumbs on that board what I just scrubbed.' So much for respecting her master.

There came a scratching at the kitchen door. It was the dog but not the lad who was supposed to be with him. No one else was in the yard. I let Gawain in and shared my cheese with him.

In the workshop, Adam was already making use of his knowledge of our craft, preparing a batch of quills. He had soaked them in water and was now heating sand over a small brazier before plunging the ends of the feather shafts into the sand to harden them. The day was already hot, and such a task was an uncomfortable one. Sweat stood out on Adam's brow, and his tunic looked damp beneath his arms.

'We'll also need ink before we do any work,' he said, wiping his forehead on his shirt sleeve. 'What was left has dried up. Do you buy it ready-made or make your own?'

'I prefer to make it up to my own receipt, especially for any high-quality work but, since that takes time and we have no prestigious commissions outstanding, I suppose I'll have to purchase some for the present. Jack can fetch it from St Paul's.'

'From the cathedral across the way?'

'Aye. There are stationers who have their stalls in the nave.'

'Then let me go. I should like the chance to see inside the place. Besides, your Jack's not here, and I'd be glad of a breath of fresh air after this.' Adam set the last quill to cool and fanned his flushed face with a rag before using it to wipe grains of sand from his hands.

'That would be a kindness, Adam,' I said, giving him a couple of coins from my purse. 'But enquire first who the Pullen brothers may be.'

'You want I buy from them?'

'Far from it. Avoid them, Adam. Their ink be so inferior, I wouldn't trust it to write a list for marketing, for fear the words would fade afore I got there. And a toothless old fellow by the name of Giles Honeywell: his wares be of a good standard but, if you purchase anything from him, don't mention that you work with me.'

'Oh? And why not?'

'Because my previous journeyman, Gabriel Widowson, upset him mightily one time by destroying the relics that he was also licensed to sell. Giles has never quite forgiven me, despite my recompensing him for his losses. Dean Wynterbourne wasn't much pleased either.'

'Then 'tis as well your new journeyman knows how to behave himself in church,' Adam said with a laugh. I heard him chuckling with Rose as he went out through the shop. I was glad that someone could bring a little merriment into the Foxley household. Ink might be in short supply, but good humour was a greater lack.

It was many months since I had last sat at my desk, but it felt good to be back in my right and proper place. My pigment brushes were like old friends well met, and I was eager to use them again. With no work requiring my attention, I decided it was time I renewed my acquaintance with my drawing board, so I took up my old leather scrip to confirm its contents. There was my small board, my supply of charcoal and both red and white chalks. There was paper also, including the sketches I had done of the Duke of Clarence – may God assoil him – preparatory to painting his portrait. I wondered if it would ever be painted now; whether Lord Richard would write to me with instructions concerning it. All was in order otherwise except for the scrip itself. I remembered the stitching of the shoulder strap had worn to a few threads and required mending. Afore we departed London in haste, I had meant to re-stitch it. I doubted it would last another outing otherwise, but it was a task I could do now.

'Sewing? Is that a task for you, husband?' Emily came into the workshop, cradling little Dickon in the crook of one arm, a dish of savoury pastries in her other hand. She set down the dish upon my desk and stood watching my efforts with needle and linen thread. 'Here. You take the babe, and I'll have that stitched in no time,' she offered.

It was as well: my handiwork with a needle was not of the best and probably wouldn't last a week. I gave up my stool to her and took Dickon in my arms. I had got used to holding him now, but it had taken a while to lose my fear of dropping him. I was pleased to see that he was awake, his blue eyes – so like his Mam's – gazing up at me. A shaft of morning sunlight through the window caught his wispy halo of hair, turning it to gold thread against the drab cloth of my old doublet. He gurgled and blew a bubble of spit. It seemed he was laughing at me. Aye, a doting Papa be a fine jest indeed.

I began to sing to him, taking him back to the kitchen and then out into our little garden across the yard. The pig greeted us with a contented grunt, wallowing in the patch of mud Nessie had created in the sty to keep her cool. Dickon blew bubbles at her too and waved his arms eagerly. Then I showed him the small hard apples ripening on our solitary tree. The tall stalks of fennel rattled their seed heads in the hint of a breeze. I picked a stem and held it for him. He seemed fascinated by the noise it made when shaken, but then grabbed at it, dispersing most of the seed so it made the pleasing sound no longer. He yawned, showing his moist, rosy tongue. I sang him a lullaby, and he was swiftly asleep, but I liked the soft weight of him in my arms and was in no hurry to put him in his woven basket back in the kitchen.

A cluster of sparrows chirruped and quarrelled on the roof of the pigsty, looking ragged as beggars in their moulting feathers – a reminder that summer was past her prime. Others might complain of the heat, but I dreaded the onset of autumn's chills and with them the return of pain in my hip. It was a penance I paid every winter, so I determined to make the most of the warm season.

Back in the workshop, Emily had repaired my scrip with her perfect stitchery and was eating one of the pastries.

'Try one, Seb: cheese and thyme. See what you think.'

I handed the babe to her.

'His nether end has been making some ripe noises,' I warned her. 'And I detect a definite fresh stink.'

She laughed.

'And you did not dare investigate further, I know.'

'That be a mother's privilege.' I helped myself and took a bite of one of the savouries.

'Poor little Dickon. What he would have to suffer, if it were left to his Papa to tend to his tailclouts. Come, my sweeting. Let Mam clean you up.'

'These pastries be delicious, Em,' I called after her as she left the workshop.

After dinner – for which meal my errant apprentices had miraculously reappeared – I determined to walk to Smithfield to watch the preparations for St Bartholomew's Fayre that would begin on the following Monday and go on for the rest of the week. I should take my drawing stuff, certain there would be plenty of subject matter in all the hustle and bustle that preceded the annual event of the largest cloth fayre in England. But a less pleasant task must take precedence: the rebuke of Tom and Jack. The application of discipline was never a skill of mine but, on this occasion, it was required. Not wishing to be heard in the shop for fear of deterring any customer, I took the pair out to the yard.

They stood before me. Tom frowned down at his shoes, kicking the dust. Jack eyed me with an air of defiance, but at least he looked me in the face.

'Explain yourselves. As soon as I went from the door this morn, you two scuttled off, not to be seen again until mealtime. There was work to be done, yet you absconded.'

'Abs-wot?' Jack said, out of habit, ever querying my choice of words. I was in no mood to enlighten him.

'Where were you? Tom, you give me answer first.' I stood, arms folded, waiting. My anger was simmering. 'Tell me!'

''Cross the bridge,' he muttered without looking up.

'To Bankside?'

He nodded.

'Why? What business have you there?'

'None.' He shrugged.

'Jack? Were you there also?'

'Wot of it, if I wos? No law 'gainst it, is there?'

'You wretched pair. Naught which occurs in Bankside can possibly be of any credit to our good reputation.'

'Wot reputation? Master Jude's dragged it in the shit long ago. We ain't got no good reputation no more, so wot's it matter wot I do?'

'It matters more now than ever, Jack. We must restore it.'

Jack snorted, and I came so close to clipping his ear – closer than I ever had afore.

'If you fink we need a beatin', you should start wiv yer bruvver. Worse than us he is, ain't he?'

'Are you telling me that Master Jude visits Bankside?'

'*The Cockpit, the Cardinal's 'At, the Blue Dolfin.* He's been t'all of 'em. We've seen him, ain't we, Tom?'

Jack had just named the most notorious gambling den, the most infamous brothel and the tavern that was the most vicious nest of crime in Southwark. If he spoke truly, then reprimanding the lads would serve little purpose when my brother was the one destroying our good name so utterly, I feared it might be beyond saving.

'Get about your work, both of you. Tom, start the preparation of ink, then rule up pages for a half dozen cheap primers. You know how well enough. Jack, you can whiten parchment for a fine book I have in mind to begin. Think you can do that without covering the workshop in chalk dust?'

'Wot for? We ain't allowed t'sell nuffink. Guild says so, don't it?'

'No longer. We be in business once more, as of this morn. I persuaded Warden Clifford to permit us to open the shop again. There is a stipulation, however, that need not concern you at present.'

'A stipilashon? Is that a good fing, then?'

'Any more shirking of your tasks or sneaking over to Bankside and I'll not be so lenient next time. Understand?'

'Aye, Master Seb,' they replied in unison. I wondered if they meant it, sighing at the urgent need to reclaim some measure of respect for the Foxley name. It would not be easily accomplished, especially if Jude was intent upon tarnishing it yet further. We would have to speak on this matter, but I dreaded confronting my brother concerning his misdeeds.

With Emily having taken little Dickon with her to collect some silkwork from Dame Ellen in Cheapside, I could not improve my humour by playing with my son. So to cheer myself, I left Tom and Jack in the workshop, under Adam's watchful eye, and went in search of inspiration for my next book – an illustrated version of *Aesop's Fables*. Folk of all ages enjoyed those short, moral tales, but I had it in mind to include marginalia of amusing figures – human bodies with animal heads, each appropriate for the story – thinking it would appeal to children as they learned to read. I suppose I envisaged little Dickon chuckling over the images when he was older and smiled at the thought. Already, I was in better humour.

When I arrived with Gawain at my heel, Smithfield was humming like a beehive, men erecting canvas tents, wooden booths and setting up trestles for their stalls. Packs of merchandise and innumerable baskets and barrels of wares for sale were stacked everywhere, some in precarious piles that looked about to topple. It was a scene of colourful chaos and so much noise. Men shouted, packhorses whinnied, donkeys brayed, and dogs yapped. Canvas awnings cracked and flapped as they were unfolded, wooden supports were hammered home into the sun-hardened ground, and laden barrows groaned and creaked as they trundled over the scorched grass. Of a sudden, a small barrel fell from a leaning stack, its lid coming loose, spilling the contents across the ground. The scent of cloves on the breeze identified the strewn spice, and a foreign tongue cursed it.

I sketched whatever took my eye whilst doing my utmost not to hinder the work in preparation for the fayre. We had a close call when a large dog took a sudden dislike to Gawain and charged at us, growling like a demon, jaws drooling. Fortunately, he was tied to a post, left to guard his master's wares, which duty he accomplished admirably. The rope pulled him up short afore he could sink his fearsome teeth into my leg or Gawain's. Poor Gawain dared not stray an inch from my side after that encounter and his tail drooped for some while as it rarely did.

Returning with a sheaf of sketches and a wealth of inspiration for my *Aesop's Fables*, I was greeted with a smile from Emily as I entered the kitchen.

'Such news, Seb,' she said even afore I had set down my scrip. 'Dame Ellen has arranged for a stall at the fayre, that we might sell our silken stuffs and Rose may sell the gloves she has been making in our absence. Is that not a most excellent opportunity to get us recognised among the finest mercers and drapers?'

'Aye, indeed it is.' I poured myself some ale. I was parched on such a day. I filled Gawain's bowl with water, certain he must be dry also. 'Do you have much to sell?'

'Well, not as much as I might have hoped, though there is the orphrey I finished just before we left London and some other few pieces of gold threadwork. I could do naught in the way of silkwork whilst we were in Norfolk, now could I? But Dame Ellen's other outworkers have been busy, and with Rose's gloves there will be plenty to sell. We will all take turns to serve at the stall. I am so excited, Seb.'

'I be glad for you, Em,' I said, taking her in my arms and kissing her lips.

'None of that, husband.' She pushed me aside. 'I have ribbons and girdles unfinished that could be ready in time for the fayre, if I work on them every minute I may. Here: you take Dickon for a half hour, and I can set up my weaving frame in the parlour afore suppertime.' She put the babe in my arms. 'He's been fed and his tailclout changed. You can manage him, can you not?'

'Aye, I suppose...'

'Nessie. Get that coney skinned and jointed and put it in the pot for supper and watch that cherry pie doesn't scorch whilst you keep it warm on the hearthstone, you hear?'

'Aye, Mistress Em,' the maid sighed and gave me a look of resignation as we both were directed in our tasks.

With Emily busy in the parlour, I took Dickon and my scrip through to the workshop. I was both pleased – and somewhat surprised – to find a scene of industry. Adam was copying out a text, Tom was ruling pages, and Jack was decanting ink from a pig's bladder into small stoppered pots, ready for use. This last was the most unusual in that he had spilled not a drop. He had also made a decent effort with four sheets of perfectly whitened parchment without the workshop being shrouded in chalk dust.

'I see you have done a good afternoon's work, all of you. I commend your diligence. Thank you.' I put my scrip on my desk and hooked the stool with my foot, pulling it out so I might sit with the babe upon my lap.

'We are in your employ. You feed us and give us a roof over our heads. In return, we work.' Adam looked up with an expression of puzzlement. 'Is that not how it's supposed to be, Seb?'

'Aye, it is. But that has not always been the case of late. Has it?' I fixed first Tom and then Jack with my eye.

Tom muttered something under his breath that I could not make out.

'We had no reason t' work when Master Jude got us shut down, did we?' Jack said, stoppering the last ink pot. 'Weren't no point us doin' fings wot would never get sold, was there?'

'Your logic is impeccable,' I said, 'But things have changed now.'

'Im-wot-able?'

'Faultless, Jack. And we have our reputation to restore.'

'Aye, 'til Master Jude picks anuvver fight wiv anuvver important fat arse 'ole.'

'Jack! I will not tolerate such speech. You will say extra prayers this eve to cleanse your mouth. Five Aves and two Paternosters at the very least.' It was fortunate my little son was deep asleep; I would not have him hear such words at so tender an age.

'Sorry, master.'

'Adam,' I said, turning to a more pleasurable subject. 'What did you think of our cathedral? Fine, is it not?'

'It took my breath away, Seb, in every way.' Adam set down his pen. 'The stained glass is a wonder indeed and far more bedazzling than the cathedral in Norwich. And the nave is so vast. The fellow from whom I bought the ink told me it's the longest nave in all of Christendom. Is that true?'

'Maybe.'

'But what robbed me of my breath was the stink of it. So many sweating bodies were hardly the worst of it. I expected that, but you never warned me about the cheese sellers, Seb. Their wares were that ripe they could stun a fellow at fifty cloth-yards distance, I swear.'

'I had forgotten about that. In hot weather, the goodwives are permitted to sell their butter and cheeses in the cool of the nave, else you'd need a bucket to carry home your purchases. The butter would be melted and rancid and the soft cheeses gone runny. It has always been the way of it every summer.'

'And such a din as all the sellers shouted out to get my attention. It seemed amiss to me in the House of God – so much yelling and distraction.'

'You must attend vespers there one evening. The choristers make a more heavenly sound. And, thinking on it, I ought to pay my respects to the precentor, letting him know I be available once more, if he requires my services.' I picked up a quill, untrimmed as yet, and tickled 'neath Dickon's dimpled chin, setting him gurgling with pleasure.

'You sing? I mean, I know you can; I've heard you in Foxley church and at your work. But you sing in St Paul's?'

'It has been known,' I said, feeling the heat rise in my cheeks. I wished I hadn't mentioned it. I lifted the babe to my shoulder to conceal my reddened face from Adam.

'Master Seb's got the best set o' lungs in London, ain't he?' Jack said, adding to my discomfiture. 'Sang fer the bishop last Christmastide, he did.'

At that moment, little Dickon stirred in my arms. Perhaps he was too hot in so many layers of swaddling and held close against me. I realised my chest was damp with sweat – his and mine.

'Dickon needs some fresh air,' I said. 'I shall be in the garden, if you need me.' Thus, I escaped from the embarrassing discussion.

Jude had returned, seemingly in a more mellow humour since he had spoken with civility to Adam and taken time to acknowledge little Dickon. After supper, he and I were alone in the kitchen. Everyone else had retired, including Adam who still kept countryman's hours and was frugal with candles. I had spread my sketches made earlier across the board, to choose the most suitable for the *Fables*, but I was only postponing the matter I dreaded. The moment had come when I could delay my conversation with my brother no longer, concerning his actions during my months of enforced absence. I poured more ale for both of us, certain we should need it. Jude took the cup and drank deep even as I braced myself to commence the speech I had been rehearsing in my head. How to reprimand my brother without having him fly into a temper?

'Jude. We must talk about...'

He held up his hands, stilling my words of reproach afore I began.

'I have to tell you: I'm going, Seb,' he said, though he still sat at the board.

'To the Hart's Horn, I suppose? Give my regards to Mistress Fletcher, but first, you must hear what I have to say.'

'No. You don't have to say anything. I mean I'm leaving. Leaving London.'

'What? But why? Why would you leave now, when we've hardly been reunited since I returned from Norfolk?'

'You've seen something of the world beyond London. Now it's my turn.'

'But that was not from choice, and I need you, Jude. I cannot manage without you.'

'You most surely can, as your months away have proved. You don't need me anymore, little brother. Besides, you've got Adam to help in the workshop now.'

'Of course I need you still! Adam is *not* my *brother.*'

'He might as well be. You two are grown close.'

'If you be jealous of him, there is no need...'

'Seb, listen to me. You have a wife, a child, a business to run. You're a good man. You work hard, and folk respect you. You've made a success of your life. Whereas I've made a bloody mess of mine from one end to the other.' He sighed with the weight of his words. 'This is my chance to begin anew; make a fresh start.'

'But, Jude...'

'You'll not persuade me otherwise, so save your breath. The others will be glad to see me gone.'

I gulped my ale; my hands a-tremble with the shock. Mayhap, that was partly true. Emily would be relieved and, most probably, the lads would not mind if he left, dreading his punishments as they did.

'Rose will not be glad at all,' I blurted out. 'She loves you, Jude.'

He laughed, but there was no humour in it.

'She should count her blessings that the wedding never came to pass, else she'd be shackled to me forever and forced to come with me.' He reached across the board and ran a melancholy finger along the bones in my hand, one by one. 'She'd hate that, seeing 'tis you she truly loves. She only said she'd wed me to be close to you. Well, now she's free of me. I shall not hold her to any promise.'

'You speak so much nonsense, Jude. None of that be the truth in the least.'

He pushed back from the board and regarded me for a long, thoughtful moment, then shook his head.

'Of course it is. 'Tis all too true: Rose loves you, little brother; not me. You must be blind, if you see it not. Anyhow, I'll be gone first thing.'

'Where will you go? What will you do for money? How will you earn your bread? How long will you be away?'

'Don't concern yourself. I haven't yet determined where I'll go.'

'Huntingdon is not so far and looked to be a goodly town when we were there a little while...'

'France, maybe?'

'No! Not there... across the Narrow Sea. To England's enemy?'

'Perhaps Bruges, then. An Englishman will get a friendlier welcome in Burgundian lands, no doubt. Or Rome?'

'I do not see you as a pilgrim, Jude. You cannot go...'

'Did I mention a pilgrimage? No. 'Tis just a city I'd like to see.'

'What about money?'

'A scrivener can earn a few pence anywhere, reading or writing letters for others.'

'In French or Dutch?'

Jude shrugged.

'Latin will serve me well enough, particularly in Rome, if I go there. I have no worries about money.'

'When do you intend to leave?'

'As I told you: first thing in the morn.'

'So soon? Oh, Jude, not yet. It is too sudden. I need to prepare myself.'

'For what? I'm leaving; not you. Besides, you left London without a word.'

'There were men attempting to kill me, as you well know. I wanted to bid you farewell, but Lord Richard's good sense prevailed: the streets were too dangerous for me then. If-if you be certain of your intent, I shall come with you as far as...'

'No, Seb. I want no miserable, long farewell. I shall be gone by first light. Have a good life, little brother.'

Of a sudden, I felt empty inside, as though I had been hollowed out. I stared at him, memorising his face to the last blemish, every bristle on his stubbled chin but, mostly, his eyes.

Would I remember them: the deepest shade of lapis lazuli, if I never saw him again?

'Jude, please. I cannot bear to...' Tears leaked and ran down my cheeks. I grasped his arm as if to save myself from drowning. 'Please. I beg you. I love you, Jude.'

'Enough! Don't try to talk me out of this. My mind is set upon it.' He pulled himself free of me. 'Don't make such a bloody fuss. You're a man, not some wet-eyed, lovelorn wench.'

I nodded and wiped my face with my palms. I made a pretence at tidying the sketches, but selecting the most suitable for the *Fables* book was of no importance any longer. My brother was leaving: I could not believe it. I sipped the last of my ale. Without looking at him, not wanting to burden him with my boundless sorrow, I touched his hand, having his warm flesh against mine. It was reassuring to feel his strength one last time.

'You are right. We both have to live as we think best. May God be with you always, Jude, my beloved brother. There will ever be a welcome for you here when your purse runs dry, which it surely will.'

Without another word, Jude nodded at me and left the kitchen to seek his bed. Long after, 'til the candle burnt down, I sat with my faithful Gawain, his head resting against my knee. I think the creature knew and understood my distress, my sense of loss, gazing up at me with dark eyes brimful of sympathy, his wet nose nuzzling my fingers. It felt like a bereavement to have Jude go from me of a sudden, and it hurt like a blade piercing my heart. But if such was his decision, who was I to speak against it? It was his life to be lived as he saw fit. I would pray God to keep him safe and guide him upon the righteous path, yet I doubted that was the way matters would betide. Jude was never one to take the straight road if there looked to be an intriguing diversion. God had granted mankind self-will, and my brother ever took full advantage of it.

# Chapter 3

## Thursday, the twentieth day of August

I arose before dawn and hastened to my brother's bedchamber. Whatever he said about not wanting any long farewells, I desperately needed to see him one last time afore he departed. Yet already I was too late. Jude's unmade bed was empty, his belongings gone. I put my hand to his sheets and coverlet, but the warmth of his body was faded. He must have left even as the first glimmers of morning had crept through his east-facing shutters. I sat upon his bed and could not help the tears that flowed. How long I remained there, I know not, but I was roused by Rose, calling Jude to break his fast.

'Seb?' she said as I stepped to the door of the bedchamber. 'I didn't expect you to be here. Where's Jude? Why the sorrowful face? Is something amiss?'

'He's gone, Rose. Gone away with no plan to return to us.'

Her eyes grew wide with shock.

'Gone? But why? Why would he leave now you've returned and set matters aright?' Tears glinted, threatening to spill. 'Why has he left us, Seb?'

'I have no sensible explanation. He said he desired to see something of the world and needed to make a new beginning, though why he could not start afresh here by marrying you, I fail to understand. You were the best thing in his life, Rose: I cannot think why he would go without you.'

'Did he say that or are those your words, about me being 'the best thing in his life'? He never really loved me, Seb, did he?' She dabbed at her eyes with her apron. 'I think he was afraid of the responsibilities of having a wife and, mayhap, children too. Perhaps it is better this way.' She sighed and looked wistful.

'But you love him, Rose...'

'Do I? Maybe. But not enough. I feel tenderness for him, but mayhap I do not love him enough to chase after him and try to persuade him to return. If he would prefer to live his life without me, then I can do likewise. Fear not, Seb, I too shall start afresh.'

I felt wonder at her words, that she was not distressed as I expected. She lifted her chin, straightened her shoulders and smiled at me, laying her hand upon my arm.

'Come,' she said, 'The bacon collops will be going cold.'


When I broke the news of Jude's departure to everyone gathered at the board to break their fast, I was stunned to realise no one else seemed the least dismayed. I never expected Emily to grieve, for she had little liking for my brother, but the others were either indifferent or even pleased that he was gone. Emily was delighted and made no secret of it. Nessie – who used to dote upon him at one time – shrugged and served the pottage.

'Bigger helpings for us then,' she said.

Tom grinned and nodded, probably relieved that the source of his constant chastisement was removed. Jack, thinking of his belly as always, simply asked if he could have the bacon that lay cooling upon Jude's trencher. I was alone in feeling any loss or regret, but at least there was a measure of understanding from Gawain who nuzzled my hand and put his paw upon my thigh in mute consolation. And then there was Adam who, despite barely an hour or two of acquaintance with Jude, was the only voice of real condolence.

'This house will miss him,' Adam said. 'I should have liked to have known him far better. I know I cannot remove your sorrow, Seb, but if I may do anything to help ease it, you but need to ask, and I shall do it.'

'My thanks, Adam, for your kindly words,' I said. Aye, the only kindly words spoken that morn. I took a bite of bread, chewed it but was hardly able to swallow it for the constriction of unshed tears in my throat. A goodly mouthful of ale was required to get it down.

'Did you hear a single word I said?' Emily nudged me hard with her elbow.

'Forgive me, Em. I fear my thoughts were elsewhere.'

'Aye, halfway to Dover with that brother of yours, no doubt. I said: I shall feed Dickon and then be away to Dame Ellen's for the rest of the morn. There is so much to do in readiness for St Bart's next week, and her other out-workers are useless at organising anything more complicated than their own Sunday veils. I'm ever surprised that Beatrice Thatcher manages to get herself out of bed each day and Peronelle Wenham couldn't arrange eggs in a basket. And as for Lizzie Knollys... Are you listening to me, husband?'

'Indeed, Em. You be going to Dame Ellen's place.'

'I'll settle little Dickon first, but you'll have to give an ear to him, if he wakes. I shall be back for dinner. Nessie, we need butter from St Paul's and see if they have any soft cheese – I have a mind to serve it in a sauce with our fish on the morrow. And pick some more chives from the garden.'

'Aye, mistress. Anything else?'

'The pastry for the pie, the parlour needs dusting, and you can strip Jude's bed, seeing he won't be needing it any longer. Remake it, and Adam can have that chamber as his own now.' Emily smiled sweetly at my nephew.

Thus was my brother dismissed in a flurry of bed linen in need of laundering. It hurt to think that he was already a matter of so little consequence as next Monday's washing and so readily replaced with a new member of the household. Dear as Adam was to me, he could not take my brother's place in my heart so easily.

After Emily had left, the babe was not yet inclined to sleep in his cradle so, despite a deal of work to be done, I endeavoured to raise my spirits by means of a deep and meaningful discussion with my son. I carried him into the shop and pointed out the fine quality of the best books, the good ones intended for discerning scholars of less affluent means and the cheap pamphlets for those without coin to spare. I told him all this would belong to him one day and chose a small hornbook for him from the counter board.

'Isn't he a little young for that, Seb?' Rose said, seeing me holding it for Dickon. She rearranged the books on the counter to fill the gap.

''Tis never too soon to learn to love books,' I said. 'See? He admires the words already.' Dickon was waving his arms enthusiastically as I read out the Ave Maria to him, pointing out the rubrics. No doubt, the red ink initials attracted his eye. I turned the paddle-shaped board over to show where the alphabet had been written out so neatly by young Kate Verney. Which reminded me that I should visit her father this afternoon, to make arrangements for her return to her apprenticeship. It was to be hoped that her time at home had been sufficient for the lass and her parent to come to terms with their unusual loss of her sister sent to Bedlam Hospital. It was a bereavement of sorts.

'And this letter here be an 'R',' I explained to my son. 'R is for Richard – your name. You will need to learn that right readily, little one.' He batted at the horn book with a plump, dimpled fist, gurgling happily. Both Rose and I were laughing at his pleasure when a woman came in to browse our wares.

'Good to see a man who isn't afraid of handling a babe,' she said, taking the trouble to straighten Dickon's linen bonnet that had gone somewhat awry in his excitement.

'God give you good day, Mistress Allen,' I said. 'How may we be of service to you this morn?'

'I heard you was returned, Master Seb, and wanted a word with Emily but, for the most part, I admit, I wanted to see your new babe. Not so newborn now, I see, and with his arms already unswaddled. Is that wise?'

'In such weather as this, he was flushed and over hot, so he be more comfortable with his arms free of the bindings.' I sounded like an old matron, discussing such matters. 'Did you wish to see our Latin primers? Your lad John must be of an age to begin to learn...'

'Indeed he is, but my husband purchased a primer last Eastertide from another stationer. Whilst you were not in business,' she added purposefully. 'You never should have left London like that, Master Seb. Your brother's way of doing things was a disaster. When my brother-by-marriage came to choose a book as a gift for my sister upon her fourth lying-in – before the guild shut your shop down – your Jude cursed him in front of others when he left without buying anything. Called him a bloody time-waster, he did. If I were you, I'd not let Jude serve customers ever again.'

'That situation has been resolved, Mistress Allen.'

'Glad to hear it and we are content to have you back. Now, my husband did mention he had little good paper left for his business correspondence, if you have some of suitable quality?'

'Most surely. I'll have Jack bring you a selection from the storeroom and Rose will serve you, if you will excuse me...'

Mistress Allen chuckled and nodded, understanding my sudden need to be excused as a large wet patch spread down my sleeve and across the front of my jerkin. Little Dickon was requiring of a dry tailclout and a change of swaddling and seemed much amused by his father's discomfiture, to judge by the merry gleam in his eyes. I would pass the task to Nessie on the grounds that I was unskilled at such things – and likely to remain so, if I had my way.

However, Nessie was busy making pastry for a pie with flour-dappled elbows and a white dusting in her dark hair. Rose was dealing with Mistress Allen and Dickon so disliked being wet he began protesting, creating such a din as seemed impossible for one so small. I might congratulate him on the power of his lungs, but it was the case, apparently, that only I was available to remedy the problem.

How fortunate was I to have a son so patient as little Dickon? He bore my fumbled ministrations without a murmur of protest, though I be certain he would let me know if I pricked him with a pin, which I took the greatest care not to do. I was still battling with yards of recalcitrant linen and legion pins, sweating profusely and cursing silently – not wanting my son to hear such ill language as the task drove me to employ – when Rose came to my rescue. Or rather she brought word of a customer insisting that he speak with me and swiftly took charge of the swaddling, to my great relief. Unfortunately, my efforts left me stinking of babe's piss and soil, as well as my own perspiration. My hair clung damply to the back of my neck and my forehead, and there was no disguising the wet stains on my attire.

'Is the customer in haste, Rose? Or may I change my clothes first, afore attending him?'

'He said it was important,' she replied, deftly finishing the swaddling in a matter of moments. Of course, I had accomplished the most part of it already.

'Did he give his name?'

'No, which is most unmannerly, but he said you would want to hear what he has to say.'

I took time to wash my face and hands in the laver bowl, adding a drop of lavender water, hoping to conceal less pleasant odours. My top shirt and jerkin would have to suffice as they were. I prayed the customer was not some fine lordling or honourable gentleman who might take offence, but Rose had given no hint of his status.

As soon as I saw that he wore an old mariner's cap, with mouse-coloured hair hacked about beneath it, I knew my appearance was of no consequence. The man was lean and of a height with me, but broad of shoulder and well-muscled under his fraying jerkin. He stood at the back of the shop, leafing through the pages of a little Book of Hours I had illuminated nigh unto a year since. Intended as a marriage gift from a father to his daughter, the wedding had never come to pass since her betrothed was thrown from his horse and killed, leaving the expensive volume languishing, unsold, on our shelf. It was not in the least suitable for a sea-going man, I should have thought, unless he too wanted it as a gift for a loved one.

'As good as I should expect of your hand, Master Seb,' he said, taking the liberty of close acquaintance with my name, to which he was not entitled. He turned a page carefully. At least he had a proper respect for the book. 'A masterly use of vermilion in this miniature of 'The Visitation', though the subject matter be not to my taste. I can see you used the likeness of your wife for the face of the Virgin Mary and Dame Ellen would appear to have inspired her Cousin Elizabeth, though 'tis hard to imagine such an elderly woman great with child, is it not?'

'It was a miracle of the Almighty,' I said, taking the book from him and replacing it on the shelf. I disliked his familiarity with my way of working and his obvious knowledge of people close to me. 'Now, you said you would have speech with me, Master er...? I fear I did not catch your name.'

He turned to face me, and I was startled to see he wore a leather patch over one eye. The other eye, brown as Thames mud, regarded me sternly for a lengthy pause. An ugly scar, pale and jagged as a lightning bolt, disfigured his sun-bronzed, salt-blasted features and pulled one corner of his mouth a little awry in a permanent half-smile. A second, lesser scar quirked one eyebrow, as if in question. His hair, brows and unkempt beard were bleached by the elements.

'What's in a name?' he said with a grin that showed a good set of strong, if unevenly coloured, teeth. 'I have news for you, but would tell it privily. Might we go into the parlour?' Such impertinence – he even led the way, as if he belonged here. 'Ale would be right welcome.'

'And wafers and cushions and a footstool, no doubt, since you invite yourself in?'

'If you offer them, aye.'

'Well, I do not, and I take exception to your effrontery.'

'Ah, Seb, am I so soon forgotten? You see the scars, the beard and not the man beneath.' He removed his cap, then a yellowish tooth and, finally, the eye patch. 'Don't like my replacement tooth much. Walrus ivory: colour doesn't match. But the eye patch serves me well, does it not, my old friend?'

I stared at him, the only man in Christendom with one eye blue and the other brown. Belatedly, I realised my mouth was agape.

'G-Gabriel? Gabriel Widowson? Is it truly you? I cannot believe...' The rest of my words were crushed in my chest as he embraced me so hard. 'I beg forgiveness for not knowing you at once,' I managed to say when I could draw breath once more. 'Of course you may have ale, sweetmeats, a fatted calf and all. It does my spirit good to see you looking so-so... alive.'

'I believe you meant to say 'battered', if not 'ugly', for I know that's the truth and you of all men, Seb, never fail to speak honestly. At least the damage to my face makes for a fine disguise, if even you with your sharp eye did not recognise me at first.'

'Aye, well, looks be of little import,' I said, feeling awkward, not wanting to acknowledge the changes to his features, despite his own admission. A little white lie could do no harm. 'Will you dine with us? There will be plenty to share since Jude is no longer...'

'Aye. I saw Jude this morn. 'Tis because of him that I decided to visit you. At dawn, he came to Queenhithe, asking passage to Burgundy upon the ship. I couldn't oblige him, since *The Eagle* – my new ship – is staying here for the duration of Bart's Fayre, but a friend of mine, master of *The Winsome Wench*, sails on the midday tide for Bruges. Jude has paid passage with him. I thought you would want to know that he's in safe hands. *The Wench* is a good stout ship and my friend an experienced captain.'

'So my brother is still in London? Time enough for him to have second thoughts. I must go to him, persuade him...'

'I'm not sure he would appreciate that, Seb. He seemed most determined.'

'But I...'

'Let him go, for now at least.' Gabriel put his hand on my shoulder. 'A single voyage may be enough to show him the error of his ways: a stormy sea crossing, encounters with brigands and uncivilised foreigners may change his mind and bring him home as your words never can. Give your brother a little space and time, my friend.'

I nodded, knowing Gabriel spoke wisely.

'Did he recognise you?' I waved Gabriel to a seat upon the settle although there was no fire kindled in the hearth, it being far too hot a day.

'Only when I lifted the eye patch, as you did. We had a brief conversation. He mentioned that Rose now lives with you. We met but for an hour or two when you rescued me, yet I recall how comely she was and is even more so now, as I saw in the shop. I came to renew her acquaintance, if you allow. Jude also said you have a new journeyman. I got the feeling he didn't like him over much. Is that true?'

'I do not understand how that could be. Their paths hardly crossed since we returned home. There has been insufficient opportunity for Jude to come to know Adam well enough to like or dislike him. Adam is our nephew, strange though it sounds since he be my elder by a few months, the son of a brother we never knew we had 'til I visited our home village of Foxley in Norfolk. We have become close.'

'Aye, so Jude told me. Might he be jealous? Could that be why he would leave?'

Dear God, I hoped that was not the reason. The possibility had not occurred to me that I might have driven Jude away by bringing Adam to dwell with us in London. What had I done? If such were true, the blame lay upon my conscience like an ingot of lead.

'You mentioned ale?'

Gabriel's words broke in upon my dark-shadowed thoughts.

'Oh, aye. I'll ask Rose to serve us.'

'Or Emily? I should like to see her again.'

'Em's not home at present.' Did I imagine it, or did his smile fade just a little when I said that? 'She will return for dinner, so you may see her then, if you stay.'

'By the by,' he said as I was about to leave the parlour, 'I use the name Gideon Waterman these days, Master of *The Eagle* out of Bristol port. Better the London authorities do not hear of Gabriel Widowson, one-time journeyman-scrivener, deceased.' He laughed when I nodded in understanding.

'How come you now have your own ship?' I asked, pausing in the doorway.

''Tis a long story, Seb. I will tell you over dinner.'

Indeed, I remembered full well just how long Gabriel's stories could be and, often as not, as enthralling as they were incredible. It would be a fine tale, no doubt, and one the whole household would be eager to hear. Tom and Jack always loved his stories when Gabriel had lived and worked with us. As a story-teller, he was unsurpassed and must have many more adventures to relate, concerning his voyages across strange seas to distant lands. I had a fondness for his tales myself, whether true or invented.

'Gabriel,' I said as a long-suppressed thought arose from my memory, 'There be a question I should wish answered from our last encounter, while none other be here to harken.'

'Oh? Well, ask it, my friend, and I shall answer if I can.'

'I know you cannot have forgotten those who did their utmost to prevent your escape upon your brother's ship: the under-sheriff and the bishop's spy...'

'You're correct. I haven't forgotten those devils, Valentyne Nox and the two guards. As for that Judas, Roger Underwood, his name is scored into my mind. He betrayed the Known Men for money. What of them? They aren't worth talking of.'

'After your brother had them taken aboard the ship, what befell them? Did you...'

'Did we hang 'em from the yard-arm? Throw them overboard? Starve them to death? Is that what you want to know?'

I nodded, although, of a sudden, I wondered if I did want to learn their fate.

'Fear not, Seb. Neither Raff nor I wanted to break God's commandment. "Thou shalt not kill" overruled our natural inclinations to be revenged upon them.'

'I am comforted to know that. So what became of them?'

Gabriel shrugged.

'I have no idea and care even less. We put them ashore on some God-forsaken coast in the Low Countries, unharmed – which they did not deserve, but why should we have them plaguing our consciences? Where they went after that or what they did was in their own hands. Does that satisfy you?'

'Aye, it does. I be grateful and relieved to know it.'

Without Emily there to chivvy the process and Rose dealing with customers in the shop – a heartening situation since I had feared none would come after the trouble with the guild – Nessie was late in serving dinner.

Emily was much annoyed to see the cloth not yet set when she returned from Dame Ellen's house in Cheapside. Yet the matter was right swiftly forgotten when my wife espied our visitor, without his eye patch.

'Gabriel! My heart! By all the saints in heaven...' She ran to him as he rose from the kitchen bench to greet her. 'Your poor dear face,' she said, cupping his cheeks in her hands. 'How greatly I-we have missed you. What has befallen you? So many scars...'

He clasped her hands in his, pulling them away from his face.

'They are of no concern now. But what of you, Em? You have a babe, I see, a fine son.'

I watched my wife and my old friend gazing at each other and felt that the rest of us, gathered in the kitchen for dinner, were no longer part of their world. They might almost have been mistaken for lovers. But then the moment passed as Gabriel turned to Nessie, enquiring as to what was for dinner since he was nigh starving.

Emily took control upon the instant, bustling about and our meal was quickly served: a mutton pie in a chive sauce, buttered sorrel, and a sweet cherry and rose-petal pottage. I was content that, by chance, it was a fine repast to welcome our friend. Then, as Rose and Nessie cleared the board and Emily sat by the hearth to feed the babe, I poured more ale for us all and reminded Gabriel of his promise to tell his story.

'Oh, aye, Master Gabe, you must tell us,' Jack insisted. 'We luv yer tales, don't we, Tom?'

'They were good stories,' Tom said, seemingly reluctant to admit that he and Jack were in agreement for once. 'Tell us about your ship. Adam won't know about that. The *St Christopher*, if I remember.'

'No longer. The *Christopher* came to grief, wrecked in a storm off the coast of Ireland last autumn. A bad day it was. Good men were lost, my brother Raff among them. You may recall Raphael Scraggs?'

'Of course. I be sorry to hear of your loss, Gabriel. I shall pray for his soul,' I said without thinking.

Gabriel frowned at me, a dark look that caused the scar to plough a crooked furrow deeply into his forehead.

'Forgive me. No insult was intended,' I murmured. Gabriel and his brother were Known Men and would have naught to do with the observances of Church ritual. Their faith had been the cause of a deal of trouble that would have taken my friend to a fiery death, if we had not succeeded in aiding his escape – as a coffined corpse. The remembrance of such acts of deception still gave me qualms, if I thought on them.

'Aye, well,' he said clearing his throat and taking a swallow of ale. 'That's a story for another day. Rather, I will tell you of the previous voyage Raff and I made together for Richard Ameryk, a merchant of Bristol, to the Island of Ice and Fire last summer. Have you heard of it?'

Everyone shook their heads. I held my tongue, not wishing to spoil the moment by airing my knowledge concerning the coldest place in the Almighty's creation.

Gabriel grinned, his missing tooth now wedged back in place after he'd finished eating. He'd jested about how it had once been lost in a marrowbone pudding, requiring every slice to be investigated with knife and spoon in order to recover it.

'The Island of Ice and Fire lies so far to the north in the Ocean Sea that the waters freeze over in winter, where the sun never rises at that season and darkness lies heavy upon the land for months on end. Yet, in summer – the only time when we could voyage there in safety – the sun does not set, but merely strokes the horizon before climbing back into the skies. Then daylight rules the stark, black rocks, the mountains of fire, the rivers of ice and the great boiling fountains that spurt from the earth itself. You have never seen such a strange place.'

Mouths hung gaping. Adam was enthralled. Tom's eyes were wide in wonder; Nessie, too, could hardly believe what she heard. Expressions of bewilderment were upon the faces of us all, as we sat around our ordinary kitchen, listening to such extraordinary things.

'The folk who bide there call it 'the Land of Ice and Fire' – as I said – and 'tis a name that suits it right well. They are hardy indeed to dwell in such a place and perhaps 'tis to be expected that their beliefs be strange also. They say they worship the Christian God, yet swear by the old gods with names like Odin and Thor. They tell of elves, whom they call the Hidden People, and trolls and other creatures as though they see them every day. Each stone and cave has a terrible troll to guard it; any mischief done is the work of the elvish folk. Raff and I were there for nigh two months and saw no sign of such beings, but we certainly learned of the existence of one fabulous beast.' Tantalising us, Gabriel paused to sip his drink.

'Tell us, Master Gabe!' Tom yelled in great excitement. 'Please tell us!'

'He won't,' said Jack. 'Like he always did make us wait 'til t'morra, didn't he?'

'Nay, Jack. Be patient, and you will hear.' Gabriel set down his cup, and Adam refilled it for him. 'It happened in this way. Our ship anchored offshore from a place called Eyrarbakki for there is no safe harbour, and a risk of shoals and rocks. Raff and I rowed to the beach of sand blacker than Satan's backside. Eyrarbakki is the main trading place for the island, and I thought to find a town the size of Bristol or the like, yet it comprised barely a dozen huts with walls and roofs of turf and a single warehouse no larger than St Michael le Querne's church. But folk were keen to trade dried fish and leather goods for the oats and barley, salt and honey that we bought. Yet we wanted other things also and had to traipse for half a day across rocks so sharp they sliced our boots, if we did not take care to keep to the path, such as it was, little more than a sheep walk – though we saw few sheep there. The land all about was black: no trees and little grass, yet strange purple spikes of flowers grew out of the very rocks: the only colour we saw.

'Our guide, Enar, told of places which smell of brimstone and the earth is hot underfoot. Pools of mud boil and bubble like cauldrons upon the fire and great spouts of steam rise into the sky, but I'm not sure how much of that is true. He took us to a fishing village along the coast from where we berthed the *Christopher*. In summer, the men fish and tend the little horses that run wild there; in winter they hunt and trap foxes and hares for their fine skins and furs. White fox furs were what we wanted to buy. The old man from whom we would buy them spoke no English, but Enar explained to him, and he spread out his wares for us to examine. The furs were of the finest quality, so soft, white and thick; good enough for a queen at least.'

I saw him glance at Emily as he said that. She smiled at him. The babe was suckling contentedly at her breast, and she stroked his golden wisps of hair, but her eyes rested upon Gabriel, not the child. Somehow, it seemed a most intimate moment betwixt my wife and another man. Best not to dwell upon it.

'Now, among these wares for sale were items of fish-leather: embroidered purses mostly and fur-lined boots and mittens. I dare say those be greatly needed in the winter when they have snow deeper than a three-storey house, as Enar described. There were walrus ivory combs and amulets, sealskin bags and shells threaded upon leather thongs as jewellery. However, among the things for sale, one particularly caught my eye: the most beautiful horn you could imagine. A perfect spiral of the finest ivory, longer than my arms could stretch – two ells or more, at least. You know from whence it came, of course? There was no doubting it was the solitary horn of a unicorn!'

'A unicorn,' Adam repeated the word. 'How I should love to see such a wonder for myself. Did you see them there in that strange land, Master Gabriel?'

I was thinking that our story-teller was spinning us a fine tale. Unicorns, indeed. I don't doubt they had once lived, but no man had reported seeing them for years. It was always a case of a friend of a cousin's wife who met a man who said his grandfather had heard tell of a unicorn glimpsed for a moment of time in the far distance. Never anything more substantial. And the cup supposedly made from a unicorn's horn that I had once seen for sale in a goldsmith's shop looked to me to be of ox horn and naught otherwise. More fool he who paid the extortionate price demanded for it too.

'No, Adam, regrettably we did not espy the creatures themselves, but then we did not expect that we should. You see, unicorns are not as I believed them to be: galloping free across the land. Enar explained that they are creatures of the sea. During a storm, the billowing foam upon the great waves that lash and thunder against a ship is known to be white horses plunging across the sea, though truly not horses – as I learned that day – but unicorns. Thus, it is clear why such beasts have been hunted in vain for so long. You will never find them in forest or meadow. You cannot hunt them with bows nor track them with hounds. Instead, you must ride the waves through howling gales and rain-drenched skies in order to see a unicorn and even then you cannot catch them.'

'Then how did this fisherman come by the horn?' I asked. I did not want to cast doubts but knowing Gabriel, this was another of his fantastic tales.

'That he would not reveal.'

Indeed. I was unsurprised at that.

'However, we bought the marvellous horn and two others beside. They are not quite so magnificent in size, but still a wonder to behold. We paid a fair price for them, and Master Ameryk expects to make an excellent profit upon them when they are sold at Bart's Fayre next week. There is more likely to be a wealthy buyer for such things in London than Bristol, maybe the king himself. That's why we're here. But, if you would like to see the horns, I can arrange it since we are keeping them aboard *The Eagle*. Such precious items are at risk of being stolen otherwise.'

'Well, I should most certainly love to see them,' Emily said. And everyone else agreed. Thus a visit to Gabriel's ship at Queenhithe was swiftly determined upon for the forenoon on the morrow. Except that I should not be joining them. The last time I set foot on shipboard was not an occasion I wished to repeat. The very memory made me feel queasy, and I would not risk appearing foolish once again for the sake of my friend's dubious mariner's tale. Unicorns! Whatever next?

# Chapter 4

## Friday, the twenty-first day of August
## Aboard the ship *The Eagle,*
## moored at Queenhithe

JACK AND TOM could hardly wait to visit Gabriel's ship,
*The Eagle,* not only to see the wondrous unicorn horns, but
to go aboard a vessel that had sailed the Seven Seas – well, a
few of them at least: the German or North Sea off the eastern
coast of England, the Irish Sea, the Narrow Sea that separated
England from France and, most exciting of all, the great Ocean
Sea to the north and west of Ireland. Gabriel had told them the
Ocean Sea was so vast, ships lost sight of land for days, even
weeks upon end. Jack had half convinced himself that, perhaps,
he too would like to become a mariner, to explore uncharted
waters in search of strange lands and new adventures. Master
Seb's workshop was a good place, apart from having to live with
Tom, but it was boring indeed. Tedinus. Aye, that was the word
for it, or something like.

Gabriel was merrily rattling off a list of facts about his fine
ship to Mistress Em and Master Adam.

''Tis a carrack, three-masted, as you see,' he told them, waving
his hand to indicate a towering mast overhead as they stepped
off the gangplank and down onto the deck. Mistress Em gave a
little squeal of delight as he lifted her down. 'When underway,
the fore- and mainmasts are square-rigged, the mizzenmast aft

is lateen-rigged. That means the sheet – the sail – is three-sided, not square. She is one-hundred-and-thirty feet in length and displaces over eight-hundred tons.'

Mistress Em, done up in her Sunday best – even to the pins in her veil, the ones with the square brass heads – was gazing at Gabriel, seemingly awestruck by the large numbers, but Jack had a feeling it was the man, not his ship, that interested her most. She had always had a soft-heart for Gabriel, if he remembered aright. For himself, Jack was trying to remember every word: it might come in useful if he did run away to sea, which he might.

'And where do you sleep, Gabriel?' Mistress Em asked.

'Usually, I share a small cabin with Rook, the first mate, but on this voyage, Master Richard Ameryk has use of the cabin, since he owns *The Eagle*. Rook and I are bunking in with the crewmen below decks, sleeping in hammocks. 'Tis rather cramped, but cosy.' He did not add that it also smelled too badly for a woman's nose. 'I can't show you because some men will be sleeping there now. You see, they have to work and rest, turn and turn about as there isn't room for everyone to sleep at the same time. Besides, some crew members have to be on watch through the night, to guard the ship and our valuable cargo.'

'Wot's that up there on the mast?' Jack asked, pointing skywards towards a basket-like contraption encircling the main mast.

'We call that the crow's nest,' Gabriel said.

'Wot? You take birds wiv you t' sea?' Jack's voice jumped from bass to treble in excitement.

'No,' Gabriel said, laughing. 'We climb up there to be on the look-out for hazardous rocks and shoals, pirate ships and to espy distant lands afar off.'

'Cor! I wager, I could see all o' London from up there, couldn't I?'

'Indeed you could, Jack. Now, as I promised, let me show you our most precious items for sale at the fayre on Monday. Master Ameryk keeps them in a locked coffer in the cabin, but has given me permission to show you. I have the key here. Come, this way.'

The timbers of the deck were heated by the sun on such a day, and Emily could feel the warmth through her thin-soled shoes. She was pleased to see everything looked scrubbed and clean, the paintwork fresh and bright in the sunshine. Ropes were neatly coiled and canvasses – sails, probably – folded away. It seemed mariners were careful as housewives concerning such things. The only aspects that didn't appeal to her were the all-pervading odours of pitch and grease.

No matter, Gabriel was holding her hand in his to guide her over the doorsill, into the cabin, and the feel of his warm, calloused skin against her fingers was all that was important in that moment. And his voice: deeper and more manly than she recalled from before, its timbre made her heart skip for joy. Inside, the cabin was too cramped to hold them all, but she was content to be pressed close against Gabriel so that Jack could squeeze in also. What a pity that was.

Gabriel pulled a coffer out from under one of the beds – bunks, he called them. The other bunk was folded up against the wall and hooked in place. He unlocked the coffer and raised the lid, turning back a leather covering to reveal three exquisite ivory spirals, each quite different in length and design, lying upon a cushion, like religious relics. Not that Gabriel, being a Known Man, would have anything to do with what he considered to be 'midden gleanings' sanctioned by the Church. These marvels were quite another matter. He lifted one out and passed it to Emily.

She took hold of it with the greatest care and turned so the light from the open doorway shone on the horn.

'It's so beautiful, Gabe,' she said, stroking her hand along its cool length. 'Like a summer icicle. I can hardly believe I am holding a real unicorn's horn. The spirals are so perfect. I never thought to see such a thing.'

Jack reached out a grubby finger and traced the grooves along the horn with wary concentration.

'Yer right, Mistress Em, it is boot'ful, ain't it?'

'Aye. Now move outside, Jack, so Master Adam and Tom can come in to see it.'

The lad huffed at being given such a short time to gaze on the horn but obeyed, muttering as Tom replaced him in the confined space. After Tom, it was Adam's turn.

'Such a privilege, master,' Adam said. 'I account myself fortunate indeed. And each one unique, you say? What sort of price do you expect them to bring at the fayre?' He held the horn in the doorway, where the sunlight glinted on its twisting form, running his nimble fingers along its length.

'All other beasts have horns in pairs but, as you see, each of these is a solitary one, as you would expect of a unicorn,' Gabriel explained. 'Thus, each is unique. As for price, I dare not hazard a guess, but the sum of five-and-twenty pounds sterling has been offered for the smallest of the three and Master Ameryk simply laughed at that, so I truly know not what he hopes for.'

Just then, the light from the doorway was gone as a dark figure blotted out the sun.

'Ah! Mistress Emily, Master Adam, may it please you to meet my first mate, Rook.' Gabriel made the formal introductions, but it wasn't until the unicorn horn was safely returned to the coffer, locked and stowed away, and they all went out on deck that Emily and Adam got a good look at the first mate.

Rook was as nigh as great a shock as the horns but, whereas they were pale as snow, he was black as the night sky. Emily had seen swarthy Spaniards and dark-skinned Moorish men, for London had visitors from across the world, but never anyone like Rook. He was so black and built like the Tower of London: a huge fellow with eyes like sea-coals. Yet when he smiled, his teeth were dazzlingly white. In truth, he scared her. Adam didn't seem to mind him though, happy enough to shake his hand.

'Rook is from Abyssinia in Africa,' Gabriel said, 'But for all that, he's as good a Christian soul as anyone here and speaks better English than most of us. Is that not so, Rook?'

'I greet you both most humbly, Mistress Emily Foxley and Master Adam Armitage. May God grant you happiness this day?' Rook bowed courteously, smiling that white-toothed smile.

'I pray God will grant you the same, Master Rook,' Adam said.

'Nay. Rook is all my name. I am no man's master, nor is anyone but God mine. But I obey Master Gideon when I have a mind to do so.' He laughed, rumbling like a cascade of rocks rolling downhill.

It took Emily a moment to recall that 'Gideon Waterman' was the name Gabriel now used.

Meanwhile, Jack and Tom, grown tired of waiting for their elders, were wandering around the deck, getting in the way of crewmen going about their tasks. Tom watched, fascinated, as a lad, much younger than themselves, suddenly leapt onto the low balustrade that went all around the deck, grabbed one of the countless ropes which seemed to be everywhere and began to climb. In no time, the lad was sitting astride a great beam that hung across the mainmast far above their heads.

'What's he doing?' Tom asked a man who was drawing up a bucket of water from the side of the ship.

'Greasin' the block-an'-tackle on the steerboard yard,' the man said, looking up and shading his eyes from the sun. 'Hey! Robin!' Hearing his name, the youngster looked down. 'And secure that ratline on the sheet when yer done.' All of which instruction meant naught to Tom.

'I could do that,' Jack said, despite having no more idea than Tom what the lad was actually supposed to do. 'I'm a good climber, ain't I? I could get up t' that bird's nest fing an' see all o' London, couldn't I? And secure the rat-sheet fing.' Then, without a moment of hesitation or the least thought about what he was doing, Jack began to climb the rigging.

'Lord's sake, Jack, are you mad?' Tom yelled out, making a grab for his companion's ankle, but Jack was out of reach and rapidly climbing higher.

'Get down 'ere, yer daft bugger!' the crewman shouted. 'Master Gideon, what's to do?'

Gabriel came running, Rook and Adam a pace behind with Emily trotting after, taking care her skirts didn't become entangled in all the bits and pieces, hooks and spikes that hindered her way. No wonder women weren't encouraged on ships.

'I couldn't stop him,' Tom said, hoping he wouldn't be blamed for his fellow's stupidity.

Emily pulled Tom out of the way so Gabriel could swing himself up among the numerous lengths of rope that disappeared upwards to the top of the mast. She had never seen Gabriel climb before, and his speed and agility enthralled her; his strength of arm impressive indeed.

Jack was up on the beam now, level with the other lad who was still smearing grease on a wooden block and wondering what all the shouting was about. Jack sat astride the beam, raising both arms in triumph at which those on the deck below gasped in horror.

At the furthest end of the beam, a short length of stout cord hung loose. Jack realised that must be the rat-sheet, or whatever it was called. He got up onto his feet, balancing on the beam which had yards and yards of rolled canvas tied in place beneath it. It was rounded but broad enough to walk along for those surer of foot than a goat. Jack, daring as ever and eager to show off, particularly once he saw the little crowd gathered on the deck below watching, made his way along the beam. Except Mistress Em wasn't watching, but hiding her face in her apron. He was now out, over the murky waters of the Thames and about to tie the loose cord in place, but it was all too easy. He would give them a bit of a fright. So he grabbed the cord and swung on it, pushing off the beam with his feet, circling outward. He was sure that he heard Mistress Em squeal and laughed out loud.

Then he spotted Gabriel coming after him and, in that moment of distraction, lost his grip and was falling backwards;

falling into nothingness. No time even to be afeared before the cold water engulfed him.

'Dear God preserve him,' Adam gasped even as they heard the splash. 'Can he swim?'

'I-I don't know. I don't think so. I never asked.' Emily was wringing her apron in her hands.

'No, he can't,' Tom said. 'Serve him right, if he drowns.'

Without discussion, Adam kicked off his boots, flung aside his cap and his jerkin and was over the balustrade before anyone could question his intent. Rook, already bare-foot, likewise dived into the river.

'Man overboard!' somebody shouted. It may have been Gabriel, now descending the shrouds.

Crewmen hastened to the side to look down. Two men were in the water, taking turns to dive beneath the surface. Finally, Rook came up, grappling with a limp form, and Adam swam to aid him. Crewmen had flung a net over the side and the heroes of the hour were climbing up it, Rook managing this feat with Jack's body over his shoulder, Adam helping by taking the weight of the lad's head somewhat. Eager hands pulled Rook's burden over the gunwales and laid the water-sodden body on the deck. Rook was swiftly on his knees beside the inert shape. He rolled Jack onto his front and pressed down betwixt his shoulder blades. Water spurted from the lad's mouth and nose, and he began coughing and spluttering. Rook stood up and backed away so Gabriel could tend the youngster. But the master of *The Eagle* had no sympathy for foolishness and hauled Jack to his feet and sat him on a coil of rope to recover even as he delivered his chastisement:

'You stupid young fool. What were you doing up there? You would have been mashed to a pulp if you'd fallen to the deck. Lucky for you that you went overboard, but you endangered other men's lives in saving you. Did you consider that for a single moment, eh? I ought to box your ears for this, but you're not worth the trouble.'

'I wanted t' see all London from the bird's-nest, didn't I?' Jack sniffed and coughed. Muddy water dripped from his hair and squelched out of his shoes; his wet clothes clung to him. He was such a sorry sight, Emily took off her apron and gave it to him to dry himself.

'Instead, you saw the bottom of the Thames. I hope that's taught you a lesson,' Gabriel added, glaring at the miscreant, his anger barely under control. A good thrashing was most certainly called for, and he wondered who should deliver it. Not Seb, that was for sure, unless he had changed much since they used to work together.

Mayhap Adam was the one to dispense discipline now Jude was gone, but perhaps not, seeing the new man was grinning, eyes closed as he held his face to the sun to dry. Adam untucked his shirt from his breeches and wrung it out, adding to the puddles on deck, before tucking it back in, wet as ever. He shook his short dark hair like a dog and water droplets sprayed everywhere, then he ran his fingers through it to comb it as best he could.

# The Foxley house

I was alarmed at the condition of my household when they arrived back at home, escorted by Gabriel and the blackest fellow I had ever seen. Adam and Jack were soaked and bedraggled, Emily was apronless, though I saw it was wrapped around Jack's shoulders, and my old friend had a thunderous look upon his face such as I had ne'er seen afore. They were all attempting to speak at once to tell me what had come to pass – except Jack, who upon this single occasion seemed to be at a loss for words and most downcast.

I had Nessie serve ale for everyone, and Rose put water on

the fire to heat, since Adam and Jack clearly needed to wash and dry themselves. Emily, wearing a fresh apron, brought clean towels and dry shirts, though we had naught of a size to fit the man called Rook. Goliath would have been required to lend him a shirt.

With the tale related at last to the satisfaction of all concerned, although Jack uttered barely a syllable even in his own defence, and everyone washed clean, dried off and respectably clad once more, I realised I had to take charge of the situation.

'You, Adam, and Master Rook have my heartfelt thanks for saving a life this morn. One that be dear to me, indeed.'

Jack glanced up as if surprised by my words.

'I did naught,' Adam said, chuckling. 'On such a hot day, I took to the water to cool myself, felt like having a swim. It was Rook who saved him, aye, and knew how to press the water out of his chest after. That's who brought him back to life, not me. 'Tis Rook deserves all credit and thanks.'

'In which case, good sir, I would shake your hand,' I said, clasping Rook's mighty hand that dwarfed mine like a child's. 'I am ever in your debt.'

'It was nothing of account, master,' Rook said with a shrug.

Little Dickon in his cradle then began to cry for his dinner and Emily took him away to our bedchamber to feed him and change his tailclout, the kitchen being so full of folk there was not room enough. Even my faithful Gawain had disappeared outside to the courtyard for fear of having his paws trodden upon.

Gabriel, wearing the eye-patch which unnerved me somewhat, took me aside, into the passage, away from others' hearing:

'That lad be in need of more than a few stern words, Seb. I know 'tis not your way, but what he did this morn was reckless, stupid and put other men's lives at hazard. 'Tis not my place to tell you how to govern and discipline your workshop, but he has to be taught a lesson, you know that.'

'Aye, I suppose... but do you not think he has learned his lesson? He must have been scared witless as well as nigh drowning. Are such sufferings not sufficient to deter him from repeating his foolish actions?'

Gabriel sighed and laid a heavy hand on my shoulder.

'I'll do it for you, if you want?' he offered, 'If you cannot face it...'

'Nay. I am his master. You be correct. And it be my place and duty to dispense discipline. I will do what must be done.'

'You know 'tis for the lad's own good.'

I nodded, but already sweat leaked from my every pore at simply contemplating what I had to do.

We returned to the kitchen. Gabriel took up his ale cup but watched me, meaningfully, over the rim.

I unbuckled the belt from around my jerkin and slipped off the purse and dinner knife that hung from it, laying them on the table, that all might comprehend my purpose.

'Jack. Outside. Behind the pigsty. Now.' I spoke sharply, hoping none noticed the quaver in my voice. The lad gave me a disbelieving glance as he left. I let him go and did not follow directly. The anticipation of the coming hurt would add to his discomfort. Everyone – Gabriel, Adam, Rook, Tom, Rose and even Nessie – was watching, waiting. Their expectation was unbearable for me, so I went out to the garden plot, steeling my nerves for actions that would be an agony for me, probably more than for Jack.

As I had ordered, he was behind the sty, sitting on the old bucket Emily used when weeding among the worts. The scent of mint arose as I brushed against the herbs overgrowing the garden plot. I breathed deeply, finding the scent soothing.

'Remove your shirt and hose,' I told him, flexing my belt so leather cracked against leather. 'Mistress Em will not thank me for ruining your attire.'

Jack undressed, revealing milk-white skin to the sun, in stark contrast to his darker face, neck and hands. The skinny, starveling waif he once had been was now muscled and hairy with adolescence, but looked vulnerable yet. The thought of the vivid red welts my belt would raise upon his flesh sickened me.

'You know how foolish you were, Jack,' I said, speaking low to disguise any tremor in my speech, 'What you did was reckless, unforgivable. Adam and Rook could have died in saving you.'

He stared at the ground, kicking at a clump of chickweed.

'Do you hear what I say?'

'S'pose so.'

'When I have dealt with you, you will go and make your abject apologies to Adam and Rook, in that you caused them to endanger their lives on your behalf.' I flexed the belt in what I hoped was an intimidating manner 'Now. Turn your back and stand to face the pigsty wall. Go on.' I swallowed hard, seeing his bare back and the indentations down his spine. I let the length of leather swing loose, gripping the buckle in my fist and drew back my arm. It made a fearful snapping sound as it struck the wall.

Jack flinched and gasped at the noise, but his skin remained unmarked. A few splinters of wood flew from the post by the corner of the pigsty. The pig inside grunted her annoyance at the disturbance of her mid-morning snooze.

I repeated the action a few times more, then girded the belt about my waist as afore.

'Get dressed,' I said. 'Then apologise.'

Gabriel awaited me in the courtyard and nodded approval.

'It was justly deserved,' he said.

I made no answer, wiping the sweat from my brow upon my sleeve. A cup of ale was thrust into my hand, and I drank it down in a single draught. Punishing the lad had proved impossible for me, but I knew that practising deception, pretending I had beaten him, was going to prove just as difficult. I never could tell a lie.

Jack came in from the garden plot, clothed once more and wearing a meek expression as he mumbled his few words of penitence to Adam and Rook. He moved awkwardly as he took his place at the board for dinner, wincing occasionally. He was a far more skilful deceiver than I. A bad moment for me occurred after our mackerel dinner, as we were eating gooseberries beaten in cream and honey. Emily called it 'gooseberry fool' and gave me a second helping I had not requested.

'You deserve that,' she whispered. 'I'm proud of you, Seb. I didn't know you were man enough to mete out such discipline, but you proved me wrong. You make me a proud wife, indeed.'

After that, I could not eat another mouthful, delicious as it was. I was a charlatan and a liar, and it curdled my humours so.


When dinner was done – to my great relief – Gabriel and Rook returned to the ship, Rose was once more dealing with customers in the shop and Emily went out to join Dame Ellen and the other silk-women in preparing the wares for their stall at the fayre, three days hence. The rest of us, bar Nessie who was instructed to tend the babe and prepare supper, went to the workshop. There had been over-much time wasted this day, and I was determined that some proper labours should be attended to.

Tom had the Latin primers to do; Jack had a design to trace onto the oaken boards for the cover to my *Aesop's Fables;* Adam was penning the text of the fables, and I was painting the miniatures and the marginalia. I had spent the morning, while the others were at Queenhithe and Rose tended the shop, roughing out the picture to illustrate the fable of the ox and the frog. The impossibility of a tiny frog so swollen with foolish pride in thinking to equal an ox in size always amused me. But of course, every fable has a moral to it and, in this tale the excess of pride causes the frog to burst asunder. I would not illustrate so gruesome an outcome, but the image of a huge frog beside a small ox should tempt any youngster to look closer and, hopefully, not only take the moral to heart but attempt to read the words. I glanced across at our own foolish 'frog', busy at his work. At least his excess of pride earlier had not destroyed him, quite, and he looked none the worse for his misadventure.

I prepared my brush and took out the sketch I had made of a frog that had obliged me by remaining still while I drew him. It had been back in the spring when we were in Norfolk. I had been making drawings in Foxley churchyard of the bluebells there and discovered the frog nestling in a clump of damp moss. Now he would give pleasure to me once more as I painted his likeness and to the readers who would see him in future. I suppose it was as close to immortality as a humble frog might aspire, achieving his prideful wish in a way.

I had been working, undisturbed, for an hour or two when running footsteps in the passage drew me from my work.

'Oh, Seb, I have so much to tell you!' Emily burst into the workshop, her pretty face flushed beneath her linen cap and her eyes bright with anticipation.

'What is it, sweetheart? Allow me just to complete this then I shall...'

'No, no. Leave your painting. Come into the parlour: we must speak privily this very minute.' She snatched the brush out of my hand and dragged me from my desk.

I was reluctant to leave my work.

'Cover the pigment pot and wash my brush for me, Tom, if you will?' I instructed him, though he groaned at having to leave his lettering to do it. 'Whatever has got you so excited, Em?' I asked her as she closed the parlour door behind us. 'You're not with child again, are you?'

'What? No, of course not. Now sit down, listen and don't interrupt until I have told you everything.'

I obeyed and sat upon the settle, bemused and wondering what this was concerning.

'Things have come to pass while we were away in Norfolk. Dame Ellen was attacked by some rascal on her way home from vespers one eve, back before Easter.'

'Poor soul. Was she injured?'

'A few bruises was all, so she said. And don't interrupt!' My wife was standing over me like a schoolmaster. 'The fiend stole her purse and knocked her down.'

'Have they apprehended the wretch?'

'Sebastian Foxley, will you be silent and hear me out. I have no idea, but that's not important.' Emily had her hands on her hips and wore her sternest expression, so I complied.

I most certainly had a different opinion on that score, but said naught.

'The truth is that Dame Ellen was not much hurt in body, but she says she has not felt easy in her mind ever since. She doesn't like to go out in the evenings now and dreads the nights drawing in as summer is passing. Her years are catching up with her, she fears, and she wishes to make arrangements for her business dealings in the future, when she is become too old. John is to take over her tailor's shop, as we expected, seeing he manages it for the most part already.'

'Your brother will make a success of the venture, no doubt. He be more than capable and hard-working.'

She glared at me, and I said naught more.

'Now we come to the crux of the matter,' Emily continued. 'Dame Ellen wants me to run her silk business. It would require me to go to Guildhall and declare myself *femme sole*, then I can take charge of the other out-workers employed by Dame Ellen and they would be answerable to me instead. Dame Ellen will leave me all her silk looms and stock of raw materials. Is that not marvellous news, husband? I shall be an independent businesswoman... but by law, I require your permission to become *femme sole*. You will say 'aye', won't you?'

I stood up and looked into her beautiful eyes agleam with enthusiasm.

'There is much to be considered afore we decide,' I said, speaking quietly. 'The implications for you and the burden of extra work and responsibilities required: little Dickon's needs are time-consuming at present. How will you care for him and manage the out-workers, the bookkeeping, the orders and purchasing and delivery to customers? Such an enterprise is not to be undertaken in haste, Em. We needs must think about it a while.'

'How typical that is of a man!' she thumped my chest with her fists. 'You would deny me any chance of independence, just because I'm a woman. You think I'm incapable because I wear skirts! Well, I'm as capable of running a business as you are.'

'I know that, sweetheart. I just want you to take time to think it through.'

'Don't you 'sweetheart' me in that tone, as if I am some silly child. There is no time to waste. Dame Ellen says she will give me three days to decide, afore she offers it to one of the other out-workers, if I don't want the business. Then where will I be? I shall find myself working for the likes of Beatrice Thatcher or Peronelle Wenham and I won't take orders from that upstart Lizzie Knollys who thinks she knows it all.'

'Three days? Is Dame Ellen not being rather unreasonable to demand such a decision be made so precipitously? Can the matter not wait a week or two or until after St Bartholomew's Fayre, at the very least?'

'Three days is what she said. So... do I have your permission or no?'

'I refuse to be rushed into this by her or by you, Em. I will take the three full days to consider the facts with care, sift through the details and come to my conclusion and you should do likewise. The decision may affect the rest of our lives. Your life, Em. As *femme sole*, you will be liable for your own debts and the pursuance through the courts of anyone indebted to you. Any legal contracts, any apprentices you take on will be your responsibility.'

'I know that. And any profits made will be mine alone. Not yours.'

'Is that what concerns you? That you want your own money? Have I not vowed at our marriage that all my worldly goods be yours also? We share every penny, Em, yet that does not content you? Have I ever withheld so much as a farthing when you asked for it?'

'That isn't the point. I shouldn't have to ask you every time I need coin. Besides, it would be an extra income if...'

'If?'

'If any mishap befell you. If you became too sick to work or if Master Caxton's printing press steals all your customers.'

'I suppose you have a valid reason there, though I do not fear William Caxton's new contraption, since it cannot do illumination, nor portraiture, nor heraldic designs, all of which we now produce to ensure he cannot put us out of business. But even so, we ought to think on it: both of us, afore I agree to you declaring yourself *femme sole*. That be my final word upon it until three days have passed and you may tell Dame Ellen that is the way it will be. Now, wife, you must allow me to return to my work.'

'But, Seb...' Emily moved to the doorway and barred my passage from the parlour.

'Em, remember when we were wed, just as I swore an oath to share all that I had, you vowed to be 'bonny and buxom in bed and at board'. Now, it is my right as your husband to demand that you keep that promise: 'to be good and obedient', as you ought. Just this once, I insist upon it.'

'Oh, I understand now.' She shoved me and stepped back. 'You punish a child afore dinner and take such courage from it, now you think to be everyone's lord and master of a sudden, asserting your new-found authority like some jumped-up petty tyrant.'

'Em, it isn't like that at all. I have no intention of asserting my authority. I want you to be aware of the possible problems, as well as the advantages...'

'Selfish! That's what you are. Self-centred, self-seeking, self-aggrandising, over-bearing...'

'Enough, Em.' I pulled her close, confining her arms though she would pummel me and fight me off. 'Still your tongue, else others will account you shrewish and scolding. Be still, I say.'

I went back to my desk, but had no heart for painting my frog now. I had noticed a customer hastening from the shop, no doubt embarrassed by our heated exchange. Everyone had heard it. Although Adam studiously continued with his penmanship, Tom was sniggering behind his ink-stained hand and Jack – who should have been shame-faced for the rest of the day at the very least – was grinning like the green-man on St Paul's doorway lintel. My cheeks were burning, and it had naught to do with the summer's heat. I could not work so. Instead, I called to Gawain, hiding 'neath my desk, and went out, hoping to find a breeze somewhere to temper my ill-humours.

Although there was no breeze there, I knew the cathedral nave would be cool and, it being Friday, the choristers should be practising. I would speak with the precentor, perhaps, and ask if I might resume my choral duties as of old, afore we went to Norfolk. Music always soothed my soul as naught else could.

# Chapter 5

## Saturday, the twenty-second day of August
## Smithfield

THE FAYRE GROUND was a-buzz, folk scurrying in all directions. Ultimately, Emily supposed, there was a purpose in their activities but, for now, Smithfield was a tapestry of chaos. The late summer grass was trampled beneath so many feet, hooves and wheels it was a wonder that none were crushed. Such a cacophony of shouts, cries and squeals, banging, thudding and hammering, made her want to cover her ears, but there was work to be done.

Dame Ellen sat upon a stool, directing Emily and the other silk-women in preparing their stall in readiness for Monday. Emily's father and brother – Stephen and John Appleyard – had constructed the wooden framework yesterday. Stephen being a fine carpenter, the booth was substantial enough to survive any windy or wet weather the coming week might throw at it. A painted canvas awning formed the roof, its blue and white stripes echoed in the boards that formed the walls. A door in the back wall gave entrance to the booth and had a stout lock so the goods could be kept safe from thieves overnight. The top half of the front wall could be lowered on leather hinges and propped on trestles to form the counter-board on which the wares would be displayed to best advantage. There were wooden pegs affixed all around, inside and out, where ribbons and girdles could be hung up so customers could see them. For the present, the counter-board was folded down to allow light into the booth.

Emily was balanced on a trestle, her skirts kilted up and her mouth full of pins as she draped a length of fine yellow silk, trimmed with gold tassels, pleating it to best effect and hanging it from the pegs.

'More to the left, my girl,' Dame Ellen waved her hand, 'The pleats are uneven and take care not to snag the tassels and pull a thread.'

Emily rearranged the pleats and looked to Dame Ellen for approval. The dame waved her hand again.

'Another pleat to the right, I think.'

Emily sighed and moved the silk back as it was before. She would have made some comment, but a mouthful of pins prevented her.

'That will serve. Now likewise with the blue. Peronelle,' Dame Ellen called to one of the other silk-women, 'Have you got that bunch of ribbons all of a length yet? Emily will be ready for them shortly. And where's Beatrice? She went for that jug of ale an hour since, I do swear, and we all be in need on such a day.' Dame Ellen fanned herself with her apron. 'And I see Mistress Knollys has absented herself yet again. Has anyone caught sight of that idle hussy this morn? She may make the finest silk lacings in London, but she's good for naught else. I don't doubt she'll expect a share of the profits without lifting one finger more than she may avoid. Ah, Beatrice: what a Godsend you are. I need that ale like my life's blood.'

Beatrice Thatcher set out four cups on the grass and poured the ale.

Emily climbed down off the trestle, took the pins from her mouth and replaced them in the pincushion, one by one.

'The stall is looking most attractive, Em,' Beatrice handed her a cup. 'Has Lizzie brought her lacings yet?'

Emily shook her head and sipped the cool ale.

'I shall be giving Lizzie Knollys a piece of my mind when she does turn up,' Dame Ellen said, 'Leaving all the work to us. Who does she think she is? The Queen of England?'

It was almost time for dinner. John Appleyard arrived, bearing gifts – well, a mutton pie, at least.

'I closed up the shop, Dame Ellen,' he said. 'Thought you fine ladies might be hungry. Come down off your perch, Em, I've brought spoons.'

Saturday was early closing day for most London shops, but business was quiet anyway, what with so many citizens preparing for the fayre. John, Emily's younger brother, ran the tailoring side of Dame Ellen's business that she had taken on when her husband died some years before. John had been her apprentice, but was now a journeyman-tailor and working towards his mastership.

They all sat cross-legged on the ground and dug spoons into the pie. John reached over and tucked a lock of his sister's hair out of the way when it threatened to dangle in the mutton juices. Her cap had gone awry during her labours, and her autumnal tresses were escaping.

'Nessie will be bringing the babe along soon, so I can feed him,' she said, trying to rearrange her hair under the cap, but there was no saving it without beginning again, so she unpinned the cap, shook out her hair and set about re-plaiting it in full view.

Dame Ellen tutted at such brazenness in a married woman, but kept her peace since there was no alternative except for Emily to look as untidy as an unmade bed.

'Oh, so we'll get to see this wondrous child at last,' Beatrice laughed. 'All we've heard of him, I shall expect him to be a marvel indeed: a prodigy reciting his catechism and penning the alphabet at the very least.'

'But he's only eight weeks of age, Beattie,' Peronelle said, taking the jest seriously, as she always did. A mouse of a woman, Emily thought 'Pen' was fearful of her own shadow, but there was no denying her silk-work was of the highest standard. Pen always looked to be disappearing into her widow's weeds, worn since her husband died of a congestion of the lungs last Shrovetide. Andrew Wenham had been much older than his bride – his third wife – and poor Pen had hardly got used to married life when she found herself attending his funeral obsequies. She mourned him with dignity, but it was never a love match, having been arranged by Pen's guardian, a distant male relation she didn't know.

'In truth, little Dickon is nigh ten weeks old now,' Emily corrected. 'And he recognises my voice already, turning his head when I say his name and waving his little fists in excitement when I go to him.' She twisted the plait and pinned it on top of her head, then settled her cap back in place, patting it until it felt as it should.

'Well, look there,' Beatrice muttered, 'See what the dog coughed up at last.'

Lizzie Knollys was strolling towards them, swinging a covered basket and looking as though the world was her Eden.

'So, you deigned to join us then?' Dame Ellen greeted the late arrival with a voice like vinegar, 'Now most of the work is done. Where were you? I said a half hour after seven of the clock and 'tis nigh four hours beyond that now.'

'I had matters to attend to,' Lizzie said airily.

'I dare say. Such as making eyes at every creature with a cod-flap. I know you well enough Elizabeth Knollys. You be careful; your reputation is not as spotless as I would wish my employees to possess. And I am planning for the future of my silk business. If you want to be a part of that, you'd best mend your ways.'

'No woman weaves finer lacings than I do: you need me, old dame, so don't pretend otherwise.'

Dame Ellen looked aghast at such a lack of courtesy. So did the others gathered there upon the grass. The trouble was Lizzie spoke the truth.

Fortunately, what could have been an uncomfortable incident was avoided because Seb arrived, carrying the babe in a basket, draped with linen to keep the sun off the little one's pale skin. He set the basket down in the shade of the striped awning and brought the swaddled bundle to Emily.

'I was expecting Nessie to bring him,' she said. 'You must have work to do.'

'Indeed. But the shop be closed, the sun shines, and I thought to walk out with my son.' Seb was smiling, and Emily realised he was just as eager as she to show off their pride and joy to those who hadn't yet had the honour of making the acquaintance of little Dickon. 'Besides, I want to see how the preparations for the fayre progress. Your stall be the most colourful I've seen. It would most assuredly tempt me to buy, if I had a mind to purchase such finery.'

But the women weren't listening to his compliments. Instead, Beatrice and Peronelle came to look more closely at the precious babe and, since he wasn't yet yelling for his dinner, Emily let Beatrice hold him. They were soon cooing and talking nonsense to the child, so Seb began chatting to John about the state of business in the city, whether tailoring, scrivening or any other. The two men wandered along the first row of stalls, towards the church of St Bartholomew the Great, Gawain trotting beside Seb.

As they paused to watch a poppet show booth being set up and spoke to the poppeteer, with Seb admiring and discussing the artistry of the painted faces on the dolls, Lizzie Knollys pushed in between them.

'Well, Master Foxley, 'tis good to see you back with us again,' she said, taking his arm. 'And Master Appleyard: how goes it with you?'

'God give you good day, Mistress Knollys,' Seb said, removing his cap. 'I did not see you there.'

John also removed his cap and nodded politely. He knew the woman rather better than his companion did and his opinion of Lizzie Knollys was coloured by Dame Ellen's. He made his excuses and slipped away.

Seb, out of courtesy, swiftly involved Lizzie in his conversation with the poppeteer, pointing out the pigments used and discussing the best-lasting lacquers and varnishes to preserve the colours on the painted faces.

'Have you considered mixing the flesh tones with walnut oil?' Seb suggested. 'Being colourless itself, it does not impart a jaundiced look as other oils do - linseed, for example.'

'Aye, I might try that,' the poppeteer said, twisting the tag end of his beard around his finger. His way of speech was not of home – more of France or Burgundy, perhaps – but his English was good for all that. 'If I could, though, I would give my children the spark of life. Meet Johannes,' he said, holding out a doll with horse-hair locks and beard, 'The hero of my tale, yet he lacks a certain er... I know not what.'

Seb grinned and laughed.

'I know precisely what you mean, Master Poppeteer, but it may soon be remedied.'

'Gerrit Heijnsbroeck of Rotterdam. Call me Gerrit, if you will? I know you English have trouble with my name.'

'Such a mouthful,' Lizzie put in, not wanting to be overlooked. 'But the poppets are well made, indeed.'

'Your goodwife is most complimentary of my efforts.'

'Mistress Kn...' Seb began to explain.

'But you say the lack of life may soon be remedied? I would be grateful to learn how.'

'It be a secret of my craft, but I suppose you too are a member of my fellowship in a way. I know not of any English poppet-makers nor to which guild they would belong. But I will tell you, Gerrit.' Seb beckoned the man closer and whispered in his ear.

'As simple as that? I shall try it this very day. Are you certain that is all it takes to give the look of life to my dolls?'

'It works for portraits and miniatures, people, animals, even saints and angels.'

'I am most grateful to you, Master...?'

'Foxley. Sebastian Foxley. If I may stop by during the fayre, I should enjoy watching your performance, Gerrit.'

'And will be most welcome and for no payment but your secret. Your goodwife too, of course. You will be able to see if the improvements you suggest work as well on poppets as on portraits.'

Lizzie giggled as they moved away.

'He thinks we be man and wife, *husband dearest.*' Then she put her hand behind Seb's head and pulled his face close, kissing him heartily, full upon the lips before he realised. He stood there, shocked, as she skipped away, still laughing.

The moment was made worse by a chorus of cat-calls and lewd gestures from a group of fellows taking their ease beside an ornate tent, its purpose as yet to be revealed. However, it was grand indeed with pennants fluttering from the tops of the poles. It must belong to a wealthy merchant from far away. At least, Seb hoped the whole assembly was from some distant land. His embarrassment would be increased, if they were Englishmen – or Londoners, God forbid.

'Come, Gawain,' he called to the dog, 'This be no place for a creature of gentle breeding like you: misfits and loose women... what is London coming to?'


Dame Ellen had gone home, claiming the heat of the day was over-taxing for one of her mature years and that the younger women could finish decorating the stall, seeing naught should be left until the morrow, it being the Lord's Day.

'Did you see that, Em?' Beatrice said, nudging Emily who was settling little Dickon to sleep in his basket.

'No. What did I miss?'

'That Lizzie just kissed your Seb, and it was no courteous

greeting either. She's trying to steal him away from you, I wager. You know no man is safe from that woman's wiles. She's a strumpet and no mistake. She tried to tempt my Hal to stray. Did I tell you of it? Aye, and it began with kisses just like that.'

'Well, her wiles will be wasted on my Seb,' Emily assured her. 'I swear he'd more likely be tempted by a saint in an illuminated manuscript.'

'Truly? What? A fine looking man as him? He got you with child, did he not?'

'After much, er, coaxing, aye. But what of your Hal?'

'She didn't get him either, not after I boxed his ears for gawping at her 'assets', but she would have stolen him away from me if she could. You best guard your man, Em.'

'Menfolk's not all she steals,' Peronelle said quietly. It was rare for her to speak at all, so Beattie and Em were eager to hear. 'Last time she came to my house to bring me some green silk thread Dame Ellen required to be worked, my ivory needle case with Our Lady carven on it – you know the one, Beattie; the one my mother gave me – well it went missing. I searched everywhere, but it's definitely gone. I know Lizzie admired it and I think she took it.'

'Mm, now you say that, Pen,' Beattie said, 'My best snips haven't been seen since she last invited herself into my home. I wonder if...'

'Come, both of you,' Emily said, bunching up the hem of her skirt and tucking it under her girdle, 'Let's get those ribbons displayed. We'll put your best ones to the front, Pen, to attract customers.' She balanced on a trestle to tie the rainbow of colourful ribbons to the bar supporting the awning, fluffing them out so they fluttered in the light breeze. 'Our Rose said she would bring her gloves later this afternoon and we must make room for them. Have you seen her work? Fine enough for royalty by any account, yet she isn't permitted to sell them by the Glovers' Guild because she's a woman. St Bart's Fayre is her best opportunity because the guilds have no say in what's sold by whom, so I want her gloves to be shown to best advantage. Dame Ellen has agreed to it.'

'Aye, well don't shove my silk kerchiefs out of sight,' Beattie said, 'I have to make a little profit for my efforts too, remember.'

'Fear not. 'Tis Lizzie's lacings that will be set aside to make space. After all, she hasn't lifted a finger to aid us all day. Why should we care if her work sells or not?'

Rose arrived soon after, bringing an ale jug, as well as a basket of her gloves for sale. All four women laboured in the sun until everything was in readiness. Two pairs of Rose's kid-leather gloves – one pale blue, the other white – and an orphrey of Emily's beautiful goldthread-work had been selected to lie upon the counter-board, taking pride of place to attract custom. For now, until the board was lowered on Monday morn, they were carefully wrapped, laid in a basketwork tray and safely stored in the booth. Just as the women closed up the counter board, locked the door behind the booth and were about to leave, Lizzie Knollys returned. The women were all sweaty, weary and bedraggled, while Lizzie was fresh as bread from the oven.

'Oh, you've closed up,' she said, 'I was about to help but... Oh, well, there will be much to do come Monday, no doubt.'

Beattie ground her teeth, but why waste breath on the lazy slut. She wasn't worth it.

'Em,' Rose said aside, 'Your gown has come unlaced. Your shift is awry too.'

Emily straightened her clothes and was about to re-tie her lacings when Lizzie espied something:

'Oh, Em, what a pretty pendant. Who gave you that?'

Emily didn't reply, but hastily concealed the amber pendant on its leather thong within her shift. It had been Gabriel's gift to her, sent from the Baltic Lands. Seb knew of it, but not how much it meant to her, nor that she'd been wearing again since Gabriel's return. She hadn't worn it for months, but now Gabe was back, the honey-hued pendant was restored to its rightful place, next to her heart.

Already, the dry late-summer grass underfoot had been nigh worn away, the earth hard packed by the passage of countless boots, wheels and hoofs. It mattered not unless it rained, in which case Smithfield would be churned to a mire of mud. It was to be hoped the fine weather continued throughout the se'en-night of the fayre. However, its unforgiving surface only made weary feet wearier, and Emily was eager to get home.

As the women trudged past the Hart's Horn tavern in Giltspur Street, a pedlar with his laden handcart nigh forced them into the tavern doorway, so heedless was he of others on the road.

'Have a care, can't you?' Emily called out, pulling her rumpled skirts out of the way of his cartwheel, but the fellow ignored her. Mayhap, he was a foreigner and understood no English.

'No manners,' Beattie complained with a huff. 'I'll certainly not buy so much as a single pin from him. Take note of that horrible knitted cap of his and avoid him like the pestilence. He doesn't deserve our custom. I wouldn't touch his tawdry rubbish with a pikestaff.'

'Since we're here at the tavern door, why don't we rest and have some ale?' Lizzie suggested.

'Nay. If I sit down, I shan't get up again,' Emily said. 'I'm going straight home, and woe betide anyone who expects me to do aught but eat supper and go to bed.'

'Same goes for me,' Beattie said, and Pen nodded agreement.

'Please yourselves. I've earned a drink.' Lizzie shrugged, pushing open the door and disappearing into the cool, ale-scented gloom of Mistress Fletcher's reputable establishment.

'Earned a drink, by my grandmother's eyeballs! She's done naught whatsoever.' Beattie expressed the disgust they all felt.

They tramped back into the city through Newgate, dragging their feet. Rose carried the babe in his basket since Emily looked so tired.

'Where is that devil, eh? Where's that slimy serpent, Jude Foxley, tell me? I see my father let him reopen the shop and that isn't right. Where is he; I haven't seen him of late, the bastard.' This tirade was thrown at Emily of a sudden by a fellow standing within the shadow of the gateway. It took her a moment to recognise Ralph Clifford, the son of the Warden Master of the Stationers' Guild. The young man's right arm hung awkwardly at his side, and one eye seemed to have a clouded veil cast upon it: Jude's doing, she recalled, on the night before the wedding that never was. Rose had said the arm was mending, but it looked to be of little use at present.

'Jude's gone and good riddance,' Emily told him, feeling sorry for the young man in his plight. It looked to her as though his days as a scrivener were over and she wondered what he might do to earn his living instead, with but one sound hand and one good eye. 'Your father allowed my husband to open the shop once more, not his brother. What Jude did has naught to do with my Seb. We weren't even in London at the time.'

'But you're all devil-damned Foxleys,' Ralph growled, stepping towards her, 'All hatched of the same nest of vipers.'

Emily shivered despite the heat, not liking the look in his solitary eye.

'Come, Rose. We are expected home in haste,' she said, pulling her friend with the babe away from this fellow. Despite their weary limbs, they broke into a run with Beattie and Pen just a yard behind.

'Who was that?' Beattie asked breathlessly. They were at the top end of Ivy Lane where their pathways divided: Beattie and Pen to Cheapside; Emily and Rose to turn down Ivy Lane towards Paternoster Row. 'I don't like the look of him, either,' she decided after Emily had explained Ralph Clifford's grudge against her household.

Adam was there to greet them, smiling as he poured ale for Emily and Rose.

'Where's Seb?' Emily asked. 'Still painting his fables, I suppose?' She sat down upon a stool, wincing as she eased off her shoes. 'Oh, just look at this: the sole's near worn through. No wonder my feet be sore. I'll need a new pair afore Monday.'

'He went to speak with someone, er, Master Verney, if I recall aright, about Kate returning to the workshop? And then to choir practice, so he said. I have a mind to attend vespers later, to hear him sing.'

'As if he has naught ten times more important to do.'

'Pass me your shoes, 'Adam said, holding out his hand for them. 'I could mend them for you this eve. I saw leather for book-binding in the store-room. Some of that would do.'

'From the store? I think not, Adam. Seb will suffer apoplexy if you use his precious stuff. 'Tis too fine for soling shoes, he'll insist.'

'For certain, he cannot expect you to wear shoes with holes?'

'He will say I can make do with my Sunday-best for now. Besides, those are what I should wear on the morrow and mayhap, I ought to look my best for the fayre on Monday also, at least for the opening ceremony, when the lord mayor inspects all the stalls and checks the cloth-yard measures to be certain no customer will be sold short.'

'Oh, aye, I can see you must wear your finest for that. By the by, Master Gideon came to see how Jack was recovering and kindly made sure I had suffered no after effects of swimming in the river yesterday.'

'Gabriel was here? And I missed him?'

Adam wondered at her wistful words.

'Aye, Gabriel, as you call him. I dare say that won't be his last visit.'

'Did he say when he would come by again?'

'No, naught so definite, but I had the feeling he would is all. Why? If you had a message for him, I could oblige...'

'There is no message,' Emily said hastily, going to the basket in the chimney corner where the babe still lay sleeping. Even so, she lifted him from his nest of blankets and held him close.

Adam was no fool. He'd seen how she looked at Gabriel on board ship that morn, all doe-eyed and winsome, and he knew now that she clutched the child to her because she felt the need to embrace another. And it wasn't little Dickon, nor even her husband she desired to hold in her arms. Seb was blind indeed if he couldn't see how she felt about that fellow. Poor Seb. Did he know she would cuckold him, given half a chance? Adam doubted it. Seb was so trusting, and he adored her; he would never believe his dearest Emily could deceive him so. But, mayhap, it was naught more than wishful thinking on her part and Gabriel was too honourable to betray his friend. Adam hoped that was the case and he would pray God it was, for Seb's sake.

He happened to look up then and saw the expression in Rose's eye: she knew as he did, but their exchanged glances sealed a contract: they would say naught of this matter to Seb – not for the present, at least.

# St Paul's Cathedral

Just as he intended, Adam went to vespers. To hear Seb sing was only part of the reason. He had much to pray about also, to thank the Almighty – as he did daily – for sending Seb to fill the void in his soul left by the death of his twin brother, Noah, a year since. The day after tomorrow would be the year's mind day of Noah's death and, in truth, he was unsure he would be able to bear the sorrow alone. But Seb had troubles enough of his own, trying to rebuild his reputation and business, discipline those unruly knaves who called themselves 'apprentices' and now, whether he knew it or no, a wife who was unfaithful in her heart, if not in body. Adam didn't want to burden Seb with his grief. Rather, he would do all he could to give due remembrance to Noah's passing, without distressing anyone else, Seb in particular. But it would not be easy. He put coins in the box, took a wax taper and lit it from one already burning, praying for strength to bear the secret pain to come. Then, upon an impulse, he paid for a second candle and lit that also.

'This is for you, Seb, because you be needful of God's aid more than you know.' He set the light in place, crossed himself and went to take his place in the nave for the vespers office.

There was no denying the choir sang most wonderfully but, since they were beyond the Rood Screen, he could not see if Seb was with them. He supposed he must be, but there was no solo singing, so he couldn't pick out Seb's voice – which was as it ought to be, that the voices should be in harmony. Yet he was disappointed to not to hear him singing alone: the man who had become a dear brother to him.


'You will let us go to the fayre, won't you, Master Seb?' Tom said in a wheedling tone across the supper board. 'We know from last year, there won't be any customers in the shop as everyone will be at the fayre too.'

I took my time over a mouthful of bread afore answering. Tom had hardly earned such an indulgence, and Jack most certainly was undeserving of any reward, after that idiotic escapade of yesterday.

'Just because there be few customers, 'tis no reason to abandon your tasks in the workshop. Once the fayre be packed up and gone, they will return to us, in need of our wares again, and it will be as well to give them choice aplenty. Those cheap Latin primers have proved popular in the past, particularly in September when the young scholars at law return to their studies and realise they have forgotten their conjugations and declensions and cannot find their primers to revise them. I want at least another half dozen completed afore the Michaelmas term commences.'

'Oh, but master, we...'

'No 'buts' Tom. The pair of you have done naught but cause trouble of late.'

'But it was Jack who...'

'Aye, so it was, yet you didn't prove yourself a shining example of commendable behaviour during my absence, did you? Some of the reports which have come to me be of a most disturbing nature and they are not all applicable to Jack alone. This very afternoon I heard tell of a brawl in a tavern upon London Bridge a fortnight since, after which one particular drunken youth required a surgeon's embroidery be done upon his ear.' I leaned over and lifted Tom's hair aside. The report was true for, sure enough, a barely healed wound was still held together by three stitches of black thread, attaching the lobe of the ear in place. 'Upon Monday morn, you'll go to Master Dagvyle and have those sutures removed,' I told him. 'I happened to meet the surgeon upon my way to see Edmund Verney, and he asked why you had not returned to him for that purpose after ten days, as he instructed you at the time.'

'I wasn't drunk!'

'Does that improve the matter or make it worse? That you were sober as a saint and still became embroiled in a fight, knowing no better how to conduct yourself?'

'Are you saying it would be less my fault if I were drunk?'

'I be saying that you disgrace the reputation of this house, whether in sobriety or inebriation, so why, in the name of good sense, should I permit either of you the licence to go to the fayre, where there will be boundless means of temptation to lead you into yet more disreputable activities?'

'That's not fair,' he whined. 'Master Collop's apprentices are all going on Tuesday next. He has given them a whole day of freedom to enjoy themselves. Harry was telling me when we were playing dice at the Green Man tav...' Tom's words tailed off as he realised he was admitting of yet another offence. 'We were only playing for straws, not coins,' he added quickly, seeing my expression.

'That's a bloody lie,' Jack said. 'Yer wos playin' fer money, I saw. An' you wos losin' an' all.'

'So you were at the Green Man also, Jack?'

'Wot if I wos? I weren't gamblin', wos I? Not like he wos.' Jack pointed an accusing finger at Tom.

'No, because you were feeling up that wench with the big tits. You had your hand up her skirts one minute and down her shift the next, you dirty lecher.'

'Well, you'd been there afore me, so yer can't say it wos only me.'

'Enough! I will not have such talk at the board, and there are women present. Where be your manners? Now apologise to Mistress Em, Mistress Rose and Nessie for your unseemly conversation then get to your beds, the pair of you. You disgust me utterly.'

The lads departed the kitchen, both wearing surly expressions that, more properly, should have been contrite.

'What am I to do with them?' I asked aloud, my head in my hands. I did not expect an answer.

'I'll take my broom to the devils,' Emily said, 'Beat some good manners into those young midden-mongers who think they can do as they please.' She was changing the babe's tailclout as she spoke around the pins in her mouth.

'You think beatings be the cure for this misbehaviour?' I asked. Rose was shaking her head.

'In truth, Seb, you may as well know that Jude punished them daily, almost, for the months you were gone, and now we see the result. They are grown worse than ever. Beatings haven't stopped them. Rather, it seems to me, they have followed his bad example. Perhaps, now you are returned to set a good example, they will do as you do.'

'I fear 'tis too late for that. Now they have tasted such sinful ways, how can I pull them back from consuming the entire dish of vice and evil-doings? If I could have prevented it to begin with, I might have kept them virtuous, but now they know of drunkenness and debauchery, gaming and gambling, I be at a loss how to repair the damage done to their morals.'

'My broom and your belt,' Emily said, seemingly having no doubts as to the wisdom and effectiveness of corporal punishment.

''Tis hardly my place to have an opinion, being an in-comer to the household,' Adam said, 'But I think you have the right of it, Seb: withholding such rewards as a visit to the fayre is likely the best punishment. When they behave, they earn a treat – just like training a dog.' He laughed and ruffled Gawain's fur. The dog indicated approval by thumping my foot with his tail as he lay beneath the board, awaiting the benevolence of any tasty morsels that might befall or be offered. 'Gawain understands that, so why not the lads?'

'That would be my preferred means of chastisement, Adam,' I said, 'But will it have any greater success, I wonder?'

Emily made a disapproving sound and shook her head in dismay, but at least I had one ally in my strategy for the redemption of those unruly youngsters – mayhap, two, if Rose agreed also?

'With Jude departed, we have an opportunity to lead by our own example, as best we may. We must be sober, upright and respectful. If the lads do good, they will be rewarded; if they misbehave, they will be denied, and bread and ale will be all they have at the board. I can think of no other remedy for their malaise. And if that fails... then I shall despair of them and resign myself to seeing them dance the hangman's jig one day and my business founder with no better reputation and far less custom than a Bankside bawdy-house.'

Thus it was with a new sense of resolve that I sought my bed. The morrow was the Lord's Day: a time for contemplation and prayerfulness. And I had much indeed to contemplate and pray for, not least the behaviour of my apprentices, but also my goodwife's intention of declaring herself *femme sole* and running her own business. I did not doubt that she was capable, but feared she might exhaust herself by attempting to do too much, what with a new babe and all. I had noted how weary she looked after just a single day of preparation for the fayre, such that her health concerned me. These things kept sleep from my eyes for the greater part of the night, and the first hint of daylight was tapping at the window glass afore I had slept more than a few moments, or that was how it seemed.

# Chapter 6

## Monday, the twenty-fourth day of August
## Smithfield

THE OPENING CEREMONY, with its traditional cups of wine served to Lord Mayor Humphrey Hayford and the approval of all the yardsticks to be used for measuring the cloth for sale, was over and done afore I arrived. I was not sorry to have missed the procession. I found crowds daunting at the best of times – bearing in mind my poor sense of balance if jostled, elbowed aside or tripped up – and such a gathering as would assemble for the occasion was better avoided. However, I had promised Emily that I would visit their booth to approve the artistry of the display of wares. Also, I suspected she wanted me to be there when Dame Ellen made her grand announcement.

Yestereve, whether rightly or wrongly – my misgivings were not to be entirely reconciled – I had given consent for Emily to declare herself *femme sole*, in order that she could take on Dame Ellen's business in the near future. The unknown consequence of whether Emily's fellow silk-women would be agreeable, jealous or even set against the prospect meant my wife wanted me to add my voice to Dame Ellen's in approval of this. When we had informed the dame of my decision after vespers at St Michael's, the elderly woman had been thrilled to learn of it. She, at least, had no doubts as to the wisdom of the venture. For myself, I was far less certain, but only time would tell if I had been correct to say 'aye' to Emily's pleas.

Earlier that morn, I had taken Tom to have the stitches removed from his ear by Surgeon Dagvyle and such a deal of protest and childish bewailing I never heard from a lad who would account himself a man. I had nigh felt obliged to cuff him about that very member which had required reattaching. Worse than a little maid ever was, the foolish lad. For the present, he and Jack were occupied in the workshop under Adam's careful eye. I knew he could be relied upon to see that they behaved. As yet, I remained undecided as to whether I would permit either of those scallywags to visit St Bart's Fayre. It seemed harsh to forbid what was, after all, a once a year recreation, but neither had they earned the boon. If I should allow it, for certain they would be given but half a day's release and most certainly not at the same time. Those two being free together was a receipt for trouble indeed.

As I arrived, Lord Mayor Hayford, a goldsmith himself, was still there, admiring the finely chased silverware of some foreign merchant. The cup he held glinted in the sun, light reflecting off the rim in dazzling flashes, forcing me to shield my eyes. Thus it was that I near tripped over young Kate Verney who was seated upon the grass, cross-legged like a tailor.

'God give you good day, Kate,' I said. 'No, do not get up. I would not disturb your work.' The lass had a drawing board upon her knees and was sketching the scene at the goldsmith's stall.

'Good day, Master Seb,' she said, setting aside her board despite my words. If my eyes had been struck by the glint of sunlight on silver, they were now bedazzled by a brighter light yet: Kate's smile put the sun to shame, as always. She stretched up, offering her smooth cheek for the kiss of greeting. It was a pleasure to oblige her.

'Are you and your father in good health?'

'Aye, we are, God be thanked. If you would speak with him again, he is hereabouts somewhere, doing business with every other mercer in the world.' She rolled her eyes at this. 'He left me to my drawing. When Papa said you were back in London, Master Seb, I was so glad of it. And then you asked about my return to your workshop. I shall be so pleased to be back with you. I've not neglected my work, as you may see.'

I had indeed visited her father at home in Walbrook, to discuss Kate's return as my apprentice. I took the sheets of paper she held out. As ever, her sketches were skilled and with elements of humour. She was a talented artist and no mistake. I had great hopes for young Kate's future as an illuminator. I had wondered if her father would be willing to allow her return to a workshop of dubious reputation, whose name was, for the present, struck from the guild's rolls. Yet he was eager enough and, after all, I hoped such ignominy would shortly be rectified but, in the meantime, things were as they were, at least until the next guild meeting at the beginning of the new month.

While I studied her drawings, Kate resumed her sketching. I could see an excellent likeness of my Gawain emerging from the charcoal upon the page. The dog was content to maintain his pose, sprawled at my feet, tongue lolling, panting as the day grew warmer. Then, typical of the lass's style, she completed the image by setting a plumed hat betwixt the dog's ears, copying one worn by some over-dressed fellow standing beside the mayor. I laughed at the jest. In truth, the hat looked better upon the dog's head than it did upon the man's.

'Fear not, Kate,' I said, still grinning with merriment, 'I have not forgotten your fine talent – as if I ever could? Now, forgive me, I too have business to attend at the silk-women's stall yonder.' I pointed to the blue and white striped booth with ribbons fluttering.

'Is Mistress Em there with the babe? I should like to see them both.'

'Mistress Em be there, but the babe be at home in Rose's care. At the dinner hour, Rose will bring him so Emily can suckle him afore Rose returns home with him. It was determined the day would likely be too hot, too busy and too crowded: no place for a tiny child. The morrow will be Rose's turn to serve at the stall and Mistress Em will stay home. 'Tis all arranged, so I'm informed.' I handed back the sheaf of drawings.

'Thank you for speaking with Papa, Master Seb.'

'It was my pleasure. Oh, one thing, Kate: I have been invited to see the poppet show by Master Gerrit. Would you like to accompany me, later? He will ring his bell when it be time.'

It was heartening to see a number of affluent-looking merchants crowded about the silk-women's stall. Even as I approached, a man grandly attired in green silk was coming away with a pair of kid-leather gloves that I recognised as Rose's work, pulling them on and admiring his hands. Another had a large package beneath his arm and looked well pleased with his purchases. At his back, I could discern that Emily's face was a picture of triumph.

'Do you see that man?' she said afore I was even close to the booth, pointing at the fellow with the package. 'He bought the orphrey I made and has ordered another to be done similarly in time for Easter next coming for his lord.' She patted at the brass-headed pins in her veil, as though to be sure she was properly presentable afore meeting this lord. 'And, you'll never guess,' she continued, 'His lord is the Bishop of Bath and Wells and Dean of St Martin's le Grand. Is that not the most excellent news, Seb, and all upon the first morning of the fayre? He hardly even haggled at the price. Do you suppose I undersold it? I pray not. At this rate, we shall have sold everything by Wednesday.' Her boundless enthusiasm was infectious, and I kissed her across the counter-board.

''Tis wondrous news indeed and you are to be congratulated. All of you,' I added to include Beatrice who was also serving and Peronelle who was replacing the sold items with others from the baskets behind the counter. 'Your booth be the most attractive I've seen.' I leaned closer to Emily and whispered: 'What of the other news? At what hour do you expect Dame Ellen to arrive and make the announcement?'

'Dinnertime. Lizzie should be here by then. She's supposed to take Pen's place for a few hours. Pen's mother had a fall last week, and Pen has to go see to her, make certain she has meat and drink. I only hope Lizzie bothers to come. She's so unreliable. Poor Pen is quite worried about it, leaving her mother untended and all.'

At that moment, I realised other customers were attempting to elbow me aside. It was most rude, but clearly I was hindering possible sales by taking up space at the counter.

'I shall be back in time for that,' I called out to Emily over the shaven head of some burly fellow determined to examine a bunch of colourful ribbons. I know not if she heard me for she was already dealing with a man and a woman on the far side and a discordant fanfare announced a juggling act about to be performed in a small area betwixt two stalls. I departed Emily's stall chuckling to myself, having imagined the bald fellow's head adorned with a plethora of ribbons like a cock's comb. I was growing fanciful as Kate, but it was good to feel my spirits lighten.

I managed to side-step an argument betwixt a draper at his stall and two toll collectors. It was the case, so the toll collectors claimed in strident voices, that his pitch straddled the boundary of the glebe land belonging to St Bartholomew's Priory and that of the City of London. Thus, the unfortunate fellow owed his fees for pickage in breaking the ground to set up his tent and stallage for erecting his stall to both the sacrist at the priory and the lord mayor. The collectors, as their representatives, were each claiming the full fees due and the argument seemed likely to be one of considerable duration.

Since I had time to spare afore the poppet show should begin, Gawain and I wandered around the fayre. Familiar Smithfield was unrecognisable beneath a veritable ocean of seething humanity and vivid colour. So much noise came as a shock after the peaceful countryside of Norfolk: I had quite forgotten how raucous the London fayre could be. I averted my gaze from an immodest exhibition of excess flesh by some wanton attempting the dance of the seven veils to the wailing of weird pipes. Mind, it would have been difficult to get a good view in any case, what with the dozens of men crowding round, their roars of approval as each veil was discarded nigh drowning out the plaintive piping.

'Come, Gawain, we both of us need refreshment,' I said, as if he understood me which, oftentimes, he seemed to. We found an ale stall set up 'neath my favoured oak tree by the Horse Pool, where I came to draw when time allowed, and in its shade, we sat and quenched our thirst – me with a quite palatable ale and Gawain from the cool water of the pool. My drink cost an entire halfpenny – a disgraceful, if not illegal, price, the assize of ale being inapplicable at the fayre – but at least Gawain was refreshed for free. This day, the squirrels had wisely retreated up into the dense, dark canopy of late-summer leaves and not a one was to be seen. Birds too had departed and if any sang, their melodies were drowned in the chaos of human noise. The scents of summer were likewise engulfed by the stink of sweaty men, beasts and the odours of foreign lands, some of which I could name, like cinnamon and pepper, lemons and frankincense, but others quite unknown and exotic taunted my senses, wafting across Smithfield on a fitful breeze. While slaking my thirst, I took out my drawing stuff from my scrip and took the opportunity, following Kate's example, to do a few sketches. I suppose it was inevitable that a fellow patron of the ale seller saw my work and took an interest. Unfortunately, he was the very subject of my drawing.

'Who's that then?' he asked, peering over my elbow. By his speech, he was a man of the West Country, maybe. I tried to fold away the paper, not wanting to cause any embarrassment to either of us. I had chosen to draw him because he was uniquely ugly, his features reminding me of the wrinkles on a dried plum. Yet he pulled the drawing from my hand, his fat little body convulsed by guffaws of laughter.

'The poor soul,' he wheezed, wiping a tear from his furrowed cheek, 'To go about life looking like that! I'll light a taper for him next time I'm in church. You've got a cruel way with charcoal there, lad.' I was unsure whether he had realised he was my subject or no, but was much relieved when he returned the image, still chortling with amusement. I hastened to conceal the offending paper in my scrip for fear he might mistake me for an entertainer at the fayre, hoping to sell a few drawings, and offer to buy it. It was a good likeness, and if he showed it to others, they would surely assess the truth, and I never meant any insult. He simply possessed, as I said, a unique face.

Still with a little time until the poppets' performance, I wandered among the stalls, sampled rosewater sweetmeats from the Land of the Turks and bought some to take home, purchased malachite green pigment from a German apothecary and a packet of finest steel needles from Sheffield town for Emily. If she had a commission for another orphrey, she would need the best embroidery needles. But a stall that caught my attention was set up within the ornate tent I had seen in the process of being set up on Saturday. I took a furtive glance around for any of those unmannerly fellows who had made rude gestures when Lizzie Knollys kissed me so blatantly while they watched. I had not forgotten my grave discomfiture at that moment and wanted none of that company to recognise me. But I could espy no one like that, mercifully.

It happened to be the stall of a Venetian merchant, selling a variety of exotic wares, from nutmegs to knife blades. The merchant was a stout fellow with a chest like an ale barrel, crimson-faced and sweating in his gold satin coat. He did not look pleased and was shouting at an underling in a tongue so rapid and incomprehensible and yet it was plain enough what he was saying. The youngster was adorned with lengths of packing straw: in his hair and clinging to his jerkin. I felt some sympathy for him since what appeared to be shards of ice glinted at his feet. A precious piece of Venice glassware lay smashed upon the ground. Thinking I might draw the merchant's attention away from the mishap, however temporarily, I went over and began admiring his wares. He immediately came to attend upon me, giving the underling some respite, as I hoped.

I had no thought of making any purchase, merely intending to show an interest. There were items of domed glass: scrying glasses such as elderly scribes use to enlarge texts that their eyes have difficulty making out – one day, I might have need of such things myself – but what caught my attention was a bright, slanting rainbow of colour illuminating the canvas at the side of the tent. How could that be, I wondered? There was sunshine aplenty, but no hint of rain. Intrigued, I made enquiry. The merchant spoke but little English and I knew naught of the Venice language, but we had Latin in common and understood one another well enough. He showed me a piece of glass, shaped like a pyramid the length of my longest finger. The instant he moved it, the rainbow danced upon the canvas two yards distant. It was quite wonderful to behold; the hues out-shining any pigment I had ever known. It was more like stained glass – well, it was glass – and yet the glass had no colour in it at all. He gave it to me, that I might see it more nearly. Even as I held it, I realised the rainbow moved as I moved the glass, but to a far greater degree. The smallest turn of the glass in my hand caused the colours to leap wildly and then, of a sudden and to my horror, they were no more. The merchant smiled at my look of panic and simply moved the glass a little. And there were all the colours returned, bright as ever.

'What alchemy is this, that you trap God's rainbow and release it at will?' I asked him, doubtful of a sudden at such trickery. Was he a sorcerer? In which case, I should depart in haste. But no. I was utterly enraptured by the magical conjuring of colours from the clear glass and eager to understand how it performed the miracle. The merchant answered my questions readily, but was it that Latin did not have the words to explain or was I too ignorant to comprehend? Mayhap, the merchant was entangling me with his arcane similes and overt obfuscation in order to keep his secrets without losing possible custom – mine. Whatever the case, I knew no more how it worked at the end of his lengthy lecture than I had at the beginning, but – *mea culpa* – I spent half a mark - an entire three shillings and eightpence - upon that device. He called the rainbow-maker a prism.

Despite feeling guilt for having spent money enough to buy food for a week upon that one beguiling item that had no use that I could think of, I was quite unable to leave the stall without it, imagining the great pleasure it would always give me to cast rainbows whenever I wished. Whether the merchant or the prism had bewitched me, I knew not. I suppose I was prideful and foolish to believe I could usurp God's own powers of creation at my whim, but the prism was duly wrapped in a soft cloth and nestled in my nigh-empty purse, while the merchant's takings were swelled considerably. He said he had another miraculous device that artists in other lands were exploring its uses, but this was the first in England: a camera obscura, he named it. He promised to demonstrate its wonders, if I returned later, but I determined I had spent too many coins already and would part with no more.

There was one last stall I should visit afore I went to watch Master Gerrit's poppets with Kate: that of the Bristol merchant, Richard Ameryk, where those unicorn horns – of which I had heard so much – were displayed for sale. The stall was marked by the crowd clustered about it, such that I could not make my way through the press of folk. Neither could I see over their heads, and a pedlar's handcart was an additional obstruction to my passage, earning me a glare and an earful of abuse from beneath his cap of faded knitting as I attempted to squeeze past. It was not to be, and I was much disappointed forwhy

Emily's description of the horns and Adam's appraisal of their virtues made me eager to set my own eyes upon their beauty. It occurred to me they might even be sold afore ever I saw them, which would be a pity indeed, they being things of such rarity. A glimpse of the black giant Rook beneath the awning was as close as I came to viewing them, yet mayhap I had garnered marvels sufficient for one day, having the rainbow-maker in my purse.

A goodly number of folk answered the summons of Master Gerrit's handbell, assembling to watch his poppets perform, but he made certain Kate and I had room to sit upon the grass at the front – no heads to obscure our view. He had greeted me as if I were a dear friend, smiling and jovial and delighted to make Kate's acquaintance. Since both were of the merriest disposition, I was in right pleasant company indeed.

The hand-poppets told a moral tale in which Master Gerrit's favoured Johannes was tempted by all manner of demons, including a ferocious green creature that made the hairs upon my arm quite stand on end. Supposed bags of gold were offered, if Johannes would but sell his soul, but our hero gave the demon a great buffet, and the crowd roared approval as the poppet fell lifeless on the counter-board. Johannes was then tempted by a golden-haired maiden under an enchantment. In the end, the hero triumphed, and the maiden was released from the spell.

'That was a fine tale, wasn't it, master?' Kate said, clapping her hands. 'And I see Master Gerrit knows the secret of the white dot of paint in the eye to bring life to his poppets.'

'Aye, he does,' I said, putting a couple of pennies in the hat that was being passed among the audience. I did not say that I had revealed the secret to him. I could not be more generous in my donation, sadly, because of my foolish purchase previously. 'His poppets be well made too, do you not think? The green creature was quite fearsome, was it not?'

'It gave me the shivers.' Kate pulled a face at the memory of it. 'The scene painted at the back reminded me of that tavern sign you made last year, for *The Woodsman,* if you recall: the path through the trees and the stormy sky.'

'Since you mention it, aye, 'tis not unlike. You be most observant, Kate. I commend you, lass. You have a good artist's eye to note such things.' With some difficulty, which I tried my best to disguise, I clambered to my feet. My hip did not take so kindly to sitting cross-legged for such a time.

I thanked Master Gerrit and congratulated him on the artistry of his play.

'Ja, the poppets look more alive, thanks to you,' he said, thumping my shoulder. 'Return this day after dinner, if you can. There will be a quite different tale told: one that will make you laugh.'

'I fear, I have other obligations, Master Gerrit. Perhaps upon the morrow, I shall have time to spare to see another play. I should like to very much.' I spoke the truth for he was a pleasant fellow indeed. It occurred to me that I should enjoy sharing a cup of ale with him, if chance befell.

With reluctance, we left the merry Dutchman, making our way by the pillory where a miscreant, labelled for a basket-dipper and cutpurse, was suffering due punishment, watched by the city beadle, Master Thaddeus Turner, and two broad-shouldered constables. Thaddeus be a friend of mine, and we exchanged greetings. I suppose 'tis a sorrowful fact that crime will show its horrid face in any gathering of humankind. No man be immune to its effects, whether as perpetrator, victim or bystander – a sad indictment upon us all.

'I must go to the silk-women's stall now. Will you come with me, Kate? Mayhap, Rose will have arrived with little Dickon by now, and you may meet him.'

At the silk-women's stall, Rose had just brought the babe from home that Emily might suckle him.

'Has Dame Ellen made the announcement yet? I whispered to her as she settled down in the small square of shade cast by the booth with little Dickon nuzzling her breast in eagerness.

'Nay. As you'd expect, Lizzie is late arriving, and Dame Ellen intends to tell the news but once. But I am quite on edge about it, not knowing how the others will receive it.'

'I be sure they will take it well enough, Em. Have you had plenty of custom this morn? There was quite a crowd earlier.'

'Aye, we were busy indeed, but it has quieted somewhat as folks have grown hot and thirsty and gone to find dinner and a place to rest. The Lord knows, my feet are grateful for this brief respite with little Dickon.'

'Kate Verney be here and would wish to greet you both. Kate! Oh, see, she is admiring the ribbons there.'

I saw that the babe was tangling his plump little hands in the leather cord of Emily's amber pendant. I had not realised she had taken to wearing it again.

'Watch that he doesn't choke you with that,' I said, laughing. 'He seems to have taken quite a liking to it.'

'Could you unfasten it for me, Seb? I wouldn't want the cord to break.'

I obliged, and she gave the warm piece of amber to the babe to play with.

Kate came over to see the babe and aided Emily in tucking him safely in his basket. The lass tied Emily's pendant to the basket handle, so that he could hold it without any danger of swallowing it. He seemed to like the smooth roundness of it, gurgling and hiccoughing as he played.

It was then that Lizzie Knollys deigned to arrive at last. Still avoiding doing any work, so it seemed to me, she also spent time admiring the babe afore Dame Ellen called everyone's attention. Seated upon a stool as if it were a throne, the elderly woman began her speech.

'Well, my girls,' she began, 'Of late, I have been forced to admit, after that wretch waylaid me in the street that one time, back in the spring – nigh at my own front door – that the affairs of business are becoming more tiring and burdensome to me. Thus, I intend to have less to do with the day to day concerns of both tailoring and silk-working. I have spoken with the Guild of Merchant Tailors, and they have agreed that John Appleyard will take on the tailoring business entirely. As to the silk-work, with the Mercers' Guild's approval, I have determined that one of you should take on the irksome duties of coordinating the out-workers, accepting and completing commissions, buying supplies and all the other tasks involved. Of course, I shall still be there to advise as required and would take one-tenth of the profits as my livelihood until my death.' She sipped from an ale cup which Rose passed to her.

I noted the expressions of expectation on the faces of the other women.

'But to whom should I entrust my business?' Dame Ellen continued. 'It has taken decades of hard work to find the best sources of silk, to build my excellent reputation for high-quality craftsmanship with orders completed on time and within costs. I have earned respect as a woman who pays her debts on time and treats her employees sternly but fairly, as I'm certain you all agree. 'Tis no easy matter to conduct a business properly. Thus I have determined my successor, and I trust you will all work as well and diligently for her in the future as you have for me in the past.' Dame Ellen stood up, easing her back as she did so. 'I am handing over my business to Mistress Emily Foxley,' she announced grandly.

Emily smiled self-consciously, I thought, but Beatrice and Peronelle came to congratulate her. Lizzie Knollys did not.

'If you think I'm working for that overbearing bitch, then think again, old dame!' Lizzie was in a fury, her fists clenched, spittle spraying as she shouted. 'I'm not her bloody servant and never will be.' Folk stopped to stare. It was all most unseemly.

'How dare you call me an overbearing bitch,' Emily cried, stepping towards the angry woman.

'Em, Em,' I said, taking my wife's arm. 'She is shocked, is all. Give her time to be reconciled.'

'But she insulted me in front of all these folk...'

'I know, but I be sure it was just a few hot words in the heat of the moment. Let it lie, lass. She be unworthy of your attention for the present.'

It was probably a good thing that Lizzie stormed off then, for Emily was rigid with anger, and I feared they might come to blows.

'Aye, well, I could call her a few things too, the lazy sow,' Emily muttered. 'Now, see, poor Pen has to go to her mother without anyone to take her place on the stall. That wretched woman shirks every task.'

'I'll stay,' Rose said, 'If Seb will take the babe home and tend the shop instead of me? After all, I still have a few pairs of gloves to sell here and, in truth, there hasn't been a single customer back at the shop all morning. I'm sure Seb will manage, won't you?' She turned to me, giving me a broad smile.

I pulled a face. Was I to be left, holding the babe and keeping shop? Was that a master's place? Oh, well, I had no money left to spend at the fayre anyhow. I may as well go home and do some work.


I left Emily, Rose and the other women at the fayre. Kate had gone off to find her father and Dame Ellen determined to stay a while, perhaps fearing trouble, if Lizzie returned. I made my way home, singing to little Dickon in his basket and contemplating with pleasure showing Adam and the lads my rainbow-maker.


Adam was a diligent example indeed, still industriously working at his desk, though he had moved it into the shop, such that he might accomplish two tasks at once: penning another of my *Aesop's Fables* and on hand if a customer required service.

'You make me look like an idle fellow, Adam,' I said, setting the babe's basket beside my desk.

'You are,' he said, grinning. 'Wasting the day, enjoying yourself, while we labour on.'

'But I did not forget you. Tom, fetch a dish from the kitchen, if you will? I have some exotic sweetmeats for you, all the way from the Land of the Turk. And it be all arranged for Kate to return to us upon Monday next.'

Jack's face lit up like a torch flame. I knew he had a fondness for the lass. He had once divulged to me that her dark eyes and hair recalled his sister to mind – the sole reference to family that he had ever made.

'I also have a device I know will enthral you,' I continued.

'Wot's infrall mean?' Jack asked, helping himself to a rose-flavoured delight even afore it got as far as the dish. Tom took one also.

'Intrigue, fascinate... fill you with wonderment.'

'Oh, is that all?'

'Aye. What more would you ask?'

'Anuvver sweetmeat,' he said, taking one and popping the whole thing in his mouth at once.

'You greedy hog!' Tom snatched away the dish afore Jack could take any more.

'Mind your manners, both of you,' Adam said sternly, removing the dish from Tom's grasp and setting it to one side. 'No more for either of you. Everyone else deserves to share them also.'

I nodded. Clearly Adam would abide no nonsense; he'd likely make a better fist of controlling the unruly pair than I could.

'Let me show you the device. 'Tis a marvel indeed,' I said, taking the triangle of Venice glass from my purse and unwrapping it. I set it on Adam's desk in the doorway, and we all gathered close. A rainbow would certainly cheer the gloom of the passageway to the shop where daylight was scarce.

Jack stared at it, prodded it with a dirty finger.

'Wot's it do then?'

''Tis a rainbow-maker; a prism, the merchant called it.'

'Where's the rainbows? I can't see none.'

I frowned. The glass sat there, stubbornly colourless. I moved it about, turning it this way and that.

'It worked very well at the fayre.'

'P'raps it's used up all the rainbows and runned out of 'em?' Jack suggested.

I persevered, changing the position of it, but no rainbows appeared.

'If I were you, I'd take it back to the merchant, on the morrow,' Adam said, leaning back and folding his arms. 'He's sold you a counterfeit, I reckon. If he won't return your coin, take him before the pie-powder court and demand recompense. How much did he charge you?'

'A couple of groats, no more than that.' The falsehood spilled from my tongue afore I was even aware of thinking the words. I was angered but, more than that, I was ashamed of my foolishness in buying a piece of useless glass that would serve no purpose but to gather dust upon a shelf. ''Tis hardly worth troubling the pie-powder for such a paltry sum.' In truth, if I accused the merchant in the market's court, afore the mayor himself, all would learn of the ridiculous amount of coin I had wasted. Everyone would know Sebastian Foxley for a witless, addlebrained dullard indeed. I would rather save face than have the money back. Despite this, telling the lie enflamed my cheeks, and I could but hope the others did not notice in the dim shadowed space.

In haste, I wrapped the offending glass in its cloth once more and took it into the little storeroom where I put it upon the higher most shelf, behind a ream of paper and some rolls of parchment. And there it would remain; my moment of weakness in buying the prism was ever to be forgotten, I hoped.

Later, when Emily and Rose had arrived home, full of excitement at the day's events, I determined that the rosewater sweetmeats, the malachite pigment and the Sheffield embroidery needles would be the only purchases mentioned. As Nessie served our supper, Rose was telling of a woman who had wished to buy a kerchief at the stall only to be pursued by her husband and dragged away, berated as a spendthrift.

'There was quite a scene,' Rose said, 'And a constable was summoned but then...' She could hardly speak for laughing. '... The woman took off her shoe and beat her husband with it and then the constable. It was so funny.'

Aye, I could imagine, yet the shoe would, quite literally, be upon the other foot: Emily would beat me if she ever found out about the rainbow-maker. I handed round the sweetmeats after the meal, and they were much appreciated by all.

'Master Seb,' Tom said in a wheedling voice, 'We worked hard all day, as Master Adam will tell you. Have we not earned a reward? Will you let us go to the fayre? It sounds so merry.'

'Aye, we deserve it, don't we, Tom?' Jack said. 'We could get more o' them sweetmeat fings, couldn't we?'

If I hadn't been overwhelmed by guilt, concerning my own shortcomings, my fall into temptation, I should have denied their request. However, they had obeyed my instruction not to mention the wretched prism, so I felt somewhat obliged to acquiesce.

'Very well,' I said, watching as their faces transformed with glee. 'But not together. Tom, you and Master Adam may go to the fayre in the morn. You will enjoy it *in his company* for I be certain Adam deserves a holy day and he will see to it that you behave in a respectful fashion. Jack, you will come with me after dinner, and there will be no running off to the ale-sellers, nor gawping at the half-naked dancer.

'Half naked?' the salacious pair echoed, eyes grown wide as platters.

'You keep away from such entertainments, so called,' I said, regretting that I'd mentioned the dancer with her too few veils attempting to conceal too much flesh. 'Master Gerrit's poppets be a more wholesome amusement. I can recommend them heartily.'

A little later, when supper was cleared away and Adam and I were about to take our ale cups out to the garden, to enjoy the warm evening airs, Emily, Rose and Nessie were gathered about little Dickon's basket. The sounds were not of a babe's making, but I heard sobbing all the same.

'What's amiss, Em? Is the babe ailing?' I asked, concerned.

''Tis naught,' she answered sharply, though there was a hint of tears for certain.

'If he be unwell...'

'Dickon is fine! Now cease your meddling, husband.'

Rose took me aside, taking my arm, leading me out into the yard and passed the pigsty.

'Em's pendant – the amber – is feared lost,' Rose explained once we were beyond my wife's hearing. 'It was tied securely to the basket handle, so little Dickon might play with it without risk of putting it in his mouth and choking. Now it is gone.' She paused, as if doubtful of what she would say next and sighed. 'I ought to tell you, Seb, Em thinks you may have been careless with it of a purpose, forwhy it was another man's gift to her.'

'Why would she think that of me? Does she account me so mean-spirited? She accepted Gabriel's gift with my blessing. Why should I have changed my mind concerning it? Besides, I don't recall noticing the pendant when I carried the basket home. Is it a surety that it was there?'

'It was tied in a double knot. I don't see how it could have come loose. Em believes you are peevish that she has taken to wearing again since Gabriel returned and lost it deliberately.'

'Oh, Rose, that be so untrue. Of course she be wearing it of late, such that if Gabriel asks after it, she may show him how greatly his gift has been appreciated. I swear upon my soul, Rose, that I never saw the pendant and would have taken pains to keep it safe, if I had, knowing she sets such store by it. If 'tis lost, then I be sorry indeed, but she accuses me falsely and mistakenly. Please tell her so.'

Seated in the garden – Adam upon the stump of the old elder tree and me upon the upturned bucket – it took all his merry wiles and good humour to drag me from my swamp of self-righteous indignation. I was angered that Emily could consider me capable of such small-minded knavery. It was unworthy of her to blame me for the loss.

'That's the way of women, Seb: unfathomable as the Ocean Sea; unaccountable as the Almighty.' He drained his ale and picked a stem from the mint plants nearby to chew on. 'You don't truly expect to understand, do you? You are but a mere man as the rest of us. When all be said and done, none of us shall ever comprehend the workings of a woman's mind. Be assured, the moment will pass, and all will be forgotten by morn. Take heart, Seb. The pendant may yet be discovered in a purse or buried amongst the babe's blankets or under a pile of linen, unless it was stolen by a basket-dipper? That could explain its disappearance.'

I nodded, but with little hope that even if he was right on any of those accounts, I might be able to prove my innocence to Emily's satisfaction.

# Chapter 7

## Tuesday, the twenty-fifth day of August
## The Foxley house

I WAS AWAKENED right early that morn by someone
pounding upon the street door. The sun had yet to give a
thought to rising. There was barely a glimpse of dawn-light in
the east, and I feared there must be a fire somewhere close by
and a considerate neighbour was giving us warning. If there
were no fire, he who hammered at my door for a lesser reason
would be told to depart in no uncertain terms. I might have
assisted him upon his way with my boot applied to his backside,
except that in my haste, I had not got so far as to put my boots
on. Thus, I padded to the door barefoot and hardly decent in
my breeches and undershirt without any lacing of points yet
accomplished, and my eyes still sanded with sleep.

'What be amiss?' I asked, opening the street door and
blinking at the fellow standing there.

'Where is Jude Foxley? Tell him to attend me straightway.'

'Master Fyssher,' I said, recognising the coroner belatedly as
the veils of slumber cleared from my wits. 'My brother is not
here. He departed London some days since.'

'He never informed me. This is most inconsiderate of him.
Still, I suppose I've come to expect such behaviour. Your brother
was never to be relied upon. However, since I require a scribe

most urgently, you'll serve the office of my assistant. Get dressed, bring your writing stuff and come with me.'

'There has been a death?' I asked him as we made our way through the Shambles, towards Newgate, having to trot to keep up with the coroner in his haste, encumbered with my scrip and writing board. As yet, the butchers were hardly about their work, the hour being so early, yet already the flies were busy, gathering on blood-stained counter-boards and investigating unwashed cleavers and knives afore any beast was brought for slaughtering. I called Gawain from nosing at a pile of yesterday's skins, stinking already as they awaited collection by the tanners.

'Of course, there's been a death. You think I'm from my bed at this hour for pleasure? Someone has been killed among the stalls at Smithfield.'

'An accident?'

'You think I'm a bloody astrologer and foreknow the future? That is what must be determined when I see the damned corpse.'

Chastened, I followed him in silence through Newgate, where a sleepy gate-keeper was only just unbarring the way, and along Giltspur Street. The Hart's Horn tavern was yet shuttered but Thaddeus Turner, the bailiff, awaited Master Fyssher's arrival there, by Mistress Fletcher's well-scrubbed doorway.

''Tis a sorry sight, Master Coroner,' Thaddeus said, mopping his brow with his cap before replacing it atop his unruly black curls. 'Quite gave me a bad moment, seeing him.' The bailiff certainly looked pallid and unwell. 'Not one of us though, God be thanked. A foreigner, here for the fayre is all.'

As if that made a difference! Was it not worse, in a way, if visitors could not feel safe in our city? And whoever had been slain was a flesh and blood man denied his rightful length of days. Citizen or in-comer, murder was an evil thing.

I checked my thoughts at that point: none had said it was a case of murder. The victim might have been struck by a falling tent pole; tripped and broke his neck or cut himself severely. Aye, and so he might – but he hadn't.

The body lay sprawled, face down upon the ground betwixt Master Richard Ameryk's booth and another next door. Both booths were, as yet, still shut up and the two constables stood watch over the scene. I saw straightway why Thaddeus had felt queasy. The poor fellow did not come by his death swiftly, but had been bludgeoned about the head repeatedly. And, as if that was insufficient, his jerkin was bloodied and torn, mayhap by a blade of some kind.

'Mm,' Fyssher grunted, 'Make a note, Foxley: beaten and stabbed. Two weapons and likely two assailants, therefore. Do we know who he is?'

Thaddeus shook his head, deliberately looking anywhere but at the lifeless form before us.

'Turn it over. Let's see the face.'

Neither the bailiff nor the constables moved to obey the order. I realised, believing I was the coroner's assistant, they assumed Fyssher was instructing me to do it. I set down my writing board on the hard-packed earth that formed the path along the line of stalls and knelt to the body. I attempted to turn it with due care and reverence, but it was beginning to stiffen in death's rigour, and I had difficulty.

'Don't be so delicate, Foxley. The dead don't bite, neither do they protest at rough handling. Get it over.'

Having succeeded, I regretted it for I recognised the victim. Despite much damage done to his head, the face was bloodied but recognisable. Gone forever was the merry smile of Master Gerrit, the poppet-master. I made the sign of the cross and murmured a prayer for a friend dead without the benefit of last rites for his dear soul. No man should suffer so in this life and then forfeit any comfort to be had in the next. I gently closed his eyes that stared, empty, at the brightening sky. The light of life I had told him of, how to put the look of living into his poppets' eyes, was now dulled forever in their master's.

'I know him,' I said, still upon my knees. 'He is – was – the Dutchman who performed the poppet-show in that booth across the way there. His name is Gerrit Heijnsbroeck of Rotterdam.'

'Write it down then.'

I admit, I frowned somewhat over the spelling of the Dutchman's name, but did my best with it: H-I-N-E-S-B-R-O-O-K. I hoped that was close enough.

'You, constables, get this unsightliness cleared away,' Fyssher was saying. 'Take it to St Bartholomew's church. Can't have the folk stepping over it when the fayre opens.' He was correct, of course. Stall-holders were already stirring from their booths and tents where many of them had slept the night. Others were arriving from lodgings in the city or else, like Master Ameryk, from ships moored at Queenhithe, though it was quite a walk uphill from there.

I did not like to hear my unfortunate friend referred to as 'an unsightliness'. Such irreverence offended me.

'Foxley. Make enquiries of those who slept here last eve, whether they saw or heard anything untoward. And if you discover the culprits, have Bailiff Turner arrest the devils. I'm going for breakfast at the Hart's Horn. Report to me there of any progress you make. Find the miscreants who did this – foreigners, no doubt. And I want the knife and cudgel that were used.' With that, William Fyssher departed.

'Hold a moment,' I said to the constables afore they should shift Gerrit's body. 'I would look more closely at his wounds.' Unpleasant as it was, I unfastened Gerrit's jerkin and shirt that I might better observe the injuries inflicted. It was apparent to me straightway that he had been stabbed with a weapon quite unlike any knife I had ever seen for the holes in both his clothing and in his poor flesh were made with something of a circular nature, not a blade. A spike of some kind, mayhap? I made notes and a sketch to show the dimensions and shapes of his chest wounds.

Then I examined his head, parting his hair. The wounds were broader than my hand, insofar as I could make out, and not rounded as they might be if he was assaulted with a club or mace. Perhaps a short log had been employed, for a staff of such breadth would have been too heavy to lift. But then I found a pale sliver of some hard substance embedded in his skull. No larger than my thumbnail, I supposed at first that it was a piece of his skull, but no hair was attached. Then I wondered if it was a flake of stone, sheared off the murder weapon. The murderer must have used a handy stone to beat Gerrit to the ground afore piercing him with a spike, but it seemed an ill-assorted choice of weapons. And why? Master Fyssher was concerned only with the 'how' and 'by whom' questions. But since I accounted Gerrit a friend – even one of such brief acquaintance – I wondered what the jovial-humoured, unassuming Dutchman could have done that angered someone sufficiently to commit this felony. There had to be a motive for such a dreadful crime.

I put the sliver of stone in my scrip and searched around for the rock from which it had come. I could find naught of the kind, although it seemed unlikely a murderer would carry a heavy, bloodied stone away with him. In truth, loose rocks or stones of any sort did not lie around Smithfield. I stood up, wincing as my hip protested.

'Cover him decently with something afore you carry him away,' I told the constables. 'Else he will attract the morbidly curious and I should not want such ghoulish persons gawping at him.' They poked around the nearby tents and stalls and found some sacking to serve the purpose, then commandeered a hurdle to take him to St Bartholomew's. It crossed my mind to wonder what would happen now to the poppets which Gerrit had regarded almost like family.

There came a commotion of a sudden at Richard Ameryk's stall, and I saw Gabriel – in his disguise as Gideon Waterman – with the black-skinned fellow, Rook, and a short, red-faced man in a fine wool coat most unsuited to the warm day. Voices and arms were raised in consternation and, fearing it might have to do with the crime the coroner had told me to investigate, I felt it beholden upon me to enquire the reason for their disquiet.

Gabriel explained in a few words, his distress apparent in his voice:

'Someone broke the locks on the door of the booth. The unicorns' horns, Seb, they're gone, stolen in the night. Master Ameryk is beside himself at such a loss.'

'It cannot be a coincidence,' I said, 'Two dire crimes so close at hand. Was someone here on watch overnight?'

'Aye and will be dismissed from Master Ameryk's employ forthwith. More drunk than an ale-taster's confessor.'

I recalled then that Gabriel's religious beliefs did not approve of priests taking confession.

'That be unfortunate. So he did not hear or see anything amiss?'

'Nay, but he felt something amiss when my foot connected to his useless nethers this morn. He was yet snoring in his blanket when we arrived. Come, Seb, I'll show you how it was.'

Behind the booth was a sorry scene, and a noisy one. Master Ameryk was shouting at a skinny fellow who stood, head hanging, as a tirade of invective poured over him like a storm surge. Gabriel coughed to attract his master's attention.

'Er, Master Ameryk, begging pardon but this is my friend, Master Sebastian Foxley. The coroner has charged him with investigating the murder, and he thinks the theft of our goods may be connected.'

'Who?' The red-faced man cupped his hand behind his ear, as one who could not hear so well. I was unable to guess at his age, but the pouches beneath his eyes, the grooves carved either side of his prominent nose and his deafness, suggested a man of years. Yet his hair hung dark as chestnuts and plentiful as a young man's, and his hands showed no evidence of thickened joints such as age might cause.

'Sebastian Foxley,' I stated clearly, 'In service at present to the deputy coroner. I be pleased to make your acquaintance,

Master Ameryk.'

'Pleased? I am most certainly not pleased. Some devilish rapscallion has made off with my most valuable pieces and this... this miserable worm did naught to prevent it.' As he spoke, he grabbed the skinny fellow's jerkin and shook him as a dog might shake a rat.

I stepped back a little and discovered the bailiff, Thaddeus Turner, standing so close behind me that I stumbled over his feet. 'What's this?' the bailiff asked, 'A theft as well? This is all too bad. I can but deal with one crime at a time.' He shook his head mournfully. 'As the coroner's assistant, Master Seb, I'll have to ask your aid with the murder, at least.'

'Aye, I expected as much, Master Turner, but I also suspect a close connection betwixt the two felonies. 'Tis too much of a coincidence, elsewise.' In truth, I had expected this. Thaddeus Turner was a diligent bailiff, but not the sharpest blade in the cutler's workshop. 'However, I must return home first. There were other matters I had intended for this day. When I return, I shall begin my enquiries, but I do have one question for Master Ameryk now.' I turned to the Bristol merchant. 'Was anything of your wares stolen apart from the unicorn horns, master?'

'No. Naught but those and there are fine things aplenty on my stall that would be easier to sell on and less difficult to hide: Spanish cinnabar, Portingale noranges and pomegranates, Castillian soap and wines, Irish linens and Icelandic fish-leather purses. But only the horns were taken. But see the damage done to the locks and the door here. They'll need replacing... more expense as if this damned fayre hasn't cost me a fortune already.'

I studied the door behind the booth. The locks had been prised off, making them useless now, and the door itself was splintered around the bolt. There were a number of what looked to be dirty and somewhat bloodied hand and finger marks upon the door, as though the thief had cut himself in the process of breaking in. Such damage must have caused enough noise to attract attention for certain. Ah, mayhap, Gerrit had been the one to investigate the disturbance and death had been his reward for an act of neighbourliness.

'Thank you, Master Ameryk. I shall return later to question the fellow you left to guard your stall, when his wits have cleared of ale fumes.' At that moment, I caught sight of Beatrice and Peronelle coming to open the silk-women's stall. They waved a greeting, and I waved back. Emily was to work this afternoon, I remembered – with Lizzie Knollys, if she consented to turn up. 'Come, Gawain. Let us go break our fast, lad,' I called to my dog.

# The Foxley house

'I apologise, Adam, Tom, but your visit to the fayre this morn cannot be. I have to attend to the coroner's business there and require someone to remain here in the workshop.'

'But that's unfair. You promised,' Tom whined, 'And I could still go. I don't need Adam to mind me.'

'I told you that you be too untrustworthy of late to go without Adam or me. That I would make concession to allow you to go at all is perhaps not my wisest decision ever. The fayre continues all week: there will be other opportunities.' I spooned up the last of the mess of eggs and herbs Emily had made for my belated breakfast and pushed the platter aside.

'But master...'

'Enough, Tom. There will be no more discussion of the matter.'

Adam nodded his agreement.

'By Master Seb's account, there will no longer be a poppet show to see anyway, sorrowfully. A pity about Master Gerrit; may God have mercy on his soul.' Adam crossed himself, as did I.

'Wot about me?' Jack put in. 'I could still come wiv yer now, 'stead of after dinner, couldn't I?'

'No, Jack. I have enquiries to make. I shall have much to concern me and no time to give eye to you.'

'I could 'elp. Yer knows folks might talk to me wot won't talk to you, ruffians an' cut-purses an' the like. I could find out wot they knows, I could. I won't be no trouble, I swear.'

'Don't believe him, master. He lies like a tupenny trollop. And it won't be fair, if you take him. I could ask questions just as well.'

'Tom! I'll not have such language used in this house. Neither of you be going to the fayre this day, so content yourselves with your work. I refuse to hear another word said about it.'

I returned to the fayre with renewed intent after my breakfast. An interview with Master Ameryk's man awaited me, if he was less befuddled than earlier. As we made our way, Gawain was startled of a sudden by a group of fire-eaters, one of whom blew a great gout of flame, dragon-like, sending the dog into a frenzy of fright, nigh tripping me and sending me headlong. When a stilt-walker was almost brought down by the poor creature, I thought I might have to leave him at home in future. The fayre was no place for my Gawain.

I interviewed the fellow behind the booth he had supposedly been guarding. His name was Arthur, but anyone less like a king was hard to imagine. I had seen bean plants with more flesh than he. His gaze still seemed somewhat vague when he looked up at me.

'How much ale did you drink last eve to render you thus?' I asked, rather to open the conversation than to make enquiry.

'A cup or two. No more than that,' he said, his tongue sounding over-large for his mouth, so the words slurred. A lie, obviously.

'You think I will believe that?'

''Tis true, whether you believe me or not. I drank a couple of cups with my supper and not another drop after that.'

'Then how come you were still senseless when Master Gab-Gideon arrived this morn to open the booth?'

'I don't know. I've got such a headache as if I drank a whole barrelful, but I never did.'

'A headache, you say?'

'Aye. All around here.' Arthur ran his hand along the left side of his head, above the ear. 'Reckon I got a lump there, too.'

I bent down to be level with him as he sat hunched on the ground.

'May I see?'

With his consent, I felt his head, parting his thick hair. I did indeed find a lump. He winced even though my touch was gently done.

'You have a nasty contusion there, Arthur. It may be that you have a concussion also.'

'What's that mean?'

'It means either that you fell and struck your head against some hard object, or else someone hit you there of a purpose to stun you, in which case they succeeded right well. Do you recall either such incident occurring?'

'No, I don't think so. My thoughts are foggy about last eve. Though I wasn't drunk, I swear on my oath.'

'I believe you,' I said, easing upright and straightening my jerkin.

'You do? Then tell Master Ameryk, will you? He accuses me of being in my cups when I should have been minding his wares. He's dismissed me from his service and made me return the keys, even though they're useless now, what with the locks all broken.'

I found Master Ameryk sorting through the wooden crates of exotic items, muttering as he pulled out blocks of scented soap, tossing them aside as worthless, followed by little carved relic boxes and pieces of Baltic amber. It seemed he still had many fine things left to sell, even without the precious unicorn horns.

'Master Ameryk. I beg pardon, Master Ameryk,' I repeated more loudly, remembering he was somewhat deaf.

'What? Can't you see I'm... oh, 'tis you Foxley. Have you found my goods yet?'

'Not as yet, good master, but I would talk to you about Arthur.'

'He is no longer in my employ. Forget about him. What of the horns?'

'I think it may be the case that Arthur was sober last eve...'

'He was drunk and slept while some scoundrel stole from me.'

'He was knocked senseless and has a contusion to prove it. He may be more deserving of a surgeon's attentions than dismissal from your service.'

'A surgeon? Why? He's not sick, is he? Is that what he claims? I have neither time nor money to spare for folk who don't do the work as I instruct them.'

'Your man was hit upon the head, Master Ameryk. He was neither drunk nor sleeping, but knocked senseless by whoever took your goods.'

'Knocked senseless? Who did such a thing?'

'The thief, most likely. Arthur would beg your forgiveness for his failure to prevent the theft and asks most humbly to be readmitted to your service. I said I would speak for him.'

Master Ameryk shrugged.

'I'll think it over. but I make no promises. He is inept if he let someone overcome him. Senselessness is no better than drunkenness.'

'He may have been attacked from behind,' I suggested.

'Is that what he says happened?'

'Nay. He remembers naught of what came to pass.'

'Then for all we know he may have been in league with the thief and will take a portion of the profits when they sell my unicorn horns for a vast sum. Why should I reinstate such a miscreant?'

'There be no evidence as to Arthur's involvement.'

'Neither is there any evidence as to his being blameless. Now I have work to do. Good day to you, Foxley.' Master Ameryk returned to rummaging through his crates, and I was dismissed by default.

I was about to walk away, to make enquiries of other stall holders concerning Gerrit's death, rather than stolen goods, though I was certain the two were connected, when Gabriel barred my way, the man Rook beside him.

'Will you be investigating the theft as well as the death?' Gabriel was pulling at his beard, somewhat distracted.

''Tis not my part to play the beadle nor the bailiff,' I said, 'I misdoubt even that the coroner be right in having me look into Gerrit's death, since Jude be his appointed assistant, not I. But if the two crimes be connected, then...'

'So you will try to discover the thief for us, Seb? We would all be so much obliged to you if you do. Those horns were our best asset and without them to sell, who knows how we'll pay our way. Even if we don't find a buyer for them here, they serve to attract customers to the stall who purchase other wares by the way. The largest horn looked so fine hanging from its tasselled cords, folk came clamouring for a closer look. Did you see it there, yesterday, glinting in the sunlight? A rare piece indeed.'

'Nay, I could not get near your stall. As you say, there was a crowd gathered around it. All I can tell you of the thief is that he is not in Master Ameryk's employ and most likely makes constant use of spade and hoe or a handcart or else is a bell-ringer or some such.'

Gabriel's one visible eye – the other being concealed by the patch – opened wide in surprise.

'How can you know?'

'Why would the thief attract attention, breaking open the door, if he worked for Master Ameryk? He would have known Arthur had the keys and, having knocked the poor fellow senseless, could take them from his person and unlock the door without causing any undue noise which might bring others to discover the reason. Besides, he was unfamiliar with the construction of the booth.'

'Aye, well the first makes sense,' Gabriel said, nodding, 'But how can you tell he didn't know much about our booth and what makes you think he's a bell-ringer?'

'Not a bell-ringer necessarily, but one who labours equally with both hands. Come, I will show you.' I led my friend to the back of the booth where the damaged door was propped open by the stool upon which Arthur still sat, looking forlorn and pale. 'Are you feeling any better?'

'Somewhat. At least Master Ameryk seems to have cooled his anger at me.'

'I explained to him about your head injury.'

'And did he believe you?'

'It gave him pause for thought concerning what came to pass last eve. What he concludes as a result, I cannot say. I have done what I can to exonerate you, but unless the guilty party be discovered, there be little else I may achieve on that score.'

'Come now, Seb, we're wasting time,' Gabriel plucked at my sleeve, 'Show me how you know what kind of fellow is our thief.'

I sighed at such impatience. Was Arthur's situation not of greater importance?

'Here, see these marks,' I explained, pointing at the grubby stains on the door. 'Having knocked Arthur senseless with some heavy implement or other, as yet undetermined, the fellow prised away the locks. His hands were stained with dust and sweat and, here, a little blood and you may see where he put both hands flat against the door forwhy it was so difficult to push it open.'

'Of course it was,' Gabriel said, 'The door opens outwardly so... ah, I see: the thief didn't realise that, thus he isn't one of us.'

'Precisely.'

''Tis not just fluff and cobwebs in that head of yours, is it, Seb? But I still don't understand how you can have the least idea about the devil's trade as a bell-ringer or whatever he is.'

'Observe the hand marks upon the door more closely, Gab-Gideon, if you will.'

'What am I supposed to see? They're about the same size as mine, so a man's hand probably, if there was ever any cause to doubt that? What of them?'

'At the base of each finger on both hands, can you note the uneven whorls? Calluses, I suspect, and since they be much of a likeness on both right and left hand, he must carry on a trade that makes equal use of both. I am hoping to observe them with a scrying glass, to see them in greater detail and make a drawing, such that we can compare them to the hands of anyone we have suspicion maybe the felon.'

'Why bother drawing them? We can simply bring him to the door here?'

'Suppose it rains and washes the marks away? Besides 'tis easier to take a sheet of paper afore the pie-powder court than to remove the door from its hinges.'

'Aye, I hadn't thought so far as that. Do you have a scrying glass?'

'No, but I know where to find one.'

I returned later with a scrying glass. The Venetian merchant, no doubt knowing me for a fool, having bought one of his worthless rainbow-makers yesterday, charged me an exorbitant deposit of two shillings just for lending me a scrying glass from his stall for the remainder of the day. And if I failed to return it in pristine condition afore the fayre closed at sunset, I should forfeit the money. It was absurd. I swear the glass was worth no more than a couple of groats at most. I may as well have purchased and kept it but, after my previous folly, I did not want another on my conscience.

With considerable care to include every detail, I drew the likeness of the handprints on the door. The glass aided my sight indeed, and I was able to copy the tiniest lines and shapes with my finest quill that I might otherwise have omitted. The glass was a most useful tool.

Gabriel came and peered over my shoulder as I worked.

'You can truly see all that?' he asked, sounding dubious. Did he think I was inventing the patterns?

'I can. Take the glass and look for yourself.'

'Well, 'tis quite a revelation, is it not?' he said, having examined the door using the glass. 'What a clever little thing it is.'

'Aye, and of more use than the Venetian's wretched rainbow-maker, that be certain.'

'His what? A rainbow-maker? What is that?'

''Tis naught at all since it fails to work. Forget I ever mentioned such a thing.'

'But I am intrigued. Does such a thing exist?'

'No. It does not. It was an utter waste of money – too much money – and I wish I never saw it, never mind bought it. Emily will skin me like a coney if she ever discovers my foolishness and intemperance. If she was half so frivolous with our hard-won coin, I should take her to task concerning the matter most certainly.'

'Would you, Seb? Knowing you as I do, I believe otherwise. You wouldn't say anything, though you might think it. Your heart is over-soft when Em is at fault.' He smiled at me.

'Aye, maybe so...' I closed the lid of my little ink pot and wiped my quill clean upon the grass, laying my paper such that the sun could dry the ink.

Gabriel put the scrying glass on one corner of the drawing, careful not to smudge my work.

'There. We don't want the wind blowing it away, do we? What say you to a cup of ale, Seb? Seems to me we both deserve one.'

The refreshment was most welcome, and we drank at the ale stall in the shade of the mighty oak. Gawain helped himself at the Horse Pool, lapping thirstily at the water's edge.

'Watch out, my friend,' I yelled to Gabriel, seeing a fellow about to snatch the purse from his belt, dagger at the ready to cut the strings.

Gabriel turned and boxed the thief's ears afore kicking him into the pool with a great splash. Others customers at the stall applauded and cheered his actions. Someone must have summoned a constable right swiftly, else one was close at hand, fortuitously. Whatever the case, the wretch was pulled from the water, dripping, and bundled off to appear at the pie-powder court. The constable asked Gabriel if he would serve as a witness. Apparently, the same fellow had been caught yesterday about his villainous occupation. Purses had been retrieved and returned to their owners, and the thief had spent five hours in the stocks as punishment. Much good had it done! Now he was apprehended once again about the same business, but the constable, so he told us, had been following him this morn. Another, longer time in the stocks would result and, since water was forbidden while thus restrained, the foolish fellow would suffer severely on a day so hot as this.

We returned to Master Ameryk's stall only to discover Arthur stamping out the remains of a small fire. It seemed Fate was looking askance at all my endeavours this day: my careful drawing of the hand marks on the door was destroyed.

'The paper caught fire all by itself,' Arthur explained. 'I know not why, but flames were licking around the scrying glass of yours.'

'May the saints aid me,' I said, kicking at the little pile of grey ash that remained. 'Everything from that Venetian's stall be cursed; bewitched! Now I have it all to do again. It truly is too bad. And see the glass: 'tis soot-caked and the scoundrel charged me two shillings by way of a deposit for the wretched thing. Now I shall forfeit my money.'

Gabriel picked up the glass and wiped it on a tussock of dry grass.

'It's not so bad, Seb. The soot comes away easily enough. We can polish it up, and the Venetian will never know.'

With a sigh, I set to do another drawing. At first, I was reluctant to take pains over the task for a second time, but reminded myself that it might be required as evidence and detail could prove essential. Thus, it was nigh the hour for dinner at home by the time my work was done. On my way, I returned the glass, thoroughly cleaned, to the merchant and received my coin in exchange. Gabriel was correct – the man noticed naught amiss with it, God be praised.

# Chapter 8

## Tuesday afternoon

IT WAS Emily's turn to serve at the silk-women's stall after dinner. Half expecting that Lizzie Knollys would not turn up to do her share, as was arranged, Rose had come along to help. In truth, Emily was pleased at the change, certain Rose's winning smile would attract a better sort of customer than Lizzie's brazen looks, folk with more intention of buying the goods for sale than merely gawping at Mistress Knollys' expanse of barely concealed bosom.

Rose was also eager to play her part and see something of the colourful and noisy fayre. Since neither woman quite trusted Nessie with the responsibility and Seb was otherwise busy about his investigations for Master Fyssher, little Dickon had had to come too. It was a wonder that he could sleep so peacefully in his basket at the back of the booth, what with the cacophony of sounds all around. Even when an itinerant hurdy-gurdy man set up his instrument just a few yards away and began turning the handle, creating his strange, plaintive music, the babe seemed not to notice and slept on. Rose succeeded in persuading an indecisive young gallant to buy a pair of her gloves for his light o' love. They were of finest lavender silk with white silk tassels and the most expensive of all her handiwork, but well worth every penny.

'You made a most excellent sale there, Rose,' Emily said, smiling. 'I be sure I could never have talked him into making the purchase as you did. 'Tis fortunate you came this afternoon.'

'Lizzie could probably have succeeded,' Rose said, but she pulled a face.

'She is not here to sell anything, is she? And I'm heartily glad of it. 'Tis a merry thing for you to have sold your best pair of gloves yourself. I hope his lady-love appreciates the superb craftsmanship of them. They're such a pretty colour. How many pairs are left to sell, now?'

'Just two.' Rose put the remaining gloves to the front of the counter-board.

'If that fellow shows his friends what he bought, mayhap they'll come hastening to buy gifts for their ladies also. I love the tiny buttons on these yellow gloves, the way they catch the light. What are they made of?'

'Mother-of-pearl they call it. I know not whence it comes but 'tis lovely, isn't it? Oh, there, Em: another customer for Pen's ribbons...'

While Emily was helping a woman to choose ribbons, Rose glanced across the crowds and espied a fayre-goer who most certainly should not be there. Jack! It seemed the young rascal had defied Master Seb, after all that had been said upon the matter. She ducked out of the booth to confront him.

'And what are you about, Jack Tabor?' Rose demanded, catching him unawares as he was inching furtively betwixt a red tent with woven baskets for sale and an ironmonger's booth.

He was startled when Rose seized his sleeve but did not appear guilty, like one who was discovered in disobedience.

'Shh!' he said, putting a finger to his lips. 'I'm after the bugger wot stoled them unicorn 'orns, ain't I? I seed him creepin' down 'ere, didn't I? Now shush.'

'Does Master Seb know you've come here?'

'Might do.'

'That is not an answer, Jack.'

'Well he ain't thought about wot I thought, has he? He don't know much about wot Ralph Clifford said to Master Jude 'cos he weren't here, wos he? He never heard Ralph swear t' get revenge on the Foxleys, did he? I reckon as I can 'elp solve the crime. Ralph did it to cause trouble for us and I been follerin' him. He went this way, all sneaky like. Now let me go!'

'I never heard such nonsense, Jack.' Rose renewed her grip upon his arm. 'Tell me why Ralph Clifford would kill a Dutchman and steal the unicorn horns? How would either crime be a means of taking vengeance upon us? We have no connection to the dead foreigner, and the loss of the horns affects Gabriel and Master Ameryk, not us. Besides, how could Ralph murder anyone with his injured arm?'

'He's a nasty piece, and I reckon he'd find a way somehow.' Jack looked obstinate, thrusting out his nether lip.

'If you have the sense God gave a sheep, you'll go home now, afore Master Seb or Mistress Em discovers what you're about. Go on: get yourself home straightway, Jack.'

'You'll tell on us.'

'No I won't, not if you do as I say and cease your foolishness. Now go! I won't give you another chance.'

Rose sighed, watching as Jack scurried off, into the crowds, roughly in the direction of home. If Emily had caught him, his punishment would have been dire indeed. Hoping for Jack's sake no one else had seen him, she went back to the stall.

'While you were gone, I sold those yellow gloves,' Emily said, beaming. 'Is aught amiss, Rose, you dashing off like that? You look distracted.'

'Needed the necessary. There was a queue is all.'

'Oh, well, now you're returned, I can see to the babe. I think he has had the same need, though no queue to inconvenience him. Come, my sweeting, let Mam change that horrid wet tailclout for you.'

I had been making enquiries around the fayre ground for what seemed to be hours, in which time I had learned naught that I didn't know already and heard the same replies time and again. No one had seen or heard anything untoward last eve. No one knew of anyone skulking about who didn't belong, but with the city brimful of strangers, it was a wonder if any odd occurrences were remarked upon. Otherwise, no one behaving suspiciously had been noticed. I was weary of asking the same questions, and folk were tired of answering them.

In the hope of some inspiration concerning the matter, I sought the ale-seller's stall beneath the oak tree by the pool. The water looked cool and refreshing even if the ale was tepid and upon the verge of turning sour in the heat. I lowered myself with care to sit on the scorched grass, leaning back on my hands to gaze up into the oak-leaf canopy above. The leaves were dull with end-of-summer dust and age with few gaps where the sun blazed through to burn green spots before the eyes. I could just make out a butterfly among the leaves, its hues impossible to determine either in the gloom or in contrast against the sun-specks. I sipped the ale and grimaced, considering whether it was drinkable or no.

'May I be joining you, master?'

I was surprised to see Gabriel's companion Rook looming over me like a mountain.

'Aye. God give you good day, Rook. Please, take your ease beside me. I would offer to buy you ale, but truly cannot recommend it.'

Rook gave a rumbling laugh from deep in his massive chest.

'Mayhap, I may oblige you, master. I have ale brought from a tavern nearby. Master Ameryk will only buy the best.' He took my cup and emptied the contents into the pool, then refilled it from a leather flask hanging at his belt.

It tasted sweet indeed – Mistress Fletcher's brewing from the Hart's Horn, if I was not mistaken. It had not taken the Bristol merchant long to discover the best tavern in town.

'Hey, you! You can't use my cups for your own drink! Give me back the cup.' Having seen what Rook did, the ale-seller was angry, rightly so, I suppose. He came running over to us, eager to snatch away the cup, but I was still drinking from it and had no intention of either hastening to finish such good ale, or allowing him to deny me.

In the event, a single, long, hard look from the towering Abyssinian stopped his angry words upon an instant. I had no need to speak, continuing to sup my drink.

'Aye, well. Return my cup when you're done,' the ale-seller said in a small voice before returning behind his stall, meek as a lamb.

I could but admire a man whose expression alone put a fellow in his proper place. I knew one other who was able to do the like: the Duke of Gloucester, my sometime patron, may God bless him.

Rook flung his great body down beside me and stretched out, closing his eyes, his arms behind his head as a pillow.

'Do your askings produce meat, Master Seb?' he said without opening his eyes.

It took me a moment to realise he was enquiring as to whether my questions had advanced my investigations.

'Nay. No meat as yet, I fear. No one saw, heard or knows anything. 'Tis to be expected in such a case, I suppose. Could it be that you remember someone or something suspicious yesterday, Rook?'

For a matter of minutes, the Abyssinian made no reply, and I feared he might have fallen asleep, but no: he was simply deep in thought for he spoke at last:

'There was a man who appeared much interested in our stall – as were so many eager to see the horns – but he returned again and again, all the while never once allowing his eyes to glance at the horns, as others did. He looked at our soaps and purses and all manner of wares, yet bought not one thing. In truth, he seemed a man of small means. I doubt he could afford our goods, so why did he come back, time and again? That is why he caught my notice. Yet he is most likely a harmless mouse, if a ragged one.'

'Can you describe him to me? I may draw his likeness, and then, if he be still hereabouts, I shall enquire of him as to his business at your stall.'

Rook laughed that rumbling laugh of his.

'He had eyes, nose, mouth and limbs, as men do. His skin was pale and, I admit, all white men look the same to me, begging your pardon, Master Seb, and meaning no offence to you and your kind.'

'Mm. None taken, but that does not aid my quest to find him,' I said, wondering how anyone could be so vague about telling one man from another. 'Perhaps he wore some distinctive item of clothing? Since you knew him to be the same fellow returning, there must have been something about him that you recognised each time.'

Again, Rook was silent for some while, and I finished my ale while awaiting his response. I was considering returning the empty cup to the disgruntled ale-seller when he spoke:

'Aye, it was his headwear. I cannot say what colour or shape it was for it was faded and battered, so it had neither tint nor form. That is what I saw each time and remembered. He may have naught to do with the theft but...'

'A hat beyond describing? Well, I suppose I might know such a one, if I see it? Was the man tall or short?'

'I saw his cap, so he was possibly of some height above others, but not so much. As I said...'

'All white men look the same to you, aye. Now I will give you my thanks for the good ale, Rook, and be about my business. Good day to you.' Discovering then that I had sat too long upon the ground, my difficulty in rising to my feet meant Rook earned further gratitude in assisting me and a second round of thanks. I returned my ale cup as required to keep the stall-holder in fair humour and resumed my enquiries, praying for some insight or morsel of useful information, notwithstanding such a clue as colourless, shapeless, indescribable headwear that amounted to no help at all.

I kept alert for just such a hat as I wound my way through the crowds among the booths and tents. I went so far as to walk all around the Horse Pool, 'neath the tall elms on the northern side. Their leaves whispered in a gentle breath of air, and I realised how quiet it was, away from the stalls. If only there had been shade here, it would be a place of respite indeed, but the sun shone full upon them, casting short shadows over Chick Lane and the walls of the buildings beyond, benefitting others there, but denying us. I returned to the fayre ground proper and, mayhap, as I was attentive to hats and caps particularly, a flash of dark, unruly hair, capless, amid the throng caught my eye. Jack? Nay. I must be mistaken. He would not dare defy me after my lectures of recent days. I did not espy the person again and put him from my mind.

One man I saw for certain, suffering a glare so malevolent from him that the hairs rose upon my neck, was Ralph Clifford. He was watching a juggling act, but as soon as he noticed me, his aspect was diverted to scowling in my direction. Mercifully, we were too far apart for speech. I turned away, discomforted, but it seemed I could still feel his eyes, like heated daggers, piercing holes betwixt my shoulder blades. Perhaps it was a need for reassurance after that encounter that caused my feet to carry me, without realising, to the silk-women's booth.

Both Emily and Rose were serving customers. Their wares looked much depleted, so business must be brisk – which was heartening news. It occurred to me that, next year, it might be as well if I set up a stall here also. For certain, customers were few indeed at the shop in Paternoster Row this week, thus far. Most folk were here at the fayre instead.

'Ah. 'Tis as well you've come, husband,' Emily said when she noticed me at last. 'Little Dickon is restless and would benefit from some attention. Tend him, will you? I am far too busy.' She did not wait upon my reply, but turned to a plump matron who was inspecting her exquisite embroidered bookmarks.

I entered the booth through the back door that had been propped open with a stool to let in more light and a whisper of cooling breeze. Even so, inside the booth was uncomfortably hot and the babe was well wrapped in a linen sheet. He looked flushed and made small grizzling noises of protest, though softly enough that none were disturbed by him. Our Dickon was a considerate infant, but no wonder he was restless. I lifted him from his basket, feeling him damp with sweat. At least, I hoped it was sweat and that he was not in need of a clean tailclout. I had long since proven that changing a babe's nether bindings was not a skill I could own.

'Come, sweeting, let Papa take you somewhere cooler.' I made certain his head, with its sparse wisps of pale hair, was covered by his bonnet, such that the sun would not burn him, and carried him to the shaded place under the oak tree where Rook and I had sat earlier. The shadow had moved since then. Now, much of the shade was cast across the Horse Pool and what little remained on the ground was already crowded with folk likewise seeking respite from the sun's heat - no room for us. The narrow band of blessed shade along the priory wall to the south of the fayre ground was also fully occupied when I reached it, having pushed through the crowds, the babe in my arms. This day, I had left Gawain at home, fearing he would be trampled, yet the fayre was no better place for an infant either.

I considered taking him home but, most like, he would want to feed sometime soon and then I should have to bring him back to Emily. Besides, I was supposed to be investigating a murder, not acting the nursemaid. Not that I begrudged a moment spent with my son, but how was a man supposed to attend to his rightful office while thus encumbered?

Eventually, having tip-toed amongst the guy-ropes with care, I found a patch of shade behind the Venetian merchant's colourful tent and the back of another which faced onto the next row of stalls. There was hardly space to stretch out my legs, but I eased down upon the grass – what little remained – and sat with Dickon upon my lap. There we played silly clapping games which set him chuckling with merriment, and I sang to him. Emily and Rose had countless childish ditties to entertain him, enough to fill a songbook, but I had never had a mother to sing to me, so knew none of that kind. Instead, little Dickon had to harken to choral pieces and the solos allocated to me by the precentor in St Paul's. It was good practice for me, and he did not seem to mind listening to Latin motets and psalms. He fell asleep in my arms, lulled by the melodies.

Time passed quickly, and the sun moved westerly until it found us out, glancing along betwixt the canvas walls and robbing us of our secret shady nook. Now I had a difficulty indeed: getting to my feet without wakening the babe as I felt the sun scorching the side of my face. I lay little Dickon down on the grass gently as maybe so as not to waken him. He snuffled and stirred, but slept on. As ever, getting up took me a few moments and then, just as I was about to retrieve my sleeping son, I was knocked down again, struck from behind by something heavy and showered in dirt. The sun was not alone in having discovered our refuge: I turned to see Ralph Clifford standing a few yards away towards the end of the row of tents, still flexing his left arm – as well his right was damaged, or his throw would have been more accurate and harder.

'How dare you assault us so, you devil!' I shouted. 'You could have injured an innocent babe. I shall summon the constables to arrest you, you miscreant.'

Dickon was now awakened and wailing, distressed by the incident. I knelt beside him, picking dirt from his linen and brushing bits of wood from his bonnet, whispering gentle words to calm him. Yet gentleness was the last thing I felt. A sizeable lump of rotting wood lay there: the stump of a knotty branch or some such. It was fortunate the rot had softened it, else it may have harmed us. I was so angered at the thought that little Dickon could have suffered hurt, against my nature as it was, I had my fists clenched in readiness to give Clifford as mighty a buffet as I could. But when I looked up, the wretch was gone. Why he held a grudge against me when I was not to blame for his troubles made no sense. It must simply be the Foxley name that offended him still. And what could I do to remedy that?

As I carried my son back through the thinning crowds, to his mother, I was seething still. I never knew I had capacity for such rage as surged in my breast in defence of little Dickon. Woe betide any man who dared cross me at that moment.

But someone did. Unfortunately, it was not Ralph Clifford.

I was considering whether I should tell Emily what had happened or no, but recalling the old wives' warning about an excess of shock or anger curdling a mother's milk, I decided caution was advisable: better that I said naught to her. As I approached the silk-women's stall who should dash out from behind a tent and nigh collide with me, but Jack?

With my free hand, I grabbed him by his hair and pulled hard, twisting it around.

'Ow! Ow! Yer bastard... lemme go!' He kicked out and caught my shin afore he recognised me.

'You defiant brat. How dare you disobey me. You've had your last warning. This time I be done with you. Go back to the streets where you belong. Forget working for me, you disobedient rascal. I won't have you under my roof ever again.'

'B-but Master S...'

'Don't speak to me. You be dismissed from my household. Get you gone from my sight. If I ever set eyes upon you again, I will not be responsible for my actions. Go!' With that, I slapped him across the ear so he leapt back in surprise. His expression was a mingling of shock and misery afore he ran off, disappearing towards St Bartholomew's church.

And what of me? Did I feel relief at venting my anger? No, for the babe was crying in my arms. I was sweating as a warrior in full armour; my heart pounded like a battering ram at my temples, and I was afflicted with a monstrous headache that threatened to cleave my skull in twain as with an axe. Such an outpouring of ire did not suit my humours in the least, and it was as if I had fought a battle – nay, rather a war. And Clifford was the cause.

I returned the babe, tears and all, to his mother, thrusting him into her embrace.

'What's this? Dirt? Splinters in his linen? And what's amiss with you? You look like Satan himself.'

'Do not ask,' I snarled. 'I be no wet-nurse. I have work to do.' With that, I left her to deal with the babe, as was befitting.

'Who's upset Master Seb? I've never heard him speak that way before,' Rose said as she wrapped some of Peronelle's ribbons in a square of linen for a customer.

Emily shrugged. 'That's men for you: never content, no matter what. Can you manage alone while I feed the babe? It would help if that idle wanton had deigned to aid us this afternoon, would it not?'

'Lizzie? Aye, it was her turn, as you say. No matter. Just look how much we've sold: we have hardly any of Beattie's kerchiefs left to sell. Only a single pair of my gloves remain and 'tis a good thing Dame Ellen brought more silk purses to make a fair display with your few bookmarks that we still have. When you sold four to a single customer, I thought we would have none of those left either. Do you have any more at home, Em? We will need something more to sell on the morrow.'

'Aye. I have a couple still requiring of tassels to finish them off. If there be time this eve...'

'I could sew them on for you, if you have them made?'

'That would be a help, Rose, if you did. By the time I've settled Dickon abed, I'll be too tired to thread a needle, and I can't think that miserable man of mine will be of a humour to aid me. That look upon his face would turn butter rancid, I swear.'

Emily lay the babe, now contentedly sleeping, in his basket and re-laced her bodice respectably. The crowd was dispersing, the weary stall-holders packing away their wares for the night. A handful of determined folk lingered here and there, but the fayre was done for the day.

'Let's close the booth and go home,' Emily said. 'I've done labour enough for a month.'

'The weight of our money chest should cheer you, Em,' Rose said, rattling the coins in their box. 'Should we lock it and leave it here, or take it with us? We know there's a thief about and so much coin could be tempting.'

'Aye. 'Tis a worry, if we leave it, yet I shan't feel safe carrying it through the streets either. If only Seb hadn't gone storming off like that, at least I'd feel reassured if he was with us, useless as he'd be if some felon tried to rob us. Let's leave the chest empty and hide the coin bags at the bottom of one of the baskets where no thief will think to look. I know: we can put them under Dickon's soiled tailclouts: that should deter any man. They can wait until the morrow for washing.' Laughing together, the women hid their profits and locked the booth.

Odds and ends of lost or discarded rubbish skipped across the ground in a rising breeze as the sun slid lower in the western sky, daubing the few wisps of cloud with the pigments of evening: purple, gold and rose. Yet even such colour barely caught my interest as I slouched home, aware that I should be required to eat a large portion of humble pie afore my wife would forgive my surliness of earlier. There was also the problem of Jack. What had I done? Where would he go? Might he return and what should I do, if he did? A troubled conscience was no remedy for a headache.

It did not improve my case in that my enquiries into Gerrit's murder had not advanced by so much as a single useful clue. What a waste of a day that could have been spent working on my illuminated *Aesop's Fables*. I cursed Master Fyssher for dragging me into his realm of death and forcing me to conduct his investigation for him. It was not my place to do so simply because my brother was gone off on his travels, leaving the coroner without an assistant. God rot them all!

The Lord be thanked: there was still a welcome for me at home. Gawain bounded from the open kitchen door, hastening across the yard to me. He woofed a greeting and wagged his tail so joyously, I had to smile at him, patting his silky head. In the kitchen, Adam and Tom sat at the board, laughing at some jest; Nessie was clattering spoons and dishes, giggling at whatever so amused them all. As I entered, the merriment ceased upon an instant.

'God save you, Seb,' Adam gave me greeting. 'I have to confess to you a great failing on my part. You gave me responsibilities concerning the lads and, well, the truth is...'

'Jack ran off to visit the fayre without a by-your-leave. I know. I saw the young toad. I have banished him from this house.'

'Oh.' That was all Adam said and gave me a strange look. I could not read its meaning.

'Why do you regard me so, Adam? I forbade him to go to the fayre without one of us to oversee his behaviour. Clearly, he defied me. Am I not within my rights as master to discharge him for his wilful act of disobedience, over and above all his legion misdemeanours aforehand?'

'Aye, but that wasn't quite the way of it. 'Tis my fault, Seb. Do not blame the lad. We had no red lead for the capitals in the primers. I gave him coin and told him to go purchase some more. I suppose I thought he would go to an apothecary for it, but I did not specify that. Not knowing who supplies you ordinarily, I left it to him. It may well be that he believed the fayre was the best place to buy it and I had not forbidden it.'

'That be no excuse: he took advantage of the opportunity. He could have got red lead from St Paul's or any number of apothecaries or grocers in Cheapside. But why was there none here? We had plenty yesterday. Whatever the case, the rogue be gone now, and you'll not see your coin again. I shall make good your loss, of course, but there's an end to it.'

'Not quite, Seb.' Adam, of a sudden, appeared to find some matter of intense interest concerning his boots, frowning at them in consternation.

'What be amiss now?' I asked, groaning inwardly, certain I truly did not want to know.

'Aye, well...' Adam cleared his throat. ''Tis like this, you see... Jack is in the workshop...'

'What! After I forbade him...'

'But I did not know that. He is scouring the storeroom floor, as I told him to,' Adam continued. 'The reason we needed more pigment was because he dropped what we had and smashed the pot. It made so great a mess. And that was my confession to you: it has ruined an entire ream of paper – the best we have, or had. There is no saving even one sheet of it. I apologise. I should have been more vigilant and attentive to my charges. I pray you can forgive me, Seb.'

'So Jack defies me yet again? I cannot believe his temerity.' With that, I strode down the passage and into the workshop. 'Jack! Get here this instant. Come out of there!'

'I'm all red an' mucky, master.'

'I don't care. Attend me at once, you knave.'

The creature that emerged, creeping from the storeroom, was an apparition from Hell. Jack was smeared with red pigment from his hair to his boots, worse than any blood-stained butcher's apprentice. The wet cloth in his hand seemed to drip gore across the floor.

'Put that down; you be making matters worse,' I told him. 'And answer me this: why are you here? Did I not make myself clear enough for you to comprehend? I told you to go. I said I never wanted to set eyes upon you again. Were those not my very words?'

'Aye, master, they wos.'

'Then why do I find you here still?'

'Cos I knowed you never meant it, Master Seb, didn't I?'

I stared at him for a long while, rendered speechless by such insolence.

'An' I promise I'll get the mess cleared up proper,' he added.

What was I to do? How was a man supposed to keep discipline in his own house? Earlier, I had clipped his ear and had it made the slightest difference? Nay. He was as incorrigible as ever. Corporal punishment achieved naught.

'There will be no supper for you until it is done to my satisfaction, you hear?'

'Aye. An' I'm sorry, master.'

I suppose an apology was something, at least. There seemed naught more to be said, and I returned to the kitchen, hoping for some of Emily's meadowsweet potion to ease my throbbing head. Apprentices! They caused me greater trouble and pain than ever.

Later, as Nessie served up a poor excuse for a supper – she claimed it was pease and bacon pottage but, if there was an element of pig's flesh in it, none was to be found upon my trencher – Emily was regaling us with the afternoon's doings at the silk-women's stall. Some at least had had a productive day. She looked exhausted when she and Rose first arrived home, but enthusiasm for the business revived her.

'We sold so much, we need more stuff for the morrow. Rose is willing to help me finish a couple more bookmarks this eve. We made so much profit, Dame Ellen will be delighted.'

'I congratulate you both,' I said. 'We must put the money away safely.'

''Tis done already, husband. Fear not. No man will rob us.' Emily and Rose exchanged a glance, and both women grinned.

'I trust you be sure?'

'We are. Come, Rose, let us be about our sewing in the parlour. Nessie, wash the pots and do not spare the elbow grease as you did yesterday. That pewter basin wasn't properly scoured clean. Use more sand this time to get a shine.'

'Aye, mistress.' Nessie wore an expression sour as verjuice and began clattering dishes as noisily as maybe to express her disapproval.

'For pity's sake, can you not do the task quietly?' I said, feeling my headache reassert itself betwixt my brows. ''Tis a warm eve: take the tub out to the yard, can you not, and spare us your annoyance and ill humour?' Who was I, in truth, to complain at another's choleric temperament? 'Give us a few minutes of peace, for the love of God.' I closed my eyes. I would rather not see the look upon her face now I had made her labours yet more arduous, having to lug the washtub outside. 'Help her move the tub, Tom.'

'Why me? It's not my job...'

'You'll do it forwhy I told you to.'

Jack, sitting at the board opposite Tom, his hands still stained red from the pigment despite a deal of scrubbing at the laver bowl, stuck his tongue out rudely.

'Time yer done some work anyways, Tom, yer lazy arse-wipe,' he said.

'I do more than you, you idle dog-turd.'

'Be silent, the pair of you.' Adam spared me the trouble of chastising them. 'We do not want your gutter slang in this house. Tom, do as you're bid. Jack, if you can't find some decent and quiet occupation 'til bedtime, you can take all our boots and shoes out to the yard and clean them, and Tom can aid you. Give Master Seb some respite, can't you?'

'My thanks, Adam,' I said when we were alone in the kitchen. 'I apologise for my earlier harsh words.'

'Aye. Have some more ale to cool your humours all the same. 'Tis not like you. You were of such mild manners in Norfolk.'

'I did not have two unruly apprentices to vex me there.'

'They are a pair of rapscallions and no mistake. Mind, I don't recall that me and Noah were much better when we were serving our 'prenticeship in Norwich. I remember one time – a Saturday in spring, it must have been – our master had given us a sound beating for back-answering him, and in retribution, we filled his Sunday best shoes with frogspawn for church next day. It earned us another beating – held over 'til Monday since our master always observed the Lord's Day most strictly – but his face was an image I'll ne'er forget when he put his shoes on, and his toes felt that cold, slimy spawn. Me and Noah laughed over it for a week or more, despite our tender backsides. Have those young demons ever played such a prank on you?'

'One or other of them – we never determined who, but Jack was the prime suspect – put flour in Jude's cap with the peacock's feather. I did find it a desperate challenge not to laugh aloud when he put it on, and flour spilled down his face and turned his hair grey. But he deserved it for it was shortly after Em and I were married, and Jude had played such a jape upon us on our wedding night. All along, my brother had been hinting that he might loosen the bed ropes, such that we and the featherbed would fall through. Therefore, to avoid such a disaster, as soon as Em and I were alone, I went under the bed to make certain the ropes were tight and secure. They were, so naught was amiss, as I thought, until I touched Em's cheek and left a great black finger mark upon her skin. The bed sheets and all were soon covered in black. My brother had smeared the bed ropes with soot, the heartless rogue. It was fully a fortnight afore I forgave him.'

Adam burst out laughing.

'Oh, I must make a note of that prank. It may be of use someday,' he chuckled over his ale.

I realised I had nigh smiled over the retelling of the tale and my headache was lessened: laughter always was a fine medicine as any.

Jack and Tom returned, carrying the washtub betwixt them, and Nessie followed with a stack of barely balanced dishes in her arms. Adam leapt from his stool just in time to catch them as they toppled, sparing us another mishap and commotion.

'We done all them shoes. They're all clean now, ain't they, Tom?' Jack looked smug.

'I shall inspect your handiwork later,' I said. 'Bring them into the kitchen. We don't want them soaked if it should rain overnight. Then you can go say your prayers and get to bed.'

'But I needs t' tell yer, Master Seb, cos I knows sumfink.'

'I do not doubt it, Jack, that you know far more than you should about too many things, I warrant. Your revelations can wait upon the morrow.'

'But it's important, ain't it?'

'I be too tired to hear of your nonsense and want no more of it. Away to your bed, Jack, afore I have second thoughts about you biding under my roof.'

'But master...'

'Master said "bed", so go!' Adam pinched Jack's ear and led him out to the yard where the wooden steps went up to the chamber that had been Jude's and to the lads' attic room. He returned, dusting off his hands as for a job well done. 'You too, Tom, unless you want I drag you also. And don't forget your prayers!' he called after, adding quietly: 'If God can spare the time to listen to such a pair of beggarly knaves.'

# Chapter 9

## Wednesday, the twenty-sixth day of August

I DID NOT sleep well last night, and Master Fyssher was a dishearteningly early riser. Once more, he was at my door afore I was hardly awake, beating the oak with an impatient fist. It was no way to ensure my humours were any improvement upon those of last eve, though mercifully the knot of pain betwixt my brows had ceased tormenting me.

'Hold! Hold, afore you break the jamb,' I called out, hopping on one foot along the passageway as I tried to pull on my other boot. Suspecting my unwelcome visitor would be the deputy coroner, I straightened my hastily-donned attire and took a deep, slow breath to calm myself afore opening the door.

'God give you good morn, Master Fyssher.' I sounded the very soul of reason.

'Good morn be damned. You did not report your progress to me last eve, as you are required to do, Foxley. There can be no excuse for your failure in this respect. It is your duty...'

'As an upstanding citizen, do you mean?'

'As my bloody assistant!'

'Yet that is not my office, sir, but my brother's. I was willing to aid you yesterday, but 'tis not my place to serve as you require. You will need to appoint a new assistant...'

'I have, and you are he. So get your things, Foxley: notes or whatever, and make your report. Now!'

'I did not agree to this...'

'Your report!'

'Aye, well, in truth,' I stammered. 'In truth, there was so little to report; I saw no reason to disturb you, sir. Apart from the unlikelihood of one of Master Ameryk's employees being involved in the robbery...'

'Robbery? You fool, we are investigating a murder, not a theft.'

'I be certain the two have some connection.'

'I do not care! I have work enough dealing with unnatural deaths. I have no interest in any lesser crimes. If I wasted my time looking into every misdemeanour and petty transgression, I'd never see my bed. Now get out there and investigate that foreigner's death and don't be distracted by anything else. You hear me?' The deputy coroner poked me repeatedly in the chest with a fat finger to emphasise his words.

'Very well. But I have business matters of my own to attend to.'

'My business – the business of law and order – takes precedence over all else. Do as I command, Foxley, or you'll get no fee. Understand?'

'Aye, I suppose so.'

Without another word, Master Fyssher stomped away, no doubt certain I would do his bidding, as if I did not have a workshop to run, commissions to fulfil and apprentices to train, never mind a family, a household and customers to keep content. Did he think his few pence remittance was compensation enough for the time I would have to give over to solving the crime? It was not. However, my friend Gerrit was deserving of justice. I would do what I could to bring that about, not for Master Fyssher's convenience nor the jingle of his coin in my purse, but for the sake of a clear conscience. I should not forgive myself if I did not do my best for Gerrit in his unquiet and untimely grave.

'What be arranged this day?' I asked Emily as we sat, breaking our fast on bread and ale, it being a fast day.

141

'Beattie and Lizzie are at the booth until dinner, then I'll be there with Pen this afternoon, but I must go there directly after this to take those few bookmarks Rose helped me finish last eve.'

'I could take them for you,' I offered. 'Master Fyssher has ordered me to continue the investigations at the fayre. He insists more questions be asked, though I cannot think who has not been interrogated already. Neither can I invent any new enquiries to make. If no man confesses to it, I know not how to solve this crime.'

'I'm sure you'll unmask the culprit, Seb, just as you did at Foxley, when Cousin Luke was slain. I have every confidence in your skills.' Adam smiled reassuringly at me around the last morsel of bread.

'I fear your confidence may be misplaced this time, Adam, but I thank you all the same. Tom, Jack, get to your work. I want those cheap primers finished by the morrow.'

'Then can we come t' the fayre?' Jack asked, 'When we've done them bloody primers? I'm sick of seein' 'em, damn fings.'

'Watch your tongue, you!' Adam said afore I could respond to such unmannerly speech.

'Come, Gawain,' I called to my dog, recalling how he had inspired my investigations at Foxley village earlier in the summer. Mayhap, he would nose out a clue or two this time also.

The fayre ground was much as afore: noisy, busy and colourful, but I was tiring of it. Gerrit's poppet booth stood forlorn and abandoned, and I wondered what would become of it. I found Beatrice opening up the silk-women's booth unaided and helped her to set the open counter-board upon its trestles.

'No sign of Mistress Knollys as yet?' I asked, giving Beatrice the new bookmarks.

'And probably won't be,' she said. 'I'll be on my own this morn, I'll wager.' She put the bookmarks to the fore on the counter where the gold threads glinted in the sunlight to attract buyers.

'I could fetch Emily or Rose to help you, if you wish?' Returning home straightway would hardly impede my investigations since I had no idea how they should proceed in any case.

'Aye, that would help, but no need for haste. The crowds seem somewhat less today. And you can never tell: Lizzie may deign to arrive later... at her convenience, of course.' Beatrice balanced precariously on a wobbling stool to hang a bunch of ribbons from a peg under the awning. 'Not many of these left to sell anyway; little choice of colours remain. Still, I'm sure someone will buy plunkett ribbons,' she said, pulling the blue-grey lengths of woven silk until they hung evenly, 'And I think we have a few red ones left in the basket to make a show.'

'If you need my aid for naught else, then I shall be about my work,' I said, half hoping she would give me further cause to delay my investigation. I was surprised to see her sorting through something that appeared to be a disgusting pile of soiled tailclouts and removing a bulging bag of coin.

'Ah! Em's a clever lass to think of hiding our profits there. As for help, I shall do well enough for now, but another pair of hands will be needed in an hour or so, Master Seb, and thank you.'

Thus, I had no excuse not to commence asking more questions, though my heart was not in the task. Perhaps a visit to Master Ameryk's stall and a few words with Gabriel would inspire me.

A brassy sun shone boldly from a milk-white sky this morn; not the lapis lazuli dome of heaven of recent days. Already, the heat was building, and tiny black flies annoyed me, sticking to my sweat-lathered face and making Gawain twitch his ears constantly. Such creatures oft-times betoken a coming storm, and I wondered if that would be the case later.

'God give you good day, Master Gideon,' I said, greeting Gabriel and remembering to use his assumed name.

'And to you, Master Seb. Have you broken your fast as yet? There be cheese pasties, fresh baked, if you want?' Gabriel offered me a tray of steaming pastries that gave off a most tempting, savoury aroma.

'My thanks, but no.' I would resist temptation on a fast day, if the Almighty were to assist my endeavours, as I had prayed he might in my brief morning office, said betwixt lacing my jerkin and running my fingers through my dishevelled early-morning hair. I ought to have been ashamed to think the Lord God would give ear to such hasty prayers, accomplished with so little regard for ceremony and proper devotion; they were nigh an insult to His grace. But, may He forgive me, there had been so little time this day.

'Any thoughts upon the thief and murderer?' Gabriel asked, munching on his pasty. He sounded so casual about the matter, as if such lamentable deeds were a daily occurrence in his life. I hoped they were not, but who knew how violent a mariner's existence could be? A scrivener's lot was sufficient for me; adventure did not appeal to my nature. I found excitement enough in my work.

'Nay. No new information has come to light, I fear, unless you include Rook's observations of a fellow wearing a colourless, shapeless, indeterminate sort of headwear. Did you see any man that might be thus described at your stall afore the theft?'

'Aye, a thousand of them at least.' Gabriel finished his food and wiped his sleeve across his mouth, brushing crumbs from his beard. 'I'm surprised at Rook. He's an observant fellow for the most part. Surely he can describe someone better than that? Were you hoping to draw a likeness?'

'Not from words so vague as that. Rook says all white men look the same to his eyes. Be that true, do you suppose?'

'I dare say,' Gabriel said with a laugh, 'All his kind look alike to me too, apart from Rook himself. Few Abyssinians are as tall as he, so I can recognise him, at least. Are you continuing your investigations? Master Ameryk is still hopeful of recovering the horns.'

'Master Fyssher has ordered me to seek out Gerrit's murderer as a priority. He has little interest in your losses. However, if I find the horns as well, that will be a good thing, but I doubt I'll solve either, the way matters be progressing – that is to say: not at all.'

'You can but do your utmost, Seb, and I know you will. Old Fyssher can't expect miracles of you and Master Ameryk will just have to bear his disappointment. By the by, Ameryk is impressed by your Emily's embroidered bookmarks and has placed a sizeable order for some. Did you know?'

'I think not. She may have mentioned it, but I have been somewhat distracted. 'Tis good that her work impresses and she will appreciate the order. But speaking of Emily: I promised I would arrange for either her or Rose to aid Beatrice on the stall. The crowd is growing, I see, so there will be need of another pair of hands. I must return home.'

'Give my greetings to Mistress Em and Rose,' Gabriel called out as I hastened away.

By mid morn, Emily had joined Beattie, working on the stall. After a slow beginning, business had become brisk, the sales numerous. The women's coin box was nigh full and yesterday's money bag was bursting its seams. There seemed to be a sense of urgency about the crowds, as if there was much to be done and little time to do it and, mayhap, they were correct. It was as well that Pen had also come early, rather than wait until after dinner.

Looking across the striped awnings, tents and rooftops to the west, Emily could see storm clouds building, darkly menacing as they rose higher and higher. Soon they would overpower the sun. If the rain came heavily – and it seemed that it must – the fayre ground would become a morass of squelching mud in no time. Customers would disappear as if by magic.

Later, Beattie was taking coin in exchange for a dozen plunkett ribbons – the colour was subtle, but the quality was of the best – just as the first raindrops splashed upon the edge of the counter-board, marking the pale wood with dark circles, larger than pennies. Within moments, water was pouring from pewter-grey clouds, and everyone ran for shelter wherever they might. A flash of lightning ripped the skies in twain and thunder crashed like the Devil's cymbals. Pen covered her ears and whimpered.

"'Tis but a storm, Pen. Naught to affright you,' Emily said. 'But I think we should close up the counter or everything will be ruined.' She and Beattie shut up the booth as quickly as possible while Pen cowered within, her eyes tightly closed and her fingers in her ears. Soaked through, they joined Pen, perching on trestles in the gloom.

'I'm sure it will pass soon,' Beattie said, fluffing out her skirts to dry. 'What shall we do in the meantime?'

Emily began to sing, attempting to drown out the next clap of thunder as Pen flinched. Beattie joined in, her voice making up in volume for its lack of melody.

'Come along, Pen, we must all sing the chorus.' Just as Emily spoke, thunder shattered the noise of pounding rain so loudly, they all jumped. The song was abandoned. 'How's your lad doing at Song School, Beattie?' Emily shouted above the drumming of rain on the wooden roof.

'Well enough, so I'm told, but he'll never equal your Seb's fine voice, if he's trained 'til Judgement Day. I heard your Seb last Sunday: voice of an angel.' They all winced at the next roar of thunder.

'Ah, but that's his only virtue.' Emily sighed. 'As a husband, he's as tedious as a Latin sermon and duller than ditch water. I tell you both: the only thing that brings him to life is the sight of a fine manuscript. I may as well be a painted saint, then he might notice me. I'm tired of it... of him.'

'Does he beat you?' Pen asked. 'You should be thankful, then,' she added when Emily shook her head.

'Would you take a lover?' Beattie gave her friend a most direct look. Their eyes met. It was Emily who turned away. 'Have you one in mind?'

'No. Certainly not. I'd never...' Emily's words trailed away into the sound of falling rain.

'You wouldn't, would you, Em?' Pen was horrified at the prospect.

'Indeed she would, if the chance offered.' Beattie folded her arms across her damp bodice, declaring the debate settled. 'I had to. How else was I to get another babe after eight years of trying in vain? That man of mine has a pizzle like a mouldy parsnip and about as much use. Is that Seb's trouble, Em? Do you have some fine fellow in mind?'

'Are you saying you're with child by another man?' Emily asked, both shocked and determined not to answer Beattie's last question. She did not dare allow that line of enquiry to continue for fear her friend might contrive to name a certain someone, and her blushes would betray the truth.

'I can recommend the cordwainer in Friday Street. He is most obliging and easy on the eye. His shoes are well made too.' They all laughed, the storm forgotten for a moment. 'Not that I'm another Lizzie Knollys, mind you.'

'I suppose, as a poor widow, she has to do what she can,' Pen said in her quietest voice, such that her words were barely heard above the fierce rage of the weather.

'A poor widow! Is that what she calls herself?' Beattie scoffed. 'She's no more a widow than I am. Nay. Two years or more since, one Sunday morn it was, she and her goodman had such a row in the midst of Foster Lane on the way to mass. He must have found out what she was about. Anyhow, the pair came to blows, and he walked off, shouting so all could hear that he was never coming back. It was a good thing so many folk heard him, else there would've been rumours that she'd done away with him. It was the talk of the parish for... aw, weeks... until King Edward's latest indiscretions with the Lord Mayor's lady got the gossip-mongers' apron-strings in a knot. You know me: I'm not one to spread rumours or gossip, but 'tis every word of it true.'

Just then, lightning lit up the dimness of the booth with repeated flashes of brilliance and thunder crashed deafeningly. An almighty bang like cannon fire split the air.

'May St Mary preserve us!' Emily leapt to her feet and made the sign of the cross. 'What was that?'

'P'raps St Paul's got struck like once before,' Beattie suggested as they opened the counter-board an inch or two, but a sheet of rain persuaded them to close it abruptly. Curiosity would have to wait a while.

I was waiting out the storm in the tent of an apothecary from the Island of Rhodes. The man spoke good Latin, so we had been discussing some of his more interesting wares when the deluge began. However, it seemed no tent could withstand such a torrent of rain, and I helped the man to save his more delicate items that would suffer most from damage by water, by which time we too were wet through as the tent leaked like a bottomless barrel. Among things that were unspoiled by the rain were the fabled Stones of Rhodes: sovereign protection against the pestilence, so he told me. They were pretty things: rosy-grey polished pebbles each marked throughout the stone by the cross of Our Lord, put there by God that all might know of their miraculous property and ability to ward off plague. The apothecary was so grateful for my timely aid in rescuing his herbs and spices that he gave me a pebble to keep as an amulet. But my works of rescue were not yet done.

Multiple bolts of lightning came together, and one struck an elm tree across the way on the far side of the Horse Pool. It was hard to make out through the thick curtain of rain, but it seemed that folk had, most unwisely, sought shelter beneath the trees. When a great bough came crashing down, I thought I heard cries and screams, even through the storm's tumult. The apothecary and I – being soaked already – hastened to the place, to see if any required our aid.

At first glance, it appeared that Master Fyssher would have many more cases to deal with this day but, one by one, people were pulled from the mess of leaves and branches, or else crawled out from under. There were cuts and bruises aplenty which I assisted the apothecary in dealing with, yet all breathed still, God be praised for his mercy. One fellow had a gash upon his head and appeared dazed even as the rain washed his scalp clean of blood. Another had a broken arm for certain and would need the services of a surgeon. But the loudest complaints came from a pedlar who had suffered no hurt at all, but rather the falling bough had damaged his cart. Even so, it was not beyond mending, so far as I could see. I made to help him pull the cart free of the fallen tree – which aid he allowed – but when I would retrieve his belongings, he became violent and shoved me aside, such that I fell back, landing upon a sharp spike of broken wood or similar which pierced my wrist. I excused the pedlar's unmannerly actions as being caused by shock. No thanks were forthcoming from him either, but now I required the apothecary's attention also.

The injury was not large, but seemed deep and was bleeding considerably around a long pale splinter. The apothecary said he had just the instrument to remove the splinter and a fine remedy to treat the gash back at his tent: dragon's blood! I had heard of such a thing to be used as a fine red pigment, but never as a wound treatment. I prayed he was not mistaken in this. Smearing paint upon a nasty cut did not seem a worthy idea.

The storm was passing, the rain easing as we returned to his tent. He bade me sit upon a stool while he prepared what was required. Being cowardly, I could not watch as he removed the splinter with a pair of steel tweezers, but he gave the needle-sharp object to me when he was done. It was not wood, as I had thought, but more like a shard of white glass or stone. I pondered it as he heated a pale reddish powder over a little charcoal burner and I watched, intrigued, as it melted into a thick, crimson liquid. This was dragon's blood, he told me. Having stirred and tested it to see that it was warm enough to be of the correct consistency, but not so hot as to burn my skin, he took my hand and smeared the stuff around my wrist with the back of the spoon, covering the cut. I expected pain, but there was none, just a feeling of warmth. He instructed me to let it dry and set afore I should move my hand, saying it would form a shield to protect the injury and aid its healing. It would drop off gradually, and my wound should be mended by the time it was gone. I thanked him but, in truth, I was unconvinced that his remedy might work as well as he would have me believe.

Business at the fayre had dwindled somewhat after the storm. Mud-caked shoes and slipperiness underfoot made trailing around the fayre ground hard work. The women's skirt-hems were wet, begrimed and weighty, clinging to their legs as they walked. It was most unpleasant, and they decided to shut up the booth and hope for more custom upon the morrow.

'So she never did bother to show her face, the idle slut,' Beattie moaned as they trudged beneath the arch of Aldersgate.

Although the downpour had ceased an hour since, the central gutter in the road gurgled and overflowed around the storm-washed detritus of leaves stripped from the trees and assorted rubbish. A rat, no doubt flooded out of its haven, dashed across their path, but the clean smell of rain-scoured air was refreshing after weeks of hot dustiness tainting every breath.

'Aye, and I wonder what excuse she'll have this time: a broken fingernail, a hair out of place or a scuffed shoe?' Emily leapt nimbly across a murky puddle of considerable proportions, lifting her gown to avoid a further soaking. 'Whatever her reason, she had better have finished that next batch of lacings since we've sold so many. It would be a pity to disappoint tomorrow's customers with so little choice remaining.'

They espied the man called Rook crossing the lane ahead of them: he was nigh impossible to miss being of such height, breadth and blackness of feature. He noticed them and doffed his cap courteously to the women.

'I never saw such a man before, did you Pen? Does he know you, Em?' Beattie asked, surprised at such a display of good manners.

'He is an acquaintance of mine; a friend of a friend.' Emily then explained how she knew Rook.

'And those gold-thread bookmarks of yours were an inspiration, Em,' Beattie said, returning to their previous conversation once her curiosity was satisfied. 'Little pieces of luxury that nigh anyone can afford and so pretty. The Prior of St Bartholomew's himself bought two to mark the pages in his missal, so he said, and Warden Clifford purchased one for his wife.'

'I too was surprised at how popular they were. Master Ameryk wants a dozen to take back to Bristol to sell but, of course, he asked me to reduce the price for buying that many, so he may make a goodly profit upon them. I said I might consider it, but only if any remain unsold at a higher price when the fayre is ended.'

'You'll make a wily woman of business, Em. Dame Ellen made a wise choice in deciding you should take over her work.'

'Why, thank you, Pen,' Emily said, blushing. Peronelle spoke so rarely, her words meant more than the casual exchanges of others. 'Well, here we are. What do you suppose Lizzie will have to say for herself?' Emily rapped on the door of Lizzie Knollys's house by St Leonard's church in Foster Lane. As a child, she recalled, Seb had lived just across the way.

After a third knock, the door was opened at last. Lizzie stood there, fresh as a periwinkle in her blue gown, quite untouched by rain or mud. It was galling indeed. She surveyed the women on her doorstep with a contemptuous air.

'You look like bedraggled rats,' she said by way of a greeting. Emily didn't bother to respond to the insult.

'We've come for the rest of the lacings you were supposed to be making,' she said, stepping over the threshold, followed by Beattie and Pen. 'I trust you finished Dame Ellen's order.'

'What if I haven't? What will you do about it, eh?'

'I tell you, Lizzie, when I take on Dame Ellen's business, *you* will not be receiving any out-work from me. You're too unreliable.'

'My lacings are the finest in London, Mistress High-and-Mighty, so it will be your loss, won't it? Besides, why should I want to work for you when I have far better prospects than that?'

Emily shrugged.

'That will suit me well enough. I dare say any new employer will tire of your idle ways in a short while. Now, where are the lacings?'

'Over there.' Lizzie waved at a basket in the corner. 'That's all I've had time to do.'

Emily found only seven in the basket, all of them yellow, so no choice of colours for the customers.

'Is this all?'

'Take them or leave them and remember: I want my fair share of the takings.'

'Only seven?' Emily asked, sorting through the contents of the basket. 'And this is all you have?' But it wasn't all, by any means. As she lifted away a skein of unused green silk thread, something dropped to the floor with a soft tap. She looked down. Shock was followed swiftly by anger. 'My pendant!' she cried, scooping it up. 'You thieving bitch, Lizzie Knollys! And look here: is this Pen's needle case? And this... and these...' Other items that had gone 'missing' of late were there in the basket, secreted away.

'Those are my snips,' Beattie said, snatching them and inspecting them for damage. 'I searched the house out for those, you wretched sow. And here they are. What else have you stolen, tell us that?'

'Those things are mine; all mine,' Lizzie shouted, backing away as the three women moved closer.

'I'm going to report you to the sheriffs if you don't return all the things you've stolen.' Emily continued to delve amongst the weaving materials. 'Look, here's a silver spoon and a fine knife with an enamelled handle. Where did you steal those from, Lizzie? And an amethyst ring. I wager that's not yours either.'

'Mind your own concerns, you nosy vixen,' Lizzie snarled, grabbing the basket from Emily and giving her a hard shove backwards.

Emily managed to keep her balance and pushed Lizzie in return. Beattie and Pen stepped up to aid Emily, but Lizzie grabbed Pen's cap and then her hair as it fell loose. All four women became involved in the scuffle. Lizzie clawed at Emily's face with her fingernails, drawing blood and leaving parallel gouges upon her cheek. Emily shrieked and tried to pull away, but they all overbalanced and went down in a heap by the cold hearthstone.

Slowly untangling themselves, the fight was over as soon as it had begun. Beattie got to her feet, straightened her bodice and took Emily's elbow to help her up.

'You'll need to put salve on your cheek. Those scratches look nasty,' she said.

Pen retrieved her cap and tried to restore her hair to some sort of respectable order.

'She's not moving,' she said softly, staring down at Lizzie sprawled on the floor.

'Astounded, I expect,' Beattie replied, prodding Lizzie's blue gown with a muddy shoe. 'Get up, you foolish creature. We're unconvinced by your mountebank's pretence.'

But Lizzie did not stir.

'Get up, Lizzie. Don't play the fool with us.' Emily bent down, intending to shake some sense back into her.

Lizzie groaned and moved her arm.

They all breathed a great sigh of relief, but didn't move to help her.

'Let's go home,' Emily said, putting her amber pendant about her neck, where it belonged. 'I have more important things to do than waste time on her.'

# The Foxley house

'Em!' I said, hastening to greet my wife at the side gate. 'I was looking out for you.' I put my arm around her shoulders. 'Come. Rose has made a fine supper, and we are waiting for you. What happened to your face, lass?' I paused and turned her to me, holding her towards the sinking sun that it might better illumine her features. 'The marks be deep, Em. How did you come by them?'

'An encounter with an overhanging briar when I slipped in some mud. It's naught.'

'It would be advisable to put some salve on it.'

'Beattie has told me that already,' she said in a sharp tone, shrugging out of my hold. 'I don't need you telling me what to do as well.' With that, she stalked into the kitchen, took little Dickon from his carrying basket and disappeared up the stairs with him.

'Em,' I called out to her, 'What of supper?' The only answer she gave was the distant sound of our bedchamber door slamming behind her. It seemed I was at fault yet again, but how I had erred, I could not say.

'Eat your supper, Seb,' Adam said, pushing my platter closer across the board. 'No reason to waste good food.' He cut a heel of bread in two and put half on my napkin, taking the remainder himself. 'This whitebait is excellent, Rose.'

'I wonder what be amiss with, Em,' I said, rearranging the tiny fishes in their buttery sauce upon the dish. 'Something has upset her. I hope 'tis not my doing.'

'Time of the moon's cycle, I dare say.' Adam took a generous swig of his ale. 'You know how women are, Seb: sometimes the least little thing will have them all a-pother. It'll pass. But what of your investigations this day? Have you uncovered the felons yet?'

''Tis not progressing well, I fear.'

'Master... if you ain't going t'eat yer fish, can I have it?' Jack gave me a hopeful look, and I passed him my supper.

'Rose? Is there some left for Em? She may be hungry later, after she has suckled the babe.'

'Aye. I'll put some by for her. And who wants cheese and gooseberry tart? Nessie, hand me that napkin, if you please.' Rose handled the hot dish with her usual skill and served up slices of the tart to us all. 'You will eat this, won't you, Seb? I made it especially, and it looks to me as though your clothes be hanging looser upon you every day.'

'I apologise, Rose,' I said. 'I intended no criticism of your fine cooking. I am not really hungry is all, but I will have some tart, thank you.' As I did my best to finish my portion – and it was very good – I could hear little Dickon wailing at the far end of the house. It was unlike him to cry for more than a few moments, yet the sounds continued. If Emily was attempting to comfort him, which no doubt she was, her efforts were receiving little reward. It seemed my wife was not alone in being out of sorts in her humours. I poured a cup of ale. 'I'll take this upstairs for her,' I said. 'She be most likely thirsty after nursing the babe.'

Cup in hand, I opened the chamber door. The circumstances were not as I had thought to find. Dickon was yelling from his cradle, unheeded, and Emily lay upon the bed, her head buried deep within the pillows. I set the cup down on the stool she used when changing the babe's tailclouts.

'Em, I brought you ale. Have you fed him? He sounds hungry to me.' She gave no answer, so I lifted Dickon from the cradle, and he quieted straightaway, nuzzling for milk against my jerkin. 'The babe is hungry, lass. Are you going to feed him?'

Having found a man's jerkin to be milkless, Dickon began to wail anew, protesting at the delay of his supper. I tried shushing him, bouncing him and singing to him, but only his mother could supply his needs. His tiny face was suffused red. There were no tears, just angry cries.

'Please, Em, he wants you to nurse him,' I said, sitting upon the bed and putting Dickon beside her. 'Come, sweetheart, whatever be amiss, 'tis not his fault.'

Of a sudden, she flung the pillows away and sat up.

'Why can you not leave me alone?' she demanded, putting the babe to her breast somewhat roughly, I thought.

'What be amiss, sweetheart?' A horrible thought occurred to me then. 'You're not ailing, are you, Em? You haven't taken some evil contagion, have you? Shall I fetch the surgeon straightway?'

'No. Why don't you just go away and leave me in peace? I don't want you, Seb. I don't want to see your self-righteous face any more. Get out.'

I said naught. What was there to say that would not serve but to make matters worse? With not the least notion as to how I had offended her so greatly, I left the chamber, closing the door softly after. My heart weighed like an anvil as I crept away, fearing the creak of a floorboard beneath my feet would increase my offence.


It was dark, but the air was cooler, fresher after the afternoon storm. The scent of wet herbs lay upon the breeze. The garden was a restful place, and I perched on the elder stump and gazed up at the velvet sky with its sprinkling of stars and the pale band of light we call the Virgin's Veil spread across the heavens.

'Found any answers up there?' Adam joined me, handing me a cup of ale.

'Nay. I suppose the Almighty knows them all, but I do not. Em be in a poorly way yet says not why.'

'Is she sick?'

'She says not. She has tear tracks down her face and swollen eyes, and I have my doubts concerning those scratches upon her cheek. No briar did that; they look more like wheel ruts and cut more deeply than any thorn.'

'Thorns can do damage indeed,' Adam said, and I recalled that his brother Noah had died by just such a means a year since.

'Aye, forgive me. I meant no flippant remark but, all the same, did they look like thorn scratches to you?'

'I did not see them closely but, in truth, no. A purposeful gouging seems more likely. Women fighting, mayhap? Using their fingernails?'

'You think Em may have had a quarrel with Beatrice and Peronelle?'

'The other one more like. The idle wench. What's her name? I can't recall it.'

'Lizzie Knollys,' I said, sipping my ale.

'Aye. That's her. Didn't seem to me that the others had much liking for her.'

'You may have the answer, Adam. It would explain Em's ill-humour and upset. I can but pray they mend their quarrel right swiftly. My peace of mind has been quite banished this day. If you have no objection, I will share your bedchamber this night.'

'Your peace of mind isn't all that's been banished then?'

I pulled a face.

'How can I refuse? It's your house, Seb. Just promise me you won't snore: I feel in need of a sound night's rest.'

'I doubt I shall sleep anyway, Adam. Being told that your wife does not wish to look upon you be unlikely to lead to sweet repose.'

'Em said that?'

'Her precise words to me were that she didn't want to see my self-righteous face any more.'

'Oh, by Saint Cross, you must have sinned grievously, Seb. What on God's earth have you done against her?' He patted my shoulder, and I was sure he was grinning in the darkness,

157

though there was not starlight sufficient to see and the moon was yet unrisen.

'I wish I knew, Adam. How may I make amends when I know not the crime I have committed?'

''Tis a tangled problem, Uncle,' he laughed, using our familial relationship as a jest, as always. But I'm certain you'll solve it soon enough. I'm away to my bed. Coming?'

In truth, it was neither a matter for jesting nor laughing, but he was doing his best to cheer me. Adam was a merry soul by nature and hated to see his fellows woe-begotten. It helped not at all.

'And what of your arm?' he continued as we mounted the outside stairway to his chamber. 'With so much crimson upon it, it looks grievous indeed.'

''Tis dragon's blood resin forming a shield to protect the wound. The apothecary assured me it was the best remedy.'

'You believe him?'

I shrugged.

'Mayhap. At least he refused payment for it, so I have wasted no coin, if it fails.'

'If it works, I shall wish I had known of it in poor Noah's case. If it might have saved him...'

'Do not dwell upon it, Adam. You did everything you could for your brother. You were not at fault. Do not be down-hearted. I suppose we both need cheering this night.'

'Aye, you're right.' My companion was silent for a few moments as we began to remove our attire and prepare for bed. 'Did I ever tell you about the time Noah fancied he had fallen in love? 'Tis such a tale as will make you laugh 'til your sides ache. The object of his desire was a lass so unlikely with a great wart like a carbuncle upon her nose and feet the size of kneading troughs...'

Already, my mouth was twitching at the corners.

# Chapter 10

## Thursday, the twenty-seventh day of August

EMILY WAS preparing to go out by the time I came down to breakfast with Adam.

'God's blessing upon you, lass. You be in haste so early?'

'I'd like to think you might care, but since you shunned my bed last night, I doubt that is so.' She fastened her apron about her waist with such vehemence I feared she might cut herself in twain.

'Em, you told me you did not want to see my face and to leave you in peace. I did as you wished is all. If you felt in need of company, you should have said, and I would have come to you willingly, you know that.'

'Do I? Well, 'tis too late now, husband.'

'Oh, Em, forgive me,' I said taking her hand only to have her pull it from my grasp.

'I have urgent matters to attend to,' she said. 'I've fed the babe, now you'll have to see to him.' And with that, she strode out of the kitchen.

'Have those scratches upon your cheeks seen to, Em,' I called after her, but I know not if she heard.

Emily hastened along Paternoster Row and into Cheapside. This early, there were few folk about, and she was glad of it, not wanting anyone to see the salty tears running down her face. She had thought about putting a salve on the gouges left by Lizzie's nails, but what was the point when tears would swiftly wash it away. Seb had failed to notice her distress, of course – wasn't that just typical? – but, in truth, she was unsure whether she wanted his sympathy or not. She wasn't sure of anything at present except that the terrible argument with Lizzie needed mending. It had played upon her mind all night, worrying about whether the foolish woman had been injured.

Nobody answered the door of the house in Foster Lane when she knocked. The stout stone wall of the abbey of St Martin le Grand loomed over the lane, and Emily glanced behind her, almost as though she feared God might be watching her from that hallowed place. She pushed the door and was somewhat surprised to find it was neither barred nor locked. Any miscreant might have walked in.

'Lizzie? Lizzie? Are you here?' Emily called out softly, not wanting to startle the woman if she was sleeping.

No answer came.

Emily entered the dimly lighted room where the shutters were closed. Someone must have shut them for they had been open yesterday afternoon. That was reassuring since Lizzie lived alone. It must be the case that she had recovered from her mishap. Even so, Emily had to brace herself to look towards the hearthstone, half fearful yet that Lizzie would be lying there, cold and stiff. She breathed an audible sigh upon seeing that there was naught to fear: no corpse nor any such indication that there might ever have been one.

'Blessed St Mary, thank you,' Emily whispered, making the sign of the cross. 'Lizzie, where are you?' she said more loudly. ''Tis your turn to work at the fayre this day and I want no excuses this time, you hear me?'

As before, there was no reply.

Emily searched the place. Everything looked much as it had yesterday, even to the ill-gotten contents of Lizzie's workbasket still in disarray. Naught had been touched, it seemed, but there was no sign of the woman. A ladder led up to a gallery above, an area half the size of the hall below. Emily went up, calling out again. The bed under the eaves was neat, the pillows plumped, and the coverlet straightened, but whether it was newly made or had not been slept in last night could not be determined. One thing was certain though: Lizzie Knollys was not at home.

Annoyance overcame relief as Emily returned home. She would not shed another tear for that idle and unreliable creature. If she was gone from her place in Foster Lane, then good riddance! With a new sense of resolve and no regrets, Emily determined to have a fine breakfast, tend to little Dickon and begin the working day anew and in good heart.

I was pleased to see Emily smiling when she returned, though the stripes upon her cheek looked an angry red. Knowing she would not take kindly to be reminded to attend them yet again, I fetched the pot of salve down from the shelf myself and removed its waxed linen cover.

'Let me put this on your cheek, Em, please. I cannot be easy until I know it has been treated to aid its healing.'

She looked about to protest, but then turned her face so I might smear it on. I did it gently as maybe and said naught concerning how sore and deep the gouges appeared. She neither winced nor gasped, but made all very bravely for it must have hurt her, however much care I took.

'And what is that upon your arm?' she asked, noticing for the first time the dragon's blood seal covering the injury to my wrist. I explained briefly without going into the gruesome details.

'Oh. We wondered what it was that the lightning had struck. An elm tree, you say? Beattie thought it might be St Paul's spire. Was anyone badly hurt?'

'Nay, lass. A few bumps and bruises were all. No worse than that, Lord Jesu be thanked.' I took my place at the board as we all gathered to break our fast and I included a prayer of thanks for our safe deliverance from the storm of yesterday when I said grace over our oatcakes and bacon collops.

'Seb,' Adam said, munching on an oatcake, 'I know our plans for visiting the fayre have all gone awry and you – rightly so – have forbidden the lads from going without one of us to give eye to them, but I would like to go myself, if you allow? I could take one of them for an hour or two and then return for t'other, if that will suffice. Rose and I talked it over, begging your pardon, Seb, and she is willing to oversee the shop, and whichever of the lads remains behind. You know customers have been very few this week. Would you be agreeable to our plan afore the fayre ends? I should hate to miss it entirely.'

I glanced at him. He was grinning, knowing he had backed me into a corner. Mayhap, I should have been annoyed at this conspiracy in my household, but it was no easy matter to be angry with Adam. The lads were gazing at me also, their faces a veritable picture of innocence, although I knew such an image was as false as the smile on a Bankside doxy.

'Well, I suppose...' I began but got no further.

'Thank you, master,' Tom said.

'We'll be'ave ourselves, won't we, Tom?' Jack added.

It seemed my authority was thwarted yet again.

'You had better,' I muttered, giving Adam a look which I hoped would serve as a silent reprimand. The Duke of Gloucester, my esteemed patron, could communicate an entire speech of reproof in a single glance, but I fear I had not acquired that particular skill because Adam laughed merrily and the lads joined him in excitement.

'Tom, I'll take you in a short while, then you, Jack, after dinner,' Adam said.

'But that's not fair,' Jack moaned. 'Why does Tom always get t'go first? It might rain like wot 'appened yesterd'y, and my visit'll be spoilt, won't it?'

'Come when I say, or not at all. 'Tis your choice.' Adam spoke sternly, and Jack fell silent, though his nether lip protruded ominously. Adam ignored him, telling Tom to fetch his purse, if he might wish to spend a few pence at the fayre.

Tom scampered off, poking his tongue at Jack in so rude a manner, I was nigh tempted to forbid this visit to the fayre after all. However, it did not seem worth the trouble that would most assuredly ensue if I did so: the lads' ill-will towards me would be disruptive to all concerned, so I let it pass. In truth, I would be heartily glad when this fayre closed on Saturday. As for my own problems – the necessity of solving two crimes – even they would be done with that day, whether I uncovered the perpetrators or not.

With breakfast done and Emily departed to the fayre, Rose in the shop, Jack working at carving book covers for my neglected *Aesop's Fables* and Nessie gone to the market for meat and worts for dinner, I sorted through the bits and pieces in my scrip. I read through the notes I had made at the scene of Gerrit's death, and the information gleaned from my enquiries – in truth, delaying my return to St Bartholomew's – when I discovered the sliver of stone or bone or whatever it was which I had found beside the Dutchman's body. On a whim, I took from my purse the shard that had pierced my wrist. Quite why I had kept it, I could not have said, but now I realised I was correct to have done so. The two were of the same material, if I was not mistaken, although I needs must borrow the Venetian merchant's scrying glass once more, in order to be certain. What did that mean, if it was so? That which had injured me had come from the pedlar's cart. Might he be the felon I sought? His cart would warrant a closer look indeed.

Beatrice arrived somewhat tardily at the silk-women's booth to find Emily had already opened the counter-board and their remaining wares for sale were all artfully displayed to best advantage.

'Forgive me, Em,' she puffed. 'What a morn I've had. Sick as a dog first thing, then a husband as can't find his best cap and a son who doesn't want to go to school because he would rather come to the fayre. I don't know why they can't close the school for a few days: I've seen more of his fellow pupils here than can be attending class.'

'Are you feeling better now, Beattie?' Emily asked, straightening her veil and arranging it close so as to conceal the worst of the scratches and be ready to serve customers. 'Does this look as it should? Does it hide my cheek?'

Beattie re-pinned a pleat in the snowy linen with a brass-topped pin and nodded approval.

'Aye, you are neat and spotless as ever, Em, but 'tis a pity there is no way to hide those claw marks on your face completely. Speaking of which: is the lazy bitch coming to help us this day?'

Emily shrugged.

'I don't know. I went to her house to rouse her, but she wasn't there.'

'Oh. You don't suppose...'

'Suppose what, Beattie?'

'I have no idea. Could she have moved out?'

'All her belongings were still there. I expect she had gone to market or to a neighbour's house.'

'At what hour did you go?'

'Right early, soon after it became light.'

'Too early for market or for visiting.'

'Aye. So what then? Where do you think she could be?'

'How should I know? You went to her house, Em: what do you think?'

'There was no sign of her... no blood...'

'Then she must be well enough. We have no need to worry, do we? She wasn't still there upon the floor. Did you look to the bed?'

'It was tidily made.'

'So she's not lying injured in her bed either. I admit, Em, after we left her yesterday, I was afeared that we might have...'

'Aye, Beattie, as was I. But that cannot be the case, can it? She couldn't have left the house if she was...'

'Dead?'

'Oh, don't even say that word! Of course, she isn't. But I was worried. I never slept a minute last night. That's why I had to go to her house so early. I had to know, Beattie. I just had to be sure.'

'Mm, well, we shall just have to wait and see what comes to pass, won't we? Look now, Em: our first customer... and oh, no, I have a stain upon my apron.' Beattie brushed at the mark to no avail.

'It won't notice if you stay behind the counter,' Emily whispered aside. 'God give you good day, sir.' She bobbed a little courtesy. 'How may I assist you?'


Adam, Tom and I, with Gawain trotting at my heel, entered the fayre ground.

''Tis a pity we can't see the poppets,' Tom moaned.

'Master Seb has let you come: be grateful for that,' Adam reproved him. 'Besides, I'm certain there will be any number of other entertainments to amuse a fine lad such as you.'

Adam winked at me, knowingly.

'Aye, indeed,' I said. 'Yesterday there was a wild-looking hedge-priest warning of hell-fire and damnation for us all and a relic-seller with feathers from the wings of the Archangel

Michael that anyone might purchase for a penny and a tooth-drawer whose services might be had for half the price.'

'I didn't come to see such things as those,' Tom said, his face creased in a frown. 'I want to watch acrobats and see the wonders from distant lands; not some mad preacher and a thieving feather-seller nor do I want my teeth pulled. You said there were...'

'Dancing girls and play-acting mountebanks? Talking popinjays and somersaulting dwarves?' I suggested.

'You didn't tell us lies about them being here, did you, master?'

'Nay, Tom. I would not lie. The sloe-eyed Salome who performs the dance-of-the-seven-veils usually appears beside that pie stall over there when St Bartholomew's bell tolls the hour, but you'll hear her plaintive piper play to summon a crowd afore time. The other acts move around. Fear not: there will be wonders aplenty for you.

'Now, I must be about my business on Master Fyssher's behalf, if I can find what I wrote last eve...' I rummaged in my scrip. I ought to bind my notes in a leather cover of some sort. Loose sheets of paper in such disarray were of assistance to no one. 'Ah. Indeed.' I found my list of tasks to accomplish this day. 'I have a certain pedlar's cart to inspect more closely. I shall leave you two to enjoy yourselves. Come, Gawain, you may earn your keep, lad, and put that fine nose of yours to good use.'

I saw the pedlar over by the Horse Pool, not far from the site of yesterday's lightning strike. The blackened bough still lay where it had fallen, and I could see now that the elm tree had been split asunder down its trunk. One charred half leaned away from the other, and the scent of burned wood lingered still upon the summer air. I doubted the tree would recover from such an assault, its leaves crisped and scorched beyond revival.

I kept my distance and watched the pedlar. He had hammer in hand and nails in his mouth, protruding like boars' tusks, as he worked to repair his damaged cart. The corner of the cart had been smashed when the tree had fallen, and he was making good the base and sides with short planks, nailing them over the broken bits. It was a bodged job, but would probably serve for now. He had stacked his wares for sale upon the grass and covered them with a canvas sheet while he mended the cart. I could not think that he would sell anything, keeping it hidden thus.

I approached warily for I did not much like the fellow after his reaction to my offer of aid the previous afternoon.

'God's blessings be upon you,' I said. 'Are you quite recovered from the lightning bolt?'

'What d'you care?' he said, mumbling around the nails betwixt his lips.

'I came to help you when the tree fell.'

'You, was it?' He removed the nails and eased his back. 'What d'you want now? My thanks in bloody coin, I s'pose? In which case you can go swing on a gibbet for all I care. Now, bugger off. I'm busy.'

'I want neither gratitude nor coin. I wished to know that you were well, is all. And, if you have any for sale, I would purchase a few ink- and pigment-pots from you.' I lifted the canvas from his pile of goods. It was true: I would buy some pots from him, but I had greater interest in other things. I stared at what lay there on the grass, but then I was pulled back with considerable violence by a strong, calloused hand on my arm – the same as had been pierced by the splinter previously. I cried out in pain and alarm.

Gawain sprang to my aid and received a mighty kick for his trouble.

'Get away from there, you meddling bastard busybody!' The pedlar held the hammer raised high. 'You want your damned skull smashed too? Leave my stuff alone. And get that bloody cur away from my stuff.'

I stepped away, holding my arm.

'I meant no offence. Come, Gawain; come away now.'

The fellow lowered the hammer and removed his shapeless cap to mop his brow.

'Bugger off, like I told you, Foxley. And stay away, if you know what's good for you.'

I was eager enough to do exactly as he ordered, but I would return – with Gabriel, Rook and Bailiff Thaddeus Turner. All the clues had come together in those few moments, but were they sufficient to secure a conviction, I wondered. And he knew my name: how might that be? Somewhat belatedly, I made my way to the Venetian merchant's tent, to beg the use of his scrying glass once more, although I was now certain of what its discerning eye would reveal.

Customers had been visiting the silk-women's booth in a constant stream all morning, so Emily and Beatrice were heartened when Peronelle arrived, bearing a brimming ale jug.

'What a welcome sight you are, Pen,' Emily said, taking the cups from the coffer behind the counter-board. 'We have been busy indeed. Your ribbons are all sold, and only one of Beattie's trimmed veils remains. I fear Lizzie's stuff – her lacings and plunket ribbons – have not sold so well. That colour is not much liked, it seems.'

'And still no sign of her ladyship, much as we expected,' Beattie's tone was scornful.

'She is all right… after what happened, isn't she?' Pen looked somewhat scared.

'Aye, she'll do well enough, that useless cow. Fear not, Pen. She's taken herself off somewhere. Finally realised that we have not time to spare for her idle sort. We'll be better without her – and get a greater share of the profits. Why should she get a penny?' Beattie swallowed her ale and smacked her lips appreciatively, putting a comforting arm around her friend's narrow shoulders. 'Don't worry, the likes of the ungodly Lizzie Knollys always survive. She probably spent the night in some ne'er-do-well's bed in Cock Lane, if you take my meaning.'

'I see I arrived at an opportune moment,' Dame Ellen said. The old woman was breathless and flushed of face. 'This heat be a torment to me.' She handed Emily a basket and then flapped her apron to make a cooling draught.

Emily gave the good dame her cup of ale and hastily set a stool for her to rest upon.

'What have you brought us, Dame Ellen?' she asked, uncovering the basket.

'More wares to sell and just in time by the look of it. Your stall is looking quite sparse. I went all the way to Thames Street yester morn, before the storm, mercifully, and collected stuff from old Agnes Shipton. You remember her? She's most infirm these days, but still does a fine hand's turn with the silk. And Katherine Champyon – my apprentice before your time, Emily – brought some work to me last eve. I've paid them both outright for their goods, so they will not be sharing the profits. Speaking of which, where is our other sharer?'

'If you mean Rose, she will be here this afternoon,' Emily said, shaking out a beautifully embroidered tablecloth. 'This is exquisite!'

'I told you Agnes can still produce fine stuff and, no, I did not mean Rose Glover. I meant Mistress Knollys, as you well know, Emily. Do not be obtuse with me.'

'She hasn't done a minute's worth of work here all week, dame, and that is no lie. Beattie and Pen will confirm the truth of what I say.'

The others nodded.

'In which case, she shall receive payment for her labour in making the goods and not a penny of the profits. I hope you've kept account of all such matters, Emily?'

'I have. 'Tis all noted down.'

A fine lady, accompanied by a trio of liveried servants, was approaching them, stepping daintily among the tussocks of grass. A waft of expensive perfume preceded her.

'Look to your offices, girls: a customer comes!' Dame Ellen announced unnecessarily, remaining upon her stool to observe how her employees conducted themselves with a client of high status – which the lady was, no doubt.

One of her servants stepped up to the counter-board.

'My lady will look at your ribbons,' he announced with an air so pompous Emily had difficulty stifling a giggle. 'Display them at once.'

'With pleasure, sir,' Emily said, producing the basket Dame Ellen had brought along and sorting through it. 'We have these fine blue ones.' She smoothed them out so the sun shimmered off their glossy surface. 'And crimson. What about this shade of tawny? It will match my lady's gown perfectly. Or the deep green, maybe? This paler green is quite a pretty hue also. What would my lady prefer?'

The servant glanced over his shoulder at the lady who gave an imperious wave that might have signified almost anything.

'We will take a pair of each colour,' he said, interpreting the gesture.

'That will be one shilling precisely, if you please?' Emily folded the ribbons and wrapped them in a square of linen.

'Put them on account. My lord will settle it come the week's end, when the fayre closes.'

'And who might your lord be, sir?'

'Such impertinence! How dare you ask? Do you not recognise my livery?'

'No, sir, I do not,' Emily said. 'Neither does the fayre permit credit. You could be a band of mountebanks out to gull simple traders like us. Come back for the ribbons when you have the coin. Good day to you, sir.'

His eyes grew so wide, it seemed that might start from his head.

'Well!' he exclaimed and spun on his heel. No doubt he intended a highly affronted exit, but it was spoilt utterly when he trod on the long pike of his shoe and went sprawling, landing flat on his face before his lady.

'Barnaby! You stupid idiot,' the 'lady' screeched, clipping Barnaby across the ear. 'You've ruined the whole thing. I wanted those ribbons. Get up now. You'd better make your role as Cupid an improvement on that this afternoon. I don't know why Matthew hired a wastrel like you.'

'Come, Simon, come away now,' one of the other 'servants' urged, and the party then made haste to disappear into the crowds before the silk-women could summon the constables.

'Play actors! I never saw the like, did you, Pen?' Beattie looked horrified. 'And to think they nearly walked away with our best ribbons. You did right not to let them, Em. Mind you, my heart almost leapt from my chest when you demanded to know his lord's name. I thought you'd lost all sense of propriety and courtesy.'

'You forget, Beattie, I've had dealings with the servants of His Grace, Richard, Duke of Gloucester – may God smile upon him. His servants are ever courteous and mannerly. I knew at once this was no lady and her servants. Besides...' Emily hid her laughter behind her hands. 'When did you last see a fine lady with the toes of her shoes cut away to make them fit and stubble upon her chin?'

'Truly? I didn't notice. Are you telling me she was a man? And to think I could be so mistaken.' The women were laughing heartily; even Dame Ellen was rocking with mirth upon her stool, when Rose arrived, laden with bread, cheese and cold meats for their dinner and to allow Emily to return home to feed the babe.


Afore I should accuse the pedlar of thievery or any worse crime, I had to make certain that the splinter from my wrist – which injury still wore a protective coat of dragon's blood – and the shard that I found beside poor Gerrit's skull were of the same substance. To my unaided eye, they looked as one, but I would use the scrying glass to be sure of it. I also needed to sit quietly and think through what had been revealed to me. The full meanings of the facts must be deliberated upon. For one: the pedlar had addressed me by name during our most recent encounter. How did he know me? I had never told him my name. Had he made enquiries concerning me, I wonder, and if he had, then why might I be of interest to him? The problem was perplexing indeed.

I made my way to the Venetian merchant's tent. His expression as I approached him was of weariness at sight of me. No doubt he was finding my visits tiresome, yet he forced a smile of sorts to greet me. We made brief but courteous exchanges – in Latin – and then he asked my business at his stall. In the midst of my explanation as to why I wished to borrow his scrying glass yet again, he began shaking his head. The glass had been sold to another customer! I was taken aback, never expecting such a hindrance to my investigations. Did he have other similar items? Could he recall who had purchased it? Did he know of any other merchant at the fayre who might sell such glasses? No, he did not. It appeared that particular road of enquiry was now barred to me, but mayhap, all was not lost.

Seated in a patch of shade betwixt the Venetian's tent and the booth next to it, I took out my silver-point and a sheet of paper from my scrip and made a sketch. With as few lines as possible, I drew a likeness that would serve my purpose.

At Master Ameryk's stall, I was heartened to find both Gabriel and Rook were present.

'Good day to you, Gideon,' I said, not forgetting to address him by his assumed name. 'Do you fare well this day?'

He grinned his lop-sided grin, revealing his tooth of walrus ivory to be in place.

'Hail and well met, Sebastian,' he said, touching his battered cap. 'How may we aid you or are you visiting for friendship's sake?'

'A little of both. I have a mind to ask Rook a question concerning a fellow who visited your stall more than once afore the unicorn horns were stolen.'

'Ask what you will, master.' Rook turned towards me upon hearing his name. 'If it aids the returning of our precious things...'

'In truth, that may not be possible, I fear. But we may apprehend the thief.'

'That would be something, at least,' Gabriel said. 'Better than naught.'

'Aye, better indeed if, as I believe, he also slew poor Gerrit, the poppet-master,' I added. 'Pray tell me again, Rook, all you can recall of the man who caught your notice in coming to the stall repeatedly.'

Rook obliged me and his description remained, word for word, as afore and just as vague. Yet it fitted.

'Might this be in any way a likeness of the fellow?' I gave my sketch to Rook. Unexpectedly, he took one glance and dropped the drawing, stepping away with a cry.

'Answer him, Rook,' Gabriel told him. 'Could this be the rogue?'

I retrieved the sketch and offered it to Rook for a second look, but he shied away from it, as if it was laced with venom.

'I know not how you imprison him on the page, but you have the man I saw.'

Black-skinned as he was, I swear Rook had turned paler.

''Tis but a drawing,' I explained, yet he wanted naught to do with me and moved away in haste. 'Has he never seen a likeness afore?' I asked Gabriel.

Gabriel shrugged.

'It seems not, but he says that is the man. Since you drew him, I realise you must know who he is?'

'Mayhap I do, but there be little evidence to proclaim his guilt for certain, except for these.' I took the splinter and the shard from my purse and held them out in the palm of my hand

173

for Gabriel to see. 'Could these be flakes from the unicorns' horns, do you suppose? You know how they looked, but I never saw them, if you remember. Please do not confirm it though, if you have the slightest doubt.'

'That scrying glass you used before would be helpful.'

''Tis no longer available, unfortunately,' I said with a sigh. 'Upon this occasion, I had decided I should buy the glass outright, rather than pay the merchant's exorbitant fee for hiring it, but I was too tardy, and someone else has purchased it. We will have to do our best without it, as men did afore such wonders were invented.'

My friend held them up to the light, then took them into the shade of the awning above the counter-board, squinting and screwing up his eyes.

'I cannot say, Seb. These days, my eyes are excellent for espying ships afar off, but not so good for such fine details close to.' Gabriel looked most serious and concerned.

'Oh, well... it was worth trying. Yet Adam and Tom saw the horns also, did they not? They may be hereabouts somewhere. Perhaps their eyesight might be keener than yours?'

'Don't trouble to seek them out, my friend,' Gabriel said. 'I have something that may serve us.' He unfastened his purse, his fingers questing around inside it for a long while.

'I'll find Adam...' I was becoming impatient.

'Ah! I have it here.' Gabriel took out something wrapped in linen. It was large enough that it was impossible he could not have found it straightway in his purse. He was grinning that lop-sided, mischievous grin of his as he removed the cloth with a flourish, like a sorcerer producing a popinjay from an empty box.

'The scrying glass! You bought it! Gabriel, you be a teasing rascal of the first order.'

He was laughing so loudly, folk were turning to discover the cause of so much mirth.

'Hush! 'Tis Gideon, remember?'

'*Mea culpa.* Forgive me. The shock of the moment caused me to forget you be a new man now. But I doubt you be in any danger; no one here remembers those times.'

'I pray God you're right, Seb, but don't make that error again, I beg of you. And no more church Latin, either. It offends God and me.'

'You still hold to those, er, beliefs?' I almost said 'heretical' beliefs.

'Of course. You think my close brush with death would change me? God saved me from the fire that day through you: His instrument of my escape. That proved to me that my beliefs as a Known Man, aye, *known* to God, are the truth for all time. I have prayed that you, as my friend, may also come to see the truth. It saddens me that such a revelation has not yet come to pass, but maybe God has plans for you...

'However, before we use the glass to examine your finds, Seb, I would see your drawing.'

Gabriel looked at my sketch.

'There is something about the fellow that seems familiar.'

''Tis likely you have seen him here at the fayre. Rook noticed what he called his 'colourless, shapeless cap' as I have drawn it. It looks to be knitted from wool cheaply dyed, mayhap with madder dye of poorest quality, I would hazard a guess.'

Gabriel rubbed at his bearded cheek.

'No, Seb, I think I knew him from a time before now. In some other place...'

'When he spoke to me – most discourteously, I must say – he sounded London-born to my ear. Strangely though, he knew my name. I cannot say how, but he did. Someone must have mentioned me to him for some unaccountable reason, since I be certain I know him not.'

'May the Good Lord God save us, Seb!' Gabriel clutched my arm so tightly that I winced for the pain in my wrist. 'I know this demon. He once proclaimed himself to be one of us: a Known Man. He kept the Pewter Pot tavern where we used to meet. Then, like Judas, he betrayed us all. You may recall, we took him and his traitorous fellows aboard my brother's ship, the *St Christopher*.'

'Aye, and when I lately asked of you what happened to them, you said you left them on some foreign coast.' I pulled free of his grasp, but he seemed unaware. I eased my wrist.

'We did but, mayhap, the rogue has made his way back to London.'

'Do you recall his name?'

'How could I e'er forget it? 'Tis Roger Underwood.'

'Then we may inform the constables and have the felon arrested and held to account.'

'We can't, Seb.'

'What? But he most likely killed Gerrit and stole your unicorn horns. You cannot let him get away with such crimes. We must tell the authorities, Gabriel.'

'He knows me, Seb, knows me from my old life. I would likely be joining him in gaol, aye, and upon the scaffold as an escaped prisoner or in the fire as a heretic. Would you condemn me too, old friend?'

I stared at him, my mind reeling and my conscience cleaved in twain upon the sharp horns of a dilemma.

# Chapter 11

## Later that Thursday

E MILY HAD gone home to feed little Dickon by the time I went to the silk-women's stall. I admit I was not in the best of humours, not knowing how to solve my dilemma. I hoped to discuss it with Emily, although I knew what she would say. Having so great a liking for Gabriel, she would readily agree with his solution that it was best to say naught to anyone about the wretched pedlar, Roger Underwood, for fear of imperilling our friend's life. That was understandable, of course, but it would permit a guilty man to go free.

Even when I insisted to Gabriel that we should compare those two shards from what I suspected to be the precious unicorns' horns – and they did indeed prove to be of the same appearance and texture – he desired to pursue the matter no further, to discover whether the pedlar had the remaining horns hid within his cart. This surprised me, knowing how valuable they were to Master Ameryk. To forego their recovery showed how fearful Gabriel must be that Underwood might reveal his former identity.

In truth, he had gone to the length of deciding he would return to *The Eagle,* his ship moored at Queenhithe, and remain aboard for all the while Master Ameryk chose to remain in London. My friend was sore afraid, as I had never known him afore, not even during his trial on charges of heresy. Then he had been so courageous, certain God would protect him as a Known Man, but not this time. I wondered what had changed.

It was after the hour for dinner. I had not eaten, but neither was I hungry, yet I wandered among the various food-stalls, hoping to find Adam. And there he was with Jack. Clearly, Adam had taken Tom back to the workshop and fetched Jack to take his turn, visiting the fayre. The pair were tucking into large pasties. Gravy dripped from the lad's chin, and Adam's beard was serving most admirably as a crumb-catcher. Just as a larger piece of pie-crust fell from Adam's dinner, Gawain was there to make certain it was not wasted. He wolfed it down and then sat, tail pounding the grass, awaiting more, his eyes following every movement of Adam's hands.

'You would have me feel guilty, Gawain, for enjoying my pie? I know you will not cease looking at me with those pleading eyes 'til I succumb and give you the rest. Your dog is a rogue, Seb, won't let a man eat in peace.'

'I know it well. Jack, go and enjoy yourself. I would speak privily with Adam.'

Both looked at me in surprise, as well they might after all my strictures concerning the lads being forbidden to attend the fayre, without Adam or me to watch over them.

'What's amiss, Seb?' Adam asked when Jack had gone, racing off into the throng of folk, my warnings concerning good behaviour unheard. 'What has come to pass that you break your own rulings?' He threw the remains of his pie to Gawain, and it disappeared even more swiftly than Jack had done.

'In short, Adam, I believe I have solved a murder and a theft, but have been implored to do naught concerning either. I would ask your opinion...'

I related to Adam my findings, the few certainties and the more numerous suspicions I had concerning the killer of the Dutch poppet-master, the fate of the unicorn horns and Gabriel's urging that I should not inform Master Fyssher, the sheriffs or Bailiff Thaddeus Turner of my discoveries. Adam listened attentively as we sat in the shade of the priory wall, made unsavoury by the effluent from the reredorter on the other side. At least here we were well away from any other interested ears since none could bide the stink for too long.

'Now you have told me, let's move to some sweeter spot. I cannot think with such a reek in my nostrils.' Adam took my arm and dragged me well away from the wall to a stall that was selling cups of cordial. 'What will you have, Seb?' he asked me.

I shrugged, uninterested.

He paid coin to a woman of most generous proportions in a tattered apron and handed me a treenware cup.

''Tis elderflower. I can consider the facts better over a drink.' He quaffed deeply from his cup and sighed with pleasure afore falling silent.

I sipped my cordial and found it cool and refreshing. I was somewhat thirsty after all.

'In truth, Seb,' he said after some lengthy pause for thought, 'I don't see that you have any choice in this matter. Whatever your friend's situation, a dead man is deserving of justice. Where would we be if we did but pick and choose which crimes should be punished and which not? 'Tis not our place... 'tis not even Christian to let a murderer go free.' He drained his cup and wiped his mouth on the back of his hand. 'When all's said and done, you must tell the authorities, Seb. I'm no lawyer but, elsewise, that makes you an accessory to the crime after the fact, does it not? Tell me, if I'm mistaken, but I believe that to be the case. You'll share this devil Underwood's guilt if you don't unmask him, and you'll have it upon your conscience forever.'

'But what of Gabriel? I risked the lives of our entire household to save him but a few years since. Are our past efforts to be for naught now, if the authorities arrest him once more?'

'I know 'tis a hard decision to make, Seb, but if you tell Master Fyssher the barest facts, enough for him to order Underwood's apprehension so the wretch cannot escape, then – you know how slowly such matters of law may progress –

Gabriel will have departed London for Bristol by that time. Anything the pedlar says afterwards cannot be used to indict him, can it? Besides, the felon has knowledge of someone by the name of Gabriel Widowson and who is he? I know him not. Master Gideon Waterman is an acquaintance of mine and yours, but not this other fellow.'

'Aye, 'Tis true. You give me wise counsel indeed, Adam. I am grateful to you. Will you come with me to Master Fyssher's chamber at Guildhall? It is not far, but a few streets over from Aldersgate.'

'If you wish me to, but what of Jack let loose upon the fayre? Should I not seek him out first before he finds some mischief or other?'


Jack wandered around, enraptured by the wonders of the fayre. A group of minstrels played fine music. They were not brash jongleurs making more noise than melody, but a lute-player and a harpist, their sweet airs joyful on the breeze. He purchased some of the rosewater sweetmeats Master Seb had bought a few days since, but now he wouldn't have to share them with that greedy oaf Tom. He spent time watching a troupe of acrobats, observing their antics with a knowledgeable eye. There was a time, long years ago now, after Ma had died all untimely – he'd always told how the family had died of plague, though that wasn't true, it was the better tale – when he and his sister Maudie had run away. They'd joined a band of acrobats, so Jack could tell who among the contortionists and jugglers had real talent and who could just get by. The rope-walker was no good at all. Wobbling was one thing, a bit of showmanship to make the crowd gasp at the great difficulty of such a feat, but this idiot fell off – twice. Jack felt tempted to show them a thing or two of his own abilities, but feared he was unpractised and might look foolish if he made a mess of things.

Maudie. She'd been sold off to a fat merchant in Cambridge or somewhere while Jack had stayed with the band on the way to London and there he determined to make his own way in life. It hadn't been easy until he'd helped Master Seb to save his brother, but now, mayhap, it was time to move on again. He wasn't meant to be a scrivener nor a book-binder nor a wood-carver. He might go back to being an acrobat, but this time he wouldn't be a little lad mistreated and half-starved. Now he was a man grown – well, nearly so – and would take charge of his own destiny.

All the while, he kept an ear open for the piper who, upon the hour, would announce the performance of the dance-of-the-seven-veils, over by the pie stall. He didn't want to miss that. Tom had said she was a luscious beauty – whatever that meant – and a fruit ripe for the plucking. At least he knew what that meant well enough.

Just then, the crowd jeered and heckled as the rope-walker fell off a third time and, as soon became clear, had suffered a hurt, such that he could not continue. A bald fellow stepped forth and began apologising that the show must end afore time.

'I'll do it,' Jack called out without thinking, slipping off his shoes and dashing towards the low slung rope. He paused momentarily to prepare himself and then grabbed the pole at one end and stepped up, catching the rope betwixt his big and second toes. He hadn't forgotten how after all. He ran to and fro along its length a few times and then stopped in the middle, bracing himself before leaping and turning a somersault, to land cleanly without a wobble. He did more turns and some fancy footwork, thinking what a pity it was Maudie wasn't here so they could do their act as they used to. Then with a double somersault, he flipped backwards to land on the grass, completing the act with hand-springs and a final cartwheel before taking his bow. He was grinning broadly and not even out of breath.

The bald fellow came over, a hat full of coin in hand. He took out a handful and gave them to Jack.

'You earned them,' he said. 'You want to join us? We leave on Monday. I need a new rope act; Kit's wrecked his knee and was never much good anyway. Pay's reasonable and the company's friendly. You'll get to see faraway places and perform for kings and princes. A good-looking lad like you could do very well for himself.'

'I'll fink on it, won't I?' Jack said and meant what he said.

Then the piper by the pie stall began to play and, of a sudden, his thoughts turned to veils and their artful removal. He darted off to ensure a good place to view the fayre's best spectacle.


An hour and more later, a band of us was searching the fayre for sight of Underwood. I had explained my deductions to the deputy coroner – without saying that Gabriel had identified the miscreant from my drawings – and shown the sketch to all concerned and also the slivers of unicorn horn. Armed with a sheriff's warrant, Bailiff Turner and two constables, assisted by Adam and me with Gawain – aye, and Jack – traipsed among the stalls, looking out for that infamous shapeless, colourless knitted cap. We did not find our quarry, for which fact I was secretly relieved, but we did find the pedlar's cart, abandoned.

It had not moved from its earlier position on the far side of the Horse Pool, and I now saw why it was so. Although repairs of a sort had been made to the body of the cart, I had not noticed previously that one wheel had also suffered damage when the tree bough crashed down upon it.

Jack rushed to search the canvas-covered heap of the pedlar's wares, though it was considerably smaller than when I first saw it earlier that day.

'The fellow must have taken as much as he could carry. Mayhap, he will return for the rest of it,' I said.

'Don't fink so, master.' Jack held out a cracked pot, a dented pewter ewer with a loose handle and a tangle of frayed laces. 'I wouldn't come back fer rubbish like wot this is, would I?' He dropped the items and burrowed deeper, into a pile of linen rags, soiled and stained. 'But I might fer this...' There, in my apprentice's grubby hand was a length of pale horn.

'Well done, Jack,' I said. 'Pass it to Bailiff Turner, if you will.'

'Is this the unicorn's horn we've heard so much about?' the bailiff asked, running admiring hands along its ornately twisted whiteness.

'I have not seen them,' I admitted, 'But Adam has: what say you, cousin?'

'There were three horns, and the shortest of them was not so short as this. Even so, this is certainly part of what I saw on Master Ameryk's ship when we visited. Do you agree, Jack?'

Jack gave no answer as yet for he delved a second time among the unwholesome cloth and found another piece, narrow and pointed and of about one foot in length.

Thaddeus Turner reached out to take it, but I espied two features of interest upon it.

'Hold a moment,' I said. 'Permit me to examine it more closely. Set it down on the canvas, Jack, please.' I knelt beside it and took out both the slivers of horn and the scrying glass that Gabriel had given me so generously. I made a careful comparison: the pointed spike of horn that had pierced my wrist did not match, but the small slice I had found beside poor Gerrit's broken skull fitted precisely into a place where the twist of ivory was missing. The scrying glass did not lie: this horn had beaten the Dutchman and, what was more, though I could not prove it, brown smears besmirching the tip and a hand's-span below it looked to me to be blood. Master Fyssher would be delighted to learn of the great value of this murderous weapon, despite it being no reflection of the felon's wealth. Thus, the amercement to be demanded as a fine afore the wretch paid the ultimate penalty could not be as high as the authorities might hope. But that was no affair of mine. The authorities would have to hunt down Gerrit's killer now: my task was done, thanks be to God.

'How could you do such a terrible thing, Sebastian!' Emily screeched at me when I spoke of what had come to pass that afternoon. The next moment, a pot of scorching pottage, straight off the fire, landed in my lap. I cried out as the boiling mix of oatmeal and herbs soaked through my shirt, and the pot burned my thighs. I leapt to my feet.

'Love of God, Em! Will you burn me to death? Get this off me.'

Rose, Adam and Jack scrambled to aid me in stripping off my attire, including my hose right down to my nether clouts, so Nessie passed me yesterday's unwashed shirt and drawers from the laundry basket to cover myself. Pottage splattered the wall, the bench, the board and the floor, oozing from the dented cauldron pot among the rushes.

My skin was crimson across my chest, belly and thighs. It was painful indeed, but Rose sent the lads out to the garden in search of snails. They found a dozen of them, mercifully, and Adam was swift to help me in smearing their slime upon my burns to ease them. I would be sore for days, but at least no blisters had erupted that I could see.

Eventually, I resumed my seat at the board, resplendent, I realised, in Adam's dirty shirt and Tom's drawers. I suppose, I must be grateful none belonged to Jack – but then why would they? He rarely changed his linen without a deal of nagging from the womenfolk. I wondered if I might expect an apology from my wife for her unruly and unmannerly conduct, but one glance at her face, set like a stone gorgon, warned that naught of the kind would be forthcoming. And

I dare say I was likely to be sharing Adam's chamber for a second night.

In the meantime, Gawain cleared away the spilt pottage, once it had cooled sufficiently, and we supped on bread, ewes' milk cheese and what remained to be scraped from the bottom of a honeypot. It was not much of a meal, and I had hardly eaten all day, but my discomfort of both body and mind drove aside any feelings of hunger.

Not so the others. Tom and Jack complained loudly but briefly as Emily struck the pair of them across their backs with her broom as they sat staring at their bare platters.

'An empty belly this once won't harm either of you fat, idle rascals,' she yelled. 'Now go to your beds. I'll hear not another word from you.'

'Em... no more of this, I beg you. They be young and enjoy their meat. Have pity...'

My words were cut short.

'Don't tell me what to do! You dare to put our dearest friend's life in peril by your actions this day; I should beat you black and blue with my broom. You endanger Gabriel at every turn. How could you? You heartless, wicked, thoughtless, unholy, misbegotten...' My wife ran out of breath and cast aside her broom with a clatter upon the floor. She stood there, arms folded, breathing heavily.

'*I* advised Seb to go to the authorities,' Adam said, coming to my rescue. 'If he hadn't, he would be accounted guilty of aiding and abetting a felon. He could hang for that. Is that what you want, Emily? To be left a widow-woman with a fatherless babe?'

I laid a restraining hand on his arm.

'Leave be. 'Tis said and done now.' Weary and hurting, I spoke softly, wanting no more heated words, strife and argument.

'We did very well on the stall this afternoon,' Rose said to no one in particular, mayhap hoping to divert our thoughts. 'We sold so much that we have little left for sale tomorrow. Beattie thinks we shall likely have naught remaining by dinnertime and be able to close up the stall early. We won't open at all on Saturday, which will be a shame as it's the final day of the fayre; I should have liked to be there at the last. Beattie says the final day is always the merriest with the entertainers doing their very best to earn a few more coin to tide them over until they find a new place to perform.'

'Did Mistress Knollys come this day at all to do her share?' I asked Rose, keeping the conversation upon a subject far removed from Gabriel and my work for Master Fyssher.

'No. We never saw so much as her shadow passing. I asked Beattie if she might be unwell, but she said the matter was best left alone... which seemed a strange thing to say, but 'tis none of my business.' Rose was stacking platters ready to wash, waiting as the water heated upon the fire.

Emily said naught, but lifted the babe from his basket and went upstairs to feed him, I assumed, but dared not enquire.

Once she went hence, the kitchen was, of a sudden, a more benign place to be and we all breathed more easily. My wife's ill-humour discomforted the whole household. I felt the tension in my body easing too: I had not realised I was holding my spine rigid as a pike-stave. Had I truly been so wrong in my actions this day? I did not believe I had but, clearly, Emily saw the matter otherwise – as women often do.

It occurred to me then that I was still bare-legged and quite unseemly in the presence of Rose and Nessie. I ought to put on some hose at least. But they were in the clothes press in our bedchamber, and it risked another confrontation if I ventured there. Yet it was my bedchamber also. Was this not my house? I had as much right to go where I pleased within it. I pushed back the bench and stood up.

'You going to the tavern?' Adam asked. 'We could get a pie and bring it back to share, if they have any still.'

'Like this?' I gestured at my state of undress.

'Might excite the wenches,' he laughed.

'Make them swoon in horror most likely.' My pale, spindle-shanks would enamour no woman and give the menfolk cause for jesting until Christmastide at least. 'But by all means, Adam, see if you can buy a pie from some tavern or cookshop, if you may. Take coin from my purse.' I turned and made to go up the stairs.

'Is that wise?' he asked.

I shrugged.

'I be in need of clean clothes.'

'Your purse is covered in pottage.' He held out my girdle belt with the purse attached all covered in the greenish mess that should, by rights, have been our supper. The fine leather of both looked to be ruined.

'I do not doubt but the coins within can be spent all the same, even if you must wash them first.' With that, I mounted the stairs in trepidation.

At our chamber door, I raised my hand to knock, but why should I? I braced my shoulders and entered, making straight for the clothes press by the window. From the corner of my eye, I saw my wife was sitting on the bed, the hangings drawn part way. Little Dickon lay in his cradle, wide awake, waving his tiny fists and blowing bubbles of spittle. He seemed content, and I bent to stroke his downy head. I felt Emily's eyes upon me as if they would bore into my flesh, but she said not a word. I raised the press and found a clean shirt, drawers and grey hose. They were my Sunday best ones, but I found them first and had no intention of sorting through the linen to find a workaday pair. I removed my borrowed nether clouts and began to dress. With my clean drawers in place, as I tied them close, Emily confronted me.

She threw my fresh shirt and hose aside.

'Why do you harm Gabriel in every way you can, you wretch? Why do you hate him so? Tell me!' She glared at me, and I could see she trembled with rage.

'Harm him? Hate him? The man is my friend. You make no sense, woman. Calm yourself, else your milk will curdle.'

'I am calm!' she shrieked, thumping my naked chest – already crimson from the hot pottage – with her fists.

I caught her wrists and held her fast though she tried to twist free of my grasp. Then I saw it dangling from her hand: the amber pendant Gabriel had sent as a gift for her from one of his Baltic voyages.

'You found it then? Where was it, Em?' The golden gem swung upon its leather thong betwixt us. 'I be so glad you found it.'

'Don't lie to me. You're jealous that he gave it to me. You'd like to cast it in the Thames so it cannot remind me of him.'

'Why should I be jealous? I be happy that you always have some keepsake of Gabriel. He is a fine man and a dear friend to us both. I do not understand you, Em. Now, I pray you, permit me to dress.'

'The authorities will be hunting him down now, thanks to you.'

'They will not. Roger Underwood alone might reveal Gabriel as a one-time Known Man yet he has not been apprehended and likely never will be. The miscreant is probably miles away from London by now, halfway to York or some such place afar. Gabriel has returned to his ship in any case. He is safe, Em, safe as he can be. You fret needlessly concerning him.' I tilted her chin so I might see her face. 'Look at me, Em.'

Reluctantly, she did so. Her eyes were swollen with too much shedding of tears.

'What be truly amiss, lass? You worry for our friend, but 'tis not all, is it? Some matter has you heartsick, does it not? Tell me.'

'I've told you!' She pushed me away. 'Leave me alone, can't you? I have naught more to say to you.' Thus was I dismissed.

'As you wish, Em. But if you want to confide in me – ever – I have a ready and kindly ear a-waiting. You do not have to bear this anguish alone, whatever it may be.'

Every time she closed her eyes, Emily saw Lizzie Knollys' limp form sprawled upon the packed-earth floor of her house, unmoving. She had not slept since and could think of little else. She knew her tirade against Seb had been unjust, but she felt so at a loss. She had told him she was fearful for Gabriel but, in truth, she was far more fearful for herself. Hugging the amber to her heart, it seemed Gabriel's affections – his love – were all she had left to rely upon and now he would have to leave because Seb had unmasked that devil, Underwood. Why could he not leave well alone? Who cared if some wretched dead Dutchman had justice or no? What about the living?

Emily buried her face in the pillows. The living – or mayhap the dead – worried her most.

If anything had happened to Lizzie Knollys – and not for a moment did she believe the idle bitch had run away, as Beattie insisted – Seb was so concerned for truth and justice, he would cast her out; abandon her, she knew. Damn him for being so righteous and dutiful. Curse him for his constant upholding of the law. The Devil take him for putting virtuous behaviour before love.

She ought to have listened to Dame Ellen and never wed a man who found more joy in a foolish manuscript than he did the marriage bed. He should take holy orders, join a monastery, have his head shaved and wear sackcloth and ashes. Aye, that would suit him better than being a husband. This was all his fault...

Adam lay abed, staring up at the darkness, the invisible rafters, the roof tiles and the unseen night sky beyond. He missed the wide skies of Norfolk. He hardly used to notice them at home, but here, in London, the stars were hidden by spires, towers, gables and chimneys; black shapes made by man obscuring the beauty of the heavens. And the open space of sky wasn't all he missed. Life in Foxley with its single street and humble dwellings had been simple and straightforward, but here, in the city, everything was twisted, contorted and impossible to fathom. How many times had he lost his way in the winding alleys and congested lanes? And it wasn't just the place. The people here were well suited to their city. They too were devious, deceitful and unknowable.

He sighed and pushed away the blanket. The night airs were stuffy and humid. Mayhap, another storm was brewing. Beside him, Seb was a silent bed-fellow – too silent. Not a murmur nor snuffle. Adam suspected he wasn't asleep either, probably lying there, brooding. Aye, Seb was one for brooding, as he'd discovered, living 'neath the same roof.

Seb and Emily were not the folk he'd thought them to be either. Especially Em. Such a harridan, it was a wonder Seb put up with her. In Foxley, she had seemed a quiet woman and a good wife, but in London, she was otherwise; different entirely. This whole house was a nest of deceit. He could see it, yet Seb seemed unaware. Unless he knew it all too well and was a consummate pretender.

As far as he could unravel the tangled weave that was this household, Emily was in love with that one-time journeyman of Seb's: Gabriel, Gideon, or whatever he called himself. But somehow, despite the odds, it appeared Seb still loved his wife, though passion – if it existed at all – was kept at bay behind the bedchamber door and never strayed beyond it.

And then there was Rose. Lovely Rose. What an unholy waste of a beautiful woman! From the moment he'd first seen her, he'd been smitten. How he longed to take her in his arms, aye, and into his bed, if he was honest. Jude must be the greatest fool in all God's blessed creation not to have married her when he had the chance. But then again, mayhap Jude was right not to, forwhy there was good reason: Rose loved another man. A man too blind to see it. Much as he wished to kiss and woo Rose, he never would for she had given her heart to Seb. The truth was there in her eyes, every time she looked at him; in her lips whenever she smiled at him. Yet Seb seemed not to know it. How could he not? Oh, he liked her well enough, but that was all. The silly fellow was utterly faithful to that tempestuous wife of his, even as she dreamed of another – if dreaming was all she did. Adam had his suspicions.

When it came down to the bare bones of the matter; the starkest truth: Seb was wed to the wrong woman!

But what good did so much thinking do any man? Adam was regretting his decision to come to London. Seeing Rose every day and knowing she hardly noticed him was a torment indeed. Mayhap he should go back to Norfolk. But not this night. Perhaps not the morrow either. You could never see what might come to pass. Women had been known to change their minds and even their hearts.

Upon a sigh, with that last hopeful thought, Adam turned over, pulled up the blanket and slept soundly until dawn.


Adam was not alone in wakefulness. Jack and Tom lay abed unsleeping also.


'Well? Did you see the dancer? What do you think of Salome, eh? I'd give her bed-sport any day.' Tom sweated with the thought of her hot skin against his.

Jack did not answer, but lay thinking in the darkness.

'Mind you, I didn't like the look of that bear of a fellow who plays the pipes for her.'

'He's there t' make sure the likes of you don't get their filfy paws on her, ain't he? Name's Arry. One o' them strong men; lifts ale tuns – full ones – like they was nuffink. They're wiv them acribats, boff Arry and M-the dancin' girl.'

191

'How do you know?'

'I ast him, didn't I?'

'Ooh, you've got a tender spot for her.'

'No, I ain't. Don't be stupid.'

'You must've admired her tits at least,' Tom insisted. 'A fairer pair I've never seen.'

'Shut yer mouth,' Jack said. 'Yer shouldn't talk 'bout her like she woz a milk-cow fer sale.'

'Ooh! Pardon me for saying. What's amiss with you, then? You ain't turning monkish on me, surely?'

'No I ain't an' I don't wanna talk 'bout it.'

'Where do you think Salome's from? Araby? Egypt? Rome?'

'None've 'em. She's English... most like, an' 'er name ain't Salome, neever. Go to sleep.'

'Sleep? When she's got me all lusty and afire? How can you think I could sleep? Rather, I might have to sneak over to Cock Lane and find a likely wench... not that she'll be half as lovesome as that dancer.'

'Yer wouldn't dare, Tom Bowen. Yer too big a coward after wot Master Seb's said. And the dancer wouldn't lay wiv yer, not fer ten pounds or more.'

'What do you know of the likes of her? And I am no coward. I would go, if I wanted.'

Jack sighed deeply and turned his face to the wall. He knew more about the dancer than he would tell.


The rain began some while after St Martin's bell had rung for matins, summoning the brethren within the abbey from their beds to prayer. In the small hours, the clouds released their burden and water sluiced the streets, overran the gutters and cascaded down to pour itself into the Thames.

Every creature out in the night-time streets sought shelter wherever it might. Rats were swept from their hidey-holes in the midden heaps, and stray curs abandoned their quest for scraps to crouch in any place that offered respite from the deluge.

One flea-bitten specimen, its tail stripped naked of hair by mange, huddled behind a broken barrel, under a wormed and rotting timber of use to no man any longer. It had been following a definite scent. Its body was skin and bone, but its nose remained undulled by hardship and near-starvation. It had been kicked aside and beaten so many times, its ears were torn, and its back was scarred, but midden heaps were safe and good places to scavenge.

The heap in Foster Lane, beside St Martin's Abbey, was rarely disturbed by men except to add more detritus to its stinking, ever-growing mound. The authorities had ordered the scawagers to cart it out of the city, but that was months since and naught had been done to remedy it. But a new scent was becoming stronger by the hour, enticing, beckoning London's most verminous inhabitants to find it out. That was until the rains came, sending them scurrying. Now only the mangy cur remained to watch a great slurry of waste, already undermined and loosened by the previous storm and unable to remain fast any longer, finally washed out into the central gutter. All manner of maggot-ridden unwholesomeness, much of it unseen for so long, now blocked the street. But not everything had been there for weeks, months, years even.

As the rain washed away the worst of the filth, a tumbled form was revealed: clothing; hair. A body. The source of that tantalising scent. The body of a woman lay in the lane to be a hearty meal for the cur and to be gnawed by the rats when they crept out again. Otherwise, it awaited discovery in the first light of day.

# Chapter 12

## Friday the twenty-eighth day of August

AT LEAST this morn I was dressed for the day when Master Fyssher came knocking at my door. I was growing weary of dawntide impositions and had words of protest in readiness upon my tongue – not that they had served any purpose on previous mornings. However, it was not the deputy coroner who stood upon my threshold with some new reason to demand I attend him. Rather, it was a street urchin, a crumpled paper held out in his grubby hand.

'Fer Mistress Foxley,' he said.

I reached out to take the paper, but he withheld it. I sighed.

'You best come in,' I said, realising a coin or two was required afore he would hand it over. He looked to be all sharp edges and angles, pointed elbows and knees. His clothes – rags – hung loosely on him. 'Have you broken your fast this day?'

'Nay, master.' The lad's eyes brightened as I beckoned him along the passage and into the kitchen.

Rose and Nessie were preparing pickled herrings, it being a fast day, and bread. Emily was yet to come down, feeding the babe in our bedchamber, no doubt.

'Wait here while I fetch a coin,' I told him. 'Mistress Glover will give you bread, ale and fish. Now I would have the note you brought.'

He handed it to me without further delay. Rose gave me a

look I was unable to read, perhaps querying my act of charity, but she served the skinny child with a heel of bread, three rolled fish and a cup of ale, making no comment but asking his name. He spoke with his mouth full and may have said 'Biddew' or some such. Meantime, I found my purse. Someone had cleaned it with care, removing all remnants of last supper's pottage. The leather was yet damp and smelled of lye soap.

'Where be the coins?' I asked.

'Oh, your money's in that chipped pot on the shelf there,' Rose said, waving towards the buffet. 'I've done what I may to clean your purse, but the leather will need oiling when it's dry, else it will crack. Your girdle-belt the same. That's hanging on the peg behind the door.'

'I be most grateful, Rose. Whatever hour did you leave your bed this morn to get it done?' I took a couple of pennies from the pot and put them beside the lad's swiftly-emptying platter.

'It needed to be done sooner rather later. I know how stains become ingrained in leather, if not attended to, so I cleaned your things before I went to bed last night.'

'A kindness, indeed. I thank you, Rose,' I said, my thoughts turning to the note the lad had brought for Emily. The paper was of the cheapest and not sealed, just folded and that none too neatly. In addition, it was rumpled and stained from the lad's dirty fingers. The writing was in an utterly untrained hand with ink blots and capitals strewn anyhow amidst the words, cast like pearls before swine, as the Scriptures say. But it read plainly enough:

*AwT As APPeNd. MusT sPeeK sooNesT.*
*beATTie ThATcher.*

Little enough information was given, and I wondered what could have occurred that required this nigh-unlettered woman to pen this briefest of missives. Besides, Emily would see her friend within an hour or so at the silk-women's stall on the fayre ground. Unless, of course, Beatrice was prevented from attending by some means. Somewhat concerned, but nonetheless intrigued, I took the note upstairs to Emily.

'God's blessings be upon you, Em,' I said as I entered, determined the day should not recommence as the last had ended. She was seated upon the bedside, suckling the babe and I kissed her hair and little Dickon's. 'This was delivered for you, sweetheart. 'Tis from Beatrice. It seems she would meet you in haste.' I watched as Emily read those few words and I swear she turned pale. 'Is aught untoward, lass?'

She did not answer, but pulled the babe from her breast and shoved him at me even as he began to wail.

'I cannot feed him,' I protested.

'He's had sufficient. I must go to Beattie.' Emily re-tied the neck of her shift and laced her bodice, missing an eyelet in her haste, I noticed.

'Your gown be awry.'

'No matter.' She pushed her hair under her cap anyhow and did not bother with a veil afore rushing out of the chamber and hastening down the stair. I heard the back door into the yard slam below and Dickon, startled, began to pour all his strength into his show of displeasure, bawling fit to waken the bishop in his bed in St Paul's precinct across the way.

'Hush, hush, little one. All be well,' I crooned to him, despite a discomforting feeling that all was not well. I rocked him and stroked his brow. I sang to him, but I doubt he could hear me for his own noise. He would not be quieted. His face puckered and reddened to a frightening hue of darkest crimson. Each drawn-out scream was followed by a heart-stopping silence as he gathered himself to take another breath afore the next deafening yell. I had never known the like from our placid babe and was at a loss what to do with him.

By the time Rose came to my rescue, both he and I were sweat-soaked.

Emily hitched up her skirts and ran along Paternoster Row and into Cheapside, splashing through puddles that sparkled in the light of the rising sun as it sent its beams along the thoroughfare, casting the long shadow of Cheap Cross towards her. Beattie lived close by, on the corner of Friday Street and was waiting on the doorstep.

'St Mary be thanked; you came, Em,' she gasped, putting a hand to her heart as though to steady it.

'What is it? Tell me, Beattie.'

'Not here. Too many ears. Hal's within. Let us walk...'

Emily made to turn up Foster Lane opposite, to take a shortcut to Aldersgate and the fayre ground beyond.

'No, no! Not that way.' Beattie dragged her back. 'Let's go along Cheap. Anywhere but up there.'

They walked swiftly, as though with a purpose, until Emily was breathless after running to Beattie's house and then striding along at such a pace.

'Have pity, Bea,' she panted. 'Just tell me. Here be as good a place as any. None is listening.' She drew Beattie into the porch of St Mildred's in Poultry, to sit on a bench within.

Beattie fanned her hot face with her apron for a few moments, bracing herself.

"'Tis terrible, Em... they found a body... a corpse... in Foster Lane.'

Emily put her hands to her mouth.

'I saw it, Em. It was so horrible... such a fearful sight.' Beattie paused to wipe her face upon her apron. 'Not much left, in truth, what with the mess made of it but... I saw enough: a blue gown, fair hair... Dear God have mercy on us, Em: it's Lizzie Knollys. And they've sent for Master Fyssher and the sheriff. What shall we do, Em? We killed her! We'll hang for it!' Beattie broke down and wept; great spasms of weeping shuddering through her as she rocked back and forth upon the stone bench.

Emily embraced her, saying naught. What was there to be said? But as she held Beattie close, her thoughts were in turmoil. There had to be something they could do. As her friend's heaving sobs lessened, Emily realised that, as a future *femme sole,* she would have to take charge of the situation.

'Quiet, Beattie. Cease your tears. Dry your eyes. You recall, she still breathed when we left her. Was that not so? Then 'tis not of our doing. It cannot be. She fell was all, and it was her own fault.' Emily stood up, straightening her skirts. 'We know naught of this matter other than the fact that a woman acquainted with us has been found dead. We are shocked and sorrowful, but no more than that. We are innocent, Beattie. You hear me? Innocent!'

Beattie nodded.

'Now, we must go warn Pen and tell her the same. Come, there is no time to dally. We can't have Pen hearing the ill-tidings and blurting out something untoward. Hurry up, Bea.'

Beattie nodded once more and made to run back along Poultry, but Emily grabbed her friend's hand.

'Walk,' she hissed. 'Remember: naught be amiss. We must not cause folk to notice us. Bad enough that we nigh ran all this way, but there weren't so many folk about then as now. Head up, Beattie: do not skulk like a felon. Smile at your neighbours as usual.'

'I can't, Em.'

'Indeed you can and you will.'

A little above an hour later, Emily, Beatrice and Peronelle opened up the silk-women's booth as they had every other morning of the fayre. All three were neatly attired and respectable, and if their bright smiles were somewhat forced, nobody noticed. That Pen's eyes watered overmuch might be caused by a summer rheum: a tale she had rehearsed already.

The stall was awaiting customers, although its wares for sale were few now. Bailiff Thaddeus Turner gave them 'good day', causing Beattie to almost choke upon her return of greeting, but Emily's reproving look soon restored her. When Master Ameryk did the same, Beattie was able to make a better effort.

Emily seemed perfectly calm and composed and both Beattie and Pen, impressed, did their best to follow her fine example.

When Dame Ellen visited all was well as far as anyone could tell.

'No Lizzie Knollys yet again?' the old woman asked, taking a seat upon the stool Emily set for her.

'No, Dame Ellen. No sign of her.' Emily kept her voice steady, her tone even. None could know how her belly churned and her legs felt weak as a newborn's.

'Well, she'll not be getting one groat of our profits, I tell you. And I'd tell her so – in writing, if the foolish unlettered hinny could read. She's done not a hand's turn of work all week to earn it. You've done well, though, and I see our coin box is full.'

At last, I had the chance to return to my long-neglected *Aesop's Fables* in the workshop. Adam was well on with penning the texts, but my miniatures were hardly begun. The previous few days, running about the fayre on Master Fyssher's concerns, meant I had not so much as sat at my desk, never mind picked up a brush, but now that was done. The sheriffs and Thaddeus Turner could continue the search for Roger Underwood, if they deemed such efforts to be worthwhile. For myself, I wanted no part in hunting down a miscreant who might endanger Gabriel, if the devil was found. For once, I would look away from the pursuit of justice, though it went contrary to my nature. My work; my business required my attentions to the full. Aye, and my heart warned me to cause no further distress to Emily, whatever disquiet my abandonment of rightful duty might cause to my conscience.

Tom had set out my pens, brushes and pigments as I had asked and I realised my lips were curving into a smile, the knots of anxiety in my sinews easing, even as I pulled up my stool and sat down. I had before me the tale of the Fox and the Crow – always a favourite of mine since childhood, knowing a fox, or a Foxley as I used to think of it, got the better of some vain and prideful creature. For this, I should prepare a fine russet pigment for the fox's coat and a deep blue-black for the crow's plumage, but first I sketched the image within the space allocated to it. With pen in hand and the image evolving in my mind's eye, I was content.

I should have known my respite of calm would not survive the hour.

'Seb,' Rose came hastening from the shop. 'You are needed.'

'A difficult customer, Rose?' I wondered why my presence was required. She was always more than able to coax and sweet-talk the vilest of visitors.

'Not a customer at all. I'm afeared Master Fyssher is here again, demanding your assistance.'

'Oh, no. What can he want of me this time? I hoped I was done with those matters at the fayre. I want none of his business and his sixpence per day will not persuade me. He must find a new assistant to replace Jude: I have not the time to traipse around the city, solving crimes.'

'He says there is a corpse been found in Foster Lane.'

'Then let the sheriffs deal with it.' Yet even as I spoke, I was laying aside my pen and taking up my scrip. 'I will speak with him,' I said.

Master Fyssher was in the shop, huffing with impatience at my delay in attending upon him.

'Make haste, Foxley. I don't have time to waste. I was but lately informed of this.'

'And what would 'this' happen to be, if I may enquire?'

'A body, as I said. Cease your questioning and come with me. Now!'

I be sure the corpse will wait, I thought, since it has naught else to do, but I said no more. It was plain that Master Fyssher was not about to enlighten me any further.

When we reached Foster Lane, a crowd marked the spot where the body lay, all craning their necks for a better view of death. And they were welcome to it. I should have avoided it, but the coroner would have it otherwise. Recognising Master Fyssher, the beadles for the wards of both Aldersgate and Farringdon Within rushed towards him, each attempting to shout above the other. Apparently, the deceased had been discovered in the street betwixt St Vedast's Church in Farringdon ward upon the one hand, and St Leonard's in Aldersgate ward upon the other and both beadles would claim jurisdiction. If I had found myself in that situation, I would have willingly permitted the other fellow to usurp my priority.

'It must certainly have lain in Aldersgate ward and washed downhill into Farringdon. Death occurred within my ward, so I take precedence.' A short, plump man with lank grey hair pointed to himself.

'But now it is in Farringdon, so 'tis on my ground. I can't help that the rain moved it, can I?' A stick-thin fellow with a lop-sided nose looked about to strike the plump one.

I elbowed a passage through the crowd, leaving Master Fyssher to determine which of the beadles he should deal with. I would complete this unsavoury task as swiftly and briefly as possible. I cannot say what I was expecting to see, apart from a dead body, but I admit I was shocked not to find some aged and wrinkled remains. Face down and besmirched with mud as it was, one hand lay outstretched and had been rinsed clean by the rain of last night. It was a youthful hand, elegantly shaped: a woman's. A mass of bedraggled hair, individual tendrils spread floating in the puddles, was of a fair colour where the filth had washed away. The tumbled gown might once have been a goodly blue. A tingling sensation began in the pit of my belly, one I did my best to ignore, but I sensed history was about to repeat itself. As occurred when I had turned the body at the fayre and discovered I knew the victim, I suspected I might recognise this unfortunate soul also.

Yet the face was an awful shock that quite sickened me. Rats had gnawed at it. Lumps had been bitten from the arm: dog bites most like. She was once pretty, but no longer. Even so, I knew the woman who had but lately made doe's eyes at me in an unseemly manner. Lizzie Knollys would never seduce another man.

'Anyone know who she is?' the coroner asked the crowd. Though some must have recognised their near neighbour, none wished to acknowledge a woman of doubtful repute for fear her ill-fame might taint their own.

''Tis Mistress Elizabeth Knollys of Foster Lane,' I said. 'An out-working silk-woman for Dame Ellen Langton.'

'Good. That saves us a deal of time in trying to name the deceased.' Master Fyssher paused, hands on hips, looking at me expectantly. 'Well? Why wait, Foxley? Get on your hands and knees and examine the body. We need a cause of death.'

'Drowning by the look of her,' I suggested not wanting to kneel in the filth and ruin my decent hose – they being my Sunday best after last eve's incident with the pottage.

'Then make certain of it.'

I sighed, set my scrip to one side and obeyed, wincing as my hip joint complained.

Her once-fine gown, though most likely bought second-hand from a fripperer, proved as a net that had caught all kinds of unwholesome rubbish. Yards of slime that might once have been some vegetable matter, fish bones and oyster shells, a discarded glove, its leather well chewed, all were trapped in the folds of woollen cloth. I looked around. Some little way back up Foster Lane, the contents of a midden heap had spread out across the street.

'I think she may have lain once within that midden, but not so long ago. A day or two at most, else the body would be in a worse condition than is the case.'

'Decomposed and putrefying you mean. Well, note the facts as you find them, Foxley.'

Indeed I would not. My hands were so filthy, I could hardly take pen, ink and paper from my scrip without soiling everything. Note-making must wait upon a chance to wash them. In the meantime, I supposed I must do my tasks as best I might. I brushed the hair away from the remains of a face now devoid of one eye. I was forced to pause and look elsewhere while my belly settled, staring at the glint of light on the wet cobblestones. The stink did not help either. I knew she had been a woman of loose morals, but in death I would see her decent, straightening her skirts and pulling together the lacings of her bodice. It was then that I noticed the marks about her neck. Something – a cord or a lacing, mayhap – had cut deeply into the now mottled flesh, though any blood had long been washed away. And then there were the bruises. Upon one side of her neck, a deep indentation; three upon the other side and, as I looked more closely, a fourth fainter mark. I stretched out my hand – the left – and saw that my thumb and fingers could nigh fit those marks, except that the span was broader than mine.

'Not drowned,' I said. 'Strangled.' With that, I reached out for the nearest stout arm to aid me to my feet. The skinny beadle of Farringdon provided my need.

'Damn it to hell. I hoped she'd fallen into the midden and drowned, like you said firstly,' he complained. 'But since the midden is in Aldersgate ward, and it looks to be a case of unnatural death, she's yours, John.' He nodded to the plump beadle. 'I'll leave you to call out the hue-and-cry and bid you farewell, then.' And with that, he went off, and I saw him enter the nearest tavern.

'Bit late for that. She could have been dead for days.' Beadle John looked disconsolate indeed, rubbing his stomach where it protruded over his belt. He sniffed loudly. 'What say you, Master Coroner? Do we bother with the hue-and-cry with the killer long since taken to his heels?'

Once again, Fyssher seemed to expect me to provide the answer.

'I doubt it would be worthwhile,' I muttered, dismayed at the condition of my jerkin and hose. I attempted to brush away the filth, but my efforts caused it to look worse than afore, smearing a larger area of cloth than ever.

'No. No need to take the time, wasting effort,' Fyssher announced, as if it was he who had made the decision. 'Foxley will make all enquiries necessary, questioning the neighbours, doing his usual poking about in other folks' business. Make a start, Foxley, soon as you've finished with the body.' Then he made to stroll away, but turned back: 'Oh, and search the midden thoroughly. We don't want to miss any useful clues, do we?'

We? He meant 'me', of course. He would leave me to attempt to solve another crime on his behalf. His audacity never ceased to amaze me, but whatever the case, I could not work looking like a begrimed beggar. I would wash and change my hose afore I began: no one would pay me the least respect as I was and if I wanted honest answers to my enquiries, then I should appear as an honest citizen myself. Besides, my attire stank of the midden and I could not abide it. As for examining the disgusting pile of refuse in detail, I would find some other way.

Some while later – in truth, I was in no hurry – I returned to Foster Lane. I was cleanly dressed and had washed thoroughly in lavender-scented water. Despite this, I did not feel entirely rid of the stench. Worse yet, my hose were most certainly still damp. Dearest Rose had washed them clean of pottage last eve, but what with so much rain overnight, they were by no means dry this morn. But what choice did I have? It was to be either cold, clammy hose or a state of near-nakedness. My jerkin was not much better forwhy Rose had sponged off the stains with more lavender-water. It was the best that could be done and would have to serve, although, as Rose reminded me – as if I required telling – my hip joint would not benefit from being clad in damp wool and, indeed, was already afflicted by the recent wet weather.

At Foster Lane, I was informed that the body had been removed into St Leonard's Church hard by, but Beadle John assured me it was readily available, should I require to look more nearly at some aspect of it. I thanked him, but had not the least intention of doing so if it might be avoided.

I had returned, bringing with me a scawager by the name of Dodd and a pair of scruffy urchins, including the lad who had delivered Beatrice's message to Emily so early that morn. They could investigate the midden while I oversaw the procedure... from a distance. When the task was accomplished to my satisfaction, Dodd could shovel up the mess into his cart, as he and his fellows should have done weeks earlier, possibly avoiding this disagreeable outcome altogether.

'A groat betwixt you, lads,' I said, 'If you search diligently.' I had already promised Dodd sixpence for what was, when all was said and done, simply the job he was paid to do by the city, but neglected to accomplish. I might hope I should be reimbursed, but doubted it, knowing the lid of the city's coffer weighed like the Devil's sins and could be prised open only with the greatest difficulty.

'Wot we lookin' fer, master?' one lad asked. It was the messenger.

'Any item which appears not to have been cast out as rubbish and has not lain there too long. It may be anything at all.' The lad pulled a face, and I realised my description was overly vague. 'Set aside whatever you may find and I shall examine it later. I shall likely be somewhere higher up the lane, making enquiries. There will be a pot of ale for you after.'

'As well as the groat?'

'Aye.'

I watched as all three began the vile task, yet the stench and the filth did not seem to concern them, and I wondered if I had been unnecessarily generous in my offered payment and they would have done it for less. No matter. What was promised would be paid for I was a man of my word, even to idle scawagers and street urchins.

My first enquiry was made of the priest at St Leonard's Church as to the location of Mistress Knollys' dwelling. At first, he was reluctant to admit he knew her, but I pointed out that since the higher and greater part of Foster Lane was in his parish, he was failing in his office as shepherd of the flock if he did not know her.

'There, two doors up,' he pointed out after some degree of persuasion – not least, my mention of a word to the bishop, as if I would dare presume. I thanked him.

I knew the house for we had lived opposite when I was younger. A cutler had dwelt in the place then; not a particularly wealthy fellow, but his wife had occasionally given sweetmeats to me, believing I was an underfed waif, no doubt, for so I looked in those days. She pitied me for my crippled leg and misshapen back, but she was kindly enough not to mock me as so many did back then. However, I had lost touch with our Foster Lane neighbours after our father died and Jude and I – he being a journeyman and myself having barely completed my apprenticeship – could not afford the rent demanded by St Martin's Abbey whose tenants we were. We had then gone to lodge at Dame Ellen's place in Cheapside, but that was all in the past.

I entered the cutler's old house. It appeared unchanged from what I remembered of it. It seemed Lizzie Knollys had done little to it; the cobwebs draped so heavy with dust, they might date back to when the cutler left. The packed earth floor was rutted so deep in places, it ought to have been resurfaced, but no one had troubled to do it. The central hearth and stones around it had not been swept for a long while. Apparently, the woman did no more housework than any other kind of respectable labour, preferring to earn her bread by less deserving means. It was almost the house of a pauper, but not quite.

There was little to see: a rickety board on trestles that wobbled because of the uneven floor, a stool, a ribbon-weaving loom, a few pots – one containing wilting worts for a meal never to be consumed – a treenware bowl and platter, a horn spoon and an earthenware cup. It was obvious to me that Lizzie had lived alone: no sign that another shared her meals. Up the ladder I climbed, wincing at every other step, and found the bed in the sleeping gallery was made straight. A few items of womanly apparel hung from pegs on the rafters. With a deal of effort, I crouched to look beneath the bed and was of an instant sneezing upon the dust.

I found there, pushed to the farthest corner, a small wooden chest, the kind in which ladies store their gloves, and it was of finer quality than the house seemed to warrant. What was more, there was no trace of dust upon the lid, so its recent use was probable. It was of beech wood, I thought, inset with a pattern of leaves and vines in other woods. It did not seem of English make to me, but I was no expert on such things. Emily's father would know, I did not doubt, but most like it mattered not in the least. Unfortunately, the chest proved to be locked with an ornate brass fastening, and I could not find a key to it, despite a search that took little time at all since there were so few possessions. In truth, it took rather longer for me to get up off my knees in order to conduct the search.

Returning downstairs, taking care upon the ladder since I had the chest under my arm, I looked into the pots and cup, but found no key. An untidy workbasket was a more likely hiding place, and I did uncover some unexpected items among tangled lengths of silk, oddments of cloth and unravelled spools of thread. There was a large ring with an amethyst gemstone in a heavy silver setting. It was no woman's adornment and, if I had to hazard a guess, I would say it looked like an Episcopal ring. Bishops and abbots prefer amethysts, they being a sovereign preventive against inebriation and it would not do for any churchman of rank ever to be deemed a drunkard. There was a dainty enamelled knife, a spoon and two keys, though neither was of a size to fit the lock on the chest. Delving deeper, there were more spoons and a pair of earrings with red stones: garnets or maybe rubies; it was hard to tell in the gloom of the house. An ivory needle case and a pair of snips were less surprising discoveries in a silk-woman's basket, though they were of finer quality compared to other things in the place.

I began to suspect that whoring might not have been the only illegal practice in which the dead woman had been involved. Thievery was more than likely another means of paying the rent and putting bread upon the platter. I looked around more carefully, thinking items other than a key might be found.

Mouse droppings beside a piece of mouldering bread upon the board with a rusted paring knife and a wrinkled onion beside suggested how frugal were the woman's meals. I was saddened to realise it. She was little better purveyed than those street urchins. Which reminded me: I must go and see how their task was progressing – if at all.

As I passed the hearthstone, something caught my eye among the cold, grey ashes, glinting in the light from the door. I retrieved it. It was a pin of a quite distinctive kind with a head of brass, square in shape. Of course, there could be thousands just like it in London, but when I had purchased three dozen of that design last Christmastide, as a gift for Emily, the pin-maker assured me she had made no others quite like them, which was why I chose them. Emily kept them for use with her Sunday best veil, but had been wearing them of late to look her finest at the fayre. Had she visited Lizzie recently? She had made no mention of it. Mayhap, it was another of Lizzie's ill-gotten gains, stolen from my wife? In which case, why was it not stored safely in the workbasket like all the rest? A careful examination showed the pin to be still shiny and unlikely to have been subjected to the heat of the fire. Did that mean the hearth had not been kindled since the pin had lain there? So many questions: so few answers. I could see a long day of enquiries stretched afore me.

Once more, I forced my creaking hip into a crouch, using a half-burned stick to move the ashes about. Naught else lay among them, but a brown smear, of the size of my palm, upon the hearthstone was an alarming disclosure. It looked to be blood and not so old either. As I eased myself upright, my hands were trembling and my belly disquieted as by a surfeit of sour ale, but I told myself there could be no connection betwixt the pin and the blood stain. None whatsoever.

Laden with the chest, the workbasket and my scrip, outside in Foster Lane, the day remained as dull as a dead mackerel's eye. But my midden-rakers were still at work, although Dodd stood, leaning upon his spade and did not look to have done anything to contribute. Seeing me, he nodded towards a small heap of odds and ends set to one side.

'They's finded a few bits fer ye,' he said, mumbling through broken teeth. 'Can't see as it'll 'elp any.'

I went to look just as a bent bucket handle clanged upon the cobbles at my feet, flung to join the pile.

'Sorry, master!' the lad at fault sang out from the top of the midden.

I set down my findings from the house and waved back at him, indicating that he had done me no hurt. With my foot, I parted the items they had collected, determined to bend down no more this day, until my hip was rested. The sole of a shoe was black with age and of no interest. A rusty buckle had probably lain there for years. Likewise, the remains of what might once have been a man's nether clouts which were so rotted, they fell apart as I moved them with my toe. A horn knife handle without a blade did not look so old and might be relevant, though I misdoubted it. And then there was the key, tied on a long, leather thong. Its brass showed no sign of verdigris, and it seemed to be of a size suitable for the little chest. I pulled the broken thong betwixt my thumb and forefinger. It came as a shock, but no surprise, that a reddish-brown tint stained my skin. If I was a gambling man – which I was not – I might have laid a wager that it was blood.

Although I would rather have avoided such a visit, I returned to the priest at St Leonard's and asked to look at the body once more. I would compare the leather thong to the ligature marks upon the sides of the victim's neck. It was of an appropriate thickness, and I determined the matter settled – until I lifted the victim's head. I wanted to see how the length of the thong would have hung about her neck, much as Emily wore her amber pendant. Was it long enough that she could have worn it always, keeping the key safe beneath her clothing, indicating that she valued it especially? Indeed, it was, but then I discovered something else. Beneath her hair as it fell aside, I could see a dent, a deep contusion, at the temple. The skin was broken, and the injury must have bled. Recalling the smear of blood upon the hearthstone, of a sudden, strangulation was less definite as the cause of death. Examining the cuts made by the thong, I saw how they lay either side, overprinted by the bruises I had noted earlier.

The head wound confused matters greatly. How had Lizzie Knollys met her unnatural end? A blow to the skull; a strong hand about her throat; even drowning in the midden were all possibilities. However, I might eliminate this last. Reluctantly, I prised her lips apart, examining her mouth. I also took a clean quill from my scrip and inserted it into her nostrils. Her mouth and the quill were clean. I therefore concluded that she had already ceased to breathe when she was flung into the midden. At least I could conclude that she had not drowned, but I must reconsider my previous assessment that she had died by strangulation and, in truth, I wished with all my heart, it was not necessary. I closed my eyes, not wanting to contemplate the worst of all possibilities.

# Chapter 13

## Later that Friday morn

DISQUIETED BY my findings upon the body, I went home, intending to write up my notes, but first I would investigate the objects from the house in Foster Lane. I cleaned the little key and discovered that it did indeed fit the lock of the chest Lizzie had kept 'neath the bed. To be undisturbed, I took it into the parlour where I might examine it privily.

The box was lined with green velvet. I be unsure what I expected to find within, but for certain it was not an exquisite Book of Hours, fine enough for a duchess to admire. The precious volume was of a size with my hand, written on vellum of the finest quality. Every recto page was a miniature of such artistry as I would find hard to equal even at my best, if I be honest upon the matter, making use of so much gold and lapis lazuli, it must be worth a princely sum. The cover was embossed and gilded with garnets and carnelians set within a tooled design of scrollwork, the corners protected by silver-gilt pieces with a clasp of the same. It was undoubtedly of Bruges workmanship for I recognised the style straightway. How could some nigh penniless, unlettered woman come to possess such a gem of the illuminator's and bookbinder's art? Further investigation of the book revealed that it must have been a gift to her – I suppose she could look at the gorgeous images – forwhy it was inscribed *To Lizzie with Fondest Regard. R.*

As I leafed through the folios with great care, a loose page fluttered free. Appalled to realise the book was damaged, I gasped, but I need not have feared. It was a letter with the seal unbroken. I fetched my new scrying glass, the better to observe the seal. It was somewhat smudged, as if the seal matrix had been turned slightly in the soft wax to blur it as it began to set. Was the author's hand unsteady or was it done on purpose to obscure the impression? There was no addressee. It was written upon good quality paper. I lit a candle and heated my penknife in order to slide it under the wax and lift the seal without breaking it. There was no greeting; no signature but a bold script, all of well-formed capitals in a professional scribal hand. But it could not be doubted that this was personal, every word nigh carved into the paper with anger. It read:

*RETURN THE BOOK MY SON GAVE TO YOU AND FURTHER THE ITEMS YOU PURLOINED FROM MY HOUSE. ELSEWISE STEPS WILL BE TAKEN AGAINST YOU.*

But what purpose might such an epistle serve since Lizzie could not read and had not even opened it to ask another to read it for her? I might hazard that she had some expectations as to what it said and wanted no other to know of it. I wondered if it might have some bearing upon her murder.

There was but one way to solve the mystery and, unfortunately, it involved asking more questions of Lizzie Knollys' neighbours in Foster Lane, weary as I was of making enquiries. Besides, no one liked the implication of my interrogations, namely that they might come under suspicion of having killed her. I locked the little chest, leaving the key in place. In the workshop, I put it upon a high shelf in the storeroom, out of the way, for safe-keeping, along with Lizzie's workbasket. Then back I went to Aldersgate ward, determined to spend but a single hour upon Master Fyssher's business and not one heartbeat longer afore I should be home for dinner. I had missed too many breakfasts on his account these past few days; no wonder my girdle-belt was drawn in by another notch and still hung loosely about my hips.

It was unsurprising to learn that, at first, nobody had seen nor heard aught untoward from Lizzie's house upon the day concerned. No villainous-looking visitors nor unsavoury fellows lurking near at hand. However, two doors along I found Mistress Baker – Cecily, as she insisted I must address her. I was invited into a home that was as well cared for and neat as that of her near neighbour was abandoned to dirt and disarray. She bustled about, fetching me ale and wafers and making me entirely welcome. It made a pleasant change, so much so, it occurred to me that she might be attempting to divert me from my purpose, having something to hide, but her smile appeared genuine enough. I feared I was becoming overly suspicious.

She pulled up a stool to sit facing me across the well-scrubbed board, pushing the dish of wafers closer to me.

'Have another, Master Foxley,' she said. 'Admit it: they're very good, aren't they? I make them to my grandmother's receipt.'

'Aye, mistress, indeed they are,' I managed to mumble around a mouthful of wafer. In truth, it was so dry, I was unable to swallow it without the thin, sour ale to wash it down, but if I wished her to answer my queries, a white lie could do no harm. However, though I took another, I fed it to Gawain surreptitiously as he lay by my feet. 'Tell me, mistress,' I said once rid of the wafer, 'Upon the afternoon of Wednesday last – it was the day of the thunderstorm – do you recall anyone going to Lizzie Knollys' house? Anyone at all?'

'Well, of course, I do. That woman has more comings and goings through her door than St Paul's on Easter Sunday. Sam Henslow's forever in and out. Says he helps her since she has no man. Aye, and mending the roof and fixing the shutters are the least things he does there, if you take my meaning.'

'And where might I find this man Henslow?' I asked, writing his name in my notes.

'Oh, he's not about this week.' Mistress Baker lowered her voice. 'He's in Ludgate lock-up. Got caught basket-dipping... again. In truth, he's so hopeless at pilfering, he should get himself some proper employment, if you ask me. Then there's William Waters. Another useless fellow, though not ugly by any means, but I haven't seen him so much of late. They had a row, him and Lizzie, and she told him to go to the Devil.' She crossed herself in haste. 'I could hear the argument from here, once I opened my door and stepped down the street a way. That was a few weeks back, but I've heard worse since then, and it wasn't no man's voice either. I did try to tell Master Coroner of it, but he wasn't interested.'

'Then tell me, mistress.'

'Call me Cicely, as I told you, Master Foxley, and do take another wafer.'

'What did you hear and when... Cicely?' I ignored the offered food and wrote my notes busily. At least, I made the pretence to avoid accepting another inedible pastry. A sheet of old parchment likely had more flavour and would dissolve more readily upon the tongue.

'It was those women friends of hers came by. I thought naught of it 'til the shouting and screeching began.'

'When was this?'

'Let me think... oh, aye, it must have been just after the storm the other afternoon. The women were so wet and bedraggled, it must have been that day it poured like Jeremiah's Flood.'

'Noah's,' I corrected.

'Who?'

'Noah's Flood, I believe you mean.'

'Do I? Well, whoever's flood it was, it was upon that day the women had this argument. Oh, and Lizzie's amour, Ralph What's-his-name, was in Foster Lane about that hour and then I saw that awful man.'

'An awful man?' I repeated, alert of a sudden for some relevant information, a possible insight upon the mystery at last.

'Aye. Do you know of him? Skin so black as a burnt pie crust. You'd know him if you saw him - a giant of a man. There can but be one of his kind. Blacker than them black-a-moors at the fayre, even. He quite gave me a shock, I can tell you. Set my heart a-pounding and stood my hair on end. I never saw the like of him before and never want to again. The mayor should not allow it.'

'Allow what, mistress?'

'Allow his sort in London. Strangers. Foreigners.'

'Such incomers and visitors be the lifeblood of our city's trade and commerce,' I said, alarmed at her vehemence against a man I accounted my friend, for there was little doubt she spoke of Rook.

'Well, I'll swear upon Holy Scripture it was him who must have killed Lizzie. I wouldn't trust that... that hideous monster, if my soul depended on it. From the Devil he came and back to the Devil he should go. He did it, I know.'

'Mistress Baker,' I said, rising to take my leave, ''Tis wrong to accuse any man merely upon the grounds of his appearance. Unless you saw him committing an act of villainy...'

'Black of skin: black of soul. That's my opinion.'

'Good day to you, mistress.' I touched my cap to her and walked out. I refused to harken to such pernicious and prejudicial nonsense. Gabriel had vouched for Rook as a righteous Christian, and I would not consider him otherwise without some firm evidence to the contrary. That a man could be considered guilty of a crime simply because he was passing by was absurd, else every neighbour must be a felon.

Outside in the lane, I took time to calm myself for the woman had quite roused my humours to an alarming pitch of turmoil. Sweat ran upon my face and soaked my undershirt. As I scanned the sparse notes I had written, the paper shook in my hand.

Beside Goldsmiths' Hall upon my right as I went along Foster Lane stood a tavern, *The Blue Angel.* Despite its name and the gaudy image on the painted sign above the door, angelic it was not, but I was much in need of a restorative for my ill-humours and to wet my tongue after Mistress Baker's wafers dry as sand. Gawain most likely needed something also, since his tongue looked dry as it lolled.

Unsurprisingly, as with most places of trade within the city this week – our own workshop included – there were few customers, and the taverner attended me in person. I ordered ale and a dish of water for Gawain.

'Mind if I take a stool?' The taverner set a jug and two cups upon the board.

''Tis your own place,' I said. 'You may surely sit where you wish.'

He poured ale into both cups, passing one to me and keeping the other for himself.

'Business ain't doing much, what with this bloody fayre going on. I'll be glad when it's done and we get back to usual.' He gestured, cup in hand, at the empty stools and benches. An elderly fellow with his ancient-looking dog, both dozing by the unlit fire, were the only other customers.

'I agree,' I said. I was not in need of conversation, but it would be churlish to make no answer.

'You're Foxley, ain't you? The coroner's man.'

I sipped my cup. At least the ale was cool and palatable.

'At your service, master.'

'Aye, well, I could tell you a thing or two about what went on in that house. You know the one: Lizzie Knollys' place. All sorts visited there; sorts as folk don't want to admit come to the neighbourhood. But that ain't all. Folk you'd think were respectable citizens used to slink in there after curfew and not leave 'til dawnlight. I reckon it was one of them what did for her, fearing she'd talk out of turn.'

I thought upon his words. Mayhap, he was not so wide of the mark in his conclusion. The unopened letter had certainly been penned by a literate man, and no pauper could afford paper of such quality. And the purpose had definitely been to threaten Lizzie.

'Then there was that women's falling-out the other afternoon,' the taverner continued, refilling our cups. 'It could've been them who done her in, or that black fellow. You couldn't miss seeing him, though he did naught that I saw to raise suspicion. But you never can tell with women or foreigners, can you now? You want bread and cheese with that ale? There's plenty just going to waste, if customers don't turn up.'

'I thank you, but no. The ale will suffice. I should return home for dinner; 'tis later than I realised,' I said, hearing St Martin's bell chime the hour of eleven. 'Here's a groat for the drink and your companionship. I hope you get customers enough to eat your bread afore it goes stale.'

'The pig'll have a banquet, if not.' He shrugged and drained the ale jug into his cup. 'Don't forget what I said about women and foreigners.'

I nodded and departed *The Blue Angel,* making haste to Paternoster Row, aware the hour for dinner was past.

Everyone was at the board when I arrived home, the mackerel in a mustard sauce consumed apart from a portion set aside for me and going cold upon the platter.

'I beg pardon for my tardiness,' I said, still breathless from my hastening, 'Master Fyssher's business takes a deal of time.'

'You'll be hungry then, Seb.' Adam handed me my dinner. 'How goes the investigation?'

'Painfully slowly, I fear. Oh, and where be Jack?' I asked, realising, belatedly, one place at board was empty.

'Your guess is as likely correct as any. The rascal hasn't been seen since breakfast.' Adam sounded angry, as well he might. 'And after you gave him leave to visit the fayre yesterday, this is how he repays your generosity. He'll deserve another beating when he does come home, the idle young scallywag.'

I ate the fish, my heart sinking the while. I wanted to beat no one.

'What of the stall, Em?' I asked to change the subject of discussion.

'Closed up. We sold everything. My father and John are dismantling the booth this afternoon, so we don't have to pay another day's stallage for tomorrow.'

She sat dandling the babe upon her knee. He was chuckling and batting at her amber pendant as it glistened in a shaft of late-morning sunlight from the window. Dickon was a merry little soul, so long as he was fed whenever he demanded.

'Em and I thought we might go to the fayre after dinner,' Rose said, serving me a generous portion of berries and cream. 'As customers this time. We neither of us have seen any of the other stalls and entertainments since we were too busy at our own work. We think we deserve an hour or two as a reward, a holy day. Do we not, Em?'

My wife nodded.

'I think that to be an excellent idea.' I smiled, dabbing berry juices and cream from my lips with a napkin. 'And I feel sufficiently restored now to return to Foster Lane and continue questioning the neighbours there. Mind you, they be a suspicious crowd indeed, naming more possible felons than one man alone can ever investigate. They even list Rook among them for no other reason than he happened to pass by and has skin of another colour than theirs. Is that not disgraceful? I had believed Londoners to have kinder hearts than that, but those who live in Foster Lane most assuredly do not. Then they name an assortment of ne'er-do-wells, some respectable citizens as well as a group of women, all as likely killers. I have such a list of suspects. If I discover who those women were, they most likely can assist my enquiries. Mayhap, they saw or heard something untoward...'

'Come, Rose. Let's go now,' Emily said, leaving her stool so abruptly it overturned. 'I would visit the fayre now in case it rains later.' She put Dickon into his basket. 'Watch him, Nessie,' she ordered.

'But you said I could come too,' the maid complained, her plump features puckering like a mouldy plum.

'Well, you can't. I changed my mind. Are you coming, Rose, or shall I go without you also?' Without awaiting reply, my wife went out into the yard, letting the kitchen door slam behind her.

Rose looked doubtful at Emily's sudden decision, but she took up her purse and followed, closing the door softly this time.

'Women!' Adam laughed. 'Such fickle creatures. I'll never understand them, even loving them as I do.'

'And they left me t' wash all the pots and platters and mind the babe. It ain't right, Master Seb. Mistress said I could go with them and now she says I can't.'

'On the morrow, Nessie,' I said, seeing such disappointment etched upon her face, 'You may go to the fayre, even if I have to watch the babe in your place.'

'What of washing pots, then?'

'That be no task for the man of the house.' I had no intention of scouring platters. I had attempted the task once before, a long time ago, and would not repeat the experience. If I recalled correctly, Jude and I had made such a poor effort of it, Emily had had to wash everything a second time anyway, so there was no point in my doing it again.

'Slow down, Em,' Rose panted. 'I can hardly keep up with you. Why do we need to hasten so? The fayre doesn't end until tomorrow's eve.'

'I'm weary of hearing about Master Fyssher's tedious affairs. Seb speaks of little else, and I have no interest whatsoever in the goings-on in Foster Lane.' Emily stopped by the entrance to the fayre, needing to catch her breath.

'But we knew Lizzie Knollys. For certain you must want the man who took her life to pay for his crime.'

'It won't matter, will it, Rose? Who cares? She was a disgrace to our kind and having someone hanged for her death won't undo the deed. Seb should let the matter lie, and I will hear no more of it.' With that, Emily strode onto the fayre ground with great purpose, ignoring the stalls and the stilt-walker juggling with flaming torches, even as Rose stopped to watch his perilous act.

'Where are you going, Em?' Rose ran after her. 'I thought we came to see the sights.'

'I-I have to make certain my father and John are taking down our booth properly.'

'They know the task better than we, Em. We will just be in their way and no use whatever. What's amiss? I know something is awry. Tell me, Em.' Rose took her friend's hand to halt her. 'What's wrong? Why are you upset?'

'I'm not upset. Naught is amiss.' Emily pulled free of Rose's grasp. 'Now, are we going to spend our coin on something frivolous and expensive, or not? I hear Master Ameryk and the Venetian both have exotic stuff for sale. I have a fancy for a new ivory comb. And I would see this wretched Salome the menfolk keep mentioning. What has she got that we lack, eh? Naught, I'll wager.'

'Fewer clothes, larger assets, I shouldn't wonder,' Rose said, giggling. Then she pointed across the way. 'Hey, Em, look yonder at the acrobats. Is that not...'

'Jack! Aye, indeed it is. Just wait 'til I get my hands on him.' Emily approached the acrobats, inexorable as a boulder rolling down a mountain. Other fayre-goers moved aside upon seeing her furious expression.

Jack had just completed a series of bouncing back-flips and was bowing as the crowd applauded and threw pennies at him when Emily came upon him. She grabbed his ear and twisted it.

'Ow, ow! Let go.' He clutched at his abused ear.

'You accursed beggar. You mangy miscreant. How could you...'

A bald fellow came scampering over.

'Are you his mother?' He looked Emily up and down.

'Don't you dare suggest such a thing. Do I look of an age to have birthed this wretch?'

The man shook his head and retreated a little.

'He's supposedly my goodman's apprentice, damn his eyes. And damn everything else about him.'

'I ain't his 'prentice, not proper. Nuffink's never signed, wos it?' Jack sniffed hard. He was trying to look manly, but the pain as Mistress Em continued to twist his ear made tears flow, despite his best efforts.

'The lad's quite an entertainer, mistress,' the man said. 'I'll make your goodman a fair offer for him. I'm sure we can reach an agreement on price.'

'I ain't some bloody sheep fer sale,' Jack protested. Fortunately, Mistress Em released hold of his ear which was a great relief. He rubbed it gently as it throbbed.

'How much? I warn you, he eats enough for an entire family and treats his clothes as if they were to be had for free.'

'Em! You can't sell Jack like a sack of windfalls.' Rose was horrified.

'Why not? He's good for naught at home. If he can earn his way as an acrobat, then so be it. At least he'll serve a purpose for something.'

'Seb will never forgive you if you do.'

'If I do what? Get rid of this millstone around his neck for him and make money on the bargain. There will be nothing to forgive. Name your price.' Emily turned to the bald man.

The fellow looked about. Quite a crowd was watching them.

'Perhaps I should speak with your husband first,' he said, a note of doubt in his voice.

'No need. As the wretch says, no papers were ever signed. He just bides in our house as mice do and is as much use as they and a greater nuisance. Ten shillings and he's yours.'

'Em, don't do this to Jack. You cannot. Mother of God have pity. He's just a lad; he's family. You can't sell him like a chattel.'

Emily moved Rose aside with deliberate care.

'He ain't worth that much,' the bald man was saying. 'I'll give you three.'

'Eight.'

'Four.'

'Six shillings.'

'Done!'

'Wot! Yer sold us! Yer can't 'ave, mistress.' Jack looked aghast. 'Wot about Master Seb? Wot'll 'e say when 'e finds out wot yer done?'

'In truth, Jack, I care not what Master Seb says. We feed you, clothe you and give you a bed and a roof over your head and what do you give us in return? Not a jot. You're lazy, dirty, ill-mannered and disobedient. I don't want you in my house any longer. I'm done with you and once I receive my six shillings that will be the end of the matter. You can go to Bristol or Norwich or to Hell itself, for all I care.'

The bald man counted coins into a leather bag and gave it to Emily. She did not so much as look within it, far less count the money for herself. She simply accepted it and walked away without a backward glance - not even a 'farewell' word of parting.

'Mistress Rose, yer gotta 'elp me,' Jack wailed, clutching at Rose's sleeve. 'Tell Master Seb wot she's done. He'll 'buy me back, won't he? Say he will, pleeease.'

'Too late for that,' the bald man said. 'You've got a crowd to amuse to earn your keep. Get back on the slack line and do your act. Now!' The last word was bellowed.

With a sob of despair and a last beseeching look at Rose, Jack was pulled away. His new employment with a new master, his future as an acrobat, was about to begin.

'I'll do all I can, Jack,' Rose called out. 'I'm going straight home to tell Seb and Adam. They'll put matters to rights, I know they will.'

Rose ran every step of the way, praying with what breath she had to spare that Seb and Adam would be there, though how to explain what had come to pass, she knew not. Bursting into the kitchen, only Nessie stacking platters and the sleeping babe were present.

'Where are Master Seb and Adam?' Rose gasped, leaning back against the wall, attempting to catch her breath.

'Why ask me?' Nessie muttered, still angered at being left behind to work. 'What's happened then?'

Rose didn't trouble to answer, but ran down the passage to the workshop where Adam and Tom were both at their desks.

'Where's Seb?'

'Minding the shop and going through his notes, I think.' Adam set his pen down and looked up. 'Are you in a fever, Rose?' he asked, seeing her flushed cheeks. But she was gone into the shop.


Rose rushed into the shop as though the Devil pursued her. She was in distress; I could see that.

'Seb, Seb, something terrible has-has occurred. You must

come to the fayre - you and Adam. And bring your purse. Dear God. I know not what's to be done.'

I cast my notes aside and held her close.

'Easy, sweet lass. Be calm. Regain your breath, then tell me.'

'Em... she sold him to the acrobat folk.'

'She sold what?'

'Not what – who. She sold Jack for six shillings, as if he was a pig or an ox at market. You've got to buy him back, Seb.' Rose was attempting to drag me by force.

'This be madness, Rose. Jack is no slave to be sold upon a whim. It makes no sense.'

'True enough, Seb, but Em has done it all the same. Bring your money. You'll have to buy him from the bald man, and he likely won't want to let you have Jack back.'

Adam joined us. He had overheard and was shaking his head in disbelief.

'I'll come with you,' he said. 'It sounds as though there might be trouble. We may need the bailiff and constables also if this bald fellow causes problems over this business. Whatever was Em thinking, selling the lad?'

I was wondering the same. Had my wife lost her wits and reason? Mayhap, the sun's heat of late had proved too much for her. I went into the parlour and took out the coin chest from its secret place behind a brick in the chimney. Without hesitation, I emptied every penny into my purse.

'Tom!' I called out, having made my decision. 'Close up the shop, lad, then run to Bailiff Turner at the fayre. Tell him we have need of him upon a matter of the utmost urgency.' It was better that his youthful legs make the effort than mine which would stumble at half the pace. 'Come, Rose. Direct us to these acrobat fellows, and we will set things aright.'

'You have money?' Rose asked.

'Aye. Enough, I pray.' I patted my purse.

It was mid-afternoon, and the fayre was bustling still. We had to push our way through the crowds in search of the band of acrobats. They were not difficult to find for they performed in an open space surrounded by cheering folk. In the midst of it, Jack was balancing upon a rope, leaping, dancing and turning. In truth, he was quite a wonder, and I admit to suffering a twinge of envy at the sight of a body so agile. But we had not the leisure to stand and watch the spectacle. Jack completed his performance with a flourish and bowed.

Adam and Rose, mayhap unwisely, were disinclined to wait upon the arrival of the bailiff and constables and pushed through to the front of the crowd, receiving shoves and looks of annoyance for their efforts. Against my better judgement, I did the same, keeping a firm hold upon my plainly-bulging purse for fear of cut-purses and basket-dippers. It would not do to be robbed now.

A man with a head as hairless as a newly laid egg approached us, hands on hips, glaring like a malevolent gnome.

'Thought I'd be seeing you again,' he said rudely, glaring at Rose.

'That's no way to speak to a respectable woman.' Adam sized up to the man, though the acrobat was slightly built and a head shorter.

'Brought your menfolk, have you?' He still spoke to Rose as though Adam was invisible. 'It'll take more than these two farts of wind, if they intend to make a fight of it.' He grinned horribly at us. 'Harry! Robbie! Will! Get your arses out here; I've got a task for you. One I know you'll enjoy.'

Three fellows came from a striped tent nearby. Dear God. Each one looked more stoutly constructed than a castle keep. Muscles bulged, and sinews strained.

'I saw them yesterday,' Adam whispered to me. 'They do feats of strength and take on challengers for money. The dark haired one nigh killed a foolish fellow with one blow from his fist.'

My own muscles had turned to water of a sudden, and I prayed Tom would come with Thaddeus and his constables afore Adam and I were laid out, drowning in our own blood. But there was no sign of any assistance as yet.

I steeled my courage, such as it was, and stepped forward.

'I would not make a fight of it, good sir,' I said, doing my best to maintain a steady voice and keep my knees from folding beneath me. 'Good sir,' I repeated, employing a form of address far above his status, hoping to mollify him, 'I come to buy back the lad. He should never have been sold to you in the first instance. What price do you ask for his return?'

'None. He's useful. Attracts the crowds. He'll make me rich, I shouldn't wonder.

What are you going to do about it, eh?' He stood so close that I felt his rank breath upon my face.

Queasy with dread, I unfastened my purse.

'Here. Take it all. My life savings in exchange for the lad. 'Tis all I have.'

'But if my men crush you like ants underfoot, I get to keep the lad *and* take your money. That sounds a better bargain still.'

What answer could I give to that?

Of a sudden, the bald man no longer stood there. He lay upon the grass, Adam's boot pressed hard against his throat.

The three strong men advanced menacingly. Jack also moved towards us, looking as wide-eyed as a coney cornered by foxes.

'Take another step, and I crush this bastard's skinny neck,' Adam growled. 'There'll be no payment for any of you if he's dead and this crowd shall bear witness that I had no choice.'

The man on the ground struggled feebly, and I could see his face becoming purple as in a hangman's noose.

'Let him up, Adam, afore you kill him,' I begged, but he took no notice.

'Jack! Come over here. Get behind me.' As Jack obeyed, I heard Adam whisper, 'And get ready to run.'

'No one be running away,' I told Adam softly, 'This will be a business transaction. Let the man be upon his feet.'

'That isn't wise, Seb.'

'I pray you do as I say.'

Muttering, Adam stepped away, but the bald man did no more than groan and rub at his injured neck, making little effort to rise.

'I offered you money for the lad's return.' I spoke sufficiently loud, such that the crowd could hear me. 'You refused my offer. Nonetheless, I be aware you paid the sum of six shillings for him, though it was no lawful transaction since the lad was not for sale. Therefore, as a gesture of my good will, I shall repay your money, such that you lose naught because of this unfortunate misunderstanding.' I took a gold noble from my purse – the very last of my money from Duke Richard for a commission as yet unfinished and, mayhap, never to be so. I could but hope he never demanded the coin returned. I tossed it at the bald man. It lay sparkling in the sun beside him. 'Take your coin. The matter be closed.' I turned away, feeling my legs somewhat uncertain under me. I prayed that they would bear my weight a little longer. 'Come away, Jack.' I took the lad's arm. If the worst came to pass, I should have to lean upon him.

By the time Tom arrived with Thaddeus Turner and a solitary constable, the situation of discord was ended, but I left Adam and Rose to explain. I staggered behind an unoccupied tent to cast up my dinner out of sight. The confrontation had put my humours in a fearful condition of imbalance. Only Jack's timely aid kept me from falling upon my face.

'Sorry, master,' he said, but I was uncertain for what he was apologising.

Supper that eve would have been a wordless meal if Adam had not taken to retelling the events of the afternoon in ever increasing detail, with additional fictions which most of us knew full well to be untrue. He made me out the hero of the piece. Aye, who but a hero would vomit and swoon after his ordeal? Rose was more rightly the heroine, but he said little of the part he played.

Emily said not a word, her eyes fixed upon her supper, though she ate naught. Jack sat silent also, though his pottage disappeared swiftly as ever. I would have to speak with them both upon the day's occurrences, but harsh words might have to be employed, and I could not suffer more adversity this eve. I should let it lie. My humours would be calmer by the morn.

I left my supper untouched, but took the babe from his basket and went out to the garden plot. Little Dickon, as ever, was balm for my troubled spirit. I showed him the fine palette of sunset colours in the western sky and the pale gibbous moon rising in the east. We waggled the beans swelling upon the bines, and I pointed out the darkening droplets of ripening elderberries in the back hedgerow. He liked the look of those and grabbed a handful, squelching purple juice betwixt his fingers, gurgling with pleasure at the mess it made. His mother would be angered by the stains upon his chemise, but I was tired of always considering her every emotion. Since our return to London, she had been unpredictable and ill-tempered. If she had good reason to be so, I did not know of it.

A butterfly alighted upon the lavender bush and Dickon wanted to grab that also. I laughed at his failed attempts as it fluttered away, distracting him with a dandelion seed head, showing him how to blow the fluff into the air when he would rather suck it. I realised this was the first time during a day so fraught that I had felt a smile upon my lips. He watched in wonderment as the seeds floated to who knows where, journeying on the breeze over St Paul's spire, to distant lands. Or at least as far as our neighbour's plot.

# Chapter 14

## Saturday the twenty-ninth day of August

IT WAS the final day of St Bartholomew's Fayre, and I was heartily glad of it. The event had brought little but disquiet and heartache to the household. But matters could not return to their former situation until I discovered what Emily had been thinking of, selling young Jack of all things. Even so – coward that I be – I had half a mind to say naught; to let the incident fade into history and spare my curiosity. If I let it go, mayhap, it could simply be forgotten. I should have known better.

At breakfast, I noticed Jack's ear to be much swollen and red as a cherry. He kept putting his hand to it, as though it pained him much.

'Did the bald man do that?' I asked.

'No.' Jack ceased fingering his ear and took another honeyed oatcake.

'You should put salve to soothe it. Mistress Rose will find you some, I be sure.'

'Don't need no salve, do I?'

'He got what he deserved and should suffer more beside!' Emily burst out. 'Don't waste pity on him. You should never have brought him home. We were well rid of him, the verminous wretch.'

'Hold, hold, Em. How can you be so uncharitable? Your actions yesterday were unworthy of you.' In truth, the breakfast board was no place to discuss this. 'Go to our bedchamber. We will speak privily there.'

'I will not. You think to get me alone?'

'You fear I'll beat you? Is that it? The parlour then, where you can scream to summon aid, if need be. As if I would ever harm you...'

She obeyed reluctantly, walking from the kitchen, rigid as a pikestave, glancing neither to left nor right. I followed. My heart was fluttering against my ribs like a captive bird in a cage.

Emily stood before the parlour chimney, keeping her back to me as I closed the door. A lengthy silence ensued. I suppose, like me, she knew not how to begin nor what to say. Then she turned of a sudden to face me.

'Do what you will, Sebastian Foxley. I'm not sorry for what I did, and you should have let it stand. As for throwing money away on that pest... you're the biggest fool in London. I'm ashamed to be wedded to you; to have to call you 'husband'. I should have heeded Dame Ellen. She said you weren't good enough. You're feeble and pathetic. A useless husband indeed who'd rather admire painted saints than bed a real woman.'

'Is that what this be about? What happens in our bed? By the Holy Rood, Em, what has that to do with selling Jack? The poor lad can hardly be to blame... But you weren't only getting rid of him, were you? You were punishing me. Was that what you intended?' I sat upon the settle to think. 'You wanted to cause me trouble. To upset me.'

'Isn't that typical of a man?' she screeched, her fists clenched. 'You think you must be at the heart of everything. Well, you're not. You're the least of things to me - less than a worm under my feet. I don't need you. I don't want you. I don't love you. In truth, I *despise* you.' And with those terrible words, Emily flung herself out of the parlour and mayhap, out of our marriage also.

I sat, head in hands, pierced to the heart and utterly bewildered: my life, of a sudden, a devastation.

Some while later – I neither knew nor cared when – Adam came in with a cup of ale for me.

'You didn't beat her then.'

I made no reply and ignored the cup he offered. A dead man has no need of refreshment.

''Tis over,' I said at last.

'What is?'

'Everything.'

'Ah, now, Seb. Matters cannot be so bad as that.'

'Believe me: they could not be worse. She said she does not love me; despises me, in truth.'

'That's just silly woman's talk,' he said, sitting down beside me. 'By tomorrow, she'll be telling you how much she adores you. Arguments betwixt husband and wife are like scraps betwixt cat and dog: they mean naught and are swiftly forgotten. Take her to bed and make up your quarrel 'neath the sheets like every other married couple.'

'Not this time.'

'Oh, drink your ale and be merry then. No man needs a shrew for a wife. Enjoy the peace of bachelorhood for a while. She'll come back, eventually, all repentant and willing to make amends. You'll see; I'm right.'

Clearly, Adam did not realise how serious, how deep was the breach betwixt us and I could take neither the trouble nor the effort to convince him. Our privy matters did not rightly concern others, in any wise.

When he passed me the ale again, I drank it down, thinking that I should not suffer thirst forwhy my wife was an unfeeling besom.

Rose came to the parlour door that had remained open while Adam attempted to comfort me.

'Forgive the intrusion,' she said, looking at me with eyes full of sorrow. 'But Master Fyssher is here. I know 'tis not convenient but...'

'*Miserere mei, Deus*! What now? I cannot deal with another corpse.'

'He says you have not made any report to him of your progress in Lizzie Knollys' case.'

'What progress? There has been none.' I stood up, discovering anger at the coroner put strength into my weary limbs. 'I will speak with him, Rose, thanking you. Is he waiting in the shop?'

She nodded, smiling an apology. I could never be angry with sweet Rose.

Would this damned business never end? Had I not told Fyssher more than once that I had no time to spare, working for him? Why did he think it my duty to unravel his accursed mysteries for him? Did I not have troubles enough of my own? The man was a confounded nuisance, and I must tell him so, directly.

But, of course, I did not. Discourtesy was beyond me, as ever. The coroner was fuming with impatience beside the counter-board.

'Good morn to you, Master Fyssher.'

'Good morn, you say? 'Tis bloody nigh noontide and I've yet to hear your report. Not good enough, Foxley. I must be kept informed at all times. And why are you not out, making further enquiries? Unless you have unmasked the killer already? In which case, why have I not heard of it?'

'Matters arose of a personal nature...'

'Personal nature! The maintenance of law and order is of concern to the city; to King Edward himself,' he said pompously. 'It takes precedence over your piddling privy affairs at all times. Understand?'

'Aye. But I...'

'No buts. Get your skinny backside over to Foster Lane and ask questions until you find the bloody culprit. And report to me before vespers. You hear?'

Damn you, I thought, watching him stomp out of my shop. I thumped my fists so hard upon the counter-board, the chain came off the peg at one end. All the books for sale slid sideways to the floor, covers flung open, spines bent and pages creased. It was a stationer's nightmare, and I did not care. In fact, I kicked the tumbled volumes across the floor, but it was not enough to vent my spleen. I sent entire reams of paper cascading off the shelf, piles of pamphlets swept away. I was even tempted to set fire to it all.

A heavy hand came down upon my shoulder.

'No more, Seb.'

I took a long, shuddering breath.

'I cannot do this any longer, Adam. Everything is in chaos.'

'We can clear up the mess,' he said, but I did not mean the state of disarray in the shop. I truly meant *everything*. 'Why don't you go to St Paul's, look at the stained glass, light a candle, say a prayer? You know it will calm you.'

'But Fyssher demands...'

'Sod Fyssher. You need a few hours respite, Seb. Take them, for your own sake, as well as ours. Go on.'

'Aye, I will. 'Tis wise counsel, Adam. I be most grateful for it.'


Emily hastened along Cheapside. The babe, unfed as yet, was grizzling in the basket as it knocked against her thigh with every hurried step. Soon he would be yelling, but she could not tend him now. Tears welled, and she brushed them away with her free hand. She reached Beattie's house on the corner of Friday Street and knocked frantically, pounding upon the door.

'Beattie! Beattie! Let me in for pity's sake,' she cried.

'Whatever is it?' Beattie opened the door and looked anxiously around the street. 'Is someone chasing you? Come along in, Em.' She ushered her friend within, then closed and barred her door, fearing intruders.

The babe began wailing, but Emily hardly noticed.

'Oh, Beattie, I've made matters so much worse. Seb is no fool, and now I've said such terrible things to him. When he works it all out – as he surely will soon – I've upset him so much, he'll be turned all against us...'

'Sit down and feed that infant before he deafens us both. Go into the kitchen. Hal won't disturb us; he's working elsewhere and my lad's at school, I hope, as he should be. We'll have some of my cowslip cordial, and you can tell me everything.'

'It all began to go wrong at dinnertime yesterday. Oh, Beattie, you wouldn't think I could make things go so badly.' Tears poured down Emily's cheeks, and Beattie dabbed them away with a napkin. 'You recall Seb is investigating... what happened... in Foster Lane?'

'I'm not likely to forget, am I?'

'Well, he said at dinner that neighbours there remembered seeing a group of women, wet from the storm, calling at Lizzie's house. And then a great argument.'

'They didn't name us, did they?'

'No. Seb would have said, if they had, I'm certain. But you know how he works at such mysteries, Beattie, like a dog with a bone. What do I do when he asks me if we were there?'

'You lie to him. What else can you do?'

'But folk saw us, heard us. She died, Beattie, and we were there. We'll hang for this, I know.' Emily took a mouthful of the flowery-scented cordial and moved the babe to a more comfortable position so he might suckle more easily.

'No we won't. You were the one telling me and Pen to go about as if naught were amiss. Now look at you. You must follow your own advice, Em. We know naught of Foster Lane. Rather, we came from the fayre by way of St Martin's Lane. 'Tis just as likely. And we did not call upon Lizzie Knollys. We had no reason to, did we? If folk think they saw us, they were mistaken. We can't have been the only women in London who took a soaking that afternoon, can we now?'

'That tale sounds plausible, but I did something which disproves it. I took back my pendant. I should have left it, as evidence of her thievery, but it means so much to me and how was I to know she would die? And Seb has seen it about my neck since. How could I have retrieved it unless I went to her house?'

'Does Seb know she took it?'

'I blamed him for losing it at first. But since then, he has found your snips and Pen's needle case and other stolen items in her workbasket.'

'I'll be glad to have my snips returned.'

'But Beattie, he will realise where I found my pendant. He'll know I was there. And then I was in such a distemper last afternoon, I went back to the fayre, and I sold Jack to the band of acrobats for six shillings.'

'You did what? By my grandmother's eyeballs, you can't sell a child. Are you quite mad?'

'It wasn't like that. Jack seemed to belong with their kind. It was like putting him to an apprenticeship, that's all.'

'No. If that were the case, you would pay the master to take him on, not receive money for him. You have to get him back, Em. No excuses.'

'Seb has done so. I'm not to be rid of wretch.'

'Is Seb angry with you? Is that another reason for these tears?'

'I suppose so. He was about to take me to task over it this morn. I know not why he waited so long, but I turned things around. I told him he was a useless husband, a worm underfoot and that I despised him. Then I left and came here. What have I done, Beattie? He must hate me so much; when he finds out the truth, he'll not pity me and he'll be glad to see me hang. Oh, Bea...'

'You foolish woman. You may have condemned all of us. Go home. Make love to your man. Woo him. Win his sympathy before he finds out the truth.'

'But I don't love him any longer; if indeed I ever did. What I told him this morn might have upset him, but it was true, even so.'

'What does that matter? You can pretend, can't you? This could be life or death for us. What do a few lies signify in the face of that?'

'But I already told him I don't love him.'

'What of it? All men think women are fickle creatures. Tell him you've changed your mind. A few lovesome kisses and he'll believe every word.'

A knock at the door made them both jump.

'They haven't come for us already, have they'? Emily turned pale as wet linen.

'Who's there?' Beattie called out, going to the door. She had to listen hard to hear the quiet reply. 'Fear not. It's Pen,' she said, unbarring and opening the door. ''Tis as well you came, Pen.' She replaced the bar. 'We may have problems.'

With little Dickon now sleeping contentedly in his basket, over more cups of cordial and slices of spiced bread, Beattie and Emily explained the woeful tidings to Pen. Pen's eyes grew larger and more terror-filled at each disclosure, even as she seemed to shrink deeper into her widow's hood.

'But there are still things we can do. If the worst befalls, we can all plead our pregnant bellies.' Beattie patted her own swollen abdomen. 'That will delay matters until we can think of something else to save our necks. Is there any chance that you might be with child, Em?'

Emily shook her head and sighed.

'Holy Church forbids a man lying with his wife if she be suckling a babe, you know that, because they say suckling prevents conception anyway. And Seb abides by every ruling, no matter how pointless it is.'

'Such nonsense.' Beattie made a rude noise. 'I conceived young Will when our daughter – God rest her little soul – was still at the breast. My Hal was more lusty and eager in those days. What of you, Pen?'

'How can I be? Andrew lies in his grave.' Pen crossed herself and murmured a brief prayer.

'Maybe so, but there are plenty of men still living in London. Any one of hundreds would oblige a comely widow like you with a goodly dower. You can take your choice. I told you of my handsome cordwainer, did I not?'

'I'm a respectable widow, Beattie! I cannot do that.' Pen surprised her friends with such a show of assertiveness.

'Andrew's not been gone so long; it could be his.'

'How can I suddenly be with child after six, nigh seven months?'

Beattie shrugged.

''Tis your first child. You didn't understand the signs.'

'But it won't be born until Andrew has been gone a twelve-month and more. I could not pretend I conceived by him.'

'Stranger things happen.'

'No, Beattie. I will not taint my reputation nor soil my memories of Andrew. I know we were wed but a few months, but he was a good man and kind to me... mostly. I won't do it.'

'Then it'll be your head in a noose and no chance of reprieve.'

Pen burst into tears at such dire words. Beattie simply passed her a napkin and turned to Emily.'

'The same applies to you, Em. Seb isn't the only man. In truth, I believe you have some other fine fellow in mind anyway. Am I wrong?'

'No, Beattie. There is someone else.' Emily had the grace to blush, at least.

'I knew it. Well, that solves your difficulty, doesn't it? Unless he too adheres to every foolish stricture of the Church?'

'Indeed, not. He disapproves of everything the pope insists upon.'

'Then go to him, Em. Do what you must. And then return to that overly-righteous husband of yours. Coddle him and smother him with sweetness. Be sure he loves you, then he'll not take his investigations too far, if he thinks you may suffer for the outcome.'

'Even if I am with child by another man?'

'A married woman's child is always assumed to be her husband's. That's the law.'

'Unless he knows otherwise.'

'We'll worry about that later. As for you, Pen...'


I returned from St Paul's. Adam had been correct: I felt calmer for my brief interlude in the presence of the Almighty.


'Has anyone seen Emily?' I asked. I wished to make some gesture of reconciliation with her, if she would allow, afore the day was another hour older.

'Not since she left earlier,' Adam said, cutting a fresh quill for his work.

'Nor me,' Rose admitted, as did everyone else.

'Did she take Dickon?'

'Aye.' That solitary word of reply filled me with unease. If the babe was not here, my wife might have no reason to return. Could she have truly meant what she said earlier? In the peace of the cathedral, I had convinced myself they were merely hot words spoken in anger, but now I was no longer certain.

'She'll return soon enough. She hasn't gone far, if that's what you fear.' It was as if Adam could read my thoughts. 'She took no mantle nor coverings for the babe, and since it looks as though it may rain, that will bring her home.'

'No doubt you be right, Adam. I worry needlessly. I suppose I must think through this hateful investigation, compile my notes and write Master Fyssher's report. Although I have far better things to do, he'll not let me rest until 'tis done. I shall be at work in the parlour if anyone has need of me.'

'We won't disturb you,' Adam said.

I went to my task, Gawain, my faithful companion, sprawled at my feet, half-hoping they would find some reason to interrupt me. I took a clean sheet of paper, dipped my pen and began to compile my discoveries, such as they were, for Master Fyssher, including a separate list of subjects for my own use only. I had no intention of informing him of names that might prove to be of entirely innocent folk. Since Lizzie's Book of Hours had come to her *with Fondest Regard 'R'* and the threatening letter would seem to apply to the same, any suspect whose name commenced thus with an 'R' had to be included. Forwhy I disliked him so greatly, and his nature was felonious, Roger Underwood headed the list, though, in truth, I could not think the likes of him would give away such an item as a fine book when he might sell it for a high price.

Against my inclination, I had to put the black-skinned Abyssinian upon the list also. A number of Lizzie's neighbours had mentioned him so it would be wrong to ignore their testimony. Unfortunately, Rook began with an 'R', but I could not think that such a pleasant fellow and friend of Gabriel could be guilty of murder. Against that, his employer, Master Ameryk, dealt in all manner of fine and exotic wares and a beautiful Book of Hours may have been among them. Could Rook have stolen it and given it as a gift to a woman who took his fancy? I doubted it. I was unsure if the man could even write to inscribe it and had no evidence of any dishonesty on his part. Nevertheless, his name had to be there. Yet how many other men in London had names commencing with 'R'? There were not years enough left to me to quiz every Robert, Richard, Reginald, Roger, Ralph and Raymond, never mind the foreign Ruperts and Renés or anyone whose family name or nickname might so begin.

Then there were the women, whatever their names. Of course, women were not killers by nature nor inclination, but I must identify and question them all the same. The trouble was, I thought I might know one at least, having found that distinctive veil pin in the hearth – now secreted in my purse, not with the other items from the house of crime – but how might a man interrogate his wife on such a matter without destroying every last semblance of love and trust betwixt them? If, indeed, any vestige of either yet remained. There had to be some other way.

Not long after, with but the first page of my report written, my hope of interruption was fulfilled. I heard Emily's voice in the passage. She was speaking with Rose, asking my whereabouts. I needed no better excuse to discard my pen.

'Em. I was worried, not knowing where you had gone,' I said.

'I had errands to do.' She smiled and stroked my sleeve.

Relief coursed through my veins. All was well betwixt us, God be praised. He had answered my prayers made barely an hour since.

'Where is Dickon?'

'Asleep in his basket in the kitchen, of course. Where else would he be?'

'I do not know. I was concerned, Em. You seemed so angry with me earlier...'

'And I was wrong, Seb. Can you forgive me?' She held my hand and pressed close against me. The sudden sweet kiss upon my lips surprised me, but I embraced her, revelling in the dear scent of her.

'Oh, Em. I can forgive you anything, sweetheart.'

She ran her fingers through my hair, sending shivers down my spine and, like any man, I could not prevent my body's response, no matter the impositions of the Church. I would have to concentrate on turning my mind to less sinful thoughts.

'I'm sorry for what I said, Seb,' she murmured.

'Then tell me you love me still.'

'Of course I do.'

'Say the words, then. Please. If you mean them...'

There was a long pause, and then she spoke:

'Very well. I love you, Seb.' She pulled away from me then. 'I must go out again. I still have errands to complete. I'll leave the babe. 'Tis cloudy now and smells like rain. I'll be home in an hour or two.' With that, she took her mantle from the peg behind the kitchen door and was gone.

'Told you so,' Adam said. 'There was no need to fret, was there?'

'No, I suppose not.' And yet something did not feel right. Something discomfited and disconcerted me, and I knew not what it was.

Emily hastened to Queenhithe, her lies to Seb still sour on her tongue, but she was more concerned how best to persuade Gabriel. How should she go about seducing a Known Man? She smiled to herself. He was a *man*, aye, and any man but Seb would *know* what was to be done with a willing woman, longing for love. Gabriel would not disappoint her; she was certain of that.

Her laughter turned heads upon the street, but let folk think what they would; she did not care. She had waited so long for this, believing the chance was gone when Gabriel had been forced to leave London two years ago. But now, for these brief few days, he was back, about to sail the perilous seas once more. Who could say if such a moment as this would ever come again? This time, she would not let him go without some lovesome memories to cherish and, if Mother Nature was smiling upon her, a quickening of her eager womb by which to remember him.

The first drops of rain splashed upon the dusty quayside as she called out, hailing *The Eagle,* asking for Master Gideon Waterman. She fingered the amber pendant at her throat, warm against her skin. Wet coin-sized blotches appeared upon her mantle, like blemishes upon a sinner's soul.

With the little book chest and its valuable contents in my script, I determined to eliminate one name from my list. My walk to Queenhithe was ill-judged with regard to the weather for it was raining, but the sooner I made my enquiries, the sooner Rook's name could be removed from the list.

From the quayside, I called up to the ship through the squall of rain.

'Master Waterman! Gideon Waterman! 'Tis Seb Foxley. I would speak with you, my friend.' I could see a couple of men on deck, but it seemed they could not hear me. The gangplank was in place betwixt the vessel and the wharf. I could have gone up it, but I dare not. Ships of any kind, from rowing boats to this fine sea-going three-master, did not agree with me. The very thought of the deck moving beneath my feet, however slightly, caused bile to rise and my belly to heave. I could no more board *The Eagle* than fly to the stars. 'Master Waterman!' I shouted through the rain.

Eventually, a fellow took notice of me.

'Come up, if you would speak with Gideon,' he called down. 'The man's at work on charts in his cabin.'

'No. I pray you, ask him to come to me. Tell him 'tis Seb Foxley: he will understand.' Indeed, he would. My one and only visit to his previous ship, the *St Christopher,* had not gone well with me. I was certain he would recall my abject embarrassment at that time.


The interruption was inopportune.

'Master Gideon,' a man's voice called from outside the cabin. 'A fellow named Foxley is asking to speak with you. Says he would have you go down to him. Says you'll understand why.'

'He must have followed me,' Emily squeaked, clutching her abandoned clothes to her naked body. 'What shall we do, Gabriel? He must not know.'

'It may be too late for that. Get dressed. I'll go down to him. If he asks, I shall say you, er, brought me a parting gift, a memento, a message before I depart.'

'Aye. Seb's trusting enough to believe it.' Emily pulled her rumpled shift over her head and fastened the ties. 'My hair is in such disarray...'

'Blame the weather.'

'Master Gideon? Did you hear me?'

'Aye, Daniel, I heard. Tell Master Foxley I'll be there directly.' Gabriel laced his hose to his shirt in such haste, it was badly done and then stepped into his boots. 'Stay here, Em, until I have a chance to get him away from the wharf. I'll lead him towards Bread Street. Then you go home by way of Cordwainer Street in the other direction.'

'I do love you so, Gabriel. This wasn't how I wanted it to end.' Emily's face was bleached with distress. 'I wanted it to be a beautiful memory for both of us. I should have known he would spoil it. He ruins everything.'

'It was beautiful, like you, Em.' Gabriel paused in fastening his doublet, took her face in his strong hands and kissed her. 'And it will be a treasured memory to the end of my days.' Then he left the cabin, closing the door.

As she did her best to dress in the unaccustomed cramped space, Emily was sobbing so hard, she could barely thread the laces on her gown. Some of the eyelet holes had been ripped in their earlier haste to lie skin to skin. Gabriel was right though: it had been beautiful despite the abrupt ending. She pressed a hand to her belly and prayed that once had been sufficient for her purpose.


I waited some while, the rain soaking through to my nether shirt and my hair flattened wetly about my ears and forehead afore Gabriel appeared and came down to greet me. He was much dishevelled. I had clearly called at an inconvenient moment. No doubt, perusing charts was a laborious task.

'Forgive the intrusion, my friend,' I said, smiling in the hope he was not too displeased at my interruption of his work.

''No, no, Seb. 'Tis always a pleasure to see you.'

I was relieved at his broad grin, noting the walrus ivory tooth was not in place, although the eye-patch was there, concealing his brown eye on this occasion, whereas he more usually hid the blue. Plainly, I had called upon him in a condition of unreadiness.

'I apologise for my visit unannounced, but my enquiries on behalf of the coroner have taken an unfortunate turn, concerning Rook.'

'Rook?' he repeated. 'You come to speak of him?' Gabriel laughed out loud.

"Tis naught to laugh about. I fear that a number of Lizzie Knollys' neighbours – you may not have heard that she was slain, most likely upon Wednesday last, in the afternoon or evening – they say they saw a man in Foster Lane, black of skin, close by around that time.'

Gabriel controlled his mirth swiftly and nodded.

'Aye. I think I take your meaning, Seb. You're saying Rook is a possible suspect? Come, let's find some place out of the rain to discuss this. There's a decent cookshop close by.' Gabriel put his arm around my shoulders, guiding me along Thames Street and turned up Bread Street. 'This place serves the best coney pies,' he said, pulling me into the gloomy shop. He set out a stool for me at a board. We were the sole customers. 'What will you have?'

'A cup of ale will suffice,' I told him. 'In truth, my belly has no desire for food at present.'

'Even looking at a ship still makes you feel queasy, does it? You've not improved on that score then.'

'Nay. But 'tis more that I be discomfited, having to tell you of folks'... their, er, distrust of others not of their kind. The awful things they have said of Rook that I be ashamed to repeat. But one matter at least can be resolved.'

The shop owner chose that moment to waddle out from his kitchen to ask what we would have. I grant he was a fine advertisement for his wares, rotund as a barrel, his girth tremendous, his complexion ruddy.

'I'll have a large coney and mustard pie, since I have worked up a great appetite this morn. Poring over charts,' Gabriel added.

'My friend will have a slice of your aniseed and fennel bread to settle his stomach. And a jug of ale.' He turned back to me, a frown betwixt his brows. 'Now, tell me how I may assist you in proving Rook's innocence, for I swear he is a good Christian soul, as I've said before.'

From my scrip, I took the chest I had found beneath Lizzie's bed, incongruous in its cost and beauty in such a poor hovel. I set it upon the board.

'I found this at the dead woman's house in Foster Lane. She being so poor, it had no place there. Could it have ever been amongst Master Ameryk's wares for sale, do you think?'

Gabriel ran an appreciative hand over the embellished wood. 'It is well made indeed and likely of Flemish make...'

'As I thought.'

'You know of such things?'

'I know little, but be more acquainted with the contents, as you will see.' I turned the brass key in its lock and revealed the velvet lining within. Taking great care, I lifted out the book. ''Tis this that suggests Bruges manufacture to me.'

Gabriel took it from me, but upon the instant, he realised what manner of book it was, he put it down, grimacing.

'A bloody popish Book of Hours! Seb, you know my hatred of such unrighteous nonsense. Why show it to me? Why make me sully my hands on this devilish stuff?'

'I apologise to you, but require that you look upon the flyleaf only, at the beginning.' I turned to the first page and showed it to him. *To Lizzie with Fondest Regard. R.* I read the inscription aloud. 'Tell me, can Rook read and write?'

'Of course. I schooled him myself, but he wouldn't touch a damned popish book no more than I. Like me, he is a Known Man and wouldn't taint himself so. Is that what you wanted to ask? Whether 'R' could stand for Rook? Well, it can't, and I'm disappointed that you felt able to contemplate such a possibility.'

The shop owner brought us our food and drink then, but Gabriel stood up, tossed a groat upon the board and walked out.

'Enjoy your food. I have things to do,' he snorted, quite forgetting I had not wanted any.

'Aye. Back to your charts, eh? I be sorry to have distracted you from your task.'

He grunted something I did not quite hear and departed. I was indeed remorseful that we did not part on better terms, knowing we might not meet again for years, if ever. At least, I could remove Rook's name far to the bottom of my list of suspects, though I might not remove it entirely.

Outside, the rain had eased, and my humours were better settled also, yet I was annoyed once more to return home and find Master Fyssher awaited me in my parlour. Every time he arrived at my door, it invariably meant more trouble for some undeserving soul – usually me. My greeting was not quite discourteous, but by no means fulsome in welcome.

'Well, Foxley, you might be more appreciative of my efforts in coming here,' he said, drinking ale from our best pewterware. "Tis good news, indeed, and will spare you any further investigation. You should be pleased. The culprit has been arrested.'

'Roger Underwood has been taken? That is good to hear.'

'Who?'

'The pedlar at the fayre.'

'No, not him. He is long gone, no doubt. The murderer of Lizzie Knollys has been apprehended. The citizens of Foster Lane tired of your delay in the matter and went to the sheriffs at Guildhall. They knew where to find such a one, made for the fayre ground, took the ghastly fellow straightway and arrested him.'

'Have they got the right man? Who is it they have taken?'

'Oh, there's no doubt as to his guilt, though he protested mightily, of course. The fellow be as black as sin and calls himself Rook. Half a dozen and more of the folk in Foster Lane described him, having seen him lurking feloniously in the vicinity at the appropriate hour. 'Tis unfortunate that they had

247

not the manners to inform me first, but I blame your tardiness for that. You should have acted as soon as they told you of him.'

'But there is no evidence...'

'Nonsense. There must be. You just haven't found it: failing in your duties again, Foxley. You are hopeless. I doubt I shall require your ill-services again. Good day to you.'


That night, mayhap, Adam in his chamber above the workshop and Rose in her bed over the kitchen passed a peaceful few hours, and Nessie snoring in the chimney alcove did well enough, but little sleep was had by others in the Foxley household.

Jack tossed upon his bed, keeping Tom from his rest. Jack could not decide whether – despite all that had come to pass – he might still be allowed to join the acrobats. Working at a craft, either as a scribe or a wood-carver, was not for him. His young body could not sit for the hours Master Seb required of him. He had enjoyed showing off to the crowd at the fayre, but being sold like a sack of cabbages by Mistress Em and then bought back by master might have spoilt his chances of being an acrobat. Besides, the fellow in charge had a nasty temper, as he'd learned. But then again, there was Maudie, after all this time. Finding his sister had come as a shock.

Emily kept as still as she could, but her head and her heart were brimful of terror, anxiety, passion and hope. She must surely keep Seb awake as he lay beside her. Such a turmoil of emotions would curdle her milk if she did not calm herself. As it was, the babe was fretful and most likely that was the cause of it. The terror and anxiety at the possibility of being accused of murder warred with the hot memory of Gabriel's body against hers, his calloused hands, his burning kisses and the naked joy of being wholly his at long last. But their ecstasy had been cut short and was, mayhap, the sweeter for it. Now she hugged the secret remembrance to herself, locking it away in her heart forever. And, perhaps, she had the hope that Gabriel had left her the seed of a more tangible reminder. A hope, if realised, that might even save her from the gallows.

There was no chance of rest for me. I lay in the dark, listening to Dickon snuffling in his sleep, the sparrows chirping under the eaves and the rain returned, tapping on the window. How could I sleep, knowing an innocent man stood awaiting trial for murder – a crime I felt certain he did not commit? Yet now I was released from my duties as the coroner's assistant, no longer required nor authorised to investigate further to uncover the real killer. I could continue unofficially, but did I wish to? Perhaps I should, but then again, I had a nagging fear, a foreknowledge almost, that it might be safest to let the matter go as it would. However, whether I could live with my conscience, if I let an innocent man hang, was a question still to be answered?

And what of the woman who lay beside me? Was the brass-headed pin I had found evidence of her involvement, sufficient to prove her guilt? It could not be, I told myself, and my heart believed it. But my head had yet to be utterly convinced. It seemed impossible that I could even entertain such doubts about the woman I loved beyond all else. Yet there they were, like evil spectres, haunting the darkest corners of my mind and I could not close them out; not quite.

# Chapter 15

## Sunday the thirtieth day of August

I WAS AWAKENED from some half-remembered dream – if a dream it was – by soft hands upon my body and sweet lips pressed against my mouth.

'Love me, Seb,' Emily murmured. 'I desire you...'

'Em? What hour is it?' I blinked against the faint light through the gap in the shutters.

'Early enough.' Delicate fingers slid lower.

''Tis the Lord's Day, then. Whatever are you thinking?' I removed her caressing hand. 'We cannot do this, Em. And what of suckling? We would offend Holy Church.'

'Damn Holy Church!' she cried, sitting up of a sudden and casting aside the blanket. 'Do you love me or not, Sebastian Foxley?'

'You know that I do, with every bone in my body.'

'Then show me. Or does the Church mean more to you than I do?'

'Of course not, but...'

'There is no 'but'. Love me or lose me.'

With such an ultimatum, what choice did I have?

We were tardy in descending to the kitchen, to join the others for the walk to St Michael's to attend low mass. Our love-making had not been as I would have wished after the long months of enforced abstinence, while Emily was with child and then feeding the babe at the breast. There had been little time for tenderness and, despite the act being done at her insistence, I felt she would take as much pleasure in doing the laundry on the morrow. As for myself, far from any sense of joy or satisfaction, I felt used and soiled as an old floor-clout, aye, and cast aside after with as much affection. It might have been a business transaction and a distasteful one at that, rather than a fond demonstration of marital love. I suppose I deserved no better, having broken the rules of Holy Church.

Father Thomas greeted us at the door of St Michael le Querne on the corner of Paternoster Row. I blushed hotly even as he smiled at me, fearing he would read in my eyes, my demeanour, what I had done an hour earlier. I was no dissembler. Yet Emily looked unabashed, as if it had not occurred. She went to speak with Dame Ellen, leaving me with little Dickon in my arms. I took him to the large, brightly painted mural of St Christopher upon the south wall of the nave. He performed his usual show of pleasure: waving his fists and blowing bubbles, but I noticed how the pigments were flaking, not unlike the dragon's blood remedy upon my wrist, and the ominous signs of mould beginning to mar the image.

The congregation was all of us sweating for the air was humid and close. It was as well the incense somewhat disguised the hot stink of our gathering in the little church, and I was sure the smell of bedsport was still rank upon me, despite my hasty ablutions. They all must know of it and guilt made me perspire the more. Neither did I find my usual sense of peace in the office of low mass. In fact, I was hardly aware of the comforting Latin phrases spoken beyond the rood screen. Rather, another perplexing question had occurred to me. Why had my wife been so desperate for my attentions of a sudden? After telling me only yesterday that she despised me, why now did she crave the body she had said was 'less than a worm beneath her feet?' I know women be famed for fickleness, but a change so abrupt must have some other cause. And I misdoubted that cause to be love.

As we were leaving at the end of the office, to salve my conscience upon a number of matters – I had not forgotten poor Rook, lying innocent in gaol, made worse when I heard it was Newgate, so abhorrent to me – I would put coins in the alms box. My fingers found some sharp object afore they found a penny: Emily's veil pin from Foster Lane. I glanced across at her, standing beside Rose, the babe upon her hip. Her veil was neatly pleated and pinned in place, but could not entirely hide the scratches on her cheek. They looked to be healing, but the scabs remained vivid upon her skin. I wondered if the scratches (that I knew had naught to do with briar thorns, despite her explanation) and the lost pin were connected. Lizzie Knollys' neighbours had recalled women arguing that day. God forbid my Emily had been one of them. Praying that she was not, I would buy favour with the Almighty and put more pennies in the box for those in need of charity in the parish.

'You look pensive, Seb,' Adam said as we returned home. 'I realise, 'tis not my place to ask, but is all well betwixt you two?'

'You mean with Emily? Aye, I suppose.' I shrugged.

'You seem unsure. When you arose late this morn, I assumed...'

'Assume what you will. As you say, 'tis not your place to ask.' I realised I spoke too sharply. 'Forgive me, Adam. I mean no rebuke. I know you enquire with concern. In truth, I would prefer not to discuss such matters. I have much upon my mind at present.'

'What say you, we go to the Horse Pool? The fayre ground will be nigh empty now. The lads can run off some of their high spirits afore archery practice, and you can draw, as I know you enjoy.'

''Tis the Lord's Day.'

'But your drawing need not be considered work, rather a sovereign remedy for your disquieted humours.'

I nodded.

'Your advice be sound as always. Aye. I would rather be out of Emily's way for now. My humours may be disquieted, as you say, but hers be utterly inexplicable. I know not where I stand with her.'

We were about to turn down the side passage to our gated yard at the back of the house when someone yelled my name. A string of foul words that ought not be uttered on a Sunday, nor any other day, followed on in such a rant. It was Ralph Clifford, waving his one good fist and cursing the name of Foxley. I had not seen him of late, but he had remained in the city, still bearing a dray-load of resentment against us for my brother's sake. Unfortunately, there was naught to be done to mend the situation, but to ignore him. It was what it was: another weight to add to my burden.

St Bartholomew's Fayre was ended at last. Almost all that remained were patches of yellowed grass where yesterday tents and stalls had stood and the bare earth between, where the passage of a thousand feet had worn the turf away. A few men sat about beside a tent here, a booth there, half dismantled. Forbidden to work upon this day, they would idle the time away until the morrow, when they could complete their tasks, the bald fellow and the other acrobats among them. I saw that Master Ameryk's booth was alone in standing untouched. It appeared abandoned. I suppose with Gabriel confined to the ship at Queenhithe for fear of recognition and Rook imprisoned, the Bristol merchant had other problems to attend. Taking down his booth was of less importance, even though it would mean his continued payment of stallage to the priory would likely be demanded. The sacristan would be glad of extra coin and, no doubt, Master Ameryk could afford it, but I felt sympathy for him, even so.

Stephen Appleyard, as Warden Archer, was already setting out the butts for archery practice after dinner. Emily's father travailed alone in this – no rest for him; he worked as hard upon this day as throughout the week – and I sent Tom and Jack to aid him.

Adam and I sat 'neath my favoured oak tree by the Horse Pool. I always felt inspired here. Adam watched as I took out my charcoal and drawing board from my scrip, leaving my legion notes made in recent days flapping in the breeze. I had no use for them any longer and took a page that was written upon on one side only and affixed it to the board. In truth, inspiration would most likely elude me, but I should make the effort.

The bulrushes stood sentinel at the edge of the pool. Of noble bearing, upright as a duke's retainers in their brown velvet and green-sheen livery, they would make a fine embellishment for the margin of my *Aesop*, when I could return to it. A dragonfly alighted upon them as I sketched, iridescent in the sunlight as some magical creature not of this world. That the Almighty had created such wondrous beauty solely for mankind's appreciation never ceased to surprise me, and I praised Him for such graciousness with a few silent words.

'What do you pray for, Seb?' Adam asked, seeing me make the sign of the cross. He was lying back, chewing a juicy grass-stem.

'Naught. I was thanking the Lord God for the beauty of bulrushes and dragonflies, that he made them for our pleasure.'

'Really? You're not beseeching Him on this account, are you?' Adam waved one of my loose pages of notes.

'You should not read those!' I attempted to grab the paper from his hand, but he removed it away. 'Return it to me.'

'You leave them lying loose... anyone might see them.'

'Please, Adam. Put them back in my scrip.'

'Too late: I've read them all but the one you're drawing upon. You know who murdered Lizzie Knollys, don't you?'

'No. I do not. Not for certain. I beg you, Adam: say naught of this. Master Fyssher has his culprit. Let the matter rest.'

'But Rook isn't guilty, is he? In your notes you write of finding a woman's pin in the ashes of the fire – a singular pin indeed and you've drawn its likeness. And besides that, you record that women were heard arguing, after which event Lizzie Knollys isn't seen alive again. You've written that here plainly enough. Both you and I know who wears pins of this design.'

'"Tis a coincidence. That be all it is. Naught more than that.'

'Seb, do you think Emily could have killed that woman?'

'No. Lizzie was strangled by a hand larger than mine. Not a woman's hand. A woman would not have sufficient strength.'

'Did she not die by the blow to her temple, then? A woman could have done that, mayhap by throwing something or knocking her against a wall.'

'I do not know, Adam. As God be my witness, I cannot tell. I hate it that Rook stands wrongfully accused, but if I suggest some other did the deed, I may be naming yet another innocent. I know not what to do. As I set down in those notes, I think 'R' who wrote the inscription in the book be a more likely killer but who is he? Unless I find him out...'

'Then that is what we must do.'

Rose and Nessie betwixt them had concocted a fine Sunday dinner of roasted mutton with fresh thyme and a pease pudding, plum tart with cream and raisins of Corinth in a sweet batter. I tried my best to do it justice but, repeatedly, as I looked at Emily across the board, my heart would lurch. Was I sharing the meal with a woman who had slain her fellow? The thought should never have crossed my mind, but it had. Now Adam had put the terrible thought into words that I could not force aside.

Of a sudden, Emily threw down her knife.

'Why do you keep looking at me so?' she demanded. 'You're staring at me. Stop it, or for pity's sake leave the board. I cannot eat with you glaring at me all the while.'

I cast my eyes down, noting what a mess I was creating upon the cloth, splashing gravy and plum juices; a splotch of cream on my napkin. I was worse than a child and had eaten barely a mouthful.

'Forgive me, all of you,' I said and left the kitchen by the door to the yard. I had to take time to think, yet my thoughts had me in deep despair. How Lizzie had come by the bruises to her throat, I could not say. A man's hand, certainly, but that could have occurred earlier. Neighbours had heard *women* arguing, and Adam was correct: a woman might have caused the contusion to her head. But which had killed her? I knew death from a head injury was not always immediate. It may have taken Lizzie hours to die of it. How was I to tell? But either way, it was impossible for Lizzie to have thrown her dead self into the midden. Someone else had done that.

When dinner was done, Adam and the lads took their bows, as required by law, and returned to Smithfield for archery practice – one thing Jack did enjoy and excel at; Tom less so. Nessie washed dishes while Rose retired to the parlour, to improve her reading with a book I had given her. It was an old exemplar, much annotated and dog-eared, the tale of Sir Lancelot in English. As for my wife, she had fed the babe and settled him to sleep afore going out. I did not enquire where: Emily was a law unto herself at present.

Gabriel was in his cabin, staring at a pamphlet: the Gospel of St Luke in the English tongue. A heretical text, but aboard *The Eagle,* all knew of his beliefs and either shared them or did not care. It was safe to study the Word of God, however, whenever he had leisure to do so. But this day, the text seemed to cavort before his eyes and he could not concentrate upon it. And a woman was the cause - another man's wife. Emily.

He had always tried to live according to God's Ten Commandments, but Emily was ever his downfall. Since the day he first set eyes upon her, when he'd come as a journeyman-scrivener to Seb's workshop, he had shamefully coveted his neighbour's – or rather his employer's – wife. But he had avoided any greater sin than that by force of will alone, believing God was simply putting temptation in his way in order that he might prove his worthiness as a Known Man.

Now he had committed adultery.

But, so Gabriel reasoned, was this not also part of the Divine Purpose? God – with Seb as his instrument – had already saved him from a heretic's fate and preserved him from shipwreck when most others had perished. He must have some vital part to play in God's plans for mankind. Was not every man's destiny known to God before ever he was conceived? Aye, that was it: his coupling with Emily had been ordained by God. It was not some sordid case of succumbing to temptation, but an instance of the working out of the Divine Purpose. No doubt Emily had conceived a child in those moments of heaven-sent ecstasy, a child who was destined by God for some great role in His service. Not adultery for the sake of lust then, but obedience to the Will of God. So be it.

Having thought it through from a godly point of view, as a Known Man should, Gabriel was now content; his conscience clear. He returned to his study with renewed vigour.

# The Foxley House

Everyone else had settled to some occupation or other suitable to the Lord's Day. I alone was over restless and unable to direct my mind to anything other than brooding upon the circumstances of Lizzie Knollys' demise. A book lay open in my lap, but I could not so much as name its title, never mind relate its contents. Therefore, I was relieved at the distraction of a visitor, even if it was Warden John Clifford of the Stationers' Guild. I could not think of any reason why he should deign to honour us so, but welcomed him wholeheartedly. It would be as well to improve my standing with the guild since, upon the day after the morrow, the restoration of the Foxley name to the memoranda roll of fellowship was intended for discussion among the senior members at their monthly meeting. I supposed Warden Clifford's call was concerning this matter.

'Good day to you, Foxley,' he said as I showed him into the parlour.

Rose bobbed a courtesy to him afore scurrying out, her book beneath her arm.

'I'll fetch ale,' she whispered as we passed in the doorway.

'God grant you blessings upon this day, Master Clifford,' I said, gesturing for him to sit in the grand chair that had once belonged to the Duke of Gloucester and, somehow, was ne'er returned to him. It bore the Gloucester coat-of-arms and would serve to remind him that I had an illustrious patron, even though he be far away in the distant shire of York. 'How may I be of service to you?' I perched upon the edge of the settle.

'I-I would enquire as to your business this week past, what with the fayre and all.'

My face must have shown my surprise that he should concern himself.

'Quiet indeed, as were most other shops, no doubt. We sold a ream or two of paper, a few pamphlets and little else. Mayhap, next year, I shall rent a pitch at the fayre myself, for business there was swift.'

'Aye. A possibility worth consideration.'

Rose tapped at the door and entered, encumbered with a tray bearing our best pewter ale jug and matching cups and a dish of the raisins in batter left from dinner. She poured for us both and offered the dish to the warden. He took a handful of the dainty delicacies.

When we were alone once more, Clifford spoke with his mouthful:

'She's the one your accursed brother was supposed to wed? Yet you keep her here. Why?'

'Rose Glover works harder than anyone in this household. She assists my wife in cooking and cleaning, tends the babe, serves in the shop and still finds time to stitch the finest kid-skin gloves in London. She was in no way at fault such that my brother did not marry her.' I almost added 'as you well know', but restrained myself. 'Why would I turn her out of her home, onto the streets?'

'Keeping a one-time whore does not improve your reputation.'

'Rose be naught of the kind, sir. You mistake her utterly and speak as though she lives here as my mistress.'

'Is that not the case, then?'

'It most certainly is not, and I resent such a remark. Rose is a respectable woman.'

The expression upon the warden's features made it clear that he knew of Rose's less respectable past – a past for which she had not been to blame in the least.

'Speaking of wanton women – .'

'Which we were not,' I put in hastily, but he ignored me.

'It has come to my notice that you are investigating the death of Elizabeth Knollys on behalf of Coroner Fyssher. How is that progressing?' He reached for more raisins.

'No longer.' I frowned, in some confusion at this path taken in conversation. 'Master Fyssher does not now require my assistance. He has solved the crime to his own satisfaction, though I believe the denizens of Foster Lane and the sheriffs determined the culprit, not the coroner. I have naught further to do with the incident now, except to return the stolen items I recovered from the deceased woman's house. For the present, I keep them safely in my storeroom.'

'Ah!' He held out his cup to be refilled. 'I was unaware she was a thief also. I dare say the purloined items must enlighten you as to what class of persons she relieved of their property.'

'They may do so.'

'And was anything significant found?'

'An amethyst ring, a pair of earrings, a knife with an enamelled handle, an ivory needle-case and suchlike trinkets. Oh, and a book in its book-box. Why? Do you know of someone who has lost something of value?'

'No, no. Of course not. Naught of the kind. I did not know the woman.' Warden Clifford appeared a little flustered, dripping ale down his doublet of crimson satin.

I handed him a napkin, but he declined it, coming to his feet as though to leave with his handful of raisins only half consumed. He tipped the remainder back into the dish – an ill-mannered gesture that shocked me – and gave me his cup to return to the tray.

'Good day to you,' he said, moving to the door. 'Attend the guild meeting promptly on Tuesday next, and we shall see what can be done to reinstate your name upon the roll.' Then he left.

I wondered why he had come. Most surely he knew I would be at Tuesday's meeting upon the hour since my livelihood required it, without his need to remind me. At least he seemed to have a better opinion of me now, though he disapproved of Rose dwelling in my household. But since there was no hint, since Jude departed, of anything improper in the conduct of those 'neath my roof, he could not hold that against me.

Once again, I took up my book, but I had only just opened it when there came a hesitant tap upon the door.

'Master?' Jack sidled into the parlour as if he was unsure whether he would or no.

'Aye? What is it, lad?'

'I needs to talk wiv yer, don't I?'

'You do not have to ask. Is something troubling you?' I set my book aside once more.

'A bit. See, I didn't like bein' sold to them acribats, did I? But all the same...' He eyed the dish of battered raisins and I pushed it towards him. He took a couple and popped them in his mouth.

'But all the same?' I prompted him.

'Master, I ain't meant t' work, sittin' on me arse all day. I ain't no scribe, am I?'

'You be a fine wood-carver though.'

'Aye, but it ain't 'citin', is it, whittlin' lumps o' wood?'

'I suppose not. More satisfying than exciting.'

'I wanna leave. I wanna be an acribat like wot I wos afore I came t' London. I'm good at it and...'

I looked at him in dismay.

'You be unhappy here?'

'Not really. I like the food an' a nice bed, but I don't like Tom.'

'Tom will finish his apprenticeship in a few months.'

'Aye and most like you'll keep 'im on as a journeyman, so the bugger'll still be 'ere, won't 'e?'

'Maybe not.'

'Yer will, cos yer soft on folks an' yer won't wanna upset 'im.'

'Kate Verney be returning to work here on the morrow.' I tried an alternative means of persuasion. 'You like Kate a great deal, I know.'

'Aye, but Tom spoils it, like 'e spoils evr'yfink.'

'Leaving: 'tis an irreparable step, Jack.'

'I don't care, whatever it means.'

'Have you given it sufficient consideration? You did but see the acrobats two days since. 'Tis hardly time to have taken into account all the possible consequences. Here you have a safe home, shelter and comfort. Upon the road, you would be homeless, at the mercy of the weather and a master you do not know. How will he treat you, Jack?'

'I don't know about no conseckitences. I jus' know I don't wanna stay 'ere no more.'

'I be sorry to hear it, Jack. I believed you to be content. Clearly, I have been mistaken. When would you wish to go?'

'In the mornin'. They're doin' the act fer the king hisself t'morra afternoon. We'll need t' practise. Lord Astings arranged it, whoever 'e is.'

'Hastings. The king's chamberlain.'

'Well, I wanna be there, don't I?'

'Of course you do, lad,' I said upon a sigh. 'But you will be greatly missed here if you go.'

'Not by Tom nor Mistress Em, I won't. They'll be glad t' be rid of us, won't they?'

'I shall miss you, Jack, very much indeed.'

The lad nodded.

'I knows yer will, don't I? But you're the on'y one. Nobody else'll care. And I'll be wiv Maudie.'

'Maudie?'

'Aye. Me sister. I founded 'er after all them years.'

'You told me she wed a merchant in Cambridge, or do I misremember it?'

'No. She did go wiv 'im, but 'e never married 'er. She was just a unpaid skivvy, weren't she, an' got used somefink so bad, she runned away an' joined these acribats.'

'I did not see a lass with them, unless you mean... Salome?'

'Aye, the veils dancer. That's Maudie.'

'Well! 'Tis quite a surprise, Jack.'

'Tom was ogglin' 'er, the filfy beast. I don't like 'im doin' that an' uvvers do it too. I wanna keep me sister safe from their kind, don't I?' The last few raisins disappeared.

'See me afore you depart in the morn, lad. I shall want to give you my blessing.' I had in mind to give him a few coin, as well as my prayers for a good life.

'I will, master.' He grinned at me, and I realised how much he wanted – nay – needed this change of direction.

My interview with Jack was done when the kitchen door slammed, and I heard footsteps racing up the stair and along the passage overhead. Our bedchamber was above the parlour where I stood and the thud of hastening feet continued, and the chamber door banged closed. Then there was silence. Emily had returned, but the omens were not good that she came home in better humour. I had news to impart that Warden Clifford would likely support me at the meeting and that Jack was leaving us. Such tidings should cheer her, but I was uncertain whether I had courage enough to go upstairs and tell her. Who could say how I might be received by a woman whose humours swung from insult to ardour and back again within hours? She might loathe me or love me, and I had no understanding of her reasoning. If women be capable of reason? Sometimes, it seems they are not.

The vespers hour was nigh, and I readied myself to return to St Michael's, but our party was much depleted. Jack had other matters to deal with in readiness for his departure upon the morrow. Tom had gone to Deptford to visit his sister Bella's family and was not yet returned. Adam said he wished to attend vespers in St Paul's. I considered joining him, but thought Emily, in her present uncertain humour, would prefer the more intimate surroundings of St Michael's. As matters befell, she did not come at all, so Rose and I walked together with Gawain at my side and Nessie trailing behind.

Rose was in good cheer, the Lord Jesu be praised, for I was much in need of a few smiles and merry words. Betwixt Jack's decision and Emily's contrariness, the pair had caused a cloud of gloom to descend upon me, and I fear I was not good company. However, by the time we returned to a simple supper of cold meats, bread and cheese, Rose had brought about a lift in my spirit, and we were laughing together.

Over the meal, with all now at board bar Emily, I had Jack tell of his plan for the morrow. The reception was mixed. Tom was elated, as might be expected; Rose was cautious in her approval and more so upon learning of Maudie. Nessie burst into snotty tears, and noisy lamentations while Adam told him to enjoy the venture, clapping him upon the back most heartily.

Supper was done, and I could find no excuse to delay the moment any longer. With heavy tread, aye, and a heavy heart, I went upstairs to our bedchamber. It was not yet dark, the window shutters were still open, and the sounds of the street could be heard. A cockerel with no sense of the hour was crowing somewhere, perhaps mistaking the colours of sunset for those of sunrise. A group of revellers passed below the window, shouting good-natured obscenities in their drunkenness and roaring with laughter as one of their number went sprawling in the dirt. Such rowdiness was unseemly upon the Lord's Day, but they were young and cared not. Watching them, I realised they were much of an age with me, yet I felt old and encumbered by responsibility and, for a few moments, I was envious of them.

Emily did not stir upon the bed when I entered. Despite the warm evening, she had pulled the blanket and coverlet up over her head. Had it not been for a few stray tendrils of gold and russet hair across the pillows, it was hard to know that she was there. I glanced into the cradle at the foot of the bed. Little Dickon slept soundly, sucking his thumb – a habit he had taken to of late.

I was not ready for sleep myself and sat upon a stool 'neath the window, watching the street fall quiet. St Paul's steeple opposite stood dark against the fading sunset, upright sentinel and guardian of our Christian souls. We lived so close by, I could not see the cross at the pinnacle high above. I took comfort in this view, knowing the Almighty, like the great steeple, oversaw our safety through the night and warded evil from us in the day.

A movement of the bed coverings drew my attention.

'Em? Be you unwell, lass? May I fetch you something since you missed supper?'

She did not answer, but settled again with her back now turned to me, as one would close a portal. Yet I did not believe she was sleeping. I sat upon the bed and touched her hair.

'Speak to me, Em, I beg you. What be amiss? I cannot aid you if I know not the cause of your sorrow. Tell me, sweetheart.'

For some while she lay still, making no sound as the light dimmed and night stole in upon the streets. I stroked her hair, my gentle fingers the only movement in the chamber.

''Tis the worst thing,' she said at long last in the smallest voice without coming from under the blanket. 'They questioned poor Pen.'

'Peronelle, do you mean? Who questioned her and concerning what matter?'

'Lizzie Knollys. Oh, Seb... it was us: we killed her!'

'Of course you did not, Em. That be foolish talk.'

'I know what I did,' she cried, casting off the covers. 'I shoved her. She fell and struck her head. I killed her. I'm a murderer and will hang for it.'

'No, no, Em.' I took her in my arms, stifling her sobs against my heart. 'You be no killer. Someone else...'

'She lay dying, and we fled. If we'd summoned a surgeon, she might have lived, but we left her to die...'

'Shh, lass. You be mistaken. We will sort this out. It was not as you think. Hush now.'

'We had our tale all rehearsed, but Pen lost her nerve. She got it wrong. Her story was not as Beattie and I told it.'

'When was this?'

'This afternoon. The neighbours in Foster Lane went to the sheriffs.'

'Aye, and they implicated Rook, claiming he was the murderer.'

'One of the sheriffs asked Pen if she had seen a black man there. Foolishly, she admitted that we all did. We saw him true enough in Foster Lane, but our tale should have been that we'd come to Beattie's house that afternoon by way of St Martin's Lane. That was what we decided we should say. When the sheriff came to Beattie's this day, and I was there, he close questioned us both. We spoke of hastening through the rain down St Martin's.

265

He listened and then told us our friend's version did not tally with ours and we had been seen in Foster Lane. He demanded to know why we lied about it if we were innocent. He has learned that we knew Lizzie and that we argued. 'Tis only a matter of time until they arrest us. Oh, Seb... such a terrible thing. I don't want to hang. You must help me.'

'I will, Em. You know I shall do all within my power to set this aright.' Tears ran down my face.

'Don't fail me, Seb, I beg you.'

'I love you, dearest Em, heart and soul, bone and sinew, to the very marrow of my being. I will not let them take you. Trust me.'

We sat, thus entwined, hour upon hour, until there were no tears left.

# Chapter 16

## Sunday night into Monday morn,
## the thirty-first day of August

I SAT AT my desk. A solitary candle illuminated the darkness of the workshop. A pale moth danced about the flame, and a breath of air from the unshuttered window caused the flame to catch its wings. It fell, scorched and wounded beside my ink pot. I ended its agony with the flat of my hand. I thought how swiftly, upon an instant, could death be come by and what a weapon was a man's bare hand.

My cheeks were stiff with the salt of dried tears, and my pen was unsteady as I wrote the letter. I addressed it to the lord mayor and sheriffs, informing them of the bruises on Lizzie Knollys' neck, how they were undoubtedly caused by a man's hand. I stated that she had been strangled for certain and – most importantly – how I knew it to be so. She had indeed suffered an injury to her head. As a result, dazed and bewildered, she succumbed swiftly to a hand about her throat. Her corpse was then dragged out after curfew and half buried in the midden. It was an act of unbridled rage, of lust turned sour.

The letter was a meddling of truth and speculation, but I ended it with a lie. I could not have maintained such a gross untruth face to face. Hence, my epistle. I dried the ink with a little pounce powder and shook it off, back into its pot. I read the words through again. They were clear enough and required no alteration. I dipped my pen for the last time and signed my name.

Sebastian Foxley.

There was an uncertainty in the final 'y', its tail shaky and longer than it ought to be for good penmanship, but it mattered not. It was legible and most definitely in my hand. That was all that was important. I folded it, addressed it to the appropriate authority and left it on my desk beside my unfinished manuscript of *Aesop's Fables*. Adam would discover it later and deliver it as required.

I believe I slept a little after that, still at my desk, but when the cockerel crowed again – rightly this time – I went out, silently, by the kitchen door. I did not look back.

# London Bridge

I did not recall the walk there, only that the Watch did not prevent me. The sun was yet a faint suggestion of paler sky in the east. Below me, the river thundered and roared, foaming around the starlings of the bridge. It terrified me. Always had. So I gazed at the sky one last time. The deepest blue-black, still star-studded overhead, it mocked me. It ought to have been dismal grey with misery.

I looked down. The bridge was not so high, but it would suffice. What choice did I have? The river surged below in a sweeping, swirling torrent, foam-flecked. The waters' tumult was the only sound to be heard in the silent city. Even the gulls had not yet roused themselves to screech my funeral oration.

That nagging voice at the back of my mind was wordless at last, the one that kept warning me 'Think of your soul. It will mean an eternity of torment.' And I had thought, long and deep, 'til my head teemed with self-argument and naught was resolved.

The letter was written, confessing to the crime I did not commit. It was for the best. The dead could not be questioned. I knew if I attempted to mislead them, whatever the colour of my lies, the authorities would find me out, for I had no skill at deception. Yet everyone believes a man's dying words to be the truth. This way, my Emily, whether guilty or no, would be spared. Rook would be known as innocent and released. My name would be abhorrent forever, but I must be content with that.

No more delay. No more thought. Not a single wasted prayer. Oblivion beckoned. God forgive me.

I inched towards the edge of parapet where workmen had obligingly left wooden scaffolding to make repairs. Dawn would see them return to their labours. I must be gone by then. My foot slipped upon a loose stone, and I clutched desperately at the scaffold poles. I was a fool. If I fell by mischance, my soul might not be condemned to hell-fire everlasting. Why did I save myself? I took another faltering step and naught remained betwixt me and the waters of my death. One last long breath. I closed my eyes, leaned out into the void and let go.

# The Foxley House

Jack was too excited to remain abed any longer. His few possessions were bundled up, tied with string and ready to leave. It was not yet dawn, but he went down to the kitchen to wait for Master Seb's blessing, as arranged last eve. Nessie was snoring and snorting in her sleep in the chimney corner behind the curtain, but Jack's sharp ears caught other sounds.

The scratching and whimpering seemed to be coming from the workshop. From the storeroom, to be precise. When he lifted the latch and opened the door, Gawain bolted out as if the Devil was on his tail. Whining and barking, the dog ran from room to room, rousing the household with such commotion.

'Lord's sake, Jack. What's going on?' Adam came into the kitchen, yawning and still fastening his shirt.

'It's G'wain, ain't it. Gone mad 'e 'as.'

'Where's Seb? If the dog be up and about this early, then so must he be?'

'The dog was shut in the storeroom, weren't it?'

'Why would Seb leave him there?' Adam strode along to the workshop as though to see for himself where Gawain had been imprisoned.

'Don't ast me. 'Ow would I know?'

There was no sign of Seb, but the dog had caused quite a tempest of papers to swirl to the floor. Adam began to collect up the scattered pages of Aesop. And then he saw the letter. Addressed to the Lord Mayor as Chief Magistrate of the City, it hadn't been sealed and had fallen open, so he began to read.

'Dear God in Heaven. This cannot be.' Adam crossed himself and stood a moment, dumbfounded. 'Come, Jack. Bring the dog. Make all haste.'

'Where we goin'?'

'I don't know. Where would you go to leap to certain death?' Adam pushed the lad out through the shop door, into the near-dark street where daylight did not yet rule.

'Wot?'

'You know London better than I. How would you kill yourself?'

'I bloody wouldn't, would I?'

'Paul's steeple?' Adam suggested, pausing in Paternoster Row to secure the boot he hadn't put on properly. 'Seb could climb up and...'

'No, 'e couldn't, not wiv 'is 'ip.'

But Gawain had no interest in St Paul's and raced away into Cheapside. Adam and Jack could not keep pace.

'Gawain! Hold!' Adam shouted, and the dog waited in the deserted street. But before they reached him, he was off once more, turning down Friday Street.

'Ow does 'e know where t' go?' Jack panted.

'Following his master's scent... I hope.'

They pounded past All Hallows, Bread Street, and lost sight of Gawain. Then they heard him bark and saw him run into Budge Row. Adam saw spots before his eyes. He was fit as any man, but his lungs were bursting, and his legs burned with fatigue. Jack was younger and faster and stretched ahead, passed Londonstone and along Candlewick Street. Adam was utterly lost, and only the occasional glimpse of Jack's jerkin half-flying off his back guided him into Crooked Lane and out into Fish Street.

Tattered fish-wives from nearby Billingsgate, laden with baskets of herring, hampered his route, but Adam barged a passage down to St Magnus by the Bridge. He prayed briefly in his thoughts – no breath for words – then braced himself to plunge into the dark tunnel that was the way across London Bridge. Shops and houses leaned in on either hand, shutting out the first glimmers of dawn.

Guided by Gawain's barking, he found a narrow gap betwixt two crumbling buildings on the downstream side of the bridge. Jack was yelling, but the thunderous river noise, no longer shut out by walls, made his words meaningless.

The lad was wrestling with a man.

It was Seb.

Jack clung onto him, fiercely tenacious and determined, but only when Adam was able to help, did they manage to overcome Seb and drag him from the brink. Yet he continued to do all he might to wrench free of them, writhing in their grasp, tearing his shirt as he tried to get away, leaving them holding ripped cloth.

Screaming at them to let him do what he must, it required Gawain to seize his master's ankle in his jaws and bring him down before they could finally subdue him. Sobbing and pleading with them still, he sat, slumped against the wall of one of the buildings.

It took a while for them all to recover and regain their breath. Adam wiped sweat from his brow upon the back of his hand.

'Whatever demon possessed you, Seb?' he asked, panting still and shaking his head in bewilderment.

No explanation was forthcoming.

I could fight them no more. They dragged me away from the bridge. They had ruined everything. My death would have been easier than watching Emily swing in a noose. They did not understand; congratulating themselves on saving my soul from damnation. What was that compared to seeing my beloved hanged for an accident? Or the alternative: having my conscience agonise over an innocent man executed forwhy his skin was of a different hue. I could only save them both if my confession were believed: that I had killed Lizzie Knollys with my bare hands. Now it never would be. If interrogated, my own lies would trip me. No one would be convinced and, mayhap, we would all hang together: Rook guilty of being black, Emily guilty of fleeing from an accident and me guilty of attempting to misdirect the course of justice. Aye, we were all guilty, and there was a price to pay.

Yet we three sat in some tavern or other quaffing ale with the day but barely begun. Adam and Jack were breaking their fast on bread and cheese, talking together. It was as if a black cloud separated us. I could see them and hear them – just – but I was part of their world no longer. Mayhap, I had died already without the need to hurl myself into the waters. Only the heat of Gawain's body pressed against my leg under the table maintained any connection betwixt me and this existence.

Of a sudden, Adam turned to me and took my hand. I could feel his touch against my skin, but somehow remained apart, as if at one remove: some ghostly barrier betwixt us.

'I read the letter, Seb. Remember, I too went through a time of blackest melancholy when Noah died; losing my twin like that, so I do understand why you did it.'

'Well, I bloody don't,' Jack muttered.

'Because you didn't read the letter.'

'Can't, can I?'

'Keep out of this, Jack. Me and Seb have to talk. Go home.'

'I'm bloody goin',' he said, standing up and draining his cup. 'I chase all over bloody London an' stop 'im bloody killin' hisself an' that's wot I get: "Go 'ome, Jack". But I ain't. I'm goin' t' Maudie an' Devil take all o' you buggers.' Then Jack walked out.

I heard what they were saying, but what did I care? Words meant naught to me. I shook Adam's hand off. I would sit 'til Judgement Day, if the bench I sat upon lasted so long or 'til I died of old age or some ailment. Or I starved to death.

'Leave me alone, Adam,' I said. 'The woman I love is destined to hang; that be all that concerns me and, by your actions, you have cruelly prevented me from saving her the only way I could. Leave me be.'

'Why? So you can return to the damned bridge and finish what you began? Oh, no, Seb. I didn't go to so much effort, racing across this God-forsaken city, for naught. I know you're desperate to save Em, whether she is guilty or blameless, but there must be a better way than you intended.'

'If there is, I know it not.'

'I can't believe you would confess to a murder you didn't commit.'

'I would do anything for Emily.'

'But would she do as much for you?'

'Of course she would.'

'I doubt it. For that wretched Gabriel fellow she might, but for you... You know how she feels about him.' He left the word unsaid, but I did not need to hear it spoken.

'Whatever sentiment she holds for me, I love her, Adam. Naught changes that.'

'Why would you even suppose she killed that woman?'

'Forwhy, she told me so, and she believes she be guilty.' I then told him what Emily had related to me last eve.

He paused to munch on some cheese and break off a heel of bread, never taking his eyes from me. He scratched at his beard as he did when thinking deeply, then delved within his shirt and brought out a damp, crumpled piece of paper. I recognised it. Though the ink was smudged with sweat in places, it was yet legible.

'How much of what you wrote in this letter is true?' he asked, smoothing it out upon the ale-house board among the thousand circles left by wet cups.

'All of it, insofar as I can tell. Except for the confession.'

'So there were a man's finger marks on her neck?'

'Aye. But I cannot know if she died of that or from the blow to the head.'

'Your description of killing her by strangling, then throwing her on the midden heap... you're guessing that may have happened?'

'It makes sense and fits with what I saw.'

'Em told you that after the argument and Lizzie falling and striking her head, they ran away, leaving her lying by the hearthstone?'

I nodded.

'But Lizzie's body was found half buried in the midden. So if Em and the others left her on the floor of her house, who took her outside?'

'Mayhap, she crawled from her door, hoping to summon aid. I do not know, Adam. If I did, the mystery would be solved.'

'However she died, Seb, we need to know whose finger marks were on her neck. Tell me about them.'

'Undoubtedly, a man's hand. It was of greater span than mine.'

'Just one hand?'

'Aye. The left.'

'Is that not strange?' Adam leaned towards me and put his hands around my neck to demonstrate. 'Why not use both hands?'

'Mayhap he was sufficiently strong, such that he had no need. One of those fellows with the acrobats would require but one hand.'

'Even so,' Adam went on, 'It seems an unnatural thing to do.'

'Murder is unnatural.'

'No, no. You're missing my purpose, Seb. However strong, it makes better sense to use both hands. He would be unbalanced elsewise. She might have turned away and escaped him. Unless he had no choice...'

'No choice? What mean you, Adam?'

'A man with but one arm is what I mean. But for the present, we needs must repair your state as best we may before we go home.'

'Do I look so bad?'

'Seb, you look as a man dragged through Satan's own portal and back. You have swollen eyes like cherries on stalks and what of your shirt, eh? Ripped to rags.' He lifted my sleeve to show me the large rent and the flapping of cloth. 'You will scare the women for certain with your face all puffy and your clothes torn.'

'Please do not tell them what I did.'

'I fear we can't avoid giving an explanation of some sort. 'Tis not as if they could fail to notice that some awful happening has come to pass. Unless we say the Devil himself abducted and tortured you...'


'Fear not,' Adam announced as we entered through the kitchen door, holding up his hands to still any enquiry. 'Ere anyone has a fit of the vapours, Seb has suffered somewhat of a mishap, but he is quite unharmed. We will answer your questions later, once he has washed, eaten, changed his clothes and had time enough to collect his thoughts. Do you all understand?'

Rose, Tom and Nessie were the only folk in the kitchen. They all nodded, though I espied an expression of horror upon Rose's features when she beheld my wretched condition.

Emily, poor lass, remained secluded in our chamber for fear of arrest, I supposed, but where Jack might be, I did not know. Gone to join the acrobats, most like.

Rose brought me water and towels and a clean shirt that had been destined for the linen press – a few creases were an improvement on a great tear. When I was done, she handed me an ointment pot, saying naught. I read the label attached to it. It contained the tiny plant we call eyebright – an efficacious remedy for sore eyes. I must have looked to be much in need and smeared the yellowish stuff upon my eyelids. It was soothing indeed. A pity there was no such balm for a mind likewise in distress.

Food and drink were set upon the board for me. I was not hungry, but eating might delay the time for explanations. Since I had neither desire nor courage to excuse my actions earlier, I ate the food, but could not say what passed my lips. Unfortunately, with the exceptions of my wife and Jack, they all sat watching my every mouthful, waiting until I was done that the interrogation might begin. It sounds absurd to admit it, but even as its master, at that moment I was in fear of my own household, how I should answer them. I ought to have known they were more kindly than that.

The questions did not come. I believe Adam and Rose must have exchanged some silent communication concerning this. When my platter was empty, Rose removed it and said she would go and open the shop front, and be serving there, if any needed her. Adam told Tom to set out the desks in the workshop for the day and soon followed the lad, saying we should get Gawain to see about the mice, for he was certain the vermin were nibbling at the reams of paper in the storeroom. However, his parting expression warned me against considering any further ungodly undertakings. Nessie had dishes to wash and the week's laundry was soaking in the Monday lye-tub, awaiting her attentions in the yard. Thus, they left me to my thoughts and, mayhap, that was unwise for they were melancholy and unwholesome as ever.

Emily eventually crept downstairs and joined me at the kitchen board. What a tragic spectacle we two must have made. She glanced about her like some timid forest creature fearful of the huntsman's arrow.

'There be no one here but us,' I said.

She gave no answer but sat and accepted the ale I poured for her.

'You should eat something. Where be little Dickon?'

'Sleeping. What's wrong with your eyes? They look swollen indeed.'

'Dust.'

She nodded, but I knew she did not believe me.

'Adam reckons we have mice chewing at our paper stock,' I said, attempting to make conversation. 'Gawain prefers larger prey. We may have to acquire a cat to protect our wares.'

'Kate will approve: another animal for her to draw.'

'Kate?'

'Your apprentice. Isn't she returning to work this morn?'

'Kate! Dear Heaven, but I had quite forgot.' Despite all things, the thought of Kate Verney's bright smile and sunny demeanour lifted my spirit a little. The day was less dour of a sudden, and I stood up with a sense of purpose, turning toward the workshop to prepare for the lass's arrival.

'Seb?'

'Aye?'

'I-if they come for me... y-you won't let them take me, will you?'

Could I have forgotten her fearful situation so soon? What an unfeeling wretch was I? I enfolded Emily in my arms, holding her against my heart that beat still, despite my earlier intention to have it cease forever.

'They won't come for you, sweetheart. I promise you. No one will take you, else I shall run them through with... with my penknife.'

She forced a laugh of sorts at my ridiculous jest.

'I would forfeit my life to keep you safe, Em.' She did not know how true that was; how perilously close I had come, but a short while since, to achieving that very thing. We clung together, each savouring the nearness of the other's living, breathing body. I realised then that I had been greatly at fault in my earlier actions. Adam was correct: there had to be a better way to keep Emily from the clutches of the law and spare Rook his near-certain appointment at Tyburn Tree.

Kate was come, bringing gladness into our house as she ever did. In the months since she had returned to her father in March last, after the sorrowful matter concerning her sister's madness, I could not recall what lessons I had proposed for her education at the time. No matter. I would rethink it after speaking with her.

'I've brought all the work I've been doing,' Kate said, placing a great sheaf of papers afore me on my desk. 'I've been trying to use shading to make things look more rounded and life-like, as you showed me last time before you left London. See?' She sorted through the drawings and displayed a few. 'I made this horse look plump indeed and here... look at this friar I saw at the fayre last week. I drew him even fatter than he was.' She giggled, setting her unruly dark curls bouncing.

Adam came to look also and joined in her merriment. If those two could not cheer the most forlorn of humours then there must be no cure at all.

'These be very fine, Kate,' I commended her, smiling – and the smile was genuine – as I tidied the papers. 'Have you been practising your capitals, also?'

'Not so much, master.' She pulled a face. 'They're not such fun to do.'

'But necessary all the same, if you wish to complete all aspects of a manuscript.'

'I will work on them this day.'

'Aye, and you may use the coloured inks. Take what you will from the storeroom.'

'I was drawing butterflies in the garden at home, yesterday,' Kate was saying, balancing upon a stool to reach the back of the shelf. 'I never knew there were so many kinds with spots and stripes and patterns and great eyes. I think they would look well in the margins... Oh, master, look here. Come see this. What a mess, but...'

I went into the storeroom and Kate presented me with a mouse's nest made all of shredded paper – my best quality paper. We did indeed have a problem. What was worse, the nest contained a writhing mass of tiny, naked things. Even as I took it from her, an adult mouse scurried along the shelf, bold as a rake-hell on a Saturday night.

Gawain came to observe, and I thrust the nest beneath his nose, so that he might take the scent.

'This be your job,' I told him. 'You should catch these little devils.' The dog sniffed and looked up at me curiously, as if wondering how he could possibly be at fault and what I expected him to do. 'You be hopeless, Gawain, and mayhap overfed. No dinner for you 'til you eat these damned mice. We have a plague of them.'

Having disposed of the nest at the far end of the garden plot, I determined the store would have to be scrubbed and cleaned throughout. Jude had allowed such matters to go undone in my absence, but such costly ruination could not continue.

With Tom and Kate assisting, I cleared every shelf of parchment, paper, pigments, brushes and all the paraphernalia of my craft. The stench of mice was strong, and we uncovered other abandoned nests, likewise constructed of paper. Two entire reams had been chewed around the edges, stained with mouse urine and sprinkled with their black truttles. It was a dreadful waste. As we worked, sleek dark bodies and worm-like tails were disappearing into crevices and crannies in the woodwork barely of a size to insert a quill. I must visit the skinners and purchase a cat – a live one afore they skinned it – this very day.

I passed Tom the book-box from the top-most shelf, the one I had taken as possible evidence from Lizzie Knollys' house. At least the mice had not yet spoiled that.

'Put it upon my desk, Tom.'

'What is this, master?' I saw Kate had unwrapped that wretched rainbow-maker that I had concealed and forgotten.

'No matter, lass, 'tis but a foolish trinket of no use. Go ask Nessie to heat some water for us. I know she will complain that she has the laundry to attend to, but a bowlful will suffice. And wash-cloths and a drop of lavender water, also. We need something to remove the stink of mice.'

'But look, Master Seb,' Kate said, 'How lovely the colours it casts by the window. 'Tis a wonder indeed, is it not?'

Aye. I might have known it would oblige her with its rainbows.

''Tis yours, if you wish it, lass,' I said, not wanting to be reminded of the coin I wasted upon it.

'A gift for me? Oh, master, you're so kind.' Afore I knew it, Kate stretched up on tip-toe and planted a kiss on my cheek. 'Thank you, master. I shall treasure it always.'

I felt hot blood rush to my face and turned away. Such frivolous expenditure was not deserving of gratitude.

'Ah. The infamous book in its box that I read about in your notes,' Adam said loudly, distracting me. 'May I look?'

I shrugged, seeing he had lifted the lid anyway.

''Tis finely made... beautifully penned. A Flemish hand by the look of it. For my taste, I would have used less realgar. Why do they always use it to paint Judas? Is it because the pigment is as vile and poisonous as he, the arch-betrayer?'

'The arch-betrayer? In truth, Adam, I have always wondered about Judas. If not for his actions in the Garden of Gethsemane, how could our Lord Jesu have died upon the cross in order to become the Saviour of mankind? Are we over hasty in condemning Judas for carrying out what must surely have been part of Almighty God's plan?'

'You mean, you would forgive Judas? I can't believe any man would do so.'

'Mayhap? I was not there in Gethsemane to know how matters befell precisely.'

'The Bible tells us.'

'Aye, but it does not say why Judas wanted the thirty pieces of silver, does it?'

'Greed, of course.'

'Or his family could have been going hungry. His mother may have needed medicines.'

'Then he should have asked our Lord for a miracle, like the loaves and fishes, or like curing Lazarus.'

'And our Lord would have refused his request, knowing His destiny required Judas to betray Him.'

'Aw, Seb, you argue like a Cambridge scholar. You're right. Perhaps Judas should not be cursed as he is. In which case, why does this miniature give him such a villainous expression? And see, he accepts the money in his left hand, showing he performs the task at Satan's bidding, not God's.' Adam showed me the colourful image. The artist had depicted Judas' left hand reaching out to take the bag of silver offered by the Chief Priest while his right hand seemed to hang uselessly at his side. Had Judas been afflicted by some injury that meant he could no longer earn his bread? Was that why...

'Ralph Clifford,' I said.

'What has he got to do with anything? You think he looks like this Judas?' He tapped the page with his fingernail.

'Not in his features, no. But see his right arm.'

'Poorly painted compared to your work. It looks lifeless.'

'As does Ralph Clifford's these days.' I pulled Adam a little to one side, away from Tom and Kate who were sorting through the damaged paper to see if any might yet be salvaged for making notes and scribbles, if naught else. 'A man who can use but one hand: his left.'

'And his name begins with an 'R'. But would he have strength enough? One-time scribes are not renowned for their strength.'

'You would be, Adam.'

'Aye, well I've laboured on the land, as well as at my desk, using scythe and billhook, as well as a pen.'

'You have seen Clifford. He be sturdy built enough. Besides, yester afternoon, I had a strange conversation with his father in our parlour. I could hardly determine the purpose of his visit unless to reprimand me for Rose's continued presence here, though what concern of his that might be, I know not. He seemed to think it reflected gravely upon my morals, even though our own Father Thomas has no problem with the situation.'

'Father Thomas knows your morals are above reproach, Seb. Warden Clifford does not know you so well.'

'Aye, may be so, but to return to Clifford's conversation. He spoke of whores and wanton women.'

'Following on from mentioning Rose? How dare he?'

'And from them to Lizzie Knollys. Then he enquired how my investigation was progressing. I told him it was ended, but for the necessity of finding the owners of the valuable goods I had recovered, in order to return them. When I mentioned this book and its box, he promptly spilt his drink. In truth, now I think back upon it, he became quite agitated. Then he departed in haste, and I was unsure of the reason for his coming in the first place. But now I wonder if he wished to probe my thoughts on the circumstances of her death. Could the Cliffords be involved in this, Adam, do you think?'

Adam leafed through the Book of Hours. The ornately gilded capitals had to be admired. And then he found the letter. Of course, that was now of pertinent interest.

'Read that,' I told him. 'This could be more relevant now?'

Adam unfolded the letter I had found at the dead woman's house – the one she had never opened and could not have read, even if she had.

RETURN THE BOOK MY SON GAVE TO
YOU AND THE ITEMS YOU PURLOINED
FROM MY HOUSE. ELSEWISE STEPS WILL
BE TAKEN AGAINST YOU.

'Well, someone was in a choleric humour when they penned this. And all in capitals, wasting a deal of ink. Do you recognise the seal or the hand that wrote it?' Adam asked me.

I shook my head.

'The seal impression be blurred, most likely by intent. The hand is a trained book hand, but not one familiar to me. The capital letter 'E's and 'F's be of an unusual form, made with this additional flourish, do you see? The 'F' in the word 'FROM' has that ornamental serif. 'Tis not as I was trained to write them, but then again not unknown.'

Adam squinted where I pointed.

'I could make use of your scrying glass for this, but I see it is as you say.'

'If this be Warden Clifford's own hand, then the son to whom he refers would be Ralph.'

'He has no other sons?'

'Nay. Ralph alone. But we run ahead of ourselves, Adam. There be no proof at all that they had anything to do with Lizzie Knollys' death.'

'True. But it would be a sort of divine justice if they did, and more so if we could prove it.'

# Chapter 17

## Later that Monday

BY DINNERTIME, the storeroom had been scrubbed clean and smelled wholesome once more – or leastways of lavender, rather than mice. But I would require the services of a cat afore everything was returned to its rightful place upon the shelves. I did not want the creature's pursuit of vermin to dislodge any precious pigments or inks and send them crashing to the floor, requiring it all to be washed anew.

Afterwards, I made my way down to Bow Lane off Thames Street. It used to be called Skinners Lane, and the skinners were there still. The change of name had not served to change the foetid stink of the place either. The sumptuary laws permitted anyone, whether pedlar or ploughman, to wear cat fur to line or trim their garments. Other furs were the reserve of the wealthy and titled. Sheepskin, also allowed for humbler folk, came from the butchers' slaughter in the Shambles, thus the skinners here dealt mainly with cats. I had no wish to enquire too closely as to how the creatures, destined for a fur collar or hood-lining, were dispatched and moved swiftly beyond a fellow taking up a sack that writhed and yowled and gave off a powerful odour of cats' piss.

Further along, not far from Whittington's Almshouses, a man sat in the sun, smoothing out a glossy cat skin, combing it so it gleamed. Such a fur would not have looked misplaced warming a lady's hands, despite its cheapness. The man had a face that appeared never to have smiled since birth.

'Master Skinner,' I addressed him. 'Good day to you.'

'And to you. What's your business?'

'A cat.'

'Plenty here. Make your choice.' He gestured to a line of skins hung from pegs outside his shop. 'I got tabbies, black, tawny, black and white, grey... whatever takes your fancy.'

'I require a live cat. I have a problem with mice.'

'Mary!' the man called out, and a frail little woman with a face like rancid tallow came from the shop. Little wonder if the man was not one for smiling. 'Fellow here wants a live one. What we got that ain't no good for skinning?'

The woman did not speak, but went back within, returning a few moments later with a cage. She took a stick and poked it through the willow withies at the scrawny creature crouched inside. It was obviously not worth the skinner's attentions. Its fur was matted and missing in places.

'Is it a good mouser?' I enquired.

The skinner shrugged.

'It's a cat, ain't it? Take it or leave it.'

'How much?'

'Nuthing. We'll have to feed the damn thing on butter to get its fur in condition, else it ain't worth nuthing. You'll be saving us the expense. Take it away. Not the cage, mind. That's worth more than the cat, that is.'

I regarded the animal, and it looked back at me in a most unfriendly manner. Its ears were flattened and its fur – what little it had – stood on end. It hissed horribly. Whether a good mouser or no, it would scare the vermin away. The sight of those claws and teeth certainly worried me.

'May I borrow a sack to take it home?'

The cat was put to work as soon as maybe, released from its sack straight into the empty storeroom and the door closed to keep it inside. Gawain seemed somewhat put out, as though another had usurped his role as guardian of the Foxley household. In this instance, however, I had little sympathy for him since he had failed to keep the vermin down as Jack's little dog, Beggar, used to do. Thinking of which – Jack, I mean – I wondered how the acrobats' performance would be enjoyed at Westminster this afternoon. Would Jack do his rope-walking act in front of King Edward himself? I prayed the lad might find contentment in his new profession. At least he would be with his sister Maudie.

Meanwhile, Gawain sat alert in the workshop, keeping a watch upon the storeroom door. He would tire of it, eventually, no doubt. Perhaps, like me, he was considering what went on within, whether the cat was slaying mice like a scythe lopping corn, or if it had curled up in a corner and gone to sleep. Since we heard not a sound, the latter seemed most likely. The dog could maintain his watch if he so pleased; the rest of us had work to do at our desks.

Kate sat, fine brush in hand, concentrating on filling in an ornate capital 'A' with green ink. I smiled. I had forgotten how she always worked with her tongue poking from the corner of her mouth. She glanced up as she rinsed out her brush and saw that I regarded her. She smiled back, then dipped her brush into a pot of red ink.

'Where's Jack?' she asked. 'I haven't seen him yet.'

Remembering that she and Jack had had a liking for each other, I explained how he was gone to join the acrobats, having discovered his elder sister Maudie was one of their number. I did not say that she was the exotic dancer we had seen at St Bartholomew's Fayre.

'Is that what he told you?' Tom snorted with derision. 'That she's his sister. What utter poppycock. It's all lies, every word of it. She's no more his sister than I'm the bloody Archbishop of Canterbury.'

'Mind your tongue, Tom,' I warned him. 'I will not tolerate such language in my workshop.'

He snorted even louder.

'As if Master Jude ever minded what he said?'

'You are not Master Jude. You are still my apprentice for a few months yet to come and will behave accordingly.'

'It's still true, what I said,' he muttered mutinously. 'She's not his sister, just a harlot with a shapely ar-backside that he fancies bedding. He'll get nowhere with her. She's already warming the bed of the strongman who guards her and plays the pipe for her dancing. Like as not, the great turd will return here by suppertime, disappointed and surly as ever.'

'Tom! Enough of that. Look to your work. I can see from here 'tis hardly of a high standard.'

'It's just another bloody cheap pamphlet. I don't know why you think we'll sell so many.'

'Forwhy Michaelmas term begins in a few weeks, and the scholars at the Inns of Court will need to revise their Latin. Last year, we sold above a score of little primers at a groat each and of better ones at least a dozen at sixpence per booklet. And how many have you completed thus far?' I pointed to a small pile of folios on the collating table, put there when we cleared the storeroom shelves earlier. 'I count five only.'

'I don't see why I have to do them all. It's not fair. Kate can do some.'

'Kate will, as soon as she be settled back in.'

'Fear not.' Adam, quiet all this while, straightened folios by tapping them on his desk. 'There are three more primers here, ready for stitching.' He got up and stretched, straightening his back and went over to Tom. He frowned. 'If you worked more and complained less, we would have enough primers already and could turn our hands to more interesting things. But with lettering like that, I'm not sure you're ready for anything more exacting than lists of Latin verbs. Look how uneven is that text. Your penmanship is a disgrace to this workshop.' With that scathing comment, Adam snatched the offending folio and tore it in half. 'Do it again and this time be a credit to the name of Foxley.'

I said naught, but was stunned at Adam's harsh words. He was correct, of course.

'Why should I do as you order me? You're not my bloody master.' Tom threw his pen across the room, splattering a trail of ink droplets along the floor.

A drop or two splashed upon Adam's shoe. His face as dark as those blotches, he bent down, unlaced the shoe and removed it, then clouted Tom across the back with it.

'If I were your master, you would have been searching for a new one years ago, you idle whelp. And now you've ruined a good pair of shoes. That ink will never come off.'

'I shall recompense you, Adam,' I said hastily. We needed no outbursts of ill-temper worse than this on such a day.

'I don't want your coin, Seb. Tom is going to pay for this by producing the most exquisitely written primers in all England. If our name is to be restored to the guild rolls tomorrow, then our workmanship must do justice to our standing. Is that not so, Tom?' Adam swatted his shoe across the lad's hair, disturbing it but doing no hurt.

'I suppose so,' Tom sighed in an exaggerated manner, making certain all might hear.

'He supposes so,' Adam repeated, shaking his head. 'There is no 'suppose' about it, you hear me? You *will* pen the best work you possibly can. Master Seb requires it thus, if you're ever to complete your 'prentice term, remember that. Elsewise, you'll still be 'prenticed and unwaged at the age of five-and-thirty. You want that? No. I thought not.'

I resumed my seat at my desk. In truth, I was coming to realise that Adam knew better than I how to maintain order in the workshop. I had not the least skill at directing a recalcitrant youth such as Tom had become. Mayhap, I should let Adam have charge of the lad while I trained the more talented – aye, and biddable – Kate. She showed more promise as an illuminator than Tom had ever done.

The lad's father, who had once been my employer, originally indentured his son to an apothecary. Tom had loathed the work and was sore wounded when the apothecary's place exploded, killing his master. I had then taken the lad as my apprentice, believing he might make a good stationer, having grown up in his father's book-selling business. Yet it seemed his father had the greater wisdom for I was mistaken. As with Jack, Tom had little aptitude for our painstaking work, but I must do what I could to make of him a competent scribe and book-binder, if not a shining example of either. He most certainly would never be an illuminator, his artistic talent being negligible. On the other hand, I had high hopes for young Kate Verney.

The workshop was cluttered with everything that belonged of right in the storeroom, and we were having to step over and around boxes, pots, parchment rolls and stacked paper. It was inconvenient, if not hazardous, and among it all was the bag containing the objects from Lizzie Knollys' house. I was yet hoping to return them to their owners, if any dared come forward and admit to having been robbed by a woman now dead of unnatural causes. In the meantime, a new place had to be found for the bag and, indeed, the fine book in its box. I determined that the secret hidey-hole in our bedchamber – where Jude had discovered a small hoard of coin – as the most secure place. The objects were not only important as possible evidence, but valuable in their own right.

'What are you hiding there, Seb?' Emily asked, watching as I swung back the picture of the Virgin and Child that formed the door to the aumbry. She was sitting at her little loom, weaving a silk ribbon. Of habit, she worked in the kitchen, but her fear of arrest meant she preferred to be up here in the bedchamber, out of sight.

'The stolen pieces from Foster Lane.' I did not mention the woman's name for fear of upsetting Em.

'If there's a needle-case among them and some decent snips, they belong to Pen and Beattie. I saw them in her work-basket when...' She did not finish the sentence.

'Aye. Such items are there. I shall see they are returned. Do you know who may have owned a pair of garnet or ruby earrings? I be unsure of the stones. When matters be concluded, I shall put notices upon church doors to inform folk I have these things.'

'But then anyone might claim them.'

'I shall require a detailed description afore I decide upon each rightful owner, but I have a feeling few will want to admit they paid for, er, female services with a ring or such.'

'But our things were stolen from us. Maybe all the objects were.'

'In which case, they will be reclaimed without embarrassment. How do you fare, Em? Be you of more cheerful mien now? Will you come down to dinner? Kate has returned as joyous as ever. She will cheer you.'

'Only if she may prove me innocent and send the constables elsewhere.'

'They will not come, sweetheart. As far as they be concerned, they have their man in custody already.'

'Aye. Poor Rook of all people. I'm sure he had naught to do with it. Gabriel would never be friends with a man capable of purposefully...' Again, she was unable to complete the phrase, but I knew what she meant.

'I do not believe it either. It seems to me Rook's only crime be to look different. He cannot help that any more than I can be blamed for my troublesome hip, or Gabriel for his mismatched eyes. I be desperate to find the real culprit. It most assuredly is not you, nor Beatrice and Peronelle, nor is it Rook.'

'Do you have the least idea who it might be, Seb?' Emily gazed at me beseechingly, laying aside the shuttle.

I closed the aumbry.

'It may be that I do, Em. But an idea is not proof.'

'You can't delay though, else Rook will be hanged for it.'

'We have a week's grace afore the next hanging day at Tyburn. I should have what proof I need within a day or two. It cannot be hurried, Em. Besides, even if I had certain proof here in my hand, I should not act upon it until after the morrow's September guild meeting.'

'Why ever not? Why let Rook languish in that dreadful gaol a single day longer?'

'Trust me, Em. I have good reason. By the by, I have acquired a cat to deal with the plague of mice in the storeroom.'

'Another mouth to feed? Jack is gone yet you replace him with a cat.'

'Hardly. The creature will live on the mice it catches. It will require no more food than that.'

'We'll have its fleas to annoy us instead. What's its name?'

'Name? The wretched beast looks unworthy of a name. 'Cat' will suffice. I fear you may be correct about fleas though. Its fur looks infested and mangy. I got it forwhy it possesses claws, teeth and, hopefully, an instinct for hunting. If not, it can go back to the skinner who rejected it as worthless for a fur collar.'

'Poor thing. I will come down and see to it.'

'Will you lavish affection on a cat?' I could have added 'rather than me', but I refrained. Her humours were too inconstant, and I dared not risk such words.

Afore dinner, the cat had been released from the storeroom and furnished with half a dish of cream and some sprats.

'He will not hunt unless he be hungry,' I said, but was ignored. 'Do not think to make some spoilt pet of the moth-eaten thing. I fetched it to perform a task only.'

My wife had most certainly taken to the sorry-looking creature and, aye indeed, she would lavish affection upon it.

Mice were a tedious diet, she said. It had also acquired a name: Grayling. I thought that was some kind of fish but – so Emily informed me – it suited the small grey cat perfectly. Who was I to argue against such womanly logic?

My sole supporter in this – the women were of one mind, apparently, and Adam and Tom indifferent – was Gawain. The dog, having no interest in chasing mice himself, was somewhat more keen to pursue the cat, growling whenever he saw it. But – coward that he be, the great overgrown pup – one swipe with a little taloned paw across his nose and he backed away, seeking refuge behind my legs. My Gawain be no fearless knight-errant as his namesake; 'tis for sure. Yet I owed him my life this day, as Adam had told the tale to me. A fearful, sickening tale I would tell no one, but make my confession to the Almighty.

I still shuddered anew when I recalled what I had attempted a few hours earlier. Did I regret that I had failed? I suppose that might depend on whether Emily and Rook could be proven innocent as they surely were by other means. Yet, seeing Rose and Kate at the table, smiling and laughing; Adam grinning... I bethought how they might now look if I had succeeded. They would be grave and grieving, downcast and tearful and, worse than that, little Dickon, my dearest child, would be orphaned. How could I not have considered such an outcome? I should ne'er have contemplated an act of so great wickedness, but it had seemed the only way in the cold airs of dawn. In truth, I suppose I was glad not to have achieved my unholy intent.

The remainder of that Monday afternoon passed without further incident. No constables came to arrest my Emily. I put the cat back in the storeroom and returned to my work. Aesop had been waiting overlong for my proper attention, and I determined it deserved an hour or two of my concentration. All other problems and anxieties were set aside until suppertime.

The careful application of beautiful pigments to my detailed drawings was a balm for an unquiet soul, and a better remedy than any physician's medicaments.

Gawain lay 'neath my desk, apparently dozing in the late summer heat, but any sound from the storeroom had him lift an ear, open one eye or rumble a low growl from deep within his chest.

There even came voices from the shop as Rose served customers, so it seemed business was resumed since the fayre ended. A heartening circumstance. Adam stitched the little primers he had inscribed that morn; Kate had done her alphabet of capital initials as far as 'E' and was now working upon 'F'. The lass was taking especial pains with it as the 'ff' formed the letter for the Foxley badge, entwined about a fox's head and a quill pen, that of late we used to denote the products of our workshop. I was planning to paint a sign of the same design to hang above the shop door when time allowed. Tom, for once, was diligent indeed and his lettering of a goodly standard. Adam's threats seemed to have had the desired outcome, miraculously.

Nessie was preparing the evening meal and bringing in the dried linen from off the garden hedgerow, where it had been bleaching in the sun. Her loud sniffs betokened complaint at having to accomplish two tasks at the same time and, eventually, Emily came down from our bedchamber – the sniffs were of sufficient loudness that she had heard them – to help fold sheets and table linen, shirts, shifts and the babe's numerous tailclouts.

When we sat at the board to eat our supper, I said a heartfelt grace. I was pleased with my achievements regarding *Aesop's Fables*, and the workshop had produced a decent body of work for once. I hoped it foretold of a more settled future for us all.

I called to Gawain who slept at my bedside of habit, but he was intent upon remaining by the storeroom door, so suspicious was he of the cat shut inside. It had been a long day for me with a traumatic beginning, but a quieter ending and I wasted no time attempting to persuade him to leave. I retired to bed, heavy-eyed and exhausted. Even qualms concerning the September guild meeting upon the morrow could not keep me from sleep.

My slumbers were ended abruptly by the most fearful row downstairs. There was no need to wonder at the cause of it. Such barking and yowling and the thud of overturned furniture meant I knew what I should find. Cursing the wretched creatures, I lit a taper, pulled on my night robe and went down to survey the damage. All the while, the sounds of violence continued. One would surely kill the other; my wager was upon the cat as the most likely victor. How it could have escaped the storeroom was a mystery, unless Gawain had learned to lift the latch and he was no such scholar nor ingenious.

Adam and Tom met me in the kitchen, each with a light in hand. Adam had donned a shirt and nether clouts. Tom stood naked as a newborn. Upon seeing him, Nessie began squealing, adding to the cacophony.

'Cease that, you silly wench,' Adam told her. 'If you've never seen a naked man, 'tis high time you did.' Nessie fell silent as commanded.

Ignoring her, I took up my staff, used when my hip was poorly. Adam armed himself with a roasting spit, and Tom chose a rolling pin, hefting it like a cudgel. Then we courageous warriors marched along the passageway to do battle with the enemy: a small cat that hissed like a serpent and a large dog with less spine than a lump of unbaked dough. I could not think we would have too much trouble ending their quarrel. On the other hand, both had teeth, and one had claws also. It was as well to be prepared.

Yet we were not prepared for the scene of turmoil and calamity that awaited us. The arena of devastation that had lately been our industrious workshop was miserable to behold and in its midst was such a tangle of writhing fur it was impossible to tell cat from dog. I tried to separate them with my staff. Adam simply brought down the spit upon the heaving mass. There was a yelp and a howl and the two fell apart. The cat bolted back into the storeroom and Tom hastily closed the door after, securing the latch. He rattled it a few times.

'It seems stout enough,' he said. 'I don't see how it could have come open.'

I had Gawain by the collar and took time to examine him. His hurts were many, but minor. None seemed the death sentence I half expected.

'Foolish beast,' I chided him. 'Do you know no better than to take on such a wily and well-armed opponent? And see what you have done to my workshop!' He had the grace to appear contrite. Sorry for himself, no doubt, for the bites and scratches must be sore. Those dark liquid eyes gazed up at me remorsefully. I would forgive him – later. He sprawled on the floor and licked at a bitten paw. 'I suppose you expect sympathy for your injuries?' I held the light close to see his wounds, but the dog flopped over on his side, leaving blood upon the flagstones. 'Oh, Gawain! This be no cat-scratch. Adam, look here. He's been cut with a blade.' My anger was gone, replaced by deep concern.

Holding high my taper, I realised there was blood all around, smeared and spattered. I wondered, was all of it Gawain's, or had the dog caused harm to the blade-wielding intruder? For such, I was now convinced, there must have been.

'The shutter-board in the shop has been prised away.' Adam came from the shop. 'It can be repaired, I think, but some devil got in that way. You should have heard them breaking in, Seb, what with your bedchamber being above.'

'I did not. I was tired and slept sound for once. But what of my Gawain? Will he live, do you believe?' I sat upon the floor, the dog's head resting in my lap. I knew not what to do for him, watching his lifeblood leaking away. No one gave me answer.

Tom was wandering around the place, picking things up and putting them down again.

'God's pox on the bastard,' he burst out. 'My best bloody work's ruined. Well, I'm not doing it all again, whatever you say.'

'Leave it, Tom. Return to your bed, lad. We can do naught 'til morning.' I stroked Gawain's head to comfort him as he whimpered softly. 'Hush, my faithful friend. Hush, now.'

Adam, ever practical, returned bringing a basin of water and napkins from the kitchen.

'Do we have any wine?' he asked.

'Aye. Emily keeps some in the pantry for important visitors.'

He went away again. In the uncertain light of my guttering taper, I gazed at the mess, at the pages of my Aesop strewn like autumn leaves. I did not care about the wasted effort. I sat, praying that Gawain would come through the night. I bathed the gash in his side, doing my best to cause him no further pain. Adam brought the wine. Injuries heal more cleanly if washed in wine, so the surgeon had once told me. Thinking of whom, I wondered if I should send for Master Dagvyle to stitch it. I knew he occasionally tended horses, but horses were of great value. Was a dog of sufficient worth?

'Here. Smear some honey on it,' Adam told me, thrusting the pot at me. 'Then I'll help you lift him, so we may bind him up. See? The bleeding has slowed already.'

I think he was attempting to cheer me for I could see little difference. Nevertheless, Gawain's wound was cleansed and covered, the linen tied in place around his chest. When it was done, the poor beast lay very still, hardly breathing.

'My thanks, Adam. Go to your bed, now. I will stay with him.'

Afore he left us, Adam brought a new candle and set it so I should not be left in the dark when the taper burned down. Ever thoughtful, he also put the rest of the wine and a cup within my reach. I poured some and drank a few sips afore trickling a little betwixt the dog's jaws, hoping it might give him a measure of strength to survive.

Alone, I sang softly to him. I stroked his head all the while, that he might know I was there and be comforted. It was going to be another long night.

At some time, I heard rain blowing against the window shutters. Then it ceased, though the wind continued, stirring the papers on the floor, rustling at the edges of my weary mind. Afar off, a dog howled at the night. But Gawain remained silent.

I was awakened from a kind of half-sleep by a blanket being wrapped around my shoulders.

'How is he?' Rose sat down on the flagstones beside me.

'Not good.'

'What of you? You must be numb from sitting so long.'

'It matters not.'

'I could sit with him. Let you rest a while.'

'No. He saved my life. Even if I cannot save his in return, I cannot leave him now.'

Rose put her hand upon my arm and remained with me, keeping vigil together.

# Tuesday morn

Adam found us there in the workshop at dawn.

Rose was asleep, her head resting on my shoulder as we shared the blanket. She stirred when he spoke.

I was awake, as I had been since she came to me. I had not moved. In truth, I could not, stiff and benumbed as I was. I would not disturb the creature's head from across my thighs, his nose against my knee.

'Is Gawain improved?' Adam asked, kneeling beside us.

I shook my head.

He touched the dog's chest with his palm and sighed.

'I'm not sure he's still with us, Seb.'

'Aye, he is. I feel his heart.'

Adam looked doubtful.

Gawain lay unmoving in my lap. He must not die. Our efforts to save him could not come to naught.

Rose also put her hand to the dog's chest.

'You're right, Seb. It beats still – just. I will stay with him. Let Adam aid you to your feet.'

Reluctantly, I agreed, lifting my dog's heavy head onto the folded blanket. I required much assistance as I clambered to my feet, lacking all sensation in my lower limbs. Adam set a stool beneath me while I rubbed my feet to restore feeling, and they were soon tingling painfully. Yet I never took my eyes from Gawain's unmoving form.

'Go. Break your fast,' Rose said. 'I will not leave him.'

'I have no interest in food.'

'You have much to do this morn.'

I frowned at her; my mind like a blank folio. What must I do this day?

At the board, breaking our fast, the household sat under a pall of gloom. I recalled how upset Jack had been when his dog, Beggar, died. I had hastened to acquire a replacement for him – Gawain – yet Jack had refused what I hoped would cheer him. Now I better understood that if my companion should die, he could not be replaced like a smashed pot or a broken stool. The gap it would leave in my life, my heart, was not to be so easily mended. But I had not yet abandoned all hope that he might recover. He was young and strong, and a miracle might befall.

'Do not forget, Seb, you must attend the guild meeting this morn.' Emily sounded the brightest of us all.

'Meeting?'

''Tis the first of the month. Your reinstatement. You cannot have forgotten.'

Indeed I had.

'Oh, aye. The meeting.'

The cat, Grayling, purred in Emily's lap. It had come through the night, unscathed, and it had done its duty, I grant, having left three dead mice on the storeroom floor for which she had rewarded the creature with half a dish of cream. I suppose I should not have resented the cat's obvious good health, but I did. My Gawain ought not to have suffered so at the hand of some intruder. The whole house seemed violated.

As yet, we had not reported the incident. That would be done after I had taken an inventory to discover what had been stolen. A cursory glance had failed to reveal that anything was missing, but there must be, for certain. No one broke in for the sole purpose of stabbing my dog. Unless Gawain defended our property better than we realised and had forced the thief to flee empty-handed. Mayhap, the poor beast's injuries had not been in vain. That would be a token of comfort to me, at least.

It was an effort that must be made: to wash and dress in my finest. To shave and comb my hair and appear at my most affluent and respectable. I must conceal my anxiety for Gawain and impress the guild that I was worthy of having my name restored to the memoranda rolls.

Emily was suckling the babe in our bedchamber, observing my ablutions.

'Not those hose; the grey ones,' she said.

I wondered what was amiss with the brown ones I had chosen, but did not argue. In matters sartorial, I bowed to her greater wisdom.

'Shoes; not boots. For pity's sake, Seb, do I need dress you like a child? Little Dickon knows better what to wear than you do. And wear the new cap I bought you, not that battered old thing that looks as though things live in it. 'Tis a disgrace.'

'You never complained of it afore.'

'Well, I'm complaining now. I want my husband to look as a prosperous craftsman should; not like some church-porch beggar.'

'The new one be less comfortable. I have not yet broken it in to suit me.'

'Exactly so, which is why you must wear it. Besides, the red colour stands out and will attract notice.' Emily had bought the cap for me weeks since, at the market in Huntingdon. It was of crimson wool with a trim of silver braid. It might appeal to some petty lordling clad like a popinjay, but I liked it not, though I dared not admit that to my wife. Instead, I must say how much I admired it – a lie indeed.

Which was precisely why I did not want to wear it, but I kept silent. I pulled on my Sunday doublet. A lump rose in my throat when I saw the dog hairs upon the padded sleeve. Emily would brush them away if I allowed her. Mayhap she would fail to see them, and I might leave them there as a memento – a charm for good luck in my efforts this morn. But of course, she saw them.

Eventually, brushed and buffed, laced and straightened, I set out for the Stationers' Hall in Ave Maria Lane.

# Chapter 18

## Tuesday, the first day of September
## at nine of the clock
## The Stationers Hall, Ave Maria Lane

I ARRIVED PROMPTLY just as St Paul's bell chimed for the hour of Terce. Apprehensive, I was glad to see my good friend and one-time master, Richard Collop, waiting on the steps outside.

'God give you good day, Sebastian,' he greeted me, smiling.

'And you also, Master Collop.' I touched my cap to him then, upon second thoughts, removed the gaudy thing entirely. I would rather go bare-headed than wear it like some court buffoon. 'Tell me I am not tardy?'

'Of course not. Not early; not late, as required. Come along. I am to plead your case before Warden Clifford and the Masters of the Guild.' He ushered me through to the hall. ''Tis a fine cap you have there.' His tone betrayed neither commendation nor censure.

'My goodwife's choice,' I said.

He nodded.

'I too have just such a hat. Yellow, with a lengthy feather and a gilded button.'

The hall was in half-darkness after the sunlight outside, and it took my eyes a few moments to adjust. When they did so, I saw Master Collop was grinning. His jest lifted my spirits. He knew me so well after my seven years apprenticed to him.

'How does your *Aesop's Fables* progress? I am eager to see it.'

'Too slowly, I fear. One disaster follows another, hampering me at every turn, so it seems. Last night, our shop was broken into, my work scattered. I have not yet had time to survey the damage done. My dog was nigh slain attempting to guard the premises and may not recover.'

'Not your Gawain?'

'Aye.'

'I am sorry to hear that. He has the makings of a fine dog; let us hope he comes through his ordeal.'

We were awaiting our summons to the dais, standing in an alcove at the lower end of the hall. I surveyed the assembly, perturbed by the presence of so many of high standing in the Company of Stationers. I feared my nervous condition might get the better of me, so I gazed at the windows of stained glass instead. They could not rival those of St Paul's next door, but were fine enough. The one beyond the dais had been installed a year or two earlier, made to Warden Clifford's own design and at his expense, to commemorate his appointment to that office. It pictured St Luke writing his gospel at his desk. St Luke was the patron of stationers and illuminators, and the image was correct in every detail of the craftsman's tools, down to the pot of pounce to whiten parchment and blot ink dry. Even the text before him, the decorated capital at least, was legible. I knew what it said, the opening verse of the first chapter of St Luke's gospel:

> *Forasmuch as many have taken in hand to set forth*
> *in order a declaration of those things which are most*
> *surely believed among us...*

And was that the unusual serif just visible on the 'ff' capital of 'Forasmuch'? I could not be sure, and the clerk was calling us forward to the dais.

Still cap in hand, I bowed to Warden Clifford seated in the ornate chair at the centre of the dais, flanked on the one hand by the newly promoted Senior Master, Giles Benedict, and Richard Collop, in like capacity, took his seat on the other hand. This was the triumvirate that would adjudge me worthy of reinstatement to the guild or no. Master Collop would most certainly speak well of me and sponsor me. Of Master Benedict, I had little notion of how he regarded me, but a face carven from flint might have looked the more welcoming than his unsmiling visage. Warden Clifford had seemed prepared to accept my return when we shared that odd conversation in my parlour two days since. But now his hooded eyes and thin mouth bore no vestige of kindness towards me. Thus, my position in the guild sat poised upon a knife edge, and I knew not what the outcome of this meeting was likely to be.

The meeting was conducted not unlike a court of law. Master Collop put forward the arguments in my defence, as I knew he would. Master Benedict spoke against me most eloquently and, I fear, most persuasively.

Giles Benedict told how I had abandoned my indentured apprentice, one Thomas Bowen, and deserted my business for nigh half a year, leaving both in the hands of a loutish drunkard – one Jude Foxley – who dwelt with a woman to whom he was related neither by blood nor marriage. He then went too far, to my mind, making our house sound more like a brothel-cum-insane asylum. He proceeded to describe in minute detail, using a written statement to jog his memory, the too numerous ways in which the aforesaid drunkard – Jude – had shouted at, abused and insulted would-be customers, to the great disrepute and shame of the Stationers' Company to which the Foxleys claimed membership at that time.

Finally, he reiterated the circumstances of the tavern brawl during which the warden's own son had been disabled for life by the aforementioned Jude Foxley's violent and unprovoked outburst. I was unsure whether Jude had been provoked or no;

he had never told me the full story. Whatever the truth, when Master Benedict's speech was ended, and he resumed his seat, it even crossed my mind that I might well have agreed with him, that the name of such a fellow as myself should not be restored to the roll and my membership remain in abeyance.

However, afore the gathered stationers should determine my fate, I must suffer Warden Clifford's interrogation, such that all could hear my answers and assess my worth. A milder version was borne by every hopeful young craftsman desiring acceptance into the company. In that case, the questions were concerning a man's attainments during his apprenticeship and then as a journeyman, and his suitability as attested to by his one-time master and latterly, by his employer, if they were not one and the same. This would include his standard of morals and behaviour and whether his finances could support his independent venture. It would end with the presentation for scrutiny of the master-piece, whether the degree of craftsmanship was fine enough to qualify.

I had passed that test easily, thanks to Master Collop and my esteemed patron, the Duke of Gloucester – may God bless him. The duke had not only paid me handsomely for the triptych I created for him – thus my finances were sound – but generously permitted me to show it as my master-piece, along with a letter of reference in his own hand. But now, at this second ordeal, an example of good craftsmanship and a royal duke's approval would not weight the decision in my favour. Only my honest answers and assurances could do that, if those assembled believed what I said – every word of it.

And I was not at my best this morn. I stammered, stuttered and mumbled through my answers like an idiot schoolboy. A particular difficulty occurred in that Warden Clifford demanded to know the reasons why, in March last, I had taken it upon myself to leave London in such haste. I prided myself upon speaking the truth, but I could hardly announce publicly that King Edward's brother-by-marriage,

Anthony Woodville, Earl Rivers, had been attempting to kill me because I knew the queen's dreadful secret. So I muttered same lame excuse concerning family difficulties in Norfolk. It was so much nonsense: at the time I was uncertain whether I had any family still living there or no. As to whether they had any difficulties requiring a complete stranger's attentions, I knew more of the Sultan of Barbary's situation than I knew of theirs.

'Are you certain you weren't fleeing your creditors?' the warden demanded, his voice accusing, as if he was certain of it, his finger a lance-point stabbing the air in my direction.

'Most assuredly not. My debts were then and are now all paid upon the dates due. I owe no man a penny.'

'Mayhap, you were abandoning a commission you no longer wanted to fulfil? Did you take the money for it and run?'

'I had but one commission outstanding at that time, for the Duke of Gloucester. He determined it should be held over until some future date still to be settled upon. I accepted his payment for the work insofar as it was done.' I did not mention the large sum he had paid me in addition; compensation, as he called it, for having put my life at hazard.

'If, as you insist, you went to Norfolk because your family there were in difficulties, what was the nature of the problem that your elder brother could not have gone instead?' He sneered as he spoke the words 'elder brother' and I realised how much he must loathe Jude. 'That way your business and reputation would not have been left to founder in *his* unworthy hands and bring the guild's name into disrepute.'

'I-I, er, it was a p-privy matter.'

'One for which you did not consider him to have sufficient tact and discretion to deal with?'

'It did n-not concern him.'

'How does a family matter concern one brother and not the other? Unless that other brother *was* the problem. In which case, you had no right to leave him to manage the shop and the apprentice in your absence! You would not leave a mad dog to guard a flock of sheep, would you?'

'No.' I hung my head. I had no arguments – no lies – left in me and the mention of a dog had brought a new constriction to my throat.

'Warden Clifford,' Master Collop stood up. 'Are we not straying from the purpose of this meeting? Are we trying Jude Foxley in his absence or assessing Sebastian's competency as a representative of our illustrious fellowship?'

'It is his competency as a reliable man of affairs that I call into question,' the warden said, clearly annoyed at the interruption. 'His judgement was severely at fault on numerous accounts...'

'His brother let him down is all,' Master Collop said, resuming his seat. ''Tis all in the past now since Jude Foxley has left the city. Should we not rather enquire of Sebastian concerning his plans for the future of his business and the restoration of our reputation? For myself, I am certain he will prove a great asset, as he has previously. The very name and title of his noble patron, the Duke of Gloucester, can but enhance our standing as a guild.'

'Yes, yes. But what if his brother returns? He cannot be trusted to dignify our status. He's a disgrace and a drunken brawler.'

'Then let us re-instate Sebastian alone, rather than the Foxley Brothers as a joint venture.'

A murmur went about the hall at Master Collop's suggestion. I was unsure whether it boded good or evil tidings for me.

'So tell us, Sebastian, what intentions you have concerning your position?'

I smiled. Master Collop's question was far easier to answer, as he well knew.

'I have taken on a most diligent and reliable journeyman of excellent character and great ability by the name of Adam Armitage.'

'I am unfamiliar with the name. Under which of us did he serve his term?'

'He completed his apprenticeship in Norwich, Warden Clifford, and has since served the Earl of Kent.' I did not say that, in truth, he had been scribe to the earl's bailiff and had never met the lord. I was coming to see that noble titles impressed the warden far more than any accomplishment.

'Oh. I suppose he will prove acceptable then. Does he plan to purchase his London citizenship?'

'In due course,' I said, though we had never discussed the subject. 'My current apprentice, Thomas, should complete his term after Christmas and I have taken on a young person of exceptional talent whose indenture will be enrolled at the same time.' I did not mention Jack's comings and goings. He had never been an officially recognised apprentice. 'My wife is to declare herself to be a silk-woman *femme sole* in the near future and she and Rose Glover will be working together.' I felt the need to account for Rose remaining under my roof for some legitimate purpose. I still stung from Master Benedict's sordid suggestion earlier that my house was little better than a brothel.

'Would you have work enough for another journeyman, Sebastian? I ask forwhy I also have a likely youngster about to complete his term. The lad is nephew to Alderman Gardyner who may well be our next Lord Mayor.'

I smiled anew. Master Collop was demonstrating his faith in me and the future prosperity of my workshop.

''Tis a possibility, good master, though that would mean I should employ three journeymen, if Thomas remains with me.' A business requiring that number of journeymen must be doing well indeed.

It was nigh unto two hours since the proceedings had commenced and for half that time I had been answering their questions. Most seemed to have some relevance, though when the matter of how my father used to conduct his business was raised, I could not see why that was important, unless they believed the trait might be inherited. In which case, why had my brother so little aptitude for it? I gave answer as best I might, though I had never known much of my father's dealings. I could, however, name some of his most important clients, including the Dean of St Martin le Grand, a couple of lord mayors and aldermen and one commission for the Earl of Warwick. I recalled my father had great hopes of more work for the earl, but then the man was both foolhardy and arrogant and betrayed King Edward. His treason ended at the battle of Barnet Field seven years before, dashing my parent's expectations. However, the naming of persons of significance sounded well and might impress the warden.

At last, my interrogation was done, and Warden Clifford, Master Collop and Master Benedict conferred together upon the dais. I was unsure whether to be heartened or dismayed by Giles Benedict's extravagant hand gestures and head shaking. The warden frowned a great deal, and my old master's expression proved unreadable.

I stood alone at the side of the hall. Numerous were the covert glances cast in my direction, but no one approached me, dissociating themselves from me until the outcome of the deliberations was known. And for now, the result could not be guessed at.

I reached down with my hand, seeking the companionship and solace of a furred head and a wet nose, but of course, I found neither. Remembrance of my poor Gawain washed over me like an icy tide. Would I return home to find he had died in my absence? I prayed that it should not be so.

The time of waiting seemed an age afore the meeting was once more called to order. My belly felt to be knotted, and every sinew tightened to the point of snapping. My hands trembled, and sweat lay wet upon my brow.

'We have discussed the matter, at considerable length, of the reinstatement of Sebastian Foxley as a member of this illustrious fellowship. We have considered, in due depth, his past inadequacies and the delinquency of his brother, bringing shame and disrepute upon our good name...'

The warden droned on in similar vein. This was not sounding well for me, and my spirits sank lower with every word that reiterated the shortcomings of the Foxleys. Had the assembly not heard even the smallest details of my failures already? Get this done with, for pity's sake, I thought. End my misery either way.

'However,' Warden Clifford announced, 'We, being a beneficent company, are willing to permit the aforementioned Sebastian Foxley the opportunity to redeem himself, notwithstanding certain stipulations, namely, that his brother is not included, we hereby re-instate Master Sebastian Foxley's name upon the memoranda roll and henceforth...'

I did not hear what else was said. The assembly erupted with shouts of approval, aye, and a number also of dissent. The majority though turned to me, smiling and nodding. There was much back-slapping, and also invitations to celebrate in the tavern of my choice. I declined such offers courteously and made my way through the press of folk – who were, of a sudden, my friends and fellows – to the dais.

The warden and both masters shook my hand, as was the custom in greeting new members, but only Master Collop's welcome felt sincere. Then I watched as the long parchment was unrolled across a board and the company's recorder inscribed my name at the foot of it. I could see, further up the memoranda roll, that the names 'Sebastian & Jude Foxley' had been struck through. That was in April last, I noted, for the crossing-out on the memoranda roll was dated. So no time had been wasted betwixt Jude's fight with Ralph Clifford and our removal from the company's membership. Now, only mine was restored to the list.

There was a longer time of waiting as a document of instatement, also on parchment, was completed. It was ready written with blank spaces left for names and dates to be filled in. I had a copy of the same at home which Jude and I had signed three years ago, but that was rendered void when our names were deemed unworthy. I observed closely as Warden

Clifford penned my name in the appropriate space upon the new document. I bit my lip to keep from gasping with surprise when he put that extra serif, the unusual flourish, upon the 'F' of Foxley in its double 'ff' form. Then he signed and dated it, as did Masters Benedict and Collop afore I did the same, making certain the initial of my surname was unadorned and simple as always.

The recorder checked it through for errors and, finding none, handed the document to a clerk to amend the company seal to it. Once the wax on its green ribbon was hardened, the parchment was rolled, tied about with more ribbon and presented to me by the warden. More handshakes ensued, and the matter was ended at last. I could return home: once again a full member of the Guild of Stationers and Illuminators. I should have felt joyful, but such an emotion eluded me, fearing what awaited my homecoming.

I went through the side gate and across the yard. Emily and Nessie were preparing a late dinner, deferred until my return, so they said. Emily dropped the ladle with a clatter and hastened to me.

'Well? Are you accepted back? Tell me, Seb.'

'Aye. See for yourself.' I gave her the parchment.

''Tis good news. You must tell me all about the meeting. Did everyone support you? Or were some against you? Who were they? I shall not give them 'good day' in future. Seb?'

I left her prattling and went to the workshop straightway.

'Gawain?' I asked Adam who was at his desk, scribing away industriously. He grinned, pointing to the corner where the dog lay upon the blanket. No longer sprawled on his side, he slept, nose on paws as was his ordinary way.

'He's been drinking water and took a tit-bit of cooked rabbit. I believe he's on the mend, Seb, so long as the wound doesn't fester. Rose has bathed it with wine again and smeared it with honey to prevent that. Mind you, we had to make haste replacing the bindings afore he licked off all the honey. He has acquired a taste for it.'

I knelt down and stroked Gawain.

'My thanks, Adam, to you and Rose and to the God of all innocent earthly creatures.'

Gawain opened his eyes, lifted his head and nudged my hand with his nose. My faithful companion was returned to me.

'I began an inventory, Seb,' Adam was saying, 'But I do not know the contents of your house so well that I can tell what's missing. However, from what Em, Rose, Tom and Nessie have said, we can find naught that has been taken. I don't know what to make of a thief who steals nothing. It must be that Gawain sent him off without any ill-gotten gains for his crime of hedge-breaking.'

I smiled at his use of the countryman's term. In London, it was more often a case of shutter-breaking as a means of uninvited entry.

'Mayhap, he found naught of value he might resell,' I suggested.

'That cannot be true. Our cloaks and mantles hanging on the pegs would bring a fair price from a fripperer. There are books in the shop worth a few marks each and pigments, paper and parchment could all be sold on. Yet the devil ignored all those items lying openly around that he could have taken away and went to the empty storeroom.'

'He did not know it was empty... but for a wild cat he let loose.'

'True, but what else would he expect to find among a stationer's stock that wasn't piled on our desks or stacked on the floor for him to help himself? In emptying the stockroom, we'd made a fine display of all our wares, but they did not interest him.'

'Mayhap, he preferred to see everything afore selecting what he would take, but Gawain gave him no opportunity. The cat must have given him quite a shock also afore it commenced the affray with Gawain. He would realise the commotion must wake us all and made a swift departure. Do you think that be most likely what came to pass, Adam?'

A summons from the kitchen called us to dine.

'By the by, did the guild take you back, Seb? I had forgotten where you were this morn.' Adam asked as we washed our hands at the laver bowl.

'They did.' I handed him the towel. 'They spent a deal of time debating it, but we be back in business officially now, with documents to prove it. Although Jude – should he return – is forbidden any part in it, regrettably. We were a good partnership, I thought. He penned the texts, and I did the miniatures and marginalia. It worked well.'

'You have me now. And young Tom's not so bad when he puts his mind to it. Then Kate is quite a wonder to judge from what I've seen of her work. Even Rose can write well enough, if there be a need. We can manage betwixt us, Seb.'

'Aye. I believe we can.'


We were enjoying a fine dinner – a celebration of sorts – of pork collops in a saffron sauce with the last of the season's cherries in wine. Aye, we had wine - a celebration indeed And saffron sauce had not been upon our bill of fare since Emily was with child, when she had a passion for it, to the considerable detriment of my purse.

'I reckon it was Jack,' Tom said incongruously around a mouthful of pork.

'What was Jack?' I asked.

'Who broke into the workshop.'

''Tis a foolish notion, Tom. Why would he not simply knock at our door?'

'Because Jack always causes trouble. That's why.'

'You cannot blame him this time.'

'Then tell me who else writes so badly as this.' Tom took a scrap of paper that he had tucked in his belt and tossed it to me. It landed beside my platter. 'I found it under my desk. 'Tis none of our writing.'

'I misdoubt he would even put pen to paper unless forced.' I unfolded the rumpled sheet. Tom was correct: the script was barely legible. It seemed it was a list of tasks to be done:

*Fetch boots from cordwainer*
*Visit apothecary*
*Meet G at Forester's place*
*Buy candles and parchment.*

'I know not how this came to be in our workshop. 'Tis not ours, as you say. Besides, Jack would have no difficulty remembering these few things and require no list. He could not spell 'apothecary' anyway, unless with an 'f', nor 'cordwainer' and mayhap not 'parchment' either. Yet this scribe can spell well enough, despite the ill-written letters that lean backwards. An educated fellow wrote this, however execrable the script, which seems strange indeed.'

I said naught more, but there it was again, and I believe not in so many coincidences: the flourish and serifs on the capital 'F's of 'Fetch' and 'Forester's'. This was clearly not the neat, authoritative hand of Warden Clifford yet it could well have come from someone who had trained under his guidance. I required to think more deeply on this matter, and there was one place that I might do that.

My favoured corner of the Horse Pool at Smithfield, 'neath the oak tree, was peaceful. The yellowed squares of grass where tents and booths had lately stood were already turning green once more. Soon, all sign of St Bartholomew's Fayre would disappear, the crimes of the pedlar, Roger Underwood, likewise fading from memory. I wondered where the wretch had gone, misliking that he had escaped justice and retribution for Gerrit's murder. He did not deserve to avoid punishment. Yet it was not my place to pursue Underwood. I must leave that task to the appropriate authorities, if they took the trouble, and I feared they would not. No doubt, they could find more important matters to occupy their precious time than seeing to it that a dead Dutchman received due justice.

But justice was also my concern still, regarding Rook, locked within Newgate's hellish walls. And my Emily was not yet safe from the law either.

Whatever the case, I leaned against the trunk of the oak and took my drawing stuff from my scrip. Charcoal in hand, I had already noticed something of interest to sketch. The bough, fallen from the lightning-blasted elm, made a most unusual shape, outlined against the still waters of the pool. The sky was overcast and the subdued light reflected from the water like a polished steel mirror. The charred outline of the bough, stark against it, was like the carven prow of a ship rearing up. I could imagine using the sinuous lines as border decorations in a manuscript, mayhap sprouting leaves, thus the dead wood might live anew. Or ending in a dragon-head, as a Viking vessel of old.

Mallard ducks paddled out on the pool, quacking and splashing silver droplets. Thinking to sketch them also, I moved to see them to better advantage. In doing so, the blasted bough changed shape somewhat: no longer a ship's prow but an 'F' with a serif. This letter form was haunting me. Instead of ducks, I drew a line of 'F's, varying the shape in numerous ways, adding and subtracting flourishes. I even wrote some with my left hand – the sinister or devil's hand, as they say. They tended to lean back somewhat, which would tire the eyes if read for too long.

That was it!

The note Tom had found was penned left-handedly. And who was it who must write thus with connections to Warden Clifford's workshop? None but his son, Ralph. And who would have known I kept anything of value in my storeroom? I had told Warden Clifford of the stolen items I secured from Lizzie Knollys' house with a view to returning them to their rightful owners, saying they were kept in my storeroom. Had he not been startled into spilling his wine when I mentioned the fine Book of Hours in its box? And who might own such a splendid book, if not a king or a bishop, but the Warden of the Stationers' Guild? Ralph must have given it to Lizzie *with Fondest Regard R*, as the neatly written inscription said, afore he was injured in the fight with my brother. A foolish gift for an illiterate woman, but a very saleable item, if hard times befell. Thus she would be reluctant to return it. If she even knew its return was being demanded, since the warden had done so by letter – a letter she could not read and would be most unlikely to ask anyone to read to her.

Ralph's father had accused her of 'purloining' further items from his house, as well as accepting the precious book as a gift. If she had visited Ralph at home, their relationship might have been more respectable than that of whore and client. But then she changed her mind. Perhaps she rejected Ralph with his now damaged sight and useless arm. Such a man would have been of little worth to her as either husband or lover, unless it were a true love match, which it seemed not to have been. In which case, Ralph also wanted his over-generous gift returned and went, in person, to claim it. Lizzie, who had lately suffered a blow to her head during an argument with my wife and others, refused to give it up. Ralph became enraged. In her befuddled state, once his left hand closed about her throat, Lizzie could not fight back. Alarmed at what he had done when she had fallen dead at his feet, Ralph had dragged her body to the midden and covered it as best he might, one-handed. In his haste, he had either forgotten to retrieve or failed to find the book that was the cause of the trouble, but fled the murder scene.

Last eve, he had broken into my house and made straightway for the storeroom, where his father had informed him that I kept the book. They could not know I had removed all the items to my bedchamber when the infestation of mice became apparent. It was Ralph Clifford who had nigh killed my Gawain as he did his utmost to defend the house. It was Ralph Clifford who had, unwittingly, released the cat from the storeroom. The cat and dog then fought, as such creatures will and, in doing so, roused the household. Ralph hastened away empty-handed, but must have dropped his *aide-memoire,* his list of errands, when Gawain attacked him as a trespasser.

Every piece fitted, like the tiles of St Paul's chancel floor, combining to make a sensible pattern which no individual tile could suggest alone. Was my thinking at fault in this? The more I considered it, the more I became convinced that I had unravelled the truth at last. Both Rook and the women were innocent of Lizzie Knollys' murder. Now must I assemble the evidence to prove it.

Rain splattering the line of letter 'F's upon my paper brought my thoughts back to the present. 'Neath the tree, the drops were just beginning to penetrate the dense canopy of late-summer leaves, but beyond my shelter, sheets of rain swept across Smithfield. Having come with neither mantle nor hood, I was going to suffer a soaking on my way home. Even so, that mattered as naught, knowing my quiet reverie by the Horse Pool had solved a murder at last. I was well content with such an afternoon's work.

Upon my return home, dripping rain upon the floor, I went directly to our bedchamber, still with my scrip over my shoulder. I took the book box from its hiding place behind the likeness of the Virgin and Child. I dried my hands on the bed coverlet afore opening the Book of Hours to the flyleaf. I studied the inscription closely. My scrying glass made it clear indeed. I was looking for that tell-tale serif on the 'F' of *Fondest,* and there it was: less noticeable than in Warden Clifford's script, but there all the same – a trait learned from the same workshop. I turned to the threatening letter, all in capitals. There were but two 'F's in the words *FURTHER* and *FROM:*

## RETURN THE BOOK MY SON GAVE TO YOU AND FURTHER THE ITEMS YOU PURLOINED FROM MY HOUSE. ELSEWISE STEPS WILL BE TAKEN AGAINST YOU.

Indeed, there were the flourishes once more, betraying the warden's hand. Comparing them to the 'F' of Foxley in my document of guild membership completed but a few hours ago, they were precisely the same. I concluded that Ralph Clifford had inscribed and given the book to Lizzie Knollys as a love token. Later, his father had written the letter, hoping to intimidate her into returning it, as well as items she had taken from his home dishonestly. Mayhap, the red-stoned earrings and the little knife with the enamelled handle that I had recovered also belonged to the Clifford family.

And what of the threatened *STEPS* to be taken against Lizzie? Murder may not have been intended, but came to pass even so. Ralph could have meant only to frighten her, but in her weakened condition, a hand at her neck proved sufficient to kill.

But how to prove so much supposition? An idea came to me. Indisputable proof might remain elusive, but corroborative evidence would definitely add substance to my arguments when I presented them to Coroner Fyssher upon the morrow. With this in mind, a visit to the Clifford household was required. I should feel like a Christian walking into the arena to face the lions, but I could see no other way and now was as good a time as any.

# Chapter 19

## Later that Tuesday afternoon
## Lombard Street

THE CLIFFORDS lived in an elegant house in Lombard Street, just by St Mary Wolnoth Church. The premises had such a length of street-frontage as would be coveted by any proprietor, with two counters let down either side of a central door into the shop. To the right was the luxury of a separate door to the house behind.

I was of the opinion that Warden Clifford was likely absent still forwhy my business this morn had been in addition to the usual monthly meeting of senior members. Since those illustrious fellows always included a lavish dinner as central to their agenda, I supposed the meeting would end close to suppertime. Thus I hoped to find Mistress Clifford at home without her husband. I prayed that her son would not be there either.

For a while, I observed the house from behind an ale cup in *The Pope's Head* tavern opposite. Customers came and went. An apprentice in a neat blue tabard appeared in the doorway once or twice, attending to the more important clients. In truth, I could not imagine leaving such a task to Tom, not trusting his manners. There was no sign of the warden nor his son, and the longer I delayed, the more chance they would return.

Steeling my nerve, I entered the shop. I should browse a little and, according to my ruse, I had come to repeat my thanks for the restoration of my guild membership.

The tabard-clad apprentice sidled over to me as I leafed through a pamphlet on etiquette. Sure enough, there was the workshop trait of elaborate serifs on the 'F's, as I expected. His attitude implied I was not a valued customer adjudged from my common attire – still wet – and a lack of finery. Mayhap, his manners were little improvement upon Tom's after all.

'I would speak with Warden Clifford, if he be available,' I said. 'Sebastian Foxley by name.'

'What business do you have with him?' Such a rude enquiry: my opinion of him plummeted lower yet. Apprentices had no place to interrogate a client except as to how they might assist him.

'Guild business and naught of yours.' I quite surprised myself regarding the self-assured tone my voice acquired.

'He's not here.'

I was relieved, but gave no indication – at least, I tried not to.

'Then I wish to speak with your mistress. Pray, inform her, I will not impose upon her precious time for more than a minute or two.'

For a moment, his surly expression caused me to think he would refuse, but then he went off with a gesture of ill-grace to find Mistress Clifford. He was gone briefly afore returning with an invitation to join Mistress Clifford in the parlour – an unexpected privilege indeed.

I had met her previously upon the occasion of the guild's feast day celebration, held yearly on St Luke's Day, when wives attended also. She was of middle years, plump and plain of face, but dressed befitting a duchess at the very least. Her crimson gown with gold silk cuffs and neckline gave me hope that my visit would be worthwhile.

'Master Foxley,' she greeted me, courteous but wary.

'Good Mistress Clifford, may your day be prosperous.'

'Godfrey said you wished to speak with my husband upon guild business, but he is not here. Yet you say you will speak with me in his stead. I cannot think how I might talk of guild business which is no concern of mine.' She sat on a cushioned settle, but did not invite me to sit also. Nor was any refreshment offered.

'Indeed, mistress, the term 'guild business' has little to do with my reason for coming to you.'

'In which case, you will leave this instant!' She rose and made for the door.

'Nay, I beg you. Despite gaining admittance upon false pretences, I come to return what I believe to be your rightful possessions, mistress. I have been in Coroner Fyssher's employ which led to my discovery of some stolen items. If any belong to you, I wish only to return them.' I delved into my scrip and brought out the items, one by one, including the gorgeous book-box. I placed each thing on the little table beside her, including those that I knew belonged elsewhere, for I would test her honesty. Alongside the box lay the needle-case, the pair of snips, the fancy knife, the earrings, the amethyst finger-ring and a few other pieces.

'My earrings!' Her exclamation came without hesitation. 'I was so terrified John would assume I'd lost them through carelessness. He bought them for me last New Year, knowing the garnets to be my favourite colour. How did you come by them?'

'I fear they were filched from this house, mistress. Do you recognise anything else?'

'Aye, the book-box is my son's. John gave him the Book of Hours when he gained his majority two winters since. Is the book still inside?'

'It is. And undamaged, but for a regrettable inscription.'

She opened the box and removed the book, turning the pages. ''Tis written upon the flyleaf.'

'Lizzie? Lizzie? Do I know the name? What foolishness is this of Ralph's? "Fondest regards" indeed. His father will be in apoplexy if he sees this.'

It may be worse than that, I thought.

'What of the needle-case? Is that yours?' I asked, knowing full well it belonged to Peronelle Wenham.

'No, not that, but the knife is John's favourite for shaping pens. I gave it to him when we were first wed. It was all I could afford in those days.' She fluffed out her voluminous skirts, as if to demonstrate to me her time of economies was now past.

"'Tis a pretty thing all the same,' I said smiling. 'The amethyst ring is not yours?'

'No, I have never seen that before, nor the other things.'

'Then you may keep the earrings and the knife, Mistress Clifford. Unfortunately, the book-box must remain with me for the moment since 'tis evidence of guilt in a criminal case.'

'Guilt?' She sounded anxious, her hands fluttering in consternation and I had no wish to cause her to panic.

'The thief's guilt,' I told her.

'Oh, aye. You must apprehend this felon, Master Foxley.'

'I intend to. I bid you good day, mistress.'

Returning home, I passed by Beatrice Thatcher's house by Cheap Cross and was much startled to see some disquieting activity there. I saw two constables barging in the door, followed by one of the sheriffs and the beadle for Bread Street ward in which the house lay. At first, I wondered what Hal Thatcher had been about to get himself arrested, but then my heart lurched and seemed to fall into my boots when they manhandled Mistress Thatcher across the threshold. Her cries, her goodman's protests and her young lad's wails served as no deterrent as my wife's friend and fellow silk-woman was taken away.

'Bloody arrested!' Hal Thatcher shouted, shaking his fist at the sheriff. 'As if my Beattie ever did wrong by any man. Go and find yourself some proper bloody felons to arrest, you miserable bastards. Let my Beattie alone!'

My first instinct was to go to him, to enquire and commiserate. But then his neighbours rallied around him, and I thought better of it. Rather, I must hasten home. If Mistress

Thatcher was taken into custody, how long afore they came to arrest Emily? If they had not done so already... Dear God in heaven...

Aching hip be damned. I ran the length of Cheapside and into Paternoster Row.

'Emily!' I burst into the kitchen, gasping for breath. 'Where is Em? Rose! Where is she?'

'Feeding little Dickon upstairs.' Rose turned from adding worts to the pot on the fire. Turning, she saw my face and hastened to me, wiping her hands upon her apron afore taking mine. 'Whatever's amiss, Seb? You look as though Satan's at your heel.'

'He is,' I panted. 'The sheriff... has arrested... Beatrice Thatcher. It cannot be long afore... they come here. Emily!' With just enough breath restored, I raced upstairs to our chamber.

'Em.'

'Seb? I heard you shouting.'

'Leave the babe, Em. Leave everything. We must go.'

'Go? But I can't without...'

'Then take Dickon with you. The sheriff arrested Beatrice. You have to flee, Em.'

'Oh, Holy Mary! Where to? Not Norfolk again.'

'No. St Martin le Grand. I shall take you there. You will have forty days of sanctuary in the precinct. 'Tis the safest place I can think. Cover yourself with your cloak. Make haste!'

'Oh, Seb...' Tears welled, but she fastened her lacings despite the babe's protests that he was not yet done suckling. 'I'll need linen for Dickon and...'

I grabbed a pile of clean tailclouts and stuffed them inside a folded cradle blanket, tying the corners together.

'Come. No time to waste. I shall bring more to you on the morrow.'

We had reached the kitchen when there came such a hammering upon the street door. I knew who it must be. There was no more time.

'Adam.' I shoved the babe into his arms. 'Take Em out the back way. Keep to the alleyways. Get her to St Martin's.'

'Where is that?'

'Em knows. Just get her there safely any way you can.'

The sound of hammering came again.

'Go! And God keep you safe.'

Emily was whimpering as I pushed them out into the yard.

'Rose, secure the side gate behind them, then be silent - all of you. You saw naught. You know naught. Now return to your tasks as if all be well.' I swallowed hard and squared my shoulders as the door was beaten a third time. 'Hold! Hold! I called out as I went along the passage. 'Who disturbs a citizen so rudely while at his work?'

'Open up, or we break this door down!'

'What means this outrage?' I opened the door a few inches, keeping behind it. I recognised the sheriff, knowing him well enough through my work for the coroner. 'Well, Master Colet, if Master Fyssher has need of my assistance, a messenger would suffice...'

'Stand aside, Foxley,' he growled, shoving past me. 'We come for your wife.'

'Emily? What business can you possibly have with her?'

By this time, we were crowded into the kitchen: Rose and Nessie preparing supper, Sheriff Colet throwing his considerable weight around, two constables, the beadle of Farringdon Within ward and myself.

'Where is she?' Colet demanded.

'If you allow me to explain, I could save you much trouble. Emily has been at our brother-in-law's place this week past. Her sister's recent confinement in childbed did not go well. My wife has gone to nurse her and care for the other little ones.' The lies fell from my lips, black and slick. 'At present, she bides at Deptford and will, doubtless, remain there some while. What is it you require of her?'

'She's under arrest.'

'Arrest? Nay, there must be some error. Emily be utterly law-abiding. She can have done no wrong.'

'The charge is murder, Foxley, so cease your prattling. And I know the Appleyards well enough to know she has no sister. Search the place,' Colet ordered his constables.

'Murder? 'Tis absurd; ridiculous. Your actions cannot be justified. My wife be guilty of naught.' They were already stomping up the stairs. 'You damage any of my possessions, and the mayor shall hear of it,' I shouted after them.

Colet remained in the kitchen, quizzing me. Of course, I denied everything he said; more and more lies told. It would take me a lifetime of confession to admit them all, if I could even remember so many. I had prided myself a man of truth. Now was I the worst of liars. And worse yet, I saw that he did not believe me.

'Your wife was working on the silk-women's stall at the fayre until Friday last. And I saw her myself on Sunday, in company with Beatrice Thatcher. I questioned them both on this matter, so still your lying tongue, Foxley.'

It was thus: I recalled now that Emily had told me of the questioning. I had quite forgotten in the urgency of the moment.

'She's not here,' one of the constables announced, returning to the kitchen.

'As I told you,' I said, attempting some small claim to a vestige of honesty.

'Where is she, Foxley? At her father's house, mayhap? Tell me no more of your pathetic lies.'

'A place where you cannot touch her.'

'Ah. Sanctuary, is it? Where? St Mary-le-Bow? St Martin's?' Colet looked at my face and nodded. 'In St Martin's, then.' He had read the fact in my eyes. Attempting to lie was to no avail for a man such as myself: one whose every thought might as well be written out in an open book, that anyone could see. I should have spoken the truth from the beginning. All I had achieved was to convince the sheriff how readily I might perjure myself in a court of law. I had aided Emily's cause not in the least.

'She be safe there for as long as need be. St Martin's has special privileges.'

'Not if I can help it.' Colet's expression was dire. 'Lord Mayor Hayford has dispute with the Dean of St Martin's and its liberties. 'Tis a nest of thieves, debtors, murderers and foreigners. You trust to your wife's safety amongst their kind?'

'She has a better chance there than in Newgate. I know that. The brethren will keep her safe.'

'Huh. The brothers are the worst offenders, as I hear tell: felons as bad as any. Aiding and abetting, receiving and fencing stolen goods to fill the abbey's own coffers. Why do you suppose they let the criminals stay?'

I shook my head and made no answer. I did not know if what he said was true. Mayhap, it was. It made no difference. Emily was there and would remain until I could prove her innocence.

Sheriff Colet and his men were gone by the time Adam returned.

'Is she safe?' I asked.

He grinned.

'Aye, and such a place! 'Tis a town of itself within the city: craftsmen selling their wares and trading of all kinds. I swear I saw a hussy by the gatehouse plying the lowest trade of all and in a monastery! I never thought to see the like.'

'The craftsmen be in-comers and foreigners,' I explained. 'Forbidden to work in London by the guilds, St Martin's protects them from such restrictions. There is even a small brewery within the precinct where some Dutchmen make that vile stuff they call "beer". Of course, such awful drink be illegal to brew elsewhere, yet I heard that some tavern-haunters have acquired a taste for its bitterness. Apparently, the herb 'hops' that makes it so foul upon the tongue yet preserves the drink without souring for months. I know not how they may tell, in truth, and cannot see what purpose it serves to keep so long something which be undrinkable in the first place.'

'Have you tried this beer?'

'Aye. Jude bought some once. Once was sufficient. We threw most of it away. 'Tis no drink for true Englishmen, I tell you. But what of Emily?'

'Well, matters fell out not so badly as you might have feared. Em recognised someone who bides there. As you say: a foreigner, but known to her father. A Frenchman, "Jacks" I think she said, a carver of misericords, who purchases his wood from Stephen Appleyard. He and his wife say Em and the babe may stay under their roof, such as it is. At least, I think that's what they said, for I hardly understood a word of it. I thought they must be speaking French, but Em answered them in good English, and they seemed to understand her.'

'Oh, aye, Jacques le Charpentier. I know of him. 'Tis a relief to hear that Emily will not be alone. My thanks, Adam, you have set my mind at rest. It was indeed the sheriff who came to the door afore you were gone. You departed just in time.'

We partook of supper in downcast humour.

'Will you be going to choir practice this eve, Seb?' Rose asked as I chewed long upon a morsel I could barely taste. All was as dust in my mouth.

'What? This eve?'

She nodded.

'Oh, I had quite forgot. I be not of a humour for singing. How can I be with Emily in such straits and little Dickon not here?'

'But, master, is it not the Archbishop of Canterbury's visit this Sunday?' Kate chimed in. 'Aren't you doing your solo *Miserere* for him?'

'Supposedly. And I require much practice indeed after months of absence. The precentor was not overly impressed with my efforts last week. Told me I cackled like a goose and brayed like a donkey. He has other, younger choristers in far better voice who could sing for the archbishop.'

'Can they achieve that exquisitely high note as you do though?' Rose said.

'I want to hear you sing next Sunday, Seb,' Adam said, and Kate added her pennyworth, insisting I must go to choir practice. I believe they were thinking that singing to the Lord God would cheer me and distract me from my worries over Emily. Mayhap, they were right, so I would go to St Paul's.

The incense that faintly perfumed the chancel of the cathedral proved a balm for my unquiet soul, as it always did. The fading light of early evening was yet sufficient to cast jewelled lights across the floor from the stained glass of the Jesse Tree in the great west window and upon my shoes as I trod the tiles. Such beauteous colours were entrancing, slipping away and fading as the sun sank lower. This time of day, the stationers and relic-sellers, butter-wives and cheese-mongers, who set up stalls in the nave, had gone home. The old church was returned to God as it should be: a place of quiet and contemplation – at least until the precentor had his boy blow up the bellows for the organ.

The ancient instrument wheezed and belched as it warmed up. Then the notes came more sonorously, and we of the choir were ordered to sing our scales and perform our vocal exercises. The precentor was ever hard to please, but with the archbishop coming to listen a few days hence, he was more intolerant of our shortcomings than usual. At the end of an hour, we had sung and re-sung the *Te Deum Laudamus* so many times, some of the youngest choristers were sobbing, and still we failed to meet his exacting standards.

Eventually, he slammed the huge choir book shut with such a thud it made me jump, and the youngest lad burst into noisy tears.

'Dismissed!' the precentor yelled. 'Get to your beds. If you cannot improve tomorrow, I shall hire a chorus of alley cats to replace you. I swear they can sing no worse. Now go.' He began ushering the lads towards the transept, still muttering about how our pathetic efforts would bring disgrace upon St Paul's. I did not think we had sung so badly as that, though we certainly were not at our best. A few more days of practice and we would improve. As I made for the door, the precentor summoned me back.

'You're not to leave, Sebastian. You haven't done the solo once yet, and your previous attempts were worse than mill-wheels grinding. Come, get the pitch right and I want to hear that top A note ring out to the heavens. Make the angels weep with envy, Sebastian, not with earache.'

Reluctantly, I resumed my place at the end of the choir stalls. Never having been permitted to join the Song School as other lads did, to learn to read, write and sing – my father had taught me at home – my ability had been discovered by fortune and it was not so long since I had earned my chorister's cassock. Most lads left the choir when their voices broke, or else took to singing the lower parts. My voice was an oddity in that I spoke as a man yet could still sing as a ten-year-old: a greater power behind a child's voice that suited the acoustics of the huge space of the cathedral.

The precentor worked me hard indeed, forcing me to sing the words *Miserere mei, Deus*. Never mind begging God for mercy; I was nigh upon my knees afore the precentor after another hour. My throat was scratchy, and I was sore in need of ale to soothe it.

'Again!' he commanded, 'And remember: you are singing to the Lord God, not to me. He will judge whether your offering is good enough. You do not want to disappoint the Almighty, do you?'

'Nay, Brother Precentor.' I braced my shoulders, raised my eyes to heaven and sang, throwing myself – heart, soul and spirit – into one last supreme effort. The top note soared up into the rafters, then faded softly, like a flower folding at sunset. It was done. I could sing no more that eve. I was relieved to see the precentor nodded approval, though not a word of commendation passed his lips – it never did.

'The morrow; same hour. Don't be tardy. You need to get that opening phrase crisper; hit that first note precisely. Get some sleep; rest your voice, Sebastian.' Thus was I dismissed.


It was late, and darkness was falling. It was as well that I lived but across the way, else the Watch might have apprehended me for being on the street without a torchlight to mark me a respectable citizen. The moon was bright enough that I managed to avoid a pile of horse dung at the entrance to our side alleyway, but not sufficient that I noticed a yet darker shadow lurking in the gloom. Until something was slipped over my head and pulled tight about my neck: a rough, hempen noose. A blade pricked betwixt my shoulder blades.

'One squeak from you, Foxley, and you're tomorrow's worm-fodder. Understand?'

I nodded. My heart was hammering; I could barely draw breath with the rope across my windpipe, and I clawed at it in desperation. It pulled tighter. The knife point pressed a little harder, urging me forward, towards our side gate.

He pushed open the kitchen door and shoved me through.

'Seb, we were wondering where you'd...' Rose's words died upon her lips when she saw I was not alone and noticed the rope around my neck.

Gawain roused himself to manage a low growl, but naught more. Nessie squealed.

'Shut your noise, or he's dead,' Ralph Clifford snarled behind me – for he was my assailant. 'I want the book. And don't deny you've got it: you showed it to my mother.' He loosened the rope a little that I might gasp a breath. 'Where is it?'

'Upstairs... the aumbry... bedchamber, behind the Virgin and Child...'

'You.' Clifford nodded at Adam. 'Fetch it and no tricks.'

A lengthy silence ensued, but for Nessie's snivelling, while Adam went upstairs. It occurred to me then to wonder how a man with a single useable hand held both a noose about my neck and a knife to my back, but I could not see what he did behind me.

Rose and Tom sat, bewildered, at the table. Rose never took her eyes from me. Tom stared at his feet. Gawain watched. The Lord God be thanked that Kate was already abed.

Adam was gone too long. Ralph was twitching the rope tighter.

'It isn't there,' Adam said upon his return. 'I'm sorry, Seb.'

'What bloody mischief is this?' Ralph pushed the knife so I felt it pierce my jerkin, shirt and then flesh.

'Ahh. It must be. It was in my scrip this afternoon...'

'Where's your scrip?' Adam asked.

'Workshop?' I truly could not recall what I had done with it. I had raced home, my every thought to get Emily to safety. I had not cared about my scrip.

'No sign of it.' Adam came back empty-handed. 'Think, Seb.'

'You'd better bloody think and quick. My patience is running out.' Another jab with the knife jogged a memory loose.

'I rushed upstairs to speak with Emily. Mayhap, I took it with me?'

Adam was off again, thundering up the wooden stairs a second time. Mercifully, he returned with my scrip.

'Under the bed,' he said, taking out the pretty book-box. 'This what you want?' he asked Ralph. 'Then have it!' He threw the box at him. The knife clattered to the floor as Ralph fumbled to catch it one-handed. He lunged for it and missed. I heard the box crash and splinter, but as my assailant fell, I was dragged backwards by the rope at my neck and fell with him.

'Summon the Watch, Tom,' I heard Adam cry as he flung himself atop of us both. I could not breathe. The noose tightened. I struggled, but blackness was closing in.

The kitchen was full of folk. I was propped on a stool at the board, my head supported by a pillow as I rested there.

'He's waking up,' someone said.

I realised they meant me. My back was sore from the knife pricks, but that was as naught compared to the agony of my throat.

'Here, Seb, sip this, if you can.' Rose held a cup to my lips. I was so thirsty, yet I could not swallow it without choking. I clutched at my neck, trying not to cough. The pain would be too much. 'Try again.' I did so, tasting honey and meadowsweet in the ale, but I could drink no more and pushed the cup away. Looking around, I saw Adam speaking with Bailiff Thaddeus Turner and Sheriff Colet.

'Where... is...' I tried to speak, but a whispered croak was the best I achieved.

'The devil is locked in the storeroom. The constables are dealing with him now; taking him away,' Rose answered. 'No need to concern yourself, Seb. As soon as these folk leave, I'll put some salve on your back. It must hurt you.'

I nodded and lay my head down upon the pillow. It seemed to weigh like lead, and my eyes closed gratefully. Somewhere, far away, it seemed, there were sounds of disturbance and shouted protests, then a thud as our front door slammed shut. After that, it went quiet. Ralph Clifford was gone from the house and good riddance to the miscreant.

'We need you to explain all this, Master Foxley.' Sheriff Colet shook me awake again. 'Master Armitage says this is about evidence of murder in this book.' He put the little Book of Hours on the board beside me. Its spine was broken, and folios hung loose. 'You must answer my questions.'

Reluctantly, I raised my head.

'I... in... ins...' My voice failed me utterly. My head returned to the welcoming pillow.

'Can your questions not wait until morning?' Rose intervened. 'He cannot speak to you now. He must rest.'

I tried once more, determined to explain. I forced myself to sit up. My head felt befuddled, and it was difficult to put my thoughts in order. Rather than speak, I opened the damaged book at the flyleaf and showed Sheriff Colet the inscription. I pointed towards the passage to the workshop.

'What is it you want?' Colet asked.

I shook my head. Pointed to my throat, then back at the passageway. Could he not comprehend my meaning? I indicated the letter 'R' that signed the inscription.

Adam pushed in.

'He's trying to tell you the man who attacked him – he who was secured in the storeroom – wrote this. 'R' for Ralph, see?'

I nodded. Then I flicked through the crushed and torn pages, searching for the letter that had been tucked inside. It was not there.

'Let-ter,' I croaked at Adam.

'Not there?'

I shook my head.

'It must have fallen out in the scuffle.'

Everyone was swiftly on their knees, searching the kitchen floor. Thaddeus found the folded paper in amongst the kindling stacked beside the fire. It must have fluttered there: fortunate indeed that it had not gone into the flames.

I unfolded it and smoothed out the creases on the board.

'Did he write this also?' Colet peered at it, squinting.

I mimed to Adam to find the scrying glass in my scrip.

Colet used it to enlarge the writing.

'A threatening letter certainly, but it doesn't look like the same hand to me.'

'No. Ward... Cliff... wrote,' I managed to say, pointing to where it said 'MY SON' in strident capitals.

'So father and son are in this together.'

I nodded agreement.

'You will have to provide us with a detailed account of everything, but it can wait 'til the morrow.' Colet regarded me with a querying frown. 'We'll do it here, in your workshop, with pen, ink and paper to hand. You can write down your explanations, if your voice is not able.'

I smiled my gratitude for his thoughtfulness.

At last, Thaddeus and Colet departed, leaving us in peace. It was late, and Tom and Nessie sought their beds. Gawain slept by the fading fire.

Adam poured ale for himself and Rose.

'You want some?' He looked over at me.

In answer, I showed him my cup, still nigh full. I attempted another sip but, as afore, it set me choking, and I spilled much of it.

Rose aided me in removing my shirt. The linen was torn here and there and spotted with blood. It appeared beyond repair with so many holes. I saw from her expression that my back was no better than my attire. I was hard put not to wince as she gently smeared salve onto the cuts, but crying out aloud was impossible anyway. She took the greatest trouble not to cause me more pain.

'How... rope and knife?' I asked Adam, hoping to distract my thoughts, 'One hand...'

'Oh, I suppose you could not see behind you,' he said, taking a hearty swallow of ale that I envied. 'The other end of the rope around your neck he'd knotted about his upper arm – the otherwise useless arm. He must have slipped the noose over your head with his left hand with it already tied in place. Then he could pull it tight with a flick of his right shoulder, leaving his left hand free to brandish the knife. Trouble was, when he tried to catch the box I threw at him, he dropped the knife, but couldn't drop the rope since it was tied to his arm. I fear that caused it to draw tight and pull you down with him. It was my fault he nigh strangled you. I'm so sorry, Seb.'

Aye, my throat was sorry also.

'What Adam is too modest to tell you,' Rose took up the story while applying salve to a gash beneath my left shoulder blade, 'Is that he wrested the knife from that devil, sliced through the rope to free you and overpowered him.'

'With help from Rose,' Adam added. 'Then we trussed him up like a Christmas goose with his own rope and wrestled him into the storeroom, latching the door after. It served as a lock-up until Tom returned with the local Watch. Meantime, we'd set about reviving you. You had us worried for a while, Seb, I can tell you. Gawain did what he could to bring you back, licking your face. I believe he was returning your efforts to save him yesterday.

Yesterday? Was it only yesterday when Ralph had injured my poor Gawain? So much had come to pass since then.

# Chapter 20

## Wednesday, the second day of September

EARLY NEXT MORN – too early, in truth – Sheriff Colet came to question me. I was dressed, though my back would have felt easier if I went naked. I had not broken my fast. Meat and drink were beyond me, my throat so swollen, swallowing my own spittle – of which there was so little, mercifully – was akin to swallowing shards of glass. Just drawing breath hurt. I could shape words with my mouth, but was unable to sound a solitary syllable. Answering Colet's questions would not be easy.

'Shall I stay?' Adam offered as we settled ourselves about my desk in the workshop. 'I may be able to help.'

I touched his arm and nodded. Thankfully, Colet also approved. Tom and Kate were to aid Rose in the shop, to let us remain undisturbed.

'Just so you know,' Colet said, 'Warden Clifford was taken into custody at dawn. As City Bailiff, Thaddeus Turner is dealing with him, but will join us later.'

That was good tidings indeed.

'He deserves it,' Adam muttered, pouring ink into a pot for me and setting a half-dozen quills beside it. It seemed he expected me to have to do much writing. I hoped he was mistaken: I did not feel of a humour to work so much this day.

I took out my untidy sheaf of notes from my scrip and began sorting them into some semblance of order. I had hoped to do this afore Colet arrived but, as I said, he came too early, and I was unprepared. I ought to have done it days ago, but never had.

Firstly, I lay aside the notes that concerned the death of Gerrit Heijnsbroeck and the theft of the unicorn horns. They were irrelevant to this case. In truth, they could be used for fire-lighting. They were of little purpose now otherwise, what with Roger Underwood disappeared and unlikely ever to return to face the consequences of his crimes.

Secondly, I found my list of items of evidence, the one Adam had read by the Horse Pool when I had not meant him to. I gave it to Colet, handing him the scrying glass, if he should have need of it. It seemed my writing was clear enough without; the daylight helped, of course.

The sheriff went through the list, point by point, asking for more details. If he knew them, Adam told him. If not, I wrote them out in full. Sometimes, my sketches assisted his understanding. My drawings of the finger marks on Lizzie Knollys' neck showed how she had been strangled one-handed. I also presented him with drawings of all the stolen items recovered, including the earrings and penknife returned to Mistress Clifford the previous afternoon. I suspected my visit there and showing the book to her was the likely cause of her son's attack upon me, but at least she had confirmed it as his possession. This information was not in my notes, since there had been no opportunity to record it. Thus, I had a good deal more to explain in writing, the details of our conversation at the house in Lombard Street. Then I demonstrated as best I could the unusual form of the capital 'F's in the inscription and the letter before showing Colet the same in my document of reinstatement to the guild of yesterday morn.

'And Warden Clifford inserted your name here himself?' Colet asked.

I nodded, putting the scrying glass over the 'F' of Foxley so he could see the detail of the serif.

'And they all have this extra flourish?'

I nodded again and wrote down that the same letterform even appeared in the design of the stained glass window in the guild hall, commissioned by Warden Clifford. It was almost a maker's mark for his workshop. I turned my paper so the sheriff might read what I had written. As I looked up from my writing, the workshop appeared to tilt and slide sideways for an instant. I blinked a few times, and it righted itself, but I flushed hot and dropped my pen, splattering ink droplets on my desk.

Adam replaced the quill in the ink pot and was frowning at me, but the moment passed, and all was well.

Then Thaddeus Turner arrived, and I feared I might be required to tell all a second time, but I was spared the ordeal. He enquired after my recovery as Rose served ale and wafers for refreshment.

Thirsty, I wanted to drink, but one sip caused a painful bout of choking, and I was forced to refrain.

'Not so good, I see.' Thaddeus answered his own question. 'Well, it should hearten you to hear, Seb, my friend, that John Clifford is now secured under lock and key. His son, being of cowardly nature, has already implicated him. Apparently, a family feud ensued when John learned that his son was so besotted with Elizabeth Knollys, he'd given her the Book of Hours as a love token, seeing its worth nigh unto the value of a decent house. John demanded Ralph get it back from her. She refused to return it and, worse yet from Ralph's point of view, she spurned him when she realised his arm and his eyesight would never mend after...' Thaddeus did not complete the sentence. He had no need. We all knew he meant "after Jude injured him in that drunken brawl". He continued: 'When Ralph used force to persuade her to give him the book, he lost his temper and went too far. Realising he'd killed her, he tried to hide her body in the midden heap. The rest you know.'

'And we have enough information here to send them both, father and son, to Tyburn Tree.' Colet tapped my pile of notes and drawings. 'Thanks to Master Foxley's assiduous attention to detail and commendable perseverance. In which case,' he smiled at me, 'I believe three silk-women and a black man must be allowed their freedom.'

'Aye?' It was the first word I had managed to croak, but it was worth the hurt as the sheriff confirmed it.

'I'll see the fellow Rook is released from Newgate this very day, along with Mistresses Thatcher and Wenham. As for Mistress Foxley, no doubt you'll be eager to fetch her yourself from St Martin's in time for dinner. You will, of course, be required to give testimony at the trial, Master Foxley. I'll let you know when we have a date. Let's hope your voice is repaired by then. In the meantime, you have Lord Mayor Hayford's gratitude and mine for removing these felons from our city's streets.' Gathering up the papers, Colet was about to stuff them back into my scrip and take it with him.

Fortunately, Adam saw this and, ever thoughtful, gave him a vegetable sack. The sheriff looked displeased.

'The sack is clean, sir,' Adam told him. 'The leather scrip is too precious to Master Foxley. He would not part with it.'

'It looks tattered enough to be used for cobbler's mendings.'

'Aye, but it's precious, all the same.'

Thus was my scrip restored to me, and I was content.

Shortly, my wife should also be returned to me. Then all would be well with the world.

With due care, I pulled on my jerkin. Thaddeus and Colet were gone, and I would go to St Martin's to fetch Emily and little Dickon home. I missed them greatly. My back was stiff as scabs had formed over the cuts, but I ignored it, my heart light.

'I'm coming with you,' Adam said. It was not a question, and I saw in his eyes there was no point in arguing. Besides, a written argument would take time and lack any persuasive tone. 'That thieves' den is no place for you as you are at present. They could knock you down with a glance and rob you naked. Besides, I know which is this French Jacks' place. I'll save you time searching for it.'

It was a short walk along Cheapside to St Martin's. The weather was warm, but by no means hot, yet I felt over-hot and somewhat unsteady on my feet. In truth, I was glad Adam was with me.

Jacques was not difficult to find, sitting outside his ramshackle dwelling. I had seen sheep-pens which looked more comfortable, but it was his home of sorts and rent free. In return, he was carving new misericords for the choir stalls in the abbey church. He was working on a piece of sturdy oak across his lap as we approached, his mop of white hair concealing his face.

'Good day to you, Master Jacks,' Adam said, touching his cap in greeting. Jacques returned the gesture. I did likewise.

'Ah! Sebastien, it ez you.'

I smiled and nodded.

'You know each other?'

'Mais oui, Adam. We meet at Monsieur Etienne's 'ouse one time.'

'Who? Oh, no matter. Seb cannot speak; his throat hurts too much. We've come to take Mistress Emily home.'

'My Claude she weel be sorry. She like ze company of anuzzer woman. Zay are inside.' He put down his work. It looked like some mythical beasts entangled. I would have asked about it, but could not. He ushered us within.

The place was gloomy with but a single tiny window. Nevertheless, I was able to make out two figures; both women, one stirring a pot upon the fire. My Emily was bending over, settling Dickon in a nest of blankets.

'Claude, we 'ave visitors,' Jacques called out.

The women looked up. Catching sight of me, Emily rushed to me, flinging herself at me and embracing me with such fervour as I could not withstand.

I staggered back with a gasp of pain as her fingers discovered the cuts upon my back. She clung to me, sobbing.

'We came to take you home, Em,' Adam explained. 'The Cliffords are in custody. You're free now.' He tried to prise her fingers away. 'You must loose your hold, Em. Seb was hurt last eve.'

'Hurt? How? Tell me, Seb.' Emily stepped away, looking me up and down. In the half-light, I misdoubt she could see the lesions that encircled my neck.

'He can't. His throat is swollen. Ralph Clifford had a noose tight around his neck; tried to strangle the life out of him. Nigh succeeded, curse him to hell and back.'

I would have told her more gently, if I could. But I was swaying on my feet. My face burned, and my head ached; my limbs weak of a sudden. A stool was placed beside me, and Adam and Jacques eased me down upon it.

Emily put a cool hand to my brow.

'He has a dry fever,' she said. 'I don't understand how a sore neck may cause it. He needs to drink to cool him. Ale or water.'

'That's the problem, Em, he can't swallow anything, but chokes upon it.'

'Don't you see? He could be dying of thirst as we watch. He must drink something, somehow.'

I realised, sluggishly, Emily might be correct. Last eve, I was already thirsty after hours of singing, afore Ralph harmed me. I had drunk not a drop since. I had not even had cause to use the jordan nor visit the privy. My body must be dry as dust. Was that what ailed me?

'Dreenk zis.' Jacques' wife, Claude, gave Emily a cup. 'Tiz ze "corne de licorne". Eet cure evyzink.'

'Cawn-deli-cawn?' Adam repeated. 'What in Our Lord Jesu's name is that? Won't kill him off, will it?'

Claude showed him a small linen bag with a drawstring. She tipped a little white powder into the palm of her hand and licked it.

'Save,' she said. 'Le colporteur 'ee sell eet say eet cure, er, toutes les maladies.'

341

'Apologies, but I have no idea what you're saying, mistress,' Adam admitted, smiling even so. 'I think it's safe, Seb. Do your best to drink some of it, if you can.'

I took the smallest sip and managed to swallow it without choking too much. A second sip went down a little more easily. It took a while, but I drank most of it, leaving only the dregs at the bottom, fearing they would set me coughing. I began to feel much restored; my mind clearer; my headache fading.

'Whatever it is, cawn-deli-cawn seems to work miracles,' Adam said. 'You look much improved already.'

'Cooler too,' Emily added, feeling my forehead again.

And so I should forwhy I had just swallowed the world's most precious medicine.

In my youth, I copied French lays and fabliaux for Richard Collop, during my apprenticeship, enough to understand the language somewhat. *Corne de licorne* meant unicorn's horn, and *le colporteur* was the pedlar. I believed I now knew the whereabouts of Roger Underwood. The wretch had not fled the city, as we thought, but was in sanctuary, right here in St Martin's, knowing full well he was safe indefinitely from any force of law. He could not be touched. If he remained within this precinct, he would escape justice. Meanwhile, he must have ground down what few pieces of horn he still possessed and was selling it as a sovereign remedy. No doubt, it had cost Jacques and Claude a good deal of money to purchase. I should repay them the cost as soon as I might enquire the price – later, when I could speak once more.

By the time we had made our way home – slowly, for I was yet recovering – Gabriel was at our door. I had not expected him to leave the safety of his ship, but now I could allay his fears, somewhat, upon that score. I so wanted to tell him there and then about Roger Underwood, but it required to be written down since my voice would not oblige me. Seated once again at my desk, Gabriel and Adam read the words over my shoulder as I wrote them, swiftly as the ink could flow.

'In St Martin's?' Gabriel queried. 'Did you see him there?'

'I certainly didn't,' Adam said, 'So I can't think how you saw him, Seb.'

The Frenchwoman told me, I wrote.

'When was this? I never understood a word of her prattle.'

I explained, word by word, what she had said.

'Ground to powder! What a waste of such beauty' Gabriel sounded horrified. 'Whatever will Master Ameryk say when I tell him you drank his unicorn horn? You swallowed his profits!'

'It worked though, didn't it, Seb?' Adam laughed, 'It had you on the mend in a few heartbeats.'

I nodded and smiled somewhat sheepishly.

'At least we know it to be as effective as claimed. That's something, I suppose.' Gabriel shrugged. 'You can write us a fine testimonial to advertise the fact when we sell the pieces you discovered by the Horse Pool. In truth, I came to ask if you wanted to come to Newgate with me. A message came from the sheriff that Rook is to be released at midday.'

Adam glanced at me, eyebrows raised in query, prepared to translate any gesture I made into words.

I shook my head.

'He's still not recovered from last eve,' Adam explained, 'But why don't I go with you and then you can bring Rook back here? We can celebrate his freedom, and he may wash. I'm sure we'll find him a clean shirt: one of mine may fit him – just about. And Emily will be delighted to prepare a decent meal for him – and for you, of course, Gabriel. I'll go ask her, but I'm certain she will. Em? What do you think if...' he called out as he went along the passage to the kitchen.

Emily had been smiling since her release from St Martin's, the more so when we returned to find Gabriel at our house. Now the thought that he no longer had to fear Underwood betraying him to the sheriff if arrested and, better yet, that our friend would dine with us this day, had broadened her smile further indeed. I knew she had an especial affection for the man with mismatched eyes.

While Adam and Gabriel were gone to Newgate, I took time at last to consider the doings of the workshop. Unsurprisingly, after days of turmoil, little work had been achieved, but at least the place might be set to rights. The cat, Grayling, had done as required and it appeared that the little storeroom was no longer overrun with mice. Thus, I instructed Tom – my voice improving all the while – to replace our stocks of paper, parchment, pigments, ink and all else back upon the shelves in their rightful places. It would be pleasant to see the floor, desks and stools without everything piled precariously on them. It goes without saying that Tom complained at being asked to do what he claimed was manual labour, as though restacking reams of paper was a task beneath his dignity.

'I don't see why I have to do it,' he grumbled, his expression like that of a fellow who had bitten into a crab apple. 'It wasn't my fault the place got full of mice. Why should I have to put everything back?'

'I'll help you,' Kate offered – as ever obliging and helpful. 'You stand on the stool, Tom, and I'll pass everything up to you.'

'Don't tell me what to do. I'm the senior apprentice here, not you.'

'But Master Seb shouldn't be lifting stuff; he'll break the healing scabs upon his back. We can do it, Tom, and then all will be neat and tidy, won't it? If you want, I'll balance on the stool, and you can fetch what needs to go on each shelf, except I'm not so tall as you and can hardly reach the back of the top shelf. It'll be neater if you do it.'

'I suppose,' he muttered with ill-grace, 'But don't you think you can order me about, Kate.'

She smiled sweetly at him. She had such a way with her; Kate always won any argument, usually by fair means. Young as she was, she knew how to use those womanly wiles on us hapless menfolk. When the time came that she should wed, her husband would needs be a fellow of sharp wit indeed to get the better of Kate Verney. For all that, he would most likely be a happy man, the envy of other Londoners, biding in a well-ordered and contented household for Kate would make it so.

Thinking to be out of their way, what with all the necessary to-ing and fro-ing, I went to the kitchen, only to be shooed from there by Emily.

'Don't get under my feet,' she scolded me, 'I have such a deal to do for this special dinner. Make yourself useful: take the babe out of the way before he gets covered in flour and if you go to the garden, pick me some rosemary and thyme to flavour the marinade for the mutton. Go on; get you gone and take the damned dog as well, else I'll trip over him.'

I obeyed, taking Dickon and calling to Gawain to follow me. The dog moved slowly, healing but hurting yet. I sympathised, having suffered from that same blade though to a lesser degree. I sat on the old elder stump with my son upon my knee and Gawain flopped at my feet. The sun was warm, and bees hummed among the few remaining marigold flowers that had self-seeded in random clumps of joyful hue around the back of the pig-sty. I looked up, enjoying the sun upon my face, watching sheep's-fleece clouds hastening downriver on a westerly breeze. Mayhap, it would rain later, but for now, the day was pleasant indeed.

Rose came to the garden, bearing an ale cup.

'You must keep drinking, Seb.' She handed me the cup.

'Be you my physician, instructing me so?' I sipped carefully.

'Aye, if you will? We must restore your voice; how else will you be able to sing for the archbishop on Sunday? At least you sound less like a croaking frog now.'

'But not good enough to please the precentor. Someone else will have to do it.'

'There is still time enough.'

I took another sip. The ale was slipping down more easily with each drop. Dickon made a grab for the cup, spilling it.

'Nay, little one,' Rose chided him, taking him from me. ''Tis milk, not ale for you as yet. A month or two and you may try some. Come, shall we say "good day" to the fat piggywig?' Dickon gurgled at her, and I thought how sorrowful it was that Rose's own babe – born out of wedlock afore I knew her – had died, for she made a fine mother. If she and Jude had married, who could say? She might have been with child by now. But that was not to be. I hoped, someday, she would find a good and kindly husband, as she deserved.

Remembering I was supposed to pick herbs for Emily's sauce or marinade, or whatever it was, I chose a few leaves of sage and sweet cicely that were still green and fresh looking. Leaving Rose talking nonsense to Dickon and the sow in her sty, I went to the kitchen with my offering of herbs.

'What's this?' Emily asked as I put them and my empty cup down beside the bowl she was mixing with a great deal of effort. 'And don't put the cup there; put it for washing can't you?' She pushed aside a stray lock of autumnal hair with the back of a flour-dusted hand.

'Herbs... for the mutton,' I managed to say.

'Rosemary and thyme, I said. Not these. Can you do naught as I tell you?'

'Sorry, I forgot which...'

'Well, go and tell Rose to bring them, instead of wasting time in the garden with you. I need her help here. There's bacon to prepare, onions to dice, leeks to wash and Nessie's far too slow. Now get out of my kitchen, else this dinner will never be cooked in time for Gabriel's return.'

With a resigned sigh, aware there was no pleasing Emily at such a time, I obeyed. But as I was about to cross the yard, the side gate was pushed open. Thinking Gabriel and Rook were in haste for their meal, I knew Emily would be upset that all was far from ready for them. However, it was not our expected guests.

It was Jack. He came furtively, like a slinking cat, as if hoping to pass unnoticed.

'Jack? You come unexpectedly.'

He jumped, so intent upon creeping in, he had failed to observe me, obvious as I was, standing by the kitchen door.

'Master Seb! I wos just goin' to...'

'What, Jack? Why come like a sneak-thief? You be welcome... Be you in need?'

'Well, I... I fink I wos... What's up wiv yer voice, master?'

'No matter. Tell me what be amiss.' I led him into the garden. He would be less appreciated than I in Emily's domain for the present.

'Jack! What a surprise,' Rose greeted him. 'Have you come for dinner?'

'Er, well, I might if...'

'Tell us, lad,' I encouraged him, accepting Dickon back from Rose and resuming my seat upon the stump.

'Aye, see, it's Maudie, ain't it? There I wos, finking she needed me t' lookout fer 'er, but she don't. She's soft on that fella Arry. Says she and im's gettin' wed; told us she don't want us.' He sniffed, wiping his nose upon a grubby sleeve. 'So... I left, didn't I?'

'But you went... for an acrobat?' I said, retrieving Dickon's hand as he reached for a bramble.

'Aye, and that weren't no good, neever. "Do this, Jack. Do that, Jack. Fetch this; bring that," all day long, like I wos a skivvy.'

'Did you perform for the king, though?' I swallowed with difficulty. Too much speech was not helping my throat.

'Didn't 'appen proper, did it? Maudie did her veils dance, all inticin' like. The king watched 'er close enuff, didn't he? Then he left when she wos done an' so did them uvver lords and them. On'y the servants stayed t' watch us cos they wos told t' make sure we never stoled nuffink. The king never watched us, did he, the fat bugger?'

'Jack! Do not speak so of the king's grace.'

'Sorry, master. I wos just sayin' cos it's true: he is fat.'

'True or no. You will not...'

'I said, I wos sorry, didn't I?'

'You want to come home?'

Jack stared at his scuffed boots.

'Well?'

He nodded so slightly, I might have mistaken it for the breeze stirring his unkempt hair.

'I must speak with Mistress Em first.'

'Why? You're the master, ain't you?'

'Mind your manners; else...'

'But yer said I wos always welcome.'

'And so you are, but such talk will not endear you... to anyone.'

'Indere? Wos that mean, then?'

'No matter.'

'You mean Mistress Em an' Tom won't want us back.'

I nodded to spare my voice.

'I shouldn't 'ave comed. I'll go back wiv them ackribats, like wot I said I would.' He turned to go.

'Nay, Jack. I be a man of my word. I have missed you, lad.'

Little Dickon made a grab for Jack's mucus-stained sleeve.

'Dickon wishes you to stay also,' I said. I might have laughed at my son's action, but my throat was not yet ready for that.


After a dinner as good as a Christmas feast, Gabriel and Rook took their leave with profuse gratitude to all. They departed by way of the kitchen and the yard.

Adam frowned, noting Gabriel went bare-headed. Something was amiss here. No respectable men went about the streets, capless.

When all had returned within doors, Emily made a discovery: Gabriel's forgotten cap.

A likely mistake, indeed, Adam thought.

'I'll take it to him,' Emily said. 'He can't have gone far.'

'I can run faster. I'll do it,' Jack volunteered, hoping to ingratiate himself with the mistress of the house.

'You think I would trust you with it? You'll sell it to the nearest fripperer for a few pence.'

'I never would, would I?'

Ignoring the lad's protest, Emily hastened out, taking the cap.

Adam followed her at a discreet distance. Thus, he saw what came to pass in the alleyway at the side of the house. There had been time enough for the mariners to be south of St Paul's by now, yet Gabriel was there waiting, alone. Clearly, forgetting his cap had been intended as part of a plan.

Emily gave him his headwear, but made no move to leave. As Adam watched, Gabriel took her in his arms. A fierce exchange of passionate kisses made him look away.

'A storm is coming, Em,' he heard Gabriel say. 'We'll be a day or two more at Queenhithe to wait upon the weather, if you can find a means...'

'I will.'

Adam withdrew to the kitchen door, his suspicions confirmed.

Emily returned, flushed of cheek and smiling.

Adam barred her way through the kitchen door, his hand on her arm.

'What are you about, Em?'

'Naught that is your concern.' She shook him off, but he refused to step aside.

'You're betraying Seb. I make that my concern. Why would you do it, eh?'

'Forwhy my husband is as dull as dirty laundry and more tiresome than yet another ink-stain I can't wash out. Gabe is so alive, so... so... eager.'

'That's just lust, Em.'

'No it isn't. Gabe loves me.'

'Seb loves you more than you know.'

'Then why doesn't he show me? He treats me like a fragile flower he hardly dares to touch for fear I'll break. And so rarely, all according to Holy Church dictation. I'm tired of being regarded like a nun in a convent. Gabriel treats me like a flesh and blood woman; not some sacred image to be worshipped at a distance. He would risk his life for me.'

'I promised Seb I would never tell anyone what he did upon Monday morn last – just two days since, though it seems far longer. Seb risked far more for your sake than his life alone.'

'You speak nonsense, Adam. Seb wouldn't risk a penny wager on a cockfight, never mind his life. Now let me by; I have platters and pots to wash.'

'Not until you read this.' Adam took a crumpled paper from the purse at his belt and handed it to her. 'Seb thinks it was destroyed, but I kept it for this very reason. He was willing to risk eternal damnation to save you, and this is how you repay him: by cuckolding him with that wretch.'

Emily read her husband's letter of confession, her eyes growing wider.

'But he had naught to do with Lizzie's death. This is all lies.'

'Aye, but see to whom the letter is addressed.'

'The Lord Mayor.'

'Seb knew he couldn't lie convincingly except in writing. He intended to jump from London Bridge and drown himself to give credence to this as a dying man's final testimony. The certainty of suffering in Hell forever was preferable to him than the torment of a life lived without you, if you hanged. That's what he said.'

'Huh! Just more words. Seb is always good with words, but never with actions. So, of course, he didn't get so far as actually jumping, did he?'

'Indeed he did. It took all my strength and Jack's to pull him back. He was already falling when we grabbed him.'

'Now who's telling lies, Adam Armitage? I don't believe you. Seb may have written this piece of foolishness,' she said, thrusting the paper in his face, 'But it obviously never reached the mayor, and I doubt he ever meant that it should. I wager, he walked slowly enough to the bridge that you were able to follow him and be there at that precise moment to save him. It was all a mountebank's performance: and a fine one, I grant you, but that was all it was.'

'To what end?'

'How should I know?' Emily said with a shrug. 'What goes on in his head is of no interest to me.'

'Nay, Em. It was no pretence. You didn't see the anguish upon his face when we prevented him from leaping into the river. He meant to kill himself without any doubt.'

'Then you shouldn't have stopped him. Now take your damned letter and let me pass.'

'You're no better than a harlot with a heart of stone,' Adam muttered as she swept by, shoving the creased paper at him on her way into the kitchen.

But she heard him, turned back and glared at him before slapping him hard across the cheek.

'And is that supposed to mend matters?' Adam rubbed his cheek. 'You don't deserve to have a man like Seb.'

'I don't *want* to have a man like Seb, and that's the truth of it.'


'I have a possible solution concerning Jack's future,' I said to Emily as we readied for bed that eve. 'If you approve, that is?'

'I don't know why you let the wretch return. We were well rid of him,' she said, removing her linen cap and shaking out her beautiful tresses that I so desired to run through my fingers.

'He made an error in thinking to join the acrobats is all. He wished to be with his sister.'

'Aye, a wise woman she must be since she told him she didn't want him.'

I made no answer to that, but busied myself, unfastening my hose. It being a Wednesday and my wife still suckling, such amorous thoughts as I entertained must be put aside. Which reminded me: I had yet to confess last Sunday's sin, aye, and Monday's aberration also.

'On Jack's part,' I went on, 'It was a whim and swiftly undone, thankfully, else he might have regretted it forever. But on one score he be correct: our craft be unsuitable for him. He wants to be active in his work, so I wondered if your father's trade might not suit him better?'

'You would burden my father with that useless, good-for-nothing wastrel? How can you suppose good might come of it for anyone?'

'When I saw Jacques le Charpentier working in St Martin's, carving that misericord...' I cleared my throat carefully. 'It occurred to me the skills required be not so different from those employed when carving book covers. Of course, Jack lacks such delicate skill, but there be evidence of talent, nonetheless. If your father taught him the carpenter's art, including the labours with saw, plane and adze – actions the lad would savour more than sitting at a desk – I think he might make a success of it.' I folded my shirt and lay it on the linen press, turning my back as Emily removed her shift for fear temptation would overwhelm me. 'Also, Jack be more than a half-decent archer for his age. Your father may well appreciate some assistance in his duties as Warden-Archer. What do you think, Em? If Stephen be agreeable, the lad could live under his roof...'

'At least then he won't be in my way. I suppose my father might agree.'

'It would require Jack's consent as well.'

'Damn it, Seb. He will do as he's told for once. You know I don't want him here any longer. I've put up with his idleness for nigh three years, and I'm done with him. If necessary, I will persuade my father to take him on.'

'You approve my solution then?' I asked, surprised, since she so rarely conceded that I ever made any correct decision.

'Aye, I suppose.' She slid beneath the sheet and coverlet and turned her back to me.

The moments of temptation were past.

Thinking what an eventful day it had been and how joyful it was to have Emily home and safe, I thanked the Lord God upon my knees for his multitude of blessings. In the distance, I believe I heard thunder roll and rain pattered against the window glass. Then I lay down beside her, inhaling deep of her beloved scent, watching her breathe for a few moments afore I snuffed the candle. At last, I was undoubtedly glad that I had not succeeded in leaping from London Bridge, reaching out beneath the sheet and finding my beloved wife's hand, enclosing it in mine as surely as she held my heart.

# *Epilogue*

SEB'S VOICE improved, but not sufficiently to sing for the archbishop upon that Sunday, much to the precentor's chagrin. Another chorister was given an easier piece than the *Miserere* to sing as a solo.

Emily kept her assignation with Gabriel aboard *the Eagle* the following day, telling Seb she was visiting Beattie. The wind was howling: the first of the autumn gales, but naught could affect her joy and pleasure in the mariner's company upon that storm-tossed ship. Beattie was willing, if necessary, to support her friend's story, no matter how many lies had to be told, and Adam held his peace – for the present, at least. Gabriel sailed away from London when the storm abated.

Ralph Clifford was sent for trial a month later. The jury found him guilty of the wilful and premeditated murder of Elizabeth Knollys, silk-woman of Foster Lane. Seb's testimony was crucial to that outcome. Ralph was hanged at Tyburn within the week.

His father, John Clifford, also stood trial, charged with aiding, abetting and encouraging a felony, then harbouring the accused in an attempt to evade the law. He too was found guilty, but avoided execution because Lord Mayor Hayford determined that the city coffers would benefit from the imposition of a hefty fine instead. The sum of one thousand marks was demanded, aye, and paid without over much inconvenience – it should have been more.

At least the Stationers' Guild saw fit to deprive Clifford of his office as Warden-Master. In fact, they expelled him from the fellowship and forbade him from conducting his craft within the City of London, in perpetuity. Richard Collop replaced him, serving a second term as Warden-Master.

Roger Underwood remained in St Martin's, claiming sanctuary indefinitely. The death of Gerrit Heijnsbroeck, the Dutch puppet-master, was not avenged and justice ill-served.

# *Author's notes*

In medieval times, some words had rather different meanings from today and those used to describe incomers to a neighbourhood come into this category. Strangers and foreigners included anyone not born in the village, town or city, so someone born in north Kent or south Essex, just a few miles away from London, would be considered both strange and foreign. People from other countries, who might be termed 'foreign' today, were then called 'aliens'. Frenchmen, Dutchmen, Venetians and Rook the Abyssinian would have been 'aliens', but to avoid making such visitors to London sound like creatures from outer space, I have taken the liberty of modern usage and called them 'foreigners'. Incidentally, Abyssinia was the old name for Ethiopia in Africa.

I had the idea for Lizzie Knollys' death after reading of a true event that occurred on 12th September in an unspecified year. Elizabeth Knollys was attacked by two other London silk-women: Elizabeth Taillour and Alice Rolff. They drowned their rival in a washtub, then tried to burn the body before throwing it into a latrine pit. Unlike Lizzie's corpse, the remains lay undiscovered for weeks since the coroner's inquest was not heard until November. Unlike Emily, Beatrice and Peronelle, in this case, the perpetrators were tried and found guilty. The death sentence was passed on both women, but Rolff claimed to be pregnant, hoping to delay the inevitable – just as Beatrice had intended to do. However, a jury of midwives was summoned to examine Rolff, and they proved she was telling lies about her condition. Taillour and Rolff were hanged together.

On holiday in Iceland recently, we visited a museum in Reykjavik, 'Whales of Iceland', dedicated to whales and dolphins. I was greatly impressed by the white narwhal (*Monodon monoceros*) with its single, spiral horn. As a note to the exhibit explained, in the fourteenth and fifteenth centuries, these exquisite objects were traded with England and Europe as 'unicorn horns'. We also went to the little town of Eyrarbakki on the south coast of the island, the centre of medieval trade between England and Iceland, hoping to discover more. But we were disappointed that the locals had no records before the 'Danish Period' of the eighteenth/nineteenth century. All we learned was that the fifteenth century was referred to as the 'English Period', but there was no mention of any trading of unicorn horns, sadly.

An English mariner of the time would probably not have known about the narwhals, but might glean enough of the truth to connect unicorns with the sea in his fanciful tales, so I felt at liberty to improvise Gabriel's stories.

'Whales of Iceland', with its life-size models of each species, is well worth a visit, if you happen to go to Reykjavik, as is the Folk Museum in Eyrarbakki, even minus unicorns.

OUT LATER THIS YEAR

# THE COLOUR OF SHADOWS

ENJOY THIS PREVIEW...

# *Prologue*

THE CHILD was screaming, attracting attention even on London Bridge where there was noise enough to drown out any normal conversation. The young wretch wriggled in the man's grasp, doing all he might to break free.

Shrieking fishwives jostled them with reeking baskets; a scawager's dung cart, that by rights ought to have finished its business before dawn, forced them into a shop doorway as it negotiated its cumbersome route through the crowd of early risers, trailing a miasma of stench in its wake. A gaggle of geese up from Kent and destined for the poulterers added to the cacophony, their feet, painted with tar for the long walk, slapping the road as they waddled and honked and got in everyone's way. The fellow driving them along seemed oblivious; more interested in the wares for sale on the counter-board of a cookshop.

'Cease your bloody squealing. You sound like a stuck pig,' the man said, giving the child a vicious shake. He was dragging him by the arm but had to bend low so the child might hear him. 'Behave... son!' he added, seeing a fishwife frowning at him. Then he continued in a whisper: 'You want your Mam to suffer?'

The lad shook his head.

'Then be quiet and walk properly beside me. You try to run off again and your Mam's for worm-fodder. Understand?'

The lad nodded and trotted along at the man's side, sniffing and wiping his snotty nose on his sleeve. If it wasn't for eyes red with weeping and the blue egg of a bruise on his forehead, he could have been comely; a dimpled chin, a shock of golden curls and a pretty mouth that would look well on a girl child. But that was what one particular customer wanted. If he was willing to pay an excess of coin for the lad, the man didn't care why.

With Parliament summoned by King Edward, now was a good time to acquire new 'stock'. Delicious, soft and enticing: innocents were just what was desired by those with jaded appetites, to add spice to their tedious lives. Whores and strumpets were all very well, but the brothel at the sign of *The Mermaid* in Bankside offered more delicate fare to those who could afford it. Now that London and Westminster were brimful of lords and shire-knights come to attend Parliament, men who would be requiring of some novel entertainment during their leisure hours, the man expected to have made a sizeable profit by the time the king was done with the sitting of that illustrious body.

Illustrious! Huh. The man grimaced to himself. There was naught 'illustrious' about what those rich devils did behind the shutters at *The Mermaid*. Nigh every vice and sin under the sun went on there. The man was delighted by the revenue brought in even as he disdained his disgusting customers. He informed the Lord God of all their names if he knew them, but otherwise, he told not a soul. 'Make money and keep silent' was his motto. It had always served him well.

He glanced down at the lad as they turned to the right at the southern end of the bridge, beside the Bishop of Winchester's palatial residence. Aye, this one was special: good skin, straight of limb and with decent teeth. Bessie would be pleased with this new apprentice to the trade. She would know how best to train him, to show him off to advantage to make the greatest profit. This one had the potential to fill their purses, and the man knew just which lord was likely to appreciate such pretty merchandise. He had deep coffers and a liking for golden hair and soft flesh. Bessie said they needed just such a boy and he would be kept aside until that particular lord came by.

# Chapter 1

## Saturday the fourth day of April in the year of Our Lord 1479 Crosby Hall, Bishopsgate in the City of London: the Residence of Richard, Duke of Gloucester

THE HALL was full of petitioners, supplicants and assorted folk, all seeking an audience with his grace, the Duke of Gloucester. Sebastian Foxley and Adam Armitage had submitted their names to the steward, as required, and now it was just a matter of waiting. And Seb knew the wait could be long indeed. He and Adam stood in a corner at the back of the hall to watch the proceedings. Adam, beardless now after the London fashion, took the opportunity to admire the sumptuous hangings, the coffered and gilded ceiling, the impressive display of silverware on a huge buffet and most of all, the vast expanse of glazed windows overlooking the wind-swept gardens. Both men had had to hang onto their best Sunday caps on the walk from Paternoster Row to Bishopsgate in the gusting wind.

The duke, slim and lithe in his finely tailored doublet of murrey wool, did not dominate the gathering from the dais, but stood among the throng, although a discrete circle of space remained around him whenever he moved. It did not do to jostle royalty nor to step too close to those practical but expensive noble shoes.

Seb began to wonder if their day to visit might be ill-chosen. When they entered the hall, Lord Richard was brandishing a sheet of parchment aloft, and a man was huddled upon his knees before him.

'What does he mean by this?' Richard said. He did not raise his voice – he had no need, for the company fell silent – yet the anger was apparent. 'Explain this incomprehensible petition to me.'

'Y-your g-grace, I... I...' The man stammered. 'My Lord Pierpoint... he...'

'Cease your nonsense. Tell me.'

'My Lord Pierpoint said... he thought... 'Tis not my fault, my lord.'

'This is not Imperial Rome,' the duke said, 'We do not slay the bearers of ill-tidings. Speak plainly, man.'

'I... I do not know...'

'I have not time to waste on this. Withdraw. Compose yourself. Return when you can speak coherently. And take this piece of foolishness with you.' He thrust the sheet of parchment at the fellow. 'Leave us.' The duke dismissed the man with a flick of his hand, as if swatting away a fly or brushing off a fleck of dust.

'I don't like the look of this duke of yours,' Adam whispered in Seb's ear. 'He has a face like thunder and the eye of an executioner.'

The man got off his knees, bowed excessively a half dozen times as he backed away before turning and rushing for the door in unseemly haste.

The mutter of conversation resumed.

''Tis said he has the temper of a true Plantagenet, but I have ne'er witnessed it afore,' Seb answered, keeping his voice to a murmur. In truth, the duke had never looked so forbidding. Seb had only ever seen him courteous and gracious; this was a man of another complexion entirely.

'Master Sebastian Foxley; Master Adam Armitage; step forward and present your business with his grace!' The steward stamped his staff of office on the floor, announcing them in ringing tones and far sooner than they expected. Seb hardly felt prepared now that the moment had arrived.

He and Adam walked in step towards the duke as a way opened up through the crowd to allow them passage. Bareheaded, they bent the knee and lowered their eyes in unison. It was surprisingly well accomplished, Seb thought, seeing they had not rehearsed it.

'Master Foxley, what a pleasant happenstance is this. Be upstanding, my friend, and make introduction of your companion.'

They both stood to face the duke. Gloucester was smiling, a sparkle in his grey eyes. This was not the man who had just sent a fellow scuttling in terror.

'Your grace. May it please you: I present my relative, Adam Armitage. He is from Norfolk, but now bides and works with us at Paternoster Row.'

'Welcome, Master Armitage. 'Tis a pleasure to make your acquaintance.' Richard extended his hand, but not so that it might be kissed by lesser men – as could correctly have been the case – rather to shake them both by the hand as friends. 'And Sebastian, it has been brought to my attention that you are to be congratulated, having become a father. Is that the case? I trust I have not been misinformed.'

'Indeed, my lord. I have a fine son.'

The duke laughed.

'And no doubt he is a paragon, as are all sons until they be of an age to err. What is his name?'

'Er, forgive my impertinence, my lord...' Seb's pulse raced, and he felt over-hot of a sudden. 'We named him Richard and call him Dickon, saving your grace.'

'Well, such a compliment is this. I heartily commend your choice. Mayhap, I shall find an opportunity to visit my illustrious namesake. Now; to business, master. What brings you here to my hall?'

'We have a gift, my lord, for your children.' Seb knelt and held out the copy of *Aesop's Fables* that had taken so many months of work, complete in its protective embroidered chemise.

The duke's face lit up as if a candle flame had been kindled behind his eyes.

'How very thoughtful. What is its text?' He accepted the book with such reverence and stepped towards a table to set it down and remove the chemise. Seb felt somewhat heartened.

''Tis the moral fables of Aesop. Instructive and amusing for young readers... I hope.' Seb's nervous state had not lessened despite the duke's obvious approval of the gift, thus far.

'Your goodwife embroidered the chemise?'

'Aye, my lord, and wove the ribbon to tie the covers closed and made the tasselled bookmark within to note the page. Adam penned the text; Jack Tabor carved the wood boards; Mistress Rose Glover made the white leather covering over the boards and embossed the gilding...'

'And you painted the exquisite miniatures,' the duke said, turning the pages with care. 'I recognise your style straightway.' As he leafed through it, he paused at a page and chuckled. 'Rob!' he called, 'Come see this: it will amuse you mightily.'

A tall, broad fellow with fiery hair came from a knot of courtiers standing by the dais to join Richard at the table. It was Seb's old friend, Sir Robert Percy. The duke and his friend chuckled together.

'Does this prideful crow not remind you of someone, Rob?' Richard asked.

'Aye, but tell him not,' Sir Robert said, grinning.

''Tis a very fine book, Sebastian,' the duke said, turning back to his visitors. 'My children will love to see it – under close supervision, I warrant – but not until I have read it myself. The contents must be approved beforehand.' Seeing Seb's worried expression, the duke laughed out loud and patted the artist's shoulder. 'I too have a fondness for a moral tale and colourful picture, if King Edward allows me sufficient leisure from his sittings of Parliament. You cannot blame me if I delay in passing on your generous gift, wishing to peruse it first before less appreciative eyes see it, and grubby fingers mar the pages.'

As Seb and Adam withdrew, Seb was smiling broadly, pleased with the duke's reception of the gift. But, as they passed through the wide doors, his smile vanished.

'What's amiss?' Adam asked, noting his companion's altered expression.

''Tis naught. I thought I saw someone from long ago, but mayhap I was mistaken.' Seb felt an icy finger brush upon his spine and shivered. He prayed his eyes had deceived him; that the dark Lord Lovell – his adversary of old – had not returned to London but, thinking upon it, with all lords summoned by the king to attend Parliament, he feared it might well be the case. Lovell was to be avoided at all cost. Unfortunately, though, the devil had a fine house, Lovell's Inn, that stood at the corner of Ivy Lane and Paternoster Row. Seb would needs beware not to cross his path.

## Palm Sunday the fourth day of April in the year of Our Lord 1479
## The Foxley house,
## Paternoster Row in the City of London

Saturday night had been wild and windy indeed but, as Seb opened the window shutters and looked out, the sky was an innocent pearlescent blue, as if naught of the kind had ever come to pass. Yet the street below was littered with spring-budding twigs, ripped untimely from bushes and trees, and terracotta shards of broken roof-tiles lay strewn around like a drunken mosaic. Wisps of thatch drifted past on the now-courteous breeze, evidence of yet more damaged houses.

'I must check upon our shutters and roof, Em, afore we be away to church,' Seb said to his wife as he bent to fasten the ties on his Sunday shoes.

'If we've lost any tiles after what that wretch charged us for repairs last autumn, you must demand our money be repaid.' Emily stood before the pewter mirror to adjust and pin her best veil. She caught her breath of a sudden and put her hands to her swelling belly.

'What is it, Em?'

'The babe. What else would it be? This one kicks like a horse, as Dickon never did.'

'A lively little fellow then. 'Tis good to know.'

'Only a man could think so; you're not the one being kicked about inside like a pig's bladder at a Shrovetide football contest.'

'I shall go see that no tiles have slipped. I'll be outside if you need me.'

'See that the privy is still standing. If it's not, God help me.'

Seb unbarred the door from the kitchen and stepped out into the cobbled yard. Debris from the storm and bits of broken fence paling were scattered about, but the palings were not theirs, fortunately, but a neighbour's. Beyond, the back garden plot looked wind-blasted. Every last blushed petal was gone from the blackthorn tree. It had to be hoped the bees had done their work already, else the fruit harvest of sloes would be poor later in the year. Gawain snuffled about, investigating any new scents that might have blown in overnight. He barked at a clump of dandelions then leapt back with a yelp.

'You silly creature,' Seb said with a laugh, patting the dog to console him. ''Tis but a grasshopper and you be a hundred times its size, you great coward.'

Seb made for the end of the garden where the privy stood, ivy-shrouded and solitary, as a house of easement should. He made use of it, and all was well as he had hoped since the ivy chained it to the ground as surely as a ship's anchor rope. The pig-sty had suffered no hurt bar a mess of twigs blown into the water trough. He fished them out, and the pig appeared, grunting and eager in expectation of breakfast.

'Later, later,' he assured her. 'We have none of us had time to prepare food.' He stepped back, turning to look up at the roof and gables of the house, almost falling over Gawain who was right behind him. The dog yelped as Seb stepped on his tail. 'Sorry, lad. Give me space to tread, I beg you.' He fondled Gawain's silky black ears and was rewarded with a well-licked hand, so it seemed his clumsiness was forgiven. Seb squinted up at the roof, narrowing his eyes against the brightness of the sky. All looked well; no missing or slipped tiles and all the window shutters seemed to be undamaged. The single chimney pot still stood proud – which was as well since it, along with the glass in the window of the master bedchamber, proclaimed the Foxleys' improving place in London society.

Returning to the kitchen, Seb reported that all was in order at the back of the house. Rose smiled at him, her face as welcome as the sun to him. She always cheered him. She was giving little Dickon his breakfast of bread sops in milk, sweetened with honey. Emily's breast milk was drying up as she was great with child again, but Dickon seemed to be thriving on the goat's milk he was given instead. He had his own chair, now that he could sit up properly. Emily's father – a skilled carpenter – had made it for his first grandchild. It was finely carved with a row of ducks across the back, more of the same lined up along the removable bar at the front which prevented the child from falling out. The turned legs were of such a length that raised him to the height of the table-board, so that Dickon could share mealtimes with everyone else. But the day being Sunday, the babe broke his fast alone. The household would attend church before coming home to eat.

Upon espying his Papa, Dickon waved his hands excitedly, gurgling through a mouthful of food and sending the next spoonful, as Rose offered it, down his father's clean Sunday best doublet. Adam grinned and offered Seb a napkin.

'You'll be in trouble when Em sees you. She'll claim you bring her laundering skills into disrepute.'

'I know,' Seb said with a sigh, using the napkin to wipe Dickon's mouth. 'But how does my little man fare upon this fine morn?' The child chuckled and made babbling noises, for all the world as if he was answering Papa's question. Seb laughed. After a rough night with little sleep due to the howling storm, at least the day began on a merry note: Dickon content, Rose smiling, Adam jesting and the house intact. Things were better yet when young Kate bounced in.

'Do you approve my new ribbons, Master Seb? Are they not the finest shade of green ever made? Do you like them?' She tossed her flamboyant dark curls to show off the ribbons to best advantage.

'Indeed,' he answered, never knowing what to say when a woman asked his opinion on female matters.

'They're beautiful,' Rose said, laying down the horn spoon she had been using to feed Dickon. 'Here, let me straighten that bow for you. There: perfect.'

'I can't wait to show Jack. He will like them, won't he? I chose green because it's his favourite colour.'

'Is it? I never knew he appreciated any colour particularly above another,' Seb said, being one to whom colour mattered so much.

'He'll favour the wearer more than the ribbons if he has the least drop of red blood in his veins,' Adam added.

It was a known fact that Kate and Jack had what Seb referred to as 'an attachment' to each other, which other less-mannerly folk called 'a lusting' on Jack's part and 'a fancy' on Kate's. It was a continuing anxiety to Seb that the relationship should go no further since he was guardian to both youngsters. Kate's father would never forgive him if his daughter's reputation were sullied, but how to prevent it, short of keeping them locked in their separate chambers, he did not know. He had lectured, cajoled and warned them so many times but could words ever overrule nature? He had no choice but to trust them and hope common sense and propriety would win the day.

'I must check the shop and the roof at the front for any storm damage,' Seb said, recalling that his task was only half done. He kissed Dickon's head of soft bright hair and was rewarded with a crow of delight and a little fist catching him a buffet on the nose. 'Mind Papa's nose, little one. 'Tis a sizable target, I know, and I would have it no larger.'

'For certain, it gets stuck in everyone else's business as it is.' Adam jested. 'Has anyone seen those idle good-for-nothings yet, else they'll be late for church?' He meant Tom Bowen, one-time apprentice and now the workshop's journeyman-scrivener, and Jack Tabor, also a one-time apprentice but now learning a new trade as a joiner with Stephen Appleyard, Emily's father.

'Their door was still closed when I came down,' Kate said. 'I expect the storm kept them awake and they're still sleeping.'

'It kept us all wakeful, and that's no excuse. The rest of us will be at St Michael's in time for Low Mass this Palm Sunday and so will they, if I have to give them a dousing with a bucketful of icy water to get them out of bed.' Adam's expression implied that he might well carry out the threat.

Meanwhile, Seb had unbarred the door at the front of the shop and gone out into Paternoster Row, to check the shutters on the parlour window and the roof that faced St Paul's across the way. As with the back garden, the street was strewn with storm debris but none that looked to have come from the Foxley house. The roof tiles were all in place, and the window shutters hung straight - what a relief. A neighbour from further along the row, by Lovell's Inn, came running, chasing a hen that seemed the faster of the two.

'Catch the devil, Seb!' the man called out.

Just in time, Seb made a lunge and grabbed the bird. Squawking and lashing out with its sharp-taloned feet, it was all Seb could do to keep hold of the writhing bundle of angry feathers. He managed to tuck it under his arm, covering its yellow eyes with his free hand so it became calm.

'Damn storm brought down our old cherry tree,' the neighbour, Jonathan Caldicott, explained as he came puffing up to Seb. 'It smashed the henhouse... birds have gone everywhere... wife's spitting mad... says it's my fault.'

''Tis the fault of the storm, surely? 'Twas quite a tempest last night, Jonathan. You could do naught to prevent it.'

'Not how the wife sees it. Says I should've known the tree was like to come down and done something about it beforehand. You know how women are,' Jonathan added with a meaningful look.

'Aye, I suppose.' Seb handed the hen to his neighbour with care, not wanting to be pecked for his trouble.

'I'm grateful, Seb. I'll stand you a jug of ale in the Panyer later. Oh, and there are two more hens on the loose somewhere about, if you see them...'

Seb nodded and turned to go back within doors. There was still one more shutter to check at the east-facing window in the workshop, but that opened inwards and had a new latch, so would most likely have weathered the storm undamaged. He brushed a few stray feathers from his doublet and was dismayed to see that the fine blue cloth, previously spattered with milk sops, was now smeared with mud and chicken dung. Jonathan Caldicott was not going to be the only man in Paternoster Row to receive the sharp blade of his wife's scolding tongue this morn.

Hoping to avoid meeting Emily for a little longer – mayhap, the mud and dung would dry somewhat and brush off – Seb went straight to the workshop. The room was cast in deep gloom which was a good indication that the shutter remained in place and unharmed. In near-darkness, he felt for the wooden latch and lifted it from its hasp, opening the two halves of the shutter like the covers of a book. Spring sunlight flooded in, welcome and warm upon his face. No damage, the Lord be praised. Emily took pride in glass window panes and a tall chimney but, of all things, Seb took the greatest satisfaction in his workshop: orderly, well-stocked and a hive of industry on weekdays. Of a Sunday, it was still a joy to behold with everything set out: inks, pigments, parchment, paper and pens, awaiting an early start on Monday morn.

But there was something that did not belong.

Frowning in puzzlement, Seb wondered what on earth lay in a heap beside his desk. He went closer to look, but leapt back with a gasp, making the sign of the cross.

'Sweet Jesu have mercy,' he said aloud. A second look confirmed it. 'Adam! Adam!' he called out. 'Come to the workshop.' He was still struggling to regain his composure as Adam came down the passage, followed by everyone else from the kitchen. 'Stay back, the rest of you,' Seb warned, 'Come no closer, Em. This be no sight suitable for a woman with child to see. Go back to the kitchen. Do as I say this once, all of you but Adam.' The womenfolk obeyed – even Emily – but Tom and Jack did no more than retreat a step or two back in the passage. 'You'll be my witness, Adam, but to what, I do not know precisely. We must move my desk...'

'By all the saints, what is a lad like that doing here? How did he get in? Was a shutter broken?'

'No shutters were broken and I unbarred the doors myself this morn.'

'We have to get him to a bed, fetch the surgeon...' Adam knelt beside the lad.

'I fear 'tis too late for that. Whoever he be, he lies dead... in our house and no way he could have entered in. I know not what can be done.' Seb sat down on the nearest stool and sighed. ''Tis a mystery indeed and beyond my power to solve.'

Adam moved the body, rolling it onto its back.

'There's blood, Seb. We'll have to inform the sheriffs' office and your friend Master Fissher.' Adam referred to the Deputy Coroner of London who occasionally forced Seb to assist him at a wage of sixpence a day – an insulting recompense for the gruesome work often involved. And 'friend' was not the word Seb would use to describe the pompous, inefficient and downright idle overseer of unexpected deaths in the city. To have to be involved with Fissher on any matter was a hateful prospect and concerning a death in his own home was worse yet.

'Later. I cannot face them. After mass, mayhap. The dead will wait patiently. The body will not walk off, will it? But we must cover it decently. I would not have Em catch sight of it. Who can tell what effect it might have upon her unborn babe. You know the sight of a hare in a field can cause a babe to be born with a hare-lip, or so they say.'

'Aye, so I've heard, but I'm not convinced it's true.'

'I will take no chances, be it true or not. Em and the child must not be put at hazard in any way.'

'Of course not. But look here, Seb, he was a striking lad, was he not? Someone will recognise him, I'm certain. Why don't you draw a likeness of him while he's still fresh and wholesome – or as much as a street urchin ever is?'

Seb winced. Adam spoke of the lad as if he was a side of mutton on a butcher's stall. Turning, he saw Tom and Jack were now in the doorway.

'Did I not tell you...' Seb began. 'Oh, no matter. One of you fetch an old blanket or sheet to cover the body, then you may both escort the womenfolk to church.'

'Tom'll do it,' Jack said.

'Don't you tell me what to do, you pissing jackanapes.'

'I ain't no such fing, you fat arse-wipe. I knows stuff wot you don't an' I might knows 'im, mightn't I?'

'Cease your foul language upon the Lord's Day. I will not have such words uttered in my house, as you know full well. Have you no respect? A Christian child lies dead there, and you two make Billingsgate fishwives sound like Paul's choristers compared to your filthy tongues. Tom, go fetch a covering and be certain 'tis not Mistress Em's best tablecloth.'

'Why me? I'm a journeyman now, not a 'prentice.'

'In either case, you do it because I be master here and I tell you to.'

Tom slunk off like a whipped dog, and Jack smirked.

'And you can cease gloating, Jack, and go wash your mouth out with soap and water.'

'Wot! But he said worserer than me.'

'And he will do likewise. Then you'll go to mass, make your contrition and light a candle – both of you – for the soul you have insulted.'

'But I never said nuffink 'gainst the dead-un, did I?'

'Your behaviour was sufficiently disrespectful.'

'But, like wot I said: I might knows him, mightn't I, if'n you let me look proper. Adam says he's a street urchin, like I wos, so...'

'The lad be not of an age with you, and you have been off the streets now for nigh unto four years. How would he be any acquaintance of a respectable young man as yourself?'

'Aye, well, I still sort o' knows folks, don't I?'

'You mean, you still consort with undesirables behind my back.'

'Nah! But you said he wos a Christian soul, not a undeseribble – wot ever it is.'

'Every word you speak makes matters worse, Jack. Come. Take one good look at the poor lad and then be gone.'

Jack went over to the body where Adam had laid it out straight.

'Well? Do you know who he is?' Seb asked.

'Nah, but...'

'Then cease your gawping and get to church.'

Tom returned then with a rumpled sheet from the morrow's laundry pile and took the opportunity to see the corpse for himself.

'Do you recognise him, Tom? His hair be quite distinctive.'

'Never seen him before and I reckon I'd remember him if I had.'

'Aye, you would. Now, the pair of you, see the others safe to St Michael's. Be alert for any falling tiles or leaning trees after the storm. If he asks, tell Father Thomas that Adam and I will attend High Mass later.'

With Tom, Jack and the rest of the household gone to Low Mass, Seb and Adam were left with the problem of what to do about the body. For fully ten minutes at least, the two sat silent upon their stools, regarding the sheet-covered corpse, deep in thought. Gawain lay at Seb's feet, waiting for whatever should come to pass. In truth, Seb was not so much thinking as praying, but the Almighty must be too concerned with other matters on a busy Sunday because no divine response was forthcoming. He scratched behind Gawain's ear.

'We can't just sit, staring at it 'til it starts to stink, Seb,' Adam said at last. 'I'll fetch one of the sheriffs: we can't avoid it.'

'Which of them?' Seb asked. 'I have little faith in either of this year's sheriffs.'

Adam shrugged:

'Sheriff Byfield is less use than a blunt axe, and I don't trust the other one no more than a cat with a sparrow in a bucket.'

'I agree. Byfield will probably be the more sympathetic to our case.'

'Our case? I don't understand, Seb.'

'Oh, Adam, can you not see how this may look to others: to the authorities? A good-looking lad found dead – most probably unlawfully killed – in a room within a house with windows shuttered and doors barred. There was no way he could have got in nor out without our knowledge, nor could any outsider have left him here for those same reasons. No one but us.'

'But that isn't true. He did get in somehow, and we knew nothing of it, Seb. Are you thinking the sheriff won't believe our story?'

'Would you? Would any man of sound mind and logical reason?'

'Mm. In which case, what do we do?' Adam was pulling at his earlobe. In the past, he used to pull his beard when distracted, but was now clean shaven, his Norfolk whiskers a thing of the past. At this moment, he missed his beard.

'I wish I knew, Adam, but I fear the truth may serve us ill.'

'Suppose we take the body to the river and throw it in. Nobody need ever know it was here in this house.'

'You would deny him a decent burial? That be most un-Christian of you, Adam.'

'Well, at least we could put it out in the alley. That would spare us a legion of unanswerable questions. What if they arrest us? Have you thought of that?'

Seb straightened his stained doublet as if by doing so he might straighten his confused thoughts also.

'Aye, the possibility had occurred to me. There be but one way of discovering the truth and that necessitates the acquiring of evidence, and I cannot do that sitting here, maudlin and moping.' He stood up, and the dog that had waited at his master's feet stood up also, hoping for a walk or a titbit. 'Let us examine the lad and this room more thoroughly afore Fissher and his ilk come thundering in and destroy every clue. 'Tis all I can think to do: we must solve the mystery and then report it to the authorities. No doubt, they will have much to do elsewhere about the city in the wake of the storm. We must use the time wisely. What have you found there, Gawain?'

The dog was nosing beneath Adam's desk.

'Well done, lad. This was not here afore.' Seb showed Adam a rusted, broken blade, handleless. 'Where could this have come from unless the child brought it with him?'

''Tis certainly not ours, so that must be the case. What other explanation could there be?'

Seb shrugged.

'I know not. This mystery requires unravelling.'

'Where do we begin?'

'With the body. Out of the way, Gawain, 'tis no business of yours. You have done your part.'

Seb eased himself down to kneel beside the dead lad. His hip joint protested, but he ignored it. With due reverence, he turned back the sheet, folding it down until only the shoes were covered. On second thoughts, he uncovered them also: no point in half measures. The feet were as likely to reveal a clue as any other part.

'What think you, concerning his hair, Adam? Unusual to see hair of so pale a hue in a youngster, is it not?'

'I knew a Dutch family in Norwich. Their hair was much the same as this. Could he be Dutch, perhaps?'

'We will keep it in mind. He has a good face: fine featured. He would be accounted handsome, I believe. As you suggested, it will be worthwhile to record his likeness.' Seb made a few brief notes on scrap paper, using his thigh as a writing slope. 'Could you hazard a guess at his age?'

'Eleven or twelve years, maybe? Not much more than that.'

'I agree. What of his eyes? Dutchmen most commonly have blue eyes, as indeed do other fair-haired folk.'

He glanced at Adam who was, likewise, upon his knees. But Adam made no move to look at the closed eyes. Seb sighed and carefully raised the lid of one eye with his thumb.

'Surprisingly, his eye be dark, though 'tis hard to tell the colour exactly with death's cloud now misting it.' He made another note. 'The dead do not bite, Adam, nor do they protest. You may touch them without harm, unless they be dead of some pestilent fever.'

'Aye, I know. But it seems a violation somehow.'

'He was violated in life. Now he deserves justice, and only he can guide us by allowing us to observe the details preserved upon his person. Your squeamishness will not aid in this.'

'You're right. How may I help?'

'Describe his clothing.'

'But you can see as well as I...'

'A second opinion always adds certainty. You may notice things I miss and *vice versa*.

'A jerkin: filthy but probably once a greyish shade of green. A linen shirt...'

'Unlace the jerkin and look to the seams: colour is oftentimes better preserved there.'

Adam obeyed and was surprised to discover the original hue had been a deep green.

'And what of the fit?' Seb asked.

'The fit?'

'Does the jerkin fit him well or is it likely made for another?'

''Tis of a fair size in breadth, in that there is no sign of the laces pulling too tight and straining the holes, but it seems rather short for him.'

'And look to the belt also.'

'The belt is worn, with many holes having been used, but its present fastening has more use than any other. Seb: you think I'm getting the way of this searching business, looking for clues? The clothes have much to tell us, I see that now.'

'And what do they say to you?'

'That he's grown taller but no fatter of late. I suppose that is the way of lads his age. The sleeves of his shirt end above his wrists which agrees with my deductions.'

'Or 'tis borrowed from someone else.'

'Mm... that could explain...' Adam slapped the back of his hand. 'Hey, I'm getting bitten here. Damned fleas.'

'More likely a louse. Fleas would have jumped from the scalp as soon as the body began to cool, whereas lice get trapped in the clothing. Now you have freed them, they too desert the dead. Not an uncommon occurrence.'

'You could have warned me.'

'Searching out clues can be an occupation full of surprises,' Seb said, grinning. 'I once found a live frog within the damp folds of a dead man's cloak and as for those dragged from the Thames, the things I've discovered there...'

'Don't tell me; I don't want to know. I hope to eat a good breakfast when we're done with this.'

'Then let us continue. The jerkin be of good quality woollen cloth with no sign of moth damage nor repairs, yet it be faded and filthy. Therefore, much care has been taken of the garment until recently. It was made for the lad, as you supposed, but he is growing out of it in length yet not girth. Either his family has fallen on hard times, or they are no longer able to care for him.'

'How do you know it was made for him? Could be handed down from an older brother or bought from a fripperer or be, as you said, borrowed.'

'Neither borrowed nor second hand. See the faint lines of wear radiating from the armholes. The cloth still lies in those same worn furrows. If another had worn it, there would be other crease-marks now fading. The lad has always been the wearer, lacing and fastening it in the same way. I would also surmise that he is a scholar and carries his book tucked under his left arm. See? The wool has lost its knap there. But we must move on swiftly, else the others will be returning from church. Afore then, we must see what his wound can tell us; how the blood stains lie...'

**NEXT IN THE SERIES:** THE COLOUR OF SHADOWS

'Seb, I truly don't want to do that. I think I'll leave you to your notes, sketches and deliberations. I shall take Gawain for a walk...'

'Adam. Four eyes be far better than two. Your aid be much appreciated.'

'I know, but my eyes would rather not see any more of this.'

With Adam departed, Seb gave the dead lad his undivided attention. The wound and blood stains were examined in minute detail. The rest of the clothing, particularly the good shoes which were discovered to be too small for him, revealed more of his story. And his hands and fingernails told a great deal; a tale of misery and neglect. It was a sorry end for a fine young lad. And how had he come to lie in the shuttered workshop? Some measure of light was shed upon that mystery also, although not every aspect was made clear as yet. Mayhap, it never would be.

THE COLOUR OF
SHADOWS IS
OUT LATER THIS YEAR

Toni Mount, a member of the Crime Writers' Association, earned her Masters Degree in 2009 by researching a medieval medical manuscript held at the Wellcome Library in London. She enjoys independent academic study and has also completed a Diploma in Literature and Creative Writing, a Diploma in European Humanities and a First Class Honours Degree from the Open University.

Toni has written several well-respected non-fiction books, concentrating on the ordinary lives of people of the Middle-Ages, which allow her to create accurate, atmospheric settings and realistic characters for her medieval murder mysteries. Her first career was as a scientist, which enhances her knowledge and brings an extra dimension to her novels. Toni writes regularly for both The Richard III Society and The Tudor Society and is a major contributor to MedievalCourses.com. She is a qualified teacher and regularly speaks on a variety of topics at venues throughout the UK.

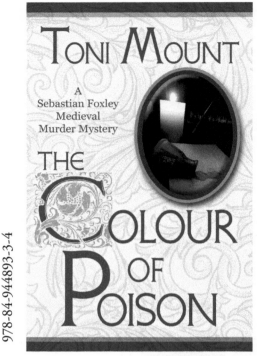

978-84-944893-3-4

**The first Sebastian Foxley
Medieval Mystery by Toni Mount.**

The narrow, stinking streets of medieval London can sometimes be a dark place. Burglary, arson, kidnapping and murder are every-day events. The streets even echo with rumours of the mysterious art of alchemy being used to make gold for the King.

Join Seb, a talented but crippled artist, as he is drawn into a web of lies to save his handsome brother from the hangman's rope. Will he find an inner strength in these, the darkest of times, or will events outside his control overwhelm him?

Only one thing is certain - if Seb can't save his brother, nobody can.

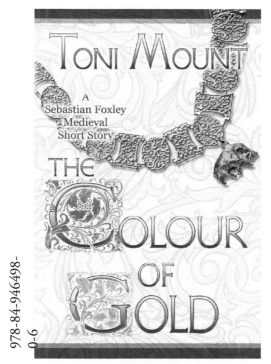

978-84-946498-0-6

**The second Sebastian Foxley
Medieval Mystery by Toni Mount.
A short story**

A wedding in medieval London should be a splendid occasion, especially when a royal guest will be attending the nuptial feast. Yet for the bridegroom, the talented young artist, Sebastian Foxley, his marriage day begins with disaster when the valuable gold livery collar he should wear has gone missing. From the lowliest street urchin to the highest nobility, who could be the thief? Can Seb wed his sweetheart, Emily Appleyard, and save the day despite that young rascal, Jack Tabor, and his dog causing chaos?

Join in the fun at a medieval marriage in this short story that links the first two Sebastian Foxley medieval murder mysteries: *The Colour of Poison* and the full-length novel *The Colour of Cold Blood*..

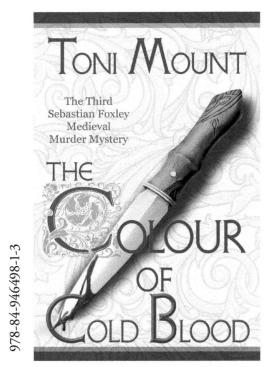

978-84-946498-1-3

**The third Sebastian Foxley
Medieval Mystery by Toni Mount.**

A devilish miasma of murder and heresy lurks in the winter streets of medieval London - someone is slaying women of the night. For Seb Foxley and his brother, Jude, evil and the threat of death come close to home when Gabriel, their well-liked journeyman, is arrested as a heretic and condemned to be burned at the stake.

Amid a tangle of betrayal and deception, Seb tries to uncover the murderer before more women die – will he also defy the church and devise a plan to save Gabriel?

These are dangerous times for the young artist and those he holds dear. Treachery is everywhere, even at his own fireside...

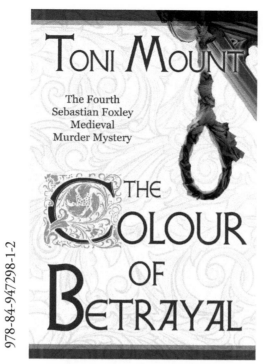

TONI MOUNT

The Fourth
Sebastian Foxley
Medieval
Murder Mystery

978-84-947298-1-2

THE COLOUR OF BETRAYAL

**The fourth Sebastian Foxley
Medieval Mystery by Toni Mount.
A short story**

Suicide or murder?

As medieval Londoners joyously prepare for the Christmas celebrations, goldsmith Lawrence Ducket is involved in a street brawl. Fearful that his opponent is dying from his injuries, Lawrence seeks sanctuary in a church nearby.

When Ducket is found hanging from the rafters, people assume it's suicide. Yet, Sebastian Foxley is unconvinced. Why is his young apprentice, Jack Tabor, so terrified that he takes to his bed?

Amidst feasting and merriment, Seb is determined to solve the mystery of his friend's death and to ease Jack's fears.

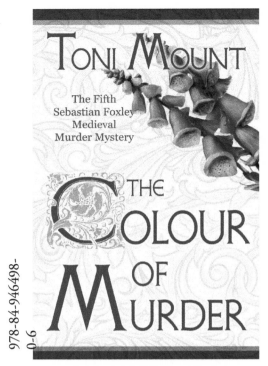

978-84-946498-0-6

**The fifth Sebastian Foxley
Medieval Mystery by Toni Mount.**

London is not safe for princes or commoners.

In February 1478, a wealthy merchant is killed by an intruder and a royal duke dies at the Tower. Neither case is quite as simple as it seems.

Seb Foxley, an intrepid young artist, finds himself in the darkest of places, fleeing for his life. With foul deeds afoot at the king's court, his wife Emily pregnant and his brother Jude's hope of marrying Rose thwarted, can Seb unearth the secrets which others would prefer to keep hidden?

Join Seb and Jude, their lives in jeopardy in the dangerous streets of the city, as they struggle to solve crimes and keep their business flourishing.